# PRAISE FOR
# THE INQUISITOR

"Smashing ER scenes, code blues, and a masked staff in orange space suits underpin a page-turner plotted for heart."
—*Kirkus Reviews*

"Hospital routine and medical procedures rendered so realistically that the book evokes the smell of bleach and alcohol wipes."
—*The Boston Globe*

"Written by a doctor, this medical thriller has lots of action and an insider's view of some of the workings and politics of a big city hospital."
—*The Oklahoman*

By Peter Clement

MORTAL REMAINS
CRITICAL CONDITION
MUTANT
THE PROCEDURE
DEATH ROUNDS
LETHAL PRACTICE

# The Inquisitor

A Medical Thriller

# Peter Clement

BALLANTINE BOOKS • NEW YORK

2006 Fawcett Books Mass Market Edition

Copyright © 2004 by Peter Clement Duffy

Published in the United States by Fawcett Books, an imprint of The Random House Publishing Group, a division of Random House, Inc., New York.

FAWCETT is a registered trademark and the Fawcett colophon is a trademark of Random House, Inc.

Originally published in hardcover in the United States by Ballantine Books, an imprint of The Random House Publishing Group, a division of Random House, Inc., in 2004.

ISBN 0-345-45781-1

Printed in the United States of America

www.ballantinebooks.com

OPM 9 8 7 6 5 4 3 2 1

*To Vyta, Sean, and James*

*Acknowledgments*

To my longtime friends Dr. Jennifer Frank and Dr. Brian Connolly for their second opinion on medical matters.

To Pat Moore for her inside information about the nasty substances on the shelves of a pathology lab.

To Father Roman Lahola for his insights into pastoral care at a large urban teaching hospital and his instruction about the nature of the Greek Orthodox Church.

To Johanna, Connie, and Betty for their eagle eyes.

To my agent, Jay Mandel, for all his help.

To my editors: Pat Peters for all her meticulous, caring work as wordsmith, and Mark Tavani for his most thoughtful input.

# Chapter 1

The air on the ward hung thick with the smell of flatulence, body odor, and sweat-soaked sheets. What little light could be seen curdled in pools of shadow. The cries that rose and fell against the outside of her door might as well have been a wail of wind, because here no one would heed them. The nurses paid attention only when the moaning stopped.

Somewhere someone retched with a force that must have stripped the stomach bare. The sound echoed along the hallway.

That might bring them.

Soon the squeak of crepe soles on linoleum would announce their approach.

None came.

"Store up all the tiny details. Let me smell, taste, hear, see, and touch through your telling of them." The command, issued to me so long ago, resurfaced, resonating in memory with the freshness of an order spoken on the spot and not to be disobeyed. As always before a mission, it marshaled a frame of mind fine-tuned to observe, the ideal state to be in for keeping myself and the records sharp.

"Can you hear me?" I whispered, holding back on the plunger of my syringe.

"Yes." Her eyes remained shut.

1

I leaned over and brought my ear to her mouth. "Any more pain?"

"No. It's gone."

"Do you see anything?"

"Only blackness." Her whispers rasped against the back of her throat.

"Look harder! Now tell me what's there." I swallowed to keep from gagging. Her breath stank.

"You're not my doctor."

"No, I'm replacing him tonight."

She didn't respond.

I gave her a gentle shake. "Mrs. Algreave?"

"Just leave me be. It doesn't hurt anymore."

Leaning back, I studied her gray, skeletal face. The moonlight cast a silvery blue tinge over her pallid skin, making her appear already dead. As for the rest of her, so much had wasted away that the soft material of her lace nightgown clung to the hollows between her ribs and reminded me of white gloves on bony fingers.

I glanced toward the closed door—the nurses shouldn't start their rounds for another half hour yet—and reapplied my thumb to the plunger. A slow push, and her pulse grew weaker. "Do you see anything yet?"

No answer.

"Mrs. Algreave!"

"Yes?"

"Tell me what you see."

"It's too dark."

"Look carefully."

"But I can't see."

"Do you sense yourself rising?"

Again no answer.

I shifted my mouth closer to her ear. "Talk to me, Mrs. Algreave." The words must have sounded like a shout.

"Leave me alone."

"Not until you tell me what you see." I gradually increased the pressure on the plunger. Her pulse diminished to clusters of barely discernible bumps, readable only to experienced fingertips, like Braille. It shouldn't be long now. Her failing circulation would abandon the lesser organs—kidneys, ovaries, digestive tracts, large and small—and reroute itself entirely to spare the more essential meats, the lungs, heart, and brain. A perfectly orchestrated sequence, designed to save neurons so that they could record the final seconds. Anyone bold enough could tap the knowledge hidden in those moments. "Are you looking down on us yet?"

At first I thought she hadn't heard me. Then her lips moved but emitted no sound. Turning my head, I hovered an inch above her mouth. She exhaled against my cheek, sending another whiff of rot drifting through my nostrils to play at the back of my tongue. "What did you say?"

"I . . . see . . . me . . ."

Her words filled my ear one breath at a time, elongated and no louder than a puff of breeze. But I could just make them out, having become a practiced listener to messages from this plane. Excitement mounting, I turned on the tiny tape recorder in my breast pocket. "What else can you make out?"

"The . . . bed . . . nightstand . . . pictures . . . all my pictures . . ."

On the small bedside table a silver-framed black-and-white shot of a young man in uniform stood propped behind an array of more recent, color snaps, the kind processed in an hour: a dark-haired couple, three grinning boys in front of a Christmas tree, a woman holding a baby. Only the soldier interested me. "Is that your husband?"

"Yes . . ."

"What's his name?"

I barely made out the word that followed. It sounded like "Frank."

"Is he dead?"

Her breath diminished to a point it wouldn't have fogged a mirror. "Yes . . ."

"Do you want to find him?" Most did. The yearning to meet up again never died.

"Yes . . ."

"Are you still looking down on yourself in bed?"

"Yes . . ."

"Let go. Allow yourself to float, escape the hospital, go high above the building. You must do this before you can see Frank."

"Yes . . ."

"Look up."

"No . . ."

"Look up and you'll see Frank. He's waiting."

"I . . . won't . . . get . . . back. . . ."

"Look up!"

No reply. Had I forced her too far? No, she still had a pulse. Nevertheless, I eased off the plunger. "Can you hear me?"

"Yes . . ."

"What do you see?"

"Too . . . vast . . ."

"What? Night? Space? Stars?"

"Gray . . ."

"Gray what?"

"Cold . . ."

"Tell me what's there."

"Nothing . . ."

My insides tightened. "You've got to see something."

"It's horrible . . ."

"What is?"

"Help me. . . ."

Damn her, why didn't she tell me? "Describe where you are, or I'll leave you there. Frank won't ever find you."

This time I heard a sharp intake of breath. "No . . . please . . ."

"Then tell me."

"Nothing . . . to . . . tell . . ."

The pulse under my fingers raced stronger. Her breath blew against my ear with more force.

"It's . . . terrible. . . . Get . . . me . . . out. . . . Please . . . get me out. . . ."

The faint sounds became a cry. Her eyes shot open, wide with terror.

No one had ever come to before now.

I clamped my palm over her mouth and watched the door again. Had one of the nurses heard?

No footsteps approached.

She looked straight at me.

"You recognize me now?" I asked, my thumb still on the plunger.

She nodded and tried to say something, but the sound vibrated against my palm. It tickled.

"Shh! Don't speak!" I advanced the plunger. Just give her a little more, enough to subdue her again. "You've been having a bad dream."

She shook her head and fixed her stare on where I'd stuck the syringe through a rubber portal in her IV. Her brows shot upward and her forehead furrowed with alarm, and the squeals she made against my hand pierced the quiet. I pressed down harder. "I said quiet!"

She started to buck, making the bed squeak.

Oh, God, where did she find the strength? The others hadn't. I leaned on her, pinning the emaciated form to the mattress. "I warn you, stop it!" I had meant to whisper, but my voice rasped out of me in a crow's squawk.

The bed rattled as she writhed under my weight.

I pushed more forcefully against her mouth.

Her movements continued. The iron frame began to creak in off-key squeals, the noises grating along the inside of my skull. Any minute a nurse would be sure to hear.

I increased the pressure on the syringe.

Flailing at me, she struck my arm, and the plunger lurched ahead, injecting the entire contents of the chamber into her IV.

I gaped at the emptied cylinder in horror.

She gradually stopped moving. Her pulse vanished. The respirations slowed to a standstill. Yet her brows remained raised, and she continued to glare at me, but with the flat dilated pupils of the dead.

Nausea swept through me, and my heart rate bounded into triple digits. I'd never killed one before. Just kept them in limbo as they died.

Swallowing until I had no more spit, I pulled out the syringe, replaced the safety cap, and pocketed it. A quick check of the covers and floor verified that nothing had been dropped or left behind. But as I bent over, the microcassette recorder slipped out of my breast pocket and clattered to the linoleum. Retrieving it, I clicked the off button. Close call. Had it hit a mat or her bedding without a sound, I might not have noticed.

I steadied my breathing and, surveying the scene, satisfied myself that everything would seem natural.

As I backed toward the door, the moonlight shone across her face at a low angle, filling the hollows and depressions with deep shadows. Her eyes, still open, glittered from the bottom of gaunt sockets. Despite my knowing better, I could have sworn they watched me every step of the way.

# Chapter 2

## Three months later

Dr. Earl Garnet sensed it the instant he stepped inside the marbled front entrance.

St. Paul's Hospital buzzed with a palpable nervousness and excitement unlike the feel of any other morning.

July 1.

Changeover day.

All over North America flocks of freshly minted medical graduates wearing crisp white coats streamed into their respective teaching hospitals, ready to begin the arduous residencies that would forge them into physicians.

And more staff doctors showed up at 7:00 a.m. than at any other time of the year. Ostensibly they'd come to welcome their charges, but he knew their early arrival had more to do with protecting patients from the newcomers and scrutinizing the latest batch of future healers for early signs of who would bear watching. Earl found himself exchanging pleasantries and brushing shoulders with colleagues he hadn't seen in months.

Except this July 1 would be like none St. Paul's had ever experienced before.

He lined up to be screened for fever alongside the rest of the employees. With four tables working, the crowd moved through quickly today. Nurses already dressed in OR gowns, shoe covers, surgical hats, goggles, gloves, and tight-fitting thick masks greeted him. One applied a thermal strip to his forehead: normal. Another asked a few quick questions that he and everyone else now knew by heart, and he just as quickly rattled off the answers: no cold symptoms, no foreign travel, no unprotected contact with suspect or probable cases. That done, he received a dated stamp on his hand, the kind that discos and theme parks use—except instead of opening the doors to fun-filled entertainment, it granted him admission to his own ER for another day on the job. He moved on to the next stop, where similarly attired porters dispensed a complete set of protective gear to every single person entering the hospital.

Welcome to the "new normal" of SARS in America.

Severe acute respiratory syndrome, the scientists had named it the year it first appeared in China. At the time residents took to calling it SCARES.

An electron microscope mug shot of the suspected cause, a smudged-looking sphere surrounded by a ring of tiny balls, had made the front pages of newspapers all over the world. The crownlike appearance allowed it to be recognized as a member of the coronavirus family, a microbe with many different strains, some responsible for up to 30 percent of common colds in people, but most infected only the lungs and bowels of livestock, such as chickens, pigs, or cows. Yet somehow one of these latter strains had acquired a genetic makeover and jumped the species barrier to take on humans in a deadly new way. Similar events with other organisms had given rise to some of our most lethal diseases—the so-called swine flu of 1918 is thought to have come from pigs, AIDS from monkeys, avian influenza from chickens. Humans, having never had prior exposure, lack immunity to these invaders, so the prospect of a brand-new bug that's highly contagious always grabs the scientific world's attention.

The real kicker is that researchers couldn't isolate the coronavirus from over half the cases, which left the possibility that this disease might be a multiheaded monster that attacked its victims in ways not yet understood, or that some other completely different unknown, a deadly X, could be floating around out there killing people.

That first year the outbreaks were beaten back. But just when the world thought itself safe, the organism mutated, the new vaccines against it were suddenly obsolete, and pockets of infections began to crop up again. Even then, until a few months ago, it had been largely the problem of other countries, the few cases that occurred in the United States being relatively mild. Everything changed after a busload of tourists returning from a religious meeting in Toronto, Canada, center stage for the initial North American endemic and center stage for its reappearance, brought back more than a few Mountie souvenirs.

According to the latest count, there were 169 confirmed cases admitted to designated Buffalo hospitals, 31 of them under treatment at St. Paul's, and most of them health care workers.

In the first wave of infections among hospital staff, two nurses and a doctor died. After that, there'd been no containing it. People broke quarantine, others lied about having symptoms or where they'd been, and while the number of new cases leveled off in the community, the virus continued to strike doctors, nurses, orderlies, and residents all over the city. Even now, every few days at St. Paul's someone with a fever would be pulled out of line at the screening station to be put in isolation for observation. Most turned out to have nothing more than a cold, but with a 15 percent mortality rate, no cure, and some survivors left so short of breath they could barely walk across a room, fear had become the norm for those who treated the sick.

Fortunately, no one who'd gone through with Earl this morning got tagged. After suiting up, they broke into smaller groups and hurried off to their respective departments.

"Heads up, guys."

"Eyes sharp."

"And cast-iron stomachs all around."

Their parting banter reminded Earl of soldiers moving out on patrol.

Upstairs, the nurses would be adopting an edgy alertness as well, scanning their wards the way ship captains keep a lookout at sea, always ready for trouble. If a rookie went alone into a patient's room, they'd keep tabs on him or her. When a novice wrote a medication order, they'd double- and triple-check it for mistakes. And during any attempt by a first-timer to perform a procedure, they'd hover over the event with the anxious scrutiny of spinster chaperones. They also would set their radars to home in on any of last year's junior trainees who might stride through the corridors a little too cockily, lording it over those who'd replaced them on the bottom level of the teaching pyramid. Arrogance could kill as readily as inexperience, and the two together were even more lethal; no one could pop them both faster than veteran nurses. Their weapon of choice: sidle up to any offender who showed off to the newfound underlings and say, "So, you finally brought me someone on the floors who actually knows less than you do. Remember, honey, that ain't saying much."

The result of it all?

Already anxious patients clutched their blankets and hoped for the best every time a new masked face with youthful eyes came near them. And they soon learned the surest way to spot a beginner: even under the surgical gowns all the clinical manuals and packets of cue cards these kids invariably kept stuffed in their pockets made telltale bulges. Earl sometimes fantasized these junior doctors pulling no end of things out from under them—suture kits, crutches, their lunch—like Harpo Marx in OR gear.

He tried not to smile as another throng filed by. The bulges of this bunch stuck out like tumors, indicating pockets laden well past the bursting point. Through the backs of their badly tied outfits he spotted their short white clinical jackets, trademark for the lowest of the low.

Medical students.

Their rapid-fire chatter, typical of first-day jitters, bounced off the walls.

". . . orientation's in the basement auditorium . . ."

". . . but where do we meet our chief residents . . ."

". . . me, I'm following my nose to the coffee . . ."

Surgical masks couldn't hide that they seemed younger than ever, he thought, indulging in a twinge of melancholy. He'd been through twenty-five changeovers and found the day marked the passing of yet another year with more impact than his own birthday.

He continued at a brisk pace toward the emergency department and pressed a large metal disc on the wall, setting off a loud hiss as the frosted glass barrier that separated his domain from the rest of the hospital slid open.

Just like Captain Kirk on the *Enterprise,* he thought, stepping through with a grin, only to have the volume of chatter coming from inside wipe it away.

That much sound meant a lot of patients. Too many.

"Morning, Dr. G.," the triage nurse greeted him. She was a cheery woman in her mid-twenties. He knew her mask hid three rings in her right nostril, and slightly spiked but short black hair stuck out from beneath her surgical cap. She glanced up from taking the blood pressure of an elderly lady who had frizzy white hair and lay gasping for breath on an ambulance stretcher, a red handbag clutched to her chest with both hands. She also was masked, and her frightened eyes stared at him over its tight-fitting rim. The material puffed in and out with each respiration.

To the left the walking wounded, equally well masked, kept their distance, prowling a waiting room meant to hold half their number. On the right another sliding door led to the inner sanctums of ER, where patients unable to sit or stand would be parked on stretchers.

"Morning, J.S.," he replied, raising his voice to make himself heard above the chatter of a hundred conversations.

The initials stood for Jane Simmons. They'd used call letters to address each other since shortly after she came on staff. It began, as did many traditions between people in ER, during the rush of a resuscitation. The intensity often cemented first impressions—for better or worse—and her impact on him had stuck for the better. Despite dressing the part of a punk rocker, she had good hands when it came to starting IVs in the worst of veins, and her calm never cracked—not then as a new kid, and not since, even during the toughest cases.

"Need any help?" he asked her. The elderly woman's rapid breathing had automatically put him on alert.

"Nah." J.S. reassuringly patted the lady's arm. "Meet Mary."

"Hi, Mary, I'm Dr. Garnet, the guy who runs the joint." He placed his gloved hand over hers and gave it a gentle squeeze.

"Only a touch of heart failure," J.S. continued, "but this little sweetie's going to be just fine as soon as we give her oxygen, relax her airways, and get her peeing."

Some of the fear drained from the old woman's gaze, and she appeared less forlorn despite the puffy circles drooping over the upper edge of her mask. An orderly whisked her through the inner door and down the hallway to a treatment room.

"Ready to whip another crop of greenhorns into shape?" Earl asked J.S. while glancing over the ambulance sheet to see what calamities the city of Buffalo had delivered up overnight. He mentally ticked off the cases that he could use as good teaching material for introducing first-year residents to ER.

The corners of her eyes crinkled, and he knew her infectious, crooked grin had appeared. She lifted an upper tie to loosen the corner of her mask and blew a strand of loose hair off her forehead. "Just let me at 'em."

Before he could remind her that she shouldn't breathe unfiltered air, even for a second, a single low growl from a siren announced the arrival of another ambulance. The signal meant they'd brought in a patient still breathing, but barely, who needed help fast.

J.S. pivoted and charged out the door leading to the garage.

Several nurses darted from the inner corridors to follow her. They passed where a teenage boy sat clutching a skateboard and doubled over in pain. J.S. must have deemed him stable enough to wait, but Earl didn't like the greenish tinge and sheen of sweat that no mask could completely hide. "Do you need to lie down?" he asked, walking over and kneeling at the young man's side.

"I need to vomit, sir."

"Just hang on." He rummaged through the equipment racks behind J.S.'s triage area, dug out a bedpan, and shoved it into the youngster's lap.

The sounds of more ambulances pulling into the unloading area reached his ears.

Busy day to break in a fresh crew, he thought, hurrying inside to marshal his staff for the onslaught. At the door he stopped to double-glove and double-gown, the added body armor required for anyone working ER. He also donned another prerequisite for anyone on the front lines of medicine these days: a cast-iron attitude of *que sera sera*.

An hour later they'd diuresed a liter of pee from the woman in heart failure, identified a ruptured spleen in the skateboard kid, and resuscitated the case that had so alarmed the ambulance technicians: a diabetic stockbroker in his fifties named Artie Baxter. He'd skipped breakfast after his morning insulin, then collapsed and seized. "I had a great tip before the market opened," he'd explained when a shot of IV glucose woke him up. "So I phoned all my clients instead of eating my usual toast and cheese. . . ."

A few of the nurses scribbled down the company's name and ran for the wall phones.

"Can I see you outside a moment?" Earl said to Susanne

Roberts, the head nurse, and led her by her elbow to a quiet spot in the hall.

"What's up?" Her pixie haircut peeking out from under her OR cap made her appear young, and only the lacework of tiny lines that fanned out at the corners of her eyes hinted at her age. She'd been on staff in ER for nearly as many years as he had, but she'd kept her passion for the job long past the point at which most lose it. Like all gifted leaders, she brought out the best in those around her.

"I'm going to try to make the end of the orientation session for the residents," he told her. "But I'm worried about this guy. Keep him on the monitor with the IV running."

"You expecting trouble?"

"His story doesn't add up. A man who's been on the needle for years and he pulls a stunt like that? I think he's not telling us something. And all that stock talk—a little too smooth for my liking. He got a wife?"

"She's on her way in."

"Ask her if he's been as well as he claims."

The speeches were almost over when he let himself in through a side door near the front of the auditorium stage. The audience occupied a steeply raked semicircle of seats, providing a wall of OR green before the speaker at the podium, Dr. Stewart Deloram, St. Paul's resident genius in critical care. His mop of jet-black hair sprang out from the sides of his headgear like burst springs, flopping about as he animatedly extolled the virtues of a quiet, calm demeanor while dealing with life-and-death situations. "Especially when working on a patient who has suffered cardiac arrest," he emphasized in a grave, sonorous voice.

As the director of the intensive care unit, and one of the hospital's biggest screamers, he ought to know.

The two-thirds of the audience who were familiar with Stewart's antics tittered. Those who weren't dutifully jotted down what he'd said. Yet every single resident who had just laughed would also willingly double their allotted time with him in ICU, so brilliantly did he teach the art of critical care, or "raising the dead," as he called it.

Earl didn't care how loud Stewart got during a resuscitation, so long as he got the job done. The patients sure were in no state to hear him, and besides, other geniuses made noises when they worked. Just listen to undoctored recordings of Glenn Gould. Or to Monica Seles when she served.

Earl spotted the chief of surgery, Sean Carrington, a giant of a man seated in the front row, and slid in beside him. He wielded enormous influence in the hospital and more than once had used it to save Earl's hide politically. But Earl appreciated him most for his zany sense of humor. Sean could cut through the suffocating bureaucracy of academic medicine like a blast of oxygen. And his bushy red eyebrows, highlighted by his mask, whipped up a laugh all by themselves when his jokes failed.

He nodded to Earl, leaned over, and whispered, "Stewart must be in anger management classes again. You know, the ones where they chant, 'Teach it, and the shit you spout will come true.' "

Earl swallowed a chuckle. "Did he brief them about SARS yet?"

The fun went out of Sean's eyes. "Yeah."

"Who's left to speak?"

"Just you, Dr. Vice President, Medical, sir, and chief poobah, or whatever it is we get to call you these days."

"Now don't you start. I get razzed enough by my department."

Sean reached over and pretended to knuckle-rub the top of his head. "Hey, what are old friends for but to keep you from getting too high and mighty up there among the ruling class?"

Earl knew that Sean took the epidemic as seriously as anyone, but apart from the mandatory discussions about it at meetings, he never dwelled on it, let alone voiced his personal fears. If anything, his joking had increased as the hospital hunkered down to meet the crisis. What with the general atmosphere of gloom, they could do with more like him. And Earl read this latest tease as a hint to lighten up himself. "High and mighty, with the bellyfull of problems you bums dump on me every day? Fat chance."

The vice president, medical held authority over all doctors in their practice of medicine at St. Paul's Hospital. Only the CEO had more power. The position also meant a mountain of trouble for whoever filled it, especially in times such as these. Yet two weeks ago, under pressure from most of the other chiefs, Earl had accepted the appointment. Why? "Because it's a responsibility I can't refuse," he'd told most people who asked. And he hadn't lied, just dressed up the real reason: it would be easier to run ER with himself in charge rather than some of the other bozos who might get the job.

"How's Janet taking you being named boss of bosses around here?"

"Cutting me down to size, as usual. I don't think she got the memo—"

A gentle cuff to the back of his head cut him off. "Hey, quit bad-mouthing your superiors," Janet whispered, loud enough for people two rows away to hear, as she slipped into a seat behind him. She whipped off her surgical cap, setting a sunburst of blond hair free with a shake. Then, quickly replacing the headgear, she gave him a masked kiss on his masked cheek. "And no memo's going to make me treat you differently."

Earl heard a few snickers.

Dr. Janet Graceton, obstetrician and recently named director of the hospital case room, held command over him as friend, lover, and wife. Some in the hospital eagerly awaited an issue where the VP, medical would have to confront the case room director over something or other. According to the rumor mill, odds of that matchup stood at eight to five for Janet.

"Hey, you look great," Sean told her.

"That's because OR greens and gowns make perfect maternity wear, don't you think?" She molded the layers of material over her abdomen, accentuating the swell of her stomach. Even with her in her thirty-fourth week of pregnancy, operating room garb hung so loosely on her tall and normally slim frame that nobody believed her due date could be six weeks away. Nor would her workload tip them off. Some women might have cut back their time on the job by now. But Janet would have gone nuts staying home at this stage under any circumstances. She relaxed through work, finding a contentment in it that her colleagues, male and female, envied. "And a happy mom usually means a contented fetus," she'd told thousands of women, helping them discover their own unique needs during pregnancy. Little wonder she gave herself the same right to decide what would be best for her baby. While carrying their first son, Brendan, now six, she'd done her last delivery a mere twenty-four hours before going into labor herself.

Not that her bravado didn't worry Earl.

"Now a word as to your night schedule." Stewart droned, and flipped open his laptop computer, where he kept house staff duty rosters. On the screen behind him a barely decipherable set of lists came into view. "As in last year, only second- and third-year residents will be on for ICU, the intensive care unit, CCU, the coronary care unit, and SICU, the surgical intensive care unit. If you learn nothing else, you'll at least be able to impress family and friends with all these neat acronyms."

A third of the audience laughed. The remainder groaned. Stewart made this same joke every year.

"And if you lose your handouts, feel free to make yourself floppies. This laptop is at your disposal, and the password is Tocco, T-o-c-c-o, my dog's name. . . ."

Earl tuned it all out, mentally preparing what he would say to sum up the session. The SARS outbreak had catapulted doctors into a level of risk that hadn't existed in North America since the 1918 flu epidemic, and forced them to adopt protective measures unprecedented in modern hospitals. No one in this room had planned to take on that kind of danger when they chose medicine as a career. How the hell did he address that?

". . . and while during the day you may be internists, surgeons, gynecologists, et cetera, residency cutbacks necessitate that at night you will cover a multitude of services, again like last year . . ."

This time Stewart got a howl of disapproval from the newcomers. High up in the back row a kid who had black Brillo pads for eyebrows and who looked lost in his voluminous OR gown leapt to his feet, teetering over the similarly attired confreres sitting in front of him. "What if we need help?" he yelled.

Equally youthful looking colleagues joined in.

". . . yeah . . ."

". . . a lack of supervision . . ."

". . . violates our contract . . ."

Earl marveled at how they could get so exercised over such a traditional complaint as the on-call roster when the new normal they faced loomed so large. Odds were that the first-year people, with so much to learn, would slip up more than anyone else when it came to all the protective measures they must practice. As a consequence, no other group in the room stood a greater chance of ending up sick, maybe even dead.

Stewart waved them quiet with the palms of his hands. "Easy, people, easy. We'll also have full-time staff doctors in the critical care areas I mentioned. That frees the R-twos and R-threes on duty there to come and assist you on the floors when you call them. It's a system that's worked well."

A few of the rookies continued to mutter, and some rolled their eyes in exasperation. The second- and third-year people remained silent and slumped in their chairs. They were all too aware that scheduling arrangements didn't matter much against an unseen threat ready to get you on any shift, at any time.

"What about ER?" a lone voice inquired from somewhere behind and above. "Will R-two and R-three people there be expected to back up arrests on the floors as in the past, or did you finally get that note from my mother saying we needed our sleep?"

This brought a much-needed laugh from everyone.

Earl smiled, recognizing the easy drawl of Dr. Thomas Biggs, his own emergency medicine protégé. He looked around and saw the lanky Tennessee native sprawled in his seat a few rows from the top with the laid-back air that he had made his trademark. Even with his mask on, the bottom margin of his black beard could be seen under his chin. On either side of him sat the other men and women in the ER program. Thomas, in his last year of training as an emergency medicine specialist, would serve as Earl's chief resident and supervise teaching during the next three months. After that he'd begin a final rotation through all the other critical care areas Stewart had just mentioned. Judging by his performance so far, he had the potential to be a real star and would undoubtedly make a major contribution wherever he ended up.

Stewart stiffened. "Right, Thomas. I should have included ER. Night coverage there will be the same as in the critical care units—a staff presence twenty-four seven plus second- and third-year folks who'll offer backup on the floors." His voice took on an edge that hadn't been there before. "Now, before I turn over these proceedings to Dr. Earl Garnet," he went on, his tone even more clipped, "our chief of ER and recently appointed VP, medical—in other words, the other guy around here whom you should listen to besides me—" He paused for the expected laugh, but the coldness in his voice had drained any fun out of the crack. He shrugged and continued. "Our hospital chaplain, Jimmy Fitzpatrick, would like to have a moment with you." Stewart unceremoniously gathered up his notes and plumped himself down in a chair behind the podium.

The atmosphere went flat.

Earl had long since stopped trying to figure out Stewart's mood swings, having concluded years ago that the man had a narcissistic personality to go with his prodigious talent. But diagnosing him didn't render him any less annoying. He could take the simplest inquiry as a personal affront, as if whoever questioned him questioned his competence. Yet everyone also excused this prickly side of him, just as they did his tendency to yell a lot, again because of his extraordinary ability to pull off miracles. Thank God, he would usually apologize afterward when he did lose his cool and pull one of his snits. "I'm just not used to anyone challenging me," he'd once told Earl. "Most of my patients have tubes down their throats." But sometimes he could prolong holding a grudge, and over the stupidest things.

Jimmy, a muscular man wearing the same protective gear as everyone else, stepped up on the stage. His square jaw stood out beneath the covering of his mask, and not even layers of green could hide his well-proportioned physique. "Top o' the mornin' to you," he began when he reached the microphone, sweeping the audience with intense black eyes that had a magnetic pull to them. "Oh, I bet you're thrilled t' hear from a preacher. The ones fresh out of medical school, having never found the human soul in all those studies, are always the most skeptical that it exists." His lilting Irish brogue and mischievous squint instantly reanimated the room. People leaned forward to hear what he had to say. "So I'll keep it short. The Pastoral Services Department is here to serve the emotional and spiritual needs of patients, family, and staff. To learn more, give me a call. I want to stress we're open to all, whether a person has a formal religious affiliation or not. Remember, people of all stripes get scared in here, and even if we just provide a sympathetic ear . . ."

But Earl kept his gaze on Stewart, then glanced back at Thomas. Presumably Stewart's display had to do with Thomas's question. Understandably the resident remained oblivious to any wrongdoing on his part, and chatted easily with the R2s immediately to either side of him, both female. No surprise there. He had a way with the ladies.

Yet Stewart kept scowling toward the young man, as if

trying to catch him in some other act of inexcusable insolence. After a few seconds, however, the ridges in his forehead flattened, and his expression softened.

Good, Earl thought.

Stewart's pique over imagined slights occasionally grew to the point that it interfered with work. One time the tension in ICU had gotten so bad that Earl slapped a notice in red ink above the entrance: PROS LEAVE THEIR GUNS AT THE DOOR. The job of setting him straight usually fell to Earl because no one else in the hospital would dare criticize Stewart about anything. Earl figured he got away with it because of the year he'd been Stewart's chief resident at New York City Hospital twenty-five years ago. That kind of seniority over a junior can stick for life.

". . . in other words, don't be shy about using our help," Jimmy said, sounding as if he'd concluded his remarks.

Janet bent forward to whisper into Earl's ear. "It's not fair, the good looks on that man. Even covered up, they might give a woman ideas."

Earl turned and raised an eyebrow at her. "You'll be making me jealous," he murmured out of the corner of his mouth.

"I'm glad I still can." She leaned back and clasped her round belly with both hands again.

"Now I have one other announcement," Jimmy continued, "but first, such a serious bunch as yourselves will frighten the sick into a relapse, so here's a joke to lighten the mood." He lifted the microphone off its stand and walked free of the podium. "Did you hear the one about the priest, the minister, and the rabbi who went to Disneyland together?"

Everybody waited for the answer.

"They got in a fight about where to go first. I mean, it got loud. The priest shouted, 'Fantasyland!' The rabbi, 'Tomorrowland!' The minister, 'Frontierland!' They even started pulling on the map, pushing and shoving each other, kicking up the dust. Grown men, squabbling like you wouldn't believe. Then Goofy walks up. 'Hey, Mickey,' he says, 'look! It's Holyland.' "

Groans filled the air again, but this time they were good-natured.

Jimmy continued to walk the stage. "Sorry, but when I entered the seminary, it was a toss-up between that and being a stand-up comic. I'm still working on my act, in case I get the call. What'd'ya think?"

"Don't give up your day job," someone shouted.

A few people chuckled.

Jimmy pointed to the heavens and shook his head. "You know, that's what He keeps telling me."

This got him a round of applause.

"Make your point, Jimmy," Earl muttered none too quietly. He was impatient to say his own piece so he could get the hell back and reassess the man he'd left in ER.

The chaplain gave him a nod. "Not to take up any more of your busy morning, but I'm here to invite you all to our annual Run for Fun this Saturday. That's when you, healthy, young, and strong, get to put your professors, weak, old, and flabby—well, some of them, anyway—to shame by humiliating them in a two-K jaunt through scenic downtown Buffalo, entirely in the name of charity. Oh, by the way, the lot of you will be pushing hospital beds, each complete with a simulated patient and half-full bedpan from which you must not spill a drop. Thanks for your time."

Earl joined in the clapping, ready to take the stage, when the overhead PA crackled to life.

"Drs. Garnet, Deloram, Biggs—ER; Father Jimmy Fitzpatrick—ER stat!"

Artie Baxter, the stockbroker, lay on his stretcher frowning and blinking furiously. He couldn't speak because of the tube in his throat, and he breathed thanks to a respiratory technician who kept ventilating his lungs with an Ambu bag, twelve squeezes to the minute. J.S. provided the chest compressions, five at a time, strands of her thick black hair slipping from under her cap and flopping over her forehead as she worked. A cloying scent of singed flesh hung in the air despite the gobs of contact gel that glistened in the tight curls on Artie's chest, and his cardiac monitor showed the zigzag line of a fibrillating heart.

"We were on him so quickly when he arrested, he never lost consciousness," Susanne whispered to Earl.

At her side stood a heavyset, pear-shaped man with worried, tired-looking eyes and the edges of a salt-and-pepper beard sticking out the bottom of his mask. Dr. Michael Popovitch was a longtime friend, director of the department's residency program, and acting chief of ER during Earl's many absences. He'd once shared the fire in the belly that's a prerequisite for long-term survival in emergency medicine, but lately the cases seemed to weigh heavily on him. Each month his gaze grew a little sadder. "We've maxed him with epi, Lidocaine, procainamide—every antiarrhythmic we have," he said, terse and to the point, "and shocked him silly. Bottom line, nothing's worked."

The causes of refractory V-fib. automatically flashed through Earl's mind. "How's his potassium, sugar—"

"No metabolic problems," Michael cut in, "other than a slightly high glucose after the bolus you gave him—"

"An overdose, maybe?" Stewart Deloram interrupted, inserting himself as part of the huddle. "Tricyclics, aminophylline, speed . . ." He rattled off the drugs that might precipitate this kind of arrest.

Thomas Biggs stood a little off to one side. He watched the proceedings but offered no suggestions.

Earl found his own attention drawn to Artie's eyes as they blinked more furiously than ever. Leaning directly over his face, he said, "Close your eyes once if you can hear me, Mr. Baxter."

The fluttering stopped. The lids closed and opened.

"Do you see me?"

They closed and opened again. Then he stared at Earl, his pupils wide with fright, seeming to want an explanation.

Earl shivered. This happened every now and then, the patient's heart not beating, the lungs not breathing, but the brain kept alive and conscious with CPR. Only he'd never seen someone in such a state remain so alert before. "Let's be careful what we say, guys," he cautioned.

Stewart continued to expound his list in a much lower voice.

"Tox screen isn't back yet," Michael interrupted, "but I emptied a vial of bicarb into him in case he'd OD'd on tricyclics. Combined with the rest of what we tried, he's had every antidote there is." Again, right to the point. Whatever sapped his spirits these days, his skill stayed as sharp as ever.

But Artie's eyes, so pained and aware, drew Earl's attention away from the discussion.

Jimmy stepped up and spoke into the man's ear. "I'm the hospital chaplain, Mr. Baxter. Is it all right if I say a prayer with you?"

Artie showed no response.

Still locked into the man's stare, Earl felt it pull him in, like a tether. Perhaps he hadn't heard Jimmy's question. "Are you Catholic, Mr. Baxter?" he asked.

Two blinks.

"Is that a no?"

One blink.

"Do you have any pain?"

No response.

The resus team kept pumping and ventilating him.

Stewart discussed options with Michael.

". . . float a pacemaker wire into his heart, hook the myocardium, and try to recapture a normal rhythm."

"Go for it," Michael said, pivoting on his heel and rushing toward the door. "I'll get the pacemaker."

Earl remained barely aware of them, transfixed instead by the black, bottomless pools at the center of Artie's eyes that beckoned him closer. What did he want? "Dr. Biggs, if you'll help me get a line through the right subclavian," Earl said, turning away, "Stewart can go in with the pacemaker from there." In order to function he must distance himself. A lifetime in ER had taught him how. But he knew that Artie was still looking at him. He could sense the patient's stare burrowing into the back of his skull.

Thomas must have felt it too. He hesitated, and the surface of his mask rippled as he clenched his teeth. Then he snapped on a sterile pair of gloves over his regular ones and got to work.

In seconds Thomas and Earl had inserted a needle the size of a three-inch nail through the skin below Artie's right clavicle and into a vein the caliber of a small hose.

Michael returned with the pacemaker equipment, and the three ER physicians stood back to let Stewart perform his magic.

Already double-gloved and -gowned, he delicately threaded a sterile pacemaker wire through the needle sticking out from beneath Artie's clavicle. Throughout the entire procedure, he eyed the monitor for evidence that he'd passed the wire through the vein, maneuvered it into the heart, and hooked its tip into the wall of the first chamber. He asked J.S. to stop pumping, and the sounds of her exertions ceased. The hiss of the ventilating bag as the technician squeezed a volley of air into Artie's lungs and the lilting beauty of Jimmy's voice while he murmured the Twenty-third Psalm became the only noises in the tiled chamber.

Earl watched the priest stroke Artie's head and thought, A special kind of man. He could laugh and joke, yet remained fearless when it came time to comfort the sick, the suffering, and the dying, and he pulled it off day after day. That took a rare brand of courage. Even people of faith could get too close to the ones they tried to help. Earl had seen the fear and suffering in ER overwhelm men and women of God as often as it broke many fine physicians. Yet Jimmy never appeared to flinch from it.

Stewart continued to manipulate the pacemaker wire, but the monitor showed no change, and the pattern remained ragged as a saw's edge.

He nodded to J.S., and she resumed pumping.

A familiar icy tightness gripped Earl in the pit of his stomach as the sense they weren't going to make it crept through him.

But Artie's eyes remained open. Imploring. Beseeching.

Stewart laid down the wire, glanced over to Earl, and silently shook his head.

J.S. continued to pump, her expression questioning him whether to stop for good.

Artie began to blink wildly again.

He knows he's going to die, Earl thought. Time to sedate him. Otherwise the instant they called off CPR, he'd suffocate, awake and aware. It would be like strangling the man.

"Get me ten milligrams of IV midazolam," he told Susanne.

Her eyes widened, but she went to the medication bin and proceeded to draw up the syringe.

"For the record," he said quietly, scanning the aghast eyes of those watching him, "I'm going to make him comfortable, then withhold any further treatment, including CPR, on the grounds it's futile." Without saying it outright, he'd declared they were not about to commit active euthanasia. To the layperson it might sound like word games, but because he was invoking a physician's right not to inflict useless interventions on a patient, Artie's resulting death would be considered natural under the scrutiny of law.

The frowns on everyone told him they felt otherwise. "Anybody have a better idea?" he asked.

Michael, Stewart, and Thomas grimly shook their heads.

Susanne, J.S., and the respiratory technician did the same.

"Mr. Baxter objects," Jimmy said.

Earl bristled. "For the love of God, Jimmy, you know the rules as well as anyone."

"At least have the decency to look at the man while you decide his fate."

Nobody else said a word.

Earl forced himself to meet that dark, fluttering stare.

Artie repeatedly blinked his eyes in couplets. No! No! No! they screamed, brimming with agony.

Earl's heart gave a wrench. "But we can't help him," he whispered to Jimmy. "At least I can make sure he doesn't suffer."

"Tell your patient, Earl."

Artie stopped blinking and glared at him.

Oh, God, thought Earl. "Mr. Baxter, you know we tried everything?"

He blinked yes.

"I'll make you comfortable—"

Two quick blinks cut him off.

"But—"

"I think he wants something," Jimmy said.

A single blink. Yes.

"You want what?" Earl asked. He couldn't think of anything else to say.

Artie responded with a scowl of disgust.

"Something medical?"

No.

"What then?"

The desperation in Artie's stare grew.

Then Earl knew.

"Your wife?"

Tears welled out of Artie's eyes. Yes, he blinked. Yes! Yes! Yes!

"Is she here?" Earl asked.

"In the waiting room," Susanne replied. Her voice sounded as if her windpipe had tightened to the size of a straw.

"You want to see her, Artie?"

The hideously slack face of the dying man had already acquired the consistency of cold mud. Yet it shifted ever so slightly, and Earl swore he glimpsed relief in those amorphous features. Yes! he blinked.

"Then we'll get her for you," Earl said.

Susanne hurriedly retrieved a chair from the corridor and placed it by the stretcher in case Artie's wife couldn't stand.

The other physicians quickly wiped the blood from IV sites and covered the needles sticking out of him with plasters, much the way they would clean up a body before letting the family view it.

Artie's eyes strained to follow the preparations, then stared at the ceiling with a spine-chilling calm.

Earl tried not to imagine his state of mind. "Your arms must be getting tired," he said to J.S., whose forehead glistened with sweat. He found the heat of the extra wear suffocating at the best of times. It would be near unbearable with the sustained physical effort she'd been making.

"I'm fine."

He believed her. She'd kept the rhythm of her chest compressions rock steady the whole time.

When they had everything set, he went to meet Mrs. Baxter. A few of Susanne's nurses had stayed with her in an interview room.

When she looked up as he entered, tiny lines feathered out from the corners of her eyes in her attempt to smile. The rest of her tanned, round forehead had the leathery look of someone who spent a lot of time outside. Petite and lean, she appeared at least a decade younger than her husband.

As he took a breath to speak, he cursed what he hated most about the new reality at St. Paul's. His gloves, mask, and gown created more than a stifling physical barrier to keep germs from passing between people. It blocked communication. She couldn't read his face any more than he could read hers, and she would hear the worst possible news from an invisible voice. He loosened the ties and tugged his mask below his chin.

Unbidden, she did the same. Her cheeks and mouth were as fine-lined as the rest of her, and rigid with fright.

As Earl explained Artie's hopeless situation, her features seemed to implode, and he took her arm to offer support. She felt as flimsy as a hollowed-out husk.

"I'm all right," she insisted.

He didn't think she even noticed when he replaced her mask and redonned his own.

At the door to the resuscitation room she gasped when she saw Artie, but her step never faltered.

Artie's eyes bulged at her approach and filled with tears again.

"Oh, baby," she whimpered, and sank into the chair, then leaned forward to cradle his face between her hands. She looked up briefly at Earl. "How long do I have?" she asked, her voice faint yet eerily smooth, almost matter-of-fact.

"For as long as he's conscious," Earl said.

J.S. nodded in agreement.

The woman once more lowered her mask and started to murmur Artie's name, over and over. Then she leaned forward and kissed his eyes, enclosing him in the privacy of her dark hair as it cascaded around his face. She began to speak of love, of all she adored in him, of forgiving the hurts they'd caused one another, of how proud she'd always been to be his wife . . .

Jimmy withdrew and herded anyone else out of the room who no longer had anything to offer.

J.S. and the respiratory technician continued to work in tandem.

Earl attempted to back out of earshot, yet stayed close enough to intervene if Artie started to seize or choke. Without trying to, he heard enough to think Mrs. Baxter couldn't have been more eloquent if she'd had years to compose her words.

Twenty minutes later Artie Baxter peacefully closed his eyes for the last time.

"I wish I could have asked him a few questions," Stewart said to Earl afterward as they wrote up the chart in the nursing station.

"What?"

"In all my research with post-cardiac-arrest survivors, I've always doubted how accurately they recall what they experienced. That's the trouble with after-the-fact retellings."

Stewart held the dubious honor of being America's expert on the near-death experience, having interviewed over a hundred patients who'd been resuscitated. Their accounts were all remarkably similar, echoing stories that individuals had related since the advent of modern resuscitation methods—rising above their own bodies, passing through tunnels, approaching bright lights—and Stewart claimed he'd demonstrated that these experiences had some basis in reality. But while his work on the topic had been in all the major newspapers and made him the toast of the afternoon talk shows on network TV, serious scientific journals savaged him for his articles. They accused him of betraying his reputation for serious science and considered his data to be the equivalent of alien abduction stories, nothing more than anecdotal evidence of mass hysteria better suited to the *National Enquirer* than the *National Science Review.*

Earl fought the urge to tell him he had the sensitivity of a rock to even think he could turn the ordeal they'd just witnessed into more fodder for his television junkets. "So what, Stewart? You still got a pile of publications out of those accounts," he said instead, hoping it would shut him up.

"But today," Stewart continued, "we could have had something I've repeatedly said this kind of research really needs."

Jesus, Earl thought, give it a rest. "What's that?" he asked, knowing he shouldn't.

"An interview with a dead man."

# Chapter 3

I crept up the back stairwell and let myself into the darkened hallway.

Empty.

So far so good. Still, better wait to see if a nurse emerged from one of the rooms.

I shrank back in the shadows.

The possibility of being spotted always worried me. I could make up a story to explain my presence, but people could see through that sort of thing, and it might invite questions.

My cover all the other times remained bulletproof. Then I became the person everyone knew me as. Not pretended it, but, like a Method actor, inhabited the role so completely that even the character's memories emerged as my own. It helped that I had invented up a past based on mine, and now that I'd lived my created history so long, it often seemed more vivid than the reality. But the real trick had been learning to believe my own lie. During those hours no one could trip me up, because I had banished my secret self to the point that what I'd been no longer existed, and the new me reigned supreme. Sometimes I even inherited the peace of mind that went with my created persona, and for those precious moments I fooled myself so completely that anyone could have

31

read my thoughts and never guessed me to be other than what I seemed. I loved those times. They let me experience hope. After they passed, I knew, once I finished what must be done, I would enter that realm forever, pull on a fresh skin, and the thing that had eaten at me for so long would be dead.

The usual chorus of muffled cries drifted toward me, stoking a sense of dread that soured the pit of my stomach.

I also heard the distant sounds of nurses talking at the far end of the corridor, their carefree voices erupting into laughter.

But no one appeared.

Occasionally a flicker from a late reveler's fireworks came through the window and illuminated the floor in front of my hiding spot, but where I stood remained pitch-black. Nevertheless, the sooner I got in the room and completely out of sight, the easier I'd feel.

I started forward, having already chosen tonight's victim. I figured the holiday meant fewer doctors, and with rookies all over the place, the nurses in other parts of the hospital should be preoccupied, riding herd on the newcomers. They'd never notice me prowling about; the bunch on duty here would be their usual lazy selves. Perfect conditions to run another subject.

Locating the room number, I slipped inside the door and softly closed it behind me.

I stood perfectly still, letting my eyes adjust to the lack of light. Someone, presumably those idiotic nurses outside, had closed the venetian blinds, blocking out the possibility that even a glimmer of illumination from the city, moon, or stars would reach the inhabitant who lay dying in the bed.

Fools, I thought. Cut off all sense of day or night, and a patient could become confused, perhaps psychotic. The observation came as a reflex, my training completely at odds with what I intended to do. The incongruity set my stomach churning, and bilious hot juices rose to the back of my tongue. I swallowed repeatedly and managed to send the acidic mix down the way it'd come up.

The ragged breathing of the woman I'd come for filled my ears. Sometimes the sound caught in her throat and ceased altogether, only to restart seconds later, when she would gasp, then exhale with a soft moan.

I tiptoed over to the blinds and opened them a sliver, just enough to admit an orange glow reflected from sodium lamps in the parking lot below. It cast her thin face in garish pumpkin shades, as if she'd applied too much makeup, and I could see that her mask had slipped down to her chest like a bib. She continued to breathe fitfully, yet remained asleep, completely unaware of my presence. But she could be roused awake. I'd made sure of that before picking her.

A cold loathing seeped through me.

I stepped over to the IV line that kept her hydrated and got to work. Even though she might die as a result of the drugs I would give her, I held with techniques instilled by years of practice and sterilized the side port with an alcohol swab so as not to risk infection. The maneuver also allowed me to think I'd given the subjects their best chance should they survive. Somehow that indulgence made it easier to get through what I did to them.

I pulled out the first of the two syringes I'd brought, removed the cap, and jabbed it in.

Slowly I began to empty half the contents, fifty milligrams of esmolol, a potent, short-acting drug that doctors used to lower pulse and pressure. It would bring her into a state of near shock. With my free hand I gently reached for her wrist and monitored her pulse with my fingers. The skin already felt clammy. She gave no reaction to my touch.

The beat slowed and grew weaker, then disappeared altogether, as it usually did once the systolic pressure fell below 90. Shifting my hand to her neck, I palpated for the carotid artery.

She stirred in protest and made little cries that sounded like mewing.

Ignoring her, I picked up the throb of the larger vessel, then continued the injection until that impulse nearly disappeared as well, which meant her pressure had fallen to just above 60.

I quickly switched syringes, and slowly gave the second ingredient, a hundred milligrams of ketamine. Normally used to induce awake anesthesia, this agent would also offset the fall in pulse and blood pressure, though not enough to reverse the near shock state. But what I really used it for had to do with a unique side effect: the blockade of certain neuroreceptors in the brain.

I finished delivering the dose, capped and pocketed both syringes so there'd be no accidents if she struggled—I'd taken that precaution ever since the Algreave woman—and waited a minute by my watch, giving time for the ketamine to have its full effect.

It felt like an hour.

The woman's breathing seemed to grow deafening as sputum rattled deep in her airway. In a treatment situation I would have suctioned her out to prevent her from choking on her own spit, an act of basic nursing. Instead I switched on the microcassette, shook her, and whispered, "Can you hear me?"

She moaned.

"Can you hear me?" I repeated.

Her reply was little more than a breath. But I could make it out.

"Yes," she said.

Showtime.

I took the microcassette out of my pocket, brought it close to her mouth, and began to coax her along with the usual questions, following my format in the same methodical way a doctor would take a medical history.

"Any more pain?"

"No . . ."

"Do you see anything?"

"No . . ."

"Look harder."

Her gravelly, faint voice seemed to exhale from a corpse. After a few minutes more she abruptly released a shrill cry, and her limbs thrashed about under the bedclothes.

"There're worms. . . ."

"What?"

"They're all over me. . . ."

"What are?"

"Oh, God, help me. . . ."

"Take it easy."

"They're under my skin. . . ."

"No, they're not."

"In my mouth . . . my nose . . ."

"You're imagining—"

". . . behind my eyes . . . coming in through my ears . . ."

"Stop it!"

"They're eating me. . . ." Her voice became a high-pitched shriek, piercing the dark like the cry of a hawk.

I snatched the syringe of ketamine from my pocket, plunged it into her IV, and pushed the plunger, giving her another twenty milligrams.

The scream died in her throat.

When they talked of heaven, it all sounded the same. But each one had a unique vision of hell.

I listened for the approach of running feet.

None came.

Would she remember? Most didn't. But some did, and that could be trouble. Already the nurses were starting to talk.

Anyway, I had enough material from her.

Snapping off the microcassette and retrieving the syringe, I closed the blinds, once more plunging myself into complete darkness. I felt my way to the door, stood there a moment, and, steadying my own breathing, listened for any sounds in the corridor.

Only the usual cries.

Behind me the old woman's respirations reverted to the fragmentary volleys of before, tapering out or choking off abruptly, then starting again. The gurgling noises made my skin crawl.

I opened the door a crack.

Nobody.

But I could still hear the nurses' voices from the far end of the hallway. No surprise there. They'd be sitting on their asses drinking coffee all night. I got ready to slip out of the room and make for the back staircase. I swung the door open another foot and carefully glanced in both directions.

The linoleum gleamed in the half-light, completely empty.

Toward the stairwell, there was only welcoming darkness.

I went to step out, and froze.

Something had moved down there, along the far wall. It had been little more than a dark shape gliding through black.

Then nothing.

Had I imagined it?

No, there it went again.

A figure emerged from the murk, tall and amorphous. It crept slowly from door to door on the opposite side of the hallway, pausing now and then, the way I had done coming in.

What the hell?

I stayed absolutely motionless and remained inside the room, watching, not moving the door, hoping the shadows would shield me as much as they did the form in the corridor. Except as the person drew closer, compared to the darker shroud of protective clothing, the white mask and upper face emanated as a pale smudge and appeared to float along by itself, like a bodiless head. Which meant I might become visible too. And behind me the noises from the old woman grew louder, certainly enough to attract attention.

My mouth went dry, and in a flash of panic I nearly leapt back into the room.

But no. This had to be done slowly.

The figure, paying no attention to the doorways on my side, continued to hug the opposite wall, focused only on the end of the passageway where the nurses' voices kept up a steady patter.

Apparently it was someone who didn't want to get caught either. It might be a man or woman. Everybody looked androgynous these days. I tried to see the eyes well enough to make an ID but couldn't with the distance and semidarkness.

The figure stopped and glanced back toward the stairs, as if making sure no one followed.

Definitely up to no good.

Nevertheless, I couldn't afford to be caught by whoever it might be, creep or not.

The person disappeared into a room twenty feet away.

I couldn't believe my luck.

But neither did I dare risk making a break now.

Whoever it had been might come back out.

I slowly closed my door, leaving a crack wide enough to see when he, or she, left.

It took me a few minutes to realize the old woman was no longer making any noise.

Her breathing had stopped completely.

Shit!

When the nurses found her, they'd call a code. It shouldn't matter, but the prospect of some eager-to-be-a-star resident getting suspicious always worried me.

Total silence now reigned at my back, and the quiet thickened around me, making it difficult to get enough air.

At that moment the person who had snuck into the far room slipped back out and stole away into the darkness, heading for the back steps.

Five minutes later I did the same.

What could be going on? I wondered once I reached the stairwell. Hearing no one below, I started downstairs.

Newspapers had accounts of the sick things male orderlies, nurses, or doctors sometimes did to comatose female patients of any age.

But this could be anyone doing anything to the patient in that room. In the morning I'd check whether an incident of some kind had been reported. No question I had to find out.

If some other scam was in the works, crossed paths might increase my own chances of getting caught. Hell, St. Paul's, with over five thousand employees, including doctors, had the population of a small town. Like any community that size, it would have its share of weirdos with black secrets. Who knew what perverted stuff went on in this place?

### Saturday, July 5, 11:00 a.m.
### Buffalo, New York

Earl loved it when doctors decided to party.

For a few hours they sloughed off the demands on them from a never-ending maze of corridors filled with patients, pain, and loss to become as goofy as schoolkids let out for vacation. The decompression—extreme at the best of times, because all physicians believed if anyone had a God-given right to play, they did—felt even more of a release than usual. Out here, away from work, they also felt freed from the threat of SARS.

But the public didn't. Despite the makings of a perfect day for another successful St. Paul's Annual Hospital Bed and Bedpan Run for Fun—blue sky, a steady breeze off Lake Erie to cool the downtown core, the good turnout by staff and residents alike—the ranks of spectators lining the curb remained sparse. Hospitals had come to be seen as reservoirs of the virus. No one wanted to be around the people who staffed them.

"At least nobody tied bells around our necks," Sean Carrington quipped, referring to the historical treatment of lepers.

Rules for the event were simple. Contestants gathered at the starting line in Buffalo's so-called theater district—two playhouses, one multiplex—and chose a standard-issue, regulation-size hospital bed from a collection slated for the scrap heap. Divided into teams of five—one to ride, four to push—they attempted to safely transport their passenger and the contents of a half-full bedpan (apple juice being the fluid of choice) over a circuit comprising two complete city blocks.

Prior to the race, local politicians and business leaders backed their favorite teams, grandiosely presenting checks the size of air mattresses bearing five-figure amounts while the various competitors christened their chariots with flying banners intended to draw in the cash donors. The Go-Go Train was Urology's entry; the Cutting Edge carried the colors for Surgery; Janet's department would attempt to do itself proud on the Baby Bucket. Earl's crew had simply called their entrant ER, blatantly capitalizing on the popular TV show. But the favorite and champion for the last five years, Jimmy's Flying Angels, brought in the most bucks. Nobody minded, because he invariably divided up the loot with the fairness of a saint. "God bless St. Paul's," he called out to the small crowd after graciously receiving a check for fifty thousand dollars from a beaming, red-faced little man who ran a well-known pest extermination company called Hasta La Vista, Baby.

Then Jimmy rivaled the sun with a flashing grin and added, "For the course of the race, however, I will not be showing Christian kindness."

The other team leaders protested and strutted their feigned indignation in a show worthy of pro wrestlers.

"Hey, Father, unfair!"

"I'll tell your boss!"

"Divine tampering!"

But they evoked only strained laughter from the audience.

"Either our jokes are worse than ever," Thomas Biggs whispered to Earl, "or the few good citizens brave enough to show up aren't that happy to be here."

"Bit of both, I'd say," muttered Sean from behind them. "I tell ya again, we'll all be in cowbells before long."

As the presentations to other teams continued, Earl mugged

for the hospital photographer, pulling deranged faces and using a grease gun like a syringe to lubricate the wheels of his team's bed.

"Set to get whipped?" Jimmy said with a sweet smile, sidling up to him.

Earl pretended to cower before him, and Jimmy flexed his muscles Atlas style, showing off a physique that most body-builders would die for. The photographer snapped away. "How about a quote?" she asked.

"In a two-K race, chaplains who run ten K a day ought to carry rocks as a handicap," Earl said.

"Nah, you're thinking of Hippomenes, and he was carrying golden apples to distract a woman he was chasing," Jimmy retorted. As soon as the woman left, his smile vanished and he glanced to where, a few feet away, Susanne Roberts, Michael Popovitch, Thomas, and J.S. were passing floppy straw hats to a half dozen spectators, enticing them to empty their pockets of small change.

"Can I have just a word with you in private?" Jimmy asked. "It won't take more than a minute."

Earl had already discovered that being VP, medical meant he'd never be lonely. He couldn't go to a hospital function without somebody collaring him for "just a word in private." But he'd hoped a zany affair where they all turned into clowns would somehow protect him from politics for at least a few hours. No such luck. And Jimmy, though on the side of the angels, could be a veritable Cardinal Richelieu when it came to exerting influence on the powers that be at St. Paul's.

"Sure."

They walked to a quiet alcove between a Starbucks and a wannabe Irish tavern with leprechauns painted on the windows.

Jimmy eyed the half-empty street. "Not the best turnout from our good citizenry."

"What's up?" Earl was impatient to dispense with whatever business the man had in mind so he could get back to his team. He'd few enough opportunities to shed his role as big boss and just be good old Earl with them.

"First let me say I thought you handled the Baxter case really well," the priest began. "That had to be the roughest case of that kind I've seen."

"Thanks, Jimmy."

"Are you going to use it for teaching rounds?"

"Of course."

"Will you invite the oncology department?"

"Anyone's welcome. Now, where's this leading?"

"Just that seeing the way you were willing to sedate Baxter so he wouldn't suffer, I knew I could come to you without being accused of overstepping my bounds."

Earl bristled at being buttered up. "Cut the stroking, Jimmy. I know you're after something," he said, comfortable enough with the man to be blunt. Although they were not close friends—they only socialized in the context of hospital business—he liked Jimmy, and sensed that Jimmy liked him. But neither man offered to extend their relationship, as if they both knew intuitively to leave their friendship within boundaries where it could remain comfortable.

The priest's face sagged, and a sadness he rarely showed settled into his eyes. "You're going to get a complaint about me from some of our oncologist colleagues."

"What?"

"These last few days I've been holding up what you did for Baxter, or at least were prepared to do, as an example of what they might well emulate, and some of them got a tad upset about it."

"You didn't."

"I just wanted to warn you—"

"Jimmy, you know damn well not to interfere in how doctors practice."

"Who's interfering? When someone does the right thing, as you did, I simply make a joyful noise about it."

"A joyful noise?"

"Right. Jesus always went on about the need to make a joyful noise. I take him at his word."

"And which doctors, specifically, did you see fit to make this joyful noise to?"

"Well, Peter Wyatt, the chief of that bunch, for one. I always figure it's best to deal with the top man. . . ."

Earl groaned. Wyatt personified the old-boy network at St. Paul's, though he himself hadn't yet reached sixty. But mentally Wyatt allied himself with those from an era where doctors were above mere mortals and not to be questioned, especially by underlings outside the medical hierarchy. "Jimmy, don't give me that naive crap. You knew going to him would stir up a hornet's nest."

"It needed doing."

"What did you say exactly?"

"That a dozen or so members of his department were dinosaurs who sucked at managing pain, and then I suggested an audit on the subject might be in order. I waited until today, of course, figuring it safer to express my opinion in a crowd, where he'd be forced to behave."

"You've got to be kidding."

Jimmy, now looking more defiant than sad, shook his head.

Earl's stomach did a pirouette at the thought of how Peter Wyatt would react, crowd or no crowd, to such a frontal assault, especially since the charge hit home. No greater hot-button issue existed in Palliative Care than proper pain management. The dilemma was, the more potent an analgesic and the bigger the dose, the more likely the medication would stop a person's breathing as well as the pain. Though some enlightened doctors advocated sufficient amounts to make a patient comfortable, even if they inadvertently hastened the person's inevitable death, some didn't. They administered instead rote, inadequate quantities rather than risk an accusation that they'd committed active euthanasia.

Then he thought Jimmy had to be ribbing him. He wouldn't

be so crazy as to pull such a stunt with Wyatt. "Come on. This is a joke, right?"

Jimmy's gaze shifted to a point behind Earl and his eyes widened. "Oh, sweet Jesus, I see the man himself headed this way."

"Quit kidding me, Jimmy, not about this."

"Oh, but I'm not. And he's flushed purple as an eggplant."

Of course Peter Wyatt wouldn't be behind him. Maybe Jimmy had never said anything to him at all, the story being just a way of making a point about a problem that he thought deserved attention from the new VP, medical. Earl loved how the priest could quick-shift from the serious to quirky, off-the-wall teasing. Delivered at the right moment, his jokes could lift the spirits of an entire ER staff and keep the craziness of what came in the door from eating at their minds. What's more, fun could be had in playing along with the man, calling his bluff, throwing out even nuttier nonsense, the game being to top him. Earl relaxed. "Yeah, right, Jimmy. And were I to turn around, there'd be the Pope as well, the pair of them coming to admonish you for sticking your nose where it had no business."

"Dr. Garnet!" rattled the gravelly voice of Dr. Peter Wyatt, the sound running down Earl's spine like knuckles on a washtub.

Jimmy winced. "Want me to stay? I will, but my presence might inflame things."

"Jesus Christ, you really did tell him off!" Earl still couldn't believe it.

Jimmy's gaze hardened, completely devoid of the sadness from minutes ago. "As I said, it needed doing. Do you want me to stay or not?"

"Garnet, I want a word with you!" Wyatt's bellow sounded twice as close as before.

"Jimmy, I swear I'll get you for this. But right now, just get out of here."

"See ya." He flashed that magic grin, gave his hamstrings a quick stretch, and jogged off.

Earl, fuming, turned to confront the chief of oncology, and had to stifle a nervous laugh at the sight of the man descending on him. Bushy eyebrows and a furrowed forehead always endowed Wyatt's grim face with more horizontal lines than the mug of an onrushing bulldog. Normally he stuffed his stocky frame into a three-piece suit, giving himself the formidable air of a Winston Churchill. Today, however, wearing a Hawaiian shirt and Bermuda shorts, he looked more like a knobby-kneed drug dealer. "Peter, good to see you." Earl force-marched his mouth into a genteel smile and held out a hand in greeting. "Fine day for a race, isn't it?"

Wyatt huffed up to where he stood and ignored the gesture. "I see that priest's already gotten to you."

Oh, brother. "Jimmy? He just promised to leave me in his dust during today's race, as usual."

"He didn't tell you what he said to me?"

At close range, Earl could see droplets of perspiration appear across Wyatt's beefy forehead despite the cool breeze. He almost suggested the man sit down somewhere but figured Wyatt would take it as an insult, he being a staunch practitioner of middle-age macho. "He never mentioned you at all, Peter. And why would he? Today's a time for fun, not business."

"Fun, my ass. That comedian in a collar had the nerve to tell me and my physicians how to treat dying patients. Even suggested that there ought to be an audit of how we practice. I never liked these modern types of chaplains, always going on about 'interfacing' and 'holistic care,' as if that's going to shrink a tumor. But Fitzpatrick crossed the line today, and I don't want him in my department anymore. You make sure he stays away."

"Now, wait a minute. I can't do that."

"No?" Wyatt drew in a sharp breath, the kind meant to show indignation, except the wheeze in his nose ruined the effect. "If you won't, then I'll go to the CEO, the board of directors, whoever it takes to get rid of him."

The man's angry voice had started to attract passersby. "Peter, this isn't the time or place."

Wyatt looked uneasily around and broke into a professional smile. "I want him to leave oncology patients alone." His voice had dropped to a whisper but had the sibilance of an angry snake.

Earl maintained the show grin he'd started with, but his cheek muscles had started to burn. "I won't do that, Peter. Jimmy's the only person some patients have to talk with, especially the terminal ones. They'd die alone if it weren't for him."

Wyatt's smile congealed a little, like cold grease. "Garnet, I didn't want you as VP, medical in the first place, and you sure as hell aren't changing my opinion any—"

"Well, I'm sure I can work with you, Peter," Earl interrupted. Despite the pain, he attempted to widen his grin, determined to take control of the situation. It felt more like a show of teeth than a smile. "How about I issue a formal reminder to him and all other Pastoral Service personnel? Something to make it clear that while their insights into patient needs are always valued, final decisions on issues of pain control and medication have forever been and forever will be the exclusive domain of doctors? A kind of 'render unto God what is God's and unto Caesar what is Caesar's' memo."

Wyatt turned a deeper shade of purple. "You're making fun of me."

Earl imagined him in a toga and sporting a crown of leaves around his head. If anyone had an emperor's complex and fantasized about possessing the power to make all of St. Paul's do his bidding with a thumbs-up or thumbs-down, it had to be Peter Wyatt. "Not at all, Peter," Earl quickly reassured him. He knew that Wyatt also held considerable sway over the other dinosaurs who'd led the anybody-but-Garnet lobby and opposed his appointment of Earl Garnet to his current post. They couldn't wait to engineer his downfall. The best defense against this bunch would be copious stroking and keeping them busy. "The truth is, Peter, you just gave me a brilliant idea."

Wyatt's heavy jaw slowly opened, as if about to swallow something whole. "Me? What kind of idea?"

"Who better to lead a hospital-wide audit on pain management than yourself? You've always showed the way in making sure St. Paul's was on the cutting edge of such protocols." And he had. The protocols gathered dust on shelves at every nursing station. "But do we really know if all of us are using them properly? It's a flaming-hot topic right now, as you're well aware, and I can't think of a better person to guide us through the minefield it's become than yourself."

"Conduct a hospital-wide audit? Why, that's a huge undertaking—"

"As far as I'm concerned, you inspired the idea, and the job's rightly yours. The Wyatt Inquiry, we could call it. You'd have the power to appoint anyone you wanted to help you, and I'd order the full cooperation of all the other chiefs. It would be your show, start to finish."

"But I'm so busy—"

"With or without you, it goes ahead, Peter. And that could be a hell of an ordeal if you have to live under somebody else making a mess of a matter you're naturally passionate about. A lot harder than doing it right yourself. Isn't that why any of us take these crazy jobs in the first place?"

Wyatt hesitated, a look of alarm pushing its way onto his thick features. "Yes, that would be hard. . . ."

Earl watched the fight go out of him.

During the man's early days in the late sixties, Wyatt had possessed the courage to take on malignant diseases at a time when they had 80 percent mortality rates. His research had even helped develop the treatments that stood the statistic on its head for lymphomas. In that category, now it was survival rates that stood at 80 percent.

How sad it was to see this tiger so diminished, his once heroic passions for epic cancer work diverted to such puny issues as perceived turf incursions by an overzealous chaplain. "So what do you say, Peter? Will you think about it?"

No answer. He looked overwhelmed.

Earl moved in with the clincher, knowing the one sweetener Wyatt wouldn't be able to resist. "There might even be a paper in it for you, Peter. After all, if you were to develop a road map that would help other hospitals actually implement current protocols in pain management, leading journals would fight to publish it."

Wyatt hadn't had anything accepted for publication for over a decade. What's more, he'd been a victim of one of the crueler spectacles in academic research. Five years ago, still chafing under his dry spell, he'd finally received an invitation to present a paper at a national conference. He'd attended, proudly presented his latest work, and then sat down, ready for questions from the audience. But the moderator, legend had it, instead of inviting inquiries, had stood, pointed at Wyatt, and declared, "This man has demonstrated exactly the type of research we don't want."

Earl had anticipated that the chance of a comeback would kindle a glow in Wyatt's eye.

It didn't.

Instead he remained stone-faced and said, "If you insist, I've no choice."

Wyatt's attitude puzzled Earl. The man he knew had an ego the size of Antarctica, and the lure of any stage generally lit him up so brightly he could be his own spotlight. "Does that mean you accept?"

"I suppose I'll have to." He might have consented to have a leg amputated, for all the enthusiasm he showed.

Weird. But what the hell, as long as the situation with Jimmy seemed defused. "Good! Then let's join the rest and enjoy the race."

"Wait! There's something else you need to hear."

Oh, God. Earl glanced at his watch, hoping Wyatt would get the message to keep this short. "I'm listening."

"The nurses tell me we've had patients complaining about near-death experiences."

"What?"

"You know. That out-of-body phenomenon, the thing Deloram wrote a paper about."

Now Earl felt really puzzled. "Peter, I don't understand the reason you're telling me this." His tone, he realized, sounded more cross than he intended, but patience had limits.

"We never got reports like that before, at least not so many. The first few months the nurses thought nothing of them. Then more patients continued to describe similar ordeals. Some, I'm told, were quite terrified. I swear it's that priest's fault. He's probably talking too much about God, heaven, and the afterlife, making his charges have nightmares about it."

Earl groaned inwardly, incredulous that Wyatt could remain so fixated on Jimmy. "Probably they're just vocalizing that kind of thing more, Peter," he said, trying to hide his exasperation, and started to walk back toward the crowd.

Wyatt followed behind. "Damn it, Garnet, it's not that simple—"

"Similar accounts have been in the media lately, thanks largely to Stewart's research," Earl cut in. If he could somehow trivialize the matter, Wyatt might drop it. "Could be that the phenomenon's been occurring with greater frequency than we knew, and patients, having seen the publicity, realize it's not just them. As a result, they feel open to talk about it now." In the distance he saw Michael wave impatiently, beckoning him to rejoin the ER crew. They were already pushing their bed into the coveted inside post position. Definitely time to ditch Wyatt. He walked faster. "Anyway, it's race time."

"But something's funny," Wyatt went on, easily picking up the pace. "Most of the people it's happened to weren't that near death yet. Oh, they're terminal, in pain, and not in good shape, but their vitals were still stable, not at all what I'd expect for a person who's seeing angels, tunnels, and bright lights."

So much for diplomacy. "Jesus, Peter. They're dying. Many of them will want to talk about that stuff. Patients always have, even atheists. It's human nature. But here isn't the place to discuss it."

"Hey!" Michael Popovitch shouted from the middle of the street thirty yards away. "We're ready to begin." He wore an industrial-strength scowl and sounded pissed.

Sheesh, what's eating him? Earl wondered. The rest of the team settled on give-it-a-break glances and tapped their watches, a far more gentle and appropriate rebuke. Michael should lighten up. "Relax! I'm coming," he shouted, and started to jog toward them.

Wyatt matched him stride for stride, clearly determined to continue their conversation.

Earl didn't intend to let him. "Look, Peter, obviously we'll have to talk about this another time. But I don't think you should make much out of it." He accelerated, pulling a few yards in front, and called over his shoulder, "Why not ask Stewart what he thinks? After all, he's the specialist in that kind of thing."

At the starting line Thomas, Susanne, and J.S. were starting to jostle good-naturedly with members of the Baby Bucket team, who'd tried to steal their spot.

"Earl Garnet," Janet yelled, eyeing him from her perch on the bed, "I'm pregnant with your baby. Chivalry demands you yield the post." She placed a hand to her forehead, adopting the melodramatic pose of a damsel in distress.

Earl laughed. He and Janet always lent their talents to the campy theatrics that were a highlight of these fund-raisers. "All's fair in love and war," he called back. "That's been my plan all along. You pregnant, us on the inside track."

"You're a scoundrel, Earl Garnet," she cried, to the delight of all.

He gave an appropriately wicked leer as he shouldered

through a last-minute rush of other competitors who were late to take their positions.

Wyatt caught up to him. "The nurses already did that, a few days ago."

Piss off, damn it! Earl nearly screamed. But they were jammed together, and rather than risk angering him again, he tried to be civil through clenched teeth. "Already did what?"

"Asked Stewart Deloram to check out the accounts that our patients have been giving. I'm told he suggested the same explanations as you did, but agreed to interview the people who were still alive."

Overhead loudspeakers crackled to life. "Ladies and gentlemen, take your marks."

Cheers broke out around them.

Teams scrambled into position.

"Let's go, Dr. G.," J.S. hollered.

Susanne and Thomas joined in.

Someone blew charge on a trumpet.

But Wyatt remained so wrapped up in his crazy story, he didn't even react to the excitement swirling around them. He just leaned in toward Earl to make himself heard. "I don't know what happened. He burst into my office yesterday, mad as hell, and accused me of trying to set him up as a fraud, then stormed out."

Oh, brother, Earl thought. Not another feud. "Peter, I'm sick as hell of being asked to sort out these kind of kindergarten spats, especially the ones involving Stewart. Now both of you act like adults and sort it out yourselves." He'd ended up shouting far more loudly than necessary to be heard above the din around him.

The rolls of flesh in Wyatt's face shifted as he assumed an injured look. "But the man refuses to even talk with me now."

Earl waved him off in exasperation and joined the welcoming arms of his ER team—all except Michael's; he still seemed upset about something as well—and mounted the bed they would push to victory. At least that's how he lustily predicted the outcome during a crude exchange of triumphant gestures with Janet, and beyond her, the surgeons in Sean Carrington's Cutting Edge mob.

God, it felt delightful—the sanest moment of his morning, when he was responsible for nothing more than the safe passage of a bedpan filled with apple juice.

# Chapter 4

**That same Saturday, 5:30 p.m.**
**The roof of Eight West, St. Paul's Hospital,**
**Buffalo, New York**

Jane Simmons sat at the picnic table, sipping a beer as she chatted with the other ER nurses. A silver medal for the ER team's closer-than-usual second-place finish behind Father Jimmy clinked against the neck of the bottle.

The so-called wind-up party, well into its fifth hour, had lasted six times longer than the race itself, and a hundred or so others still hadn't gone home. Everyone seemed glad to hang out where they could see one another's faces again. But the reason she'd stuck around stood on the other side of the dance floor among a group of residents, too many of them women.

Thomas Biggs leaned against a picnic table, his arms folded across his chest, laughing easily and listening more than talking.

She felt jealous, and hated herself for it. When he eventually came to the makeshift bar, a long cafeteria table laden with drinks in buckets of ice, she walked over to greet him.

"Hi, Thomas. Want to share a beer?"

"Hey, J.S. Sorry, I said I'd go into ER early, starting a few hours from now. Split a juice with you?"

"Cute!"

"Would you like to dance?"

"Sure."

He swung her out onto the platform, where a dozen other couples snaked around to the strains of "Lady in Red." It blared from speakers suspended in a pair of potted trees, all part of the loaned decor that turned the gravel surface on top of the hospital's west wing into what the program described as the "Roof Garden." Mauve velvet ropes strung between chrome posts to demarcate an area well away from the edge looked as if they'd been borrowed from a movie theater lobby. Behind them stood a veritable jungle of more borrowed large plants. These concealed the ten-foot chain-link fence that, according to hospital lore, had been erected around the perimeter six years earlier after the then chief of psychiatry jumped to his death. Without the greenery as camouflage, the place resembled a prison yard.

She settled comfortably into his arms, once more appreciating his ability as a dancer. She also liked the gentle way he held her, and the feel of his firm chest.

Jane knew he was covering ER tonight. She'd checked the schedule, as she often did, to see if they'd be on together. But her slot started at eleven, the regular nursing shift.

Christ! For a grown woman, sometimes she could act so lame about him, she thought, embarrassed at having looked up when he worked. Then she wondered if he ever did the same for her. She'd like that.

An early evening breeze ruffled her hair, and she relaxed her head dreamily against his shoulder. He shifted his arms ever so slightly, enfolding her. She enjoyed the sensation.

She'd barely noticed him his first rotation through ER at St. Paul's. That had been her own rookie year. Scared to death of making a mistake on duty, then preoccupied with studying possible case scenarios on her days off in order to boost her confidence at work, she'd little time for men and didn't enjoy going out much. But after six months she had gained enough competence to look beyond her job and enjoy life a little—enough to keep an open mind as far as hooking up with someone when the Christmas party rolled around. Big mistake. People decompressed so much that most behaved as if they were at Mardi Gras. Wives left their wedding rings at home, husbands forgot where they lived, and singles swung.

Except for Dr. Thomas Biggs. He not only knew a fox-trot from a waltz but also didn't use their time on the dance floor as an opportunity to grope her. Better yet, between numbers he actually seemed to enjoy talking about something besides work.

From then on she'd started checking his schedule against her own. They never ran out of anything to say. Movies, music, medicine—the topic didn't matter. And she particularly liked his easy, soft-spoken manner and barely detectable Tennessee drawl. To her mind, he sounded like someone out of *Gone with the Wind*—a man who knew how to treat a lady. Of course, she never monopolized him, again to avoid tongues wagging. Even at subsequent ER parties she'd danced with him no more than anyone else. But it had bothered her that he hadn't tried to take it further.

Initially she'd presumed he didn't want to date anyone with whom she worked, even though many residents had no such qualms and behaved like free-range rutters whenever they had the chance. Then his rotations took him to other departments—some even out of the city, to rural rotations in the Finger Lakes district, a winemaking area east of Buffalo—and she hardly saw him at all. Occasionally they ran into each other in the cafeteria and would have a coffee together. But he would never initiate anything more, not so much as a dinner invitation. She'd even begun to think he might be gay, then decided probably not. She could usually tell that about a man. It had to do with the carnality of her attraction to him, and Thomas's pull on her definitely rated a ten.

Still, frustrated at his lack of boldness and wondering about the reason, she'd finally asked him outright. "Do you prefer men, or is it me as a woman you got problems with?"

His swarthy complexion had flushed behind the closely

cropped beard. "Want to go to my apartment and find out?" His tone carried more dare than invitation.

"Yeah," she'd said, double-daring him right back.

And they'd become lovers.

"Why'd you wait so long?" she'd asked him afterward.

"Because I didn't want us to be the latest gossip morsel for the hospital to chew over. I hate that."

"Me too."

"So what do we do?" He'd seemed genuinely lost for ideas.

"Continue to act like friends in public," she'd told him, surprised at how easily he'd let her take charge. "Can you keep a secret? I mean really keep it. Not a peep about us to anyone?"

He'd shrugged. "Watch me."

So they'd sealed the bond.

That had been eight months ago, just before last Christmas.

They'd been lovers ever since, except when he'd had to go off to the Finger Lakes district again, at the beginning of the year.

The music ended, and she opened her eyes. The summer dusk promised a long, languid sunset. "I want to be more than just your chum tonight," she whispered.

"You mean in the hospital? We might blow our cover."

"There's tomorrow morning. After sign-out, come on over, and I'll make you breakfast."

His dark good looks lit up with that infectious grin of his that she loved to see.

"You mean ol' hillbilly me finally is considered house-broken enough to be allowed into that new apartment of yours?" he teased. "What happened? Someone cover it all in plastic?"

She'd just moved into a new place. For reasons of her own, she'd hesitated at inviting him over. "Something like that. How about it?"

"Love to," he said, and walked away, rejoining the residents he'd been talking with earlier.

Feeling miserable, she wandered over to the end of the table, away from her nursing friends. Did he want her as much as she did him? At times she suspected his aversion to gossip simply gave him the excuse he needed to keep her at a distance—handy when he needed her, but out of sight when it suited him.

"You look as if you've lost your best friend," said a voice behind her.

She turned to see Father Jimmy, beer in hand. He gave her a lopsided grin that lifted her spirits despite her foul mood. "Hi, Father. No, it isn't anything like that."

He glanced across the room and nodded toward Thomas. "You're sure?"

She felt her face grow warm. He couldn't possibly know about Thomas and her. They'd been so careful. "What are you talking about?"

"You seem unhappy. 'Tis a shame, a woman of your talent and beauty."

The burn in her face increased. "I'm fine."

"Are you? I'd say that the usual J.S. spark is missing tonight."

"Just tired, is all."

"Ah, well, if that's the problem, I'm not surprised. You work hard."

"No more than the next person."

"Oh, I disagree. I can tell the good ones, and you're right up there, J.S. You pour heart and soul into what you do, and haven't backed off it since the day you arrived. I like that in you."

His candid praise surprised her. While he'd always been friendly and spoke of the good job that nurses did, she'd never heard him single one out for special mention before, let alone her. Probably figured she needed cheering up. "Thank you, Father. That's very kind."

"Kindness has nothing to do with it." He walked over and

sat down beside her. "A lot of the patients talk about the special 'pierced angel of ER.' "

She started to laugh. "The what?"

He grinned again and took a swig of beer. "I've been wondering if maybe I should get an earring. What do you think?"

She laughed some more. "Come on."

"But I never get a clear answer whether right or left is a message. Needless to say, I can't go around giving the wrong idea."

"You're not serious."

"Sure. I figure it'll help bridge the gap between me and some of the street kids."

She searched his face for a hint that he'd engaged her in one of his games of zany banter, but he seemed quite pensive. And for the first time she found herself guessing about his age. Probably mid-thirties. Not at all too old for jewelry, though she couldn't remember ever seeing a priest wear any. She would have thought there'd be a rule against it.

"So which is it, right or left?"

She laughed. "Right or left ear. It doesn't matter anymore," she said. "And I could do it for you if you like." She immediately felt shy at making the offer.

But he let out a deep chuckle. "Why, I can't think of anyone I'd rather trust my earlobe to. Just tell me when and where."

His ready acceptance relaxed her. Apparently he hadn't found the offer out of line. "Good. I'll check with Susanne about using a treatment room in ER. It won't take more than a few minutes. But bring the ring with you, so I can insert it to keep the perforation open."

"Done. Let me know when you're ready. And thanks, J.S." He held out his hand to shake on the deal. The firmness of his grip didn't surprise her, given his physique, but the roughness of his palm did. It had the calluses that only years of physical labor could produce. Like her father's.

She realized her hand had lingered in his when he said, "Not the soft skin you expected?"

"Oh, sorry." She felt her cheeks grow warm.

"Hey, I'm proud when someone notices. They got like that prior to divinity school, when I bummed around out west for a few years. Worked as a ranch hand in several places. Say, you're from the prairies too, aren't you?"

"Yeah, but farther east. I grew up in wheat country—Grand Forks, North Dakota, right on the Minnesota border."

"I know where it is. Just north of where they made that movie *Fargo* a few years back, and gave everyone Norwegian accents."

She laughed again, knowing exactly the film he meant. Everyone in Grand Forks had busted a gut laughing at it. "I-ya do-on't kno-oo wh-at yo-ou me-an," she mimicked, summoning up her best singsong rendition of the lead actress's portrayal of a local female cop's speech.

He threw his head back and guffawed so loudly it stopped conversations and attracted more than a few looks. "That's perfect," he managed to say, still chortling, oblivious to the reactions around him. "Say something else."

Carried away by his exuberance, she added, "Be-ee ca-re fu-ull, o-or yo-ou wi-ill pu-uke."

This time he nearly doubled over, and she started to giggle, finding his easy enjoyment of her joke infectious.

They settled down, and he asked, "Are your mom and dad still in Grand Forks?"

A twinge of sadness cut through the happy moment. "My father died in a construction accident twelve years ago. Mom's there, though," she added, brightening, "along with my kid brother, Arliss, who's now six foot and in his final year of high school. To think I used to beat him up."

He reared back in an expression of mock horror. "Did ya now?"

His Irish brogue made her giggle again.

"And you look like you could still handle yourself," he continued, bringing his head closer to hers. His eyes alight with playfulness, he held a hand to the side of his mouth in an obvious parody of someone about to reveal a secret. "Your speed as a runner actually had me worried during the race today. Fast as a cheetah, ye are. Nobody's come so close to beatin' the Flying Angels in years."

They chatted a few more minutes about the prairie, and then he excused himself.

As he walked away, she thought it odd that she found him so likable. Her attitude toward God's existence amounted to little more than a willingness to keep an open mind on the subject. Yet during her encounters with Father Jimmy in ER, she had never once sensed that he had an underlying agenda to show her the error of her loosely held beliefs. He just seemed friendly and fun. In fact, if he weren't a priest . . . She immediately shut down that line of thought. My God, what could she be thinking?

She nevertheless continued to watch the man as he wandered the room, joking with whomever he met, until she saw Dr. G. corner him. The two exchanged a few words, their expressions tightened into frowns, and they left together, joined in an animated discussion. At the door leading back into the hospital they stopped where boxes of protective clothing had been stacked and suited up again, but the ritual failed to interfere with their conversation.

She scanned the crowd, looking for Thomas. He stood against the setting sun, head tilted in easy laughter, evidently finding the woman he talked to exceedingly funny. The pleasant warmth of her interlude with Father Jimmy vanished instantly, replaced by a longing she'd come to resent.

"Do you want him, girl?" Susanne whispered in her ear and sat down beside her. "This time next year he'll be gone."

Jane felt herself flush. "What are you talking about?"

Susanne gave a dismissive wave. "You're a lot like me," she said. "A woman who likes to keep private things private. But I can tell what's up between you two."

"Really, Susanne, you've got the wrong impression—"

Susanne cut her off with a skeptical arch of an eyebrow that made it clear further protests were pointless.

Jane shook her head and took a swig of beer. She also felt an overwhelming urge to unload her secret to a sympathetic ear. She'd once carried her feelings for Thomas effortlessly, but they'd become all too heavy lately, the price of bearing them in private. It left her isolated and lonely, and she didn't like that. Maybe the time to talk was here. "How'd you know?"

"Just by watching. There's something different between the two of you when you dance. I didn't see it before last Christmas, but since . . ." She grinned with a shrug.

"See what?"

"You're more relaxed."

"And him?"

Susanne shrugged again. "Hard to tell. He's already so loosey-goosey with that hillbilly facade he puts on."

Jane laughed, then felt depressed again. She peered through the gaps between nearby buildings and glimpsed the blue sparkle of Lake Erie. A line of dark clouds floated across the horizon, their tops swollen into great round caps like a patch of mushrooms. The sight reminded her of the prairie skyline and carefree days back home in North Dakota.

"He seems like a good guy, though," Susanne added. "I can see why you like him."

The confirmation of her own instincts picked Jane up a little. She trusted Susanne's judgment and especially liked her ability to share insights without appearing to give advice. That bond had been established early, within days of her arrival in ER.

Despite her decision not to date anyone, Jane had started to let her guard down with the guys in the department, hoping to fit in. Nothing serious, just played along with their lighthearted chatter and teasing in the way she would have with her buds back at Grand Forks. But then came the comments laced with sexual innuendos.

At first she'd taken offense. That kind of talk angered her.

As early as high school she'd had to endure the "nice T and A" comments the boys whispered behind her back but loud enough for her to hear. It drove her to start dressing tough, all the while feeling far from it inside. Even now, being what her mother called "amply endowed," whenever she wore a swimsuit the old self-consciousness about her body remained. So when the males in ER cracked that J.S. had better not go near old men with pacemakers, she might have grinned good-naturedly, but the joke set her cheeks on fire.

"They're assholes," Susanne had told her in the nurses' lounge after the first incident. "Not one of them would know what to do with a gorgeous woman like you, and that's your weapon. Zing their kind right back, and they fold."

The next time some wit resorted to that same refrain, Jane had run her fingernail down the front of his lab coat, unhooking the buttons as she went, and looked him scornfully in the crotch. "No danger letting you near the female patients, with or without pacemakers."

He'd turned tomato red.

The others had oohed and laughed.

But she'd felt elevated a notch in how the males treated her after that.

And Susanne had become a combination older sister and aunt who watched over her without ever seeming to interfere.

"He says he doesn't want to do anything more about us right now," Jane found herself admitting to her. "That he couldn't stand the busybodies picking our lives apart."

"They won't if you don't let them," Susanne said.

"And how do I manage that?"

Susanne smiled and shook her head. "I suppose the same way you already have, silly—by continuing to keep your mouth shut. It's worked."

"But you knew."

"I'm different. What I picked up on had to do with seeing a kindred spirit, you might say. No one else is likely to find out."

Jane again wondered if Father Jimmy might not suspect the truth. "Yeah, right."

"Ask yourself why you know so much about who the people in this department are sleeping with," Susanne said.

Jane shrugged. "I don't know. Word gets around."

"Because most people, when they become lonely or down enough, brag about whom they love as a way to raise their confidence. I guess it somehow makes their being loved back feel more real. So far, honey, you've resisted that urge. As a result, you fall off everyone else's radar as soon as you walk out of here."

Susanne ought to know, Jane thought. Hardly anyone in the department ever gossiped about *her* private life. Oh, a few might have guessed at the possibilities of whom she might be with, but they didn't get far, there being no rumors to feed the mill. She wore no wedding ring, never discussed anything personal, and when *she* went out the door of ER, it might as well be into a black hole.

"So it beats me why he'd still be worried about gossip this stage of the game," Susanne continued. "You've both proven you can put up a good enough front to keep your business private. What's to stop the two of you from making plans for after next year?"

Hearing someone else articulate what she'd been telling herself, Jane felt something release deep inside her. Susanne, as usual, hadn't advised her what to do, but rather nudged her to see for herself what ought to be done. Not that she didn't already know. Anyone with half a brain could see that the time had come to press Thomas for the real reason he'd been stalling about their future. What held her back had to do with her fear of the truth and the practical prairie philosophy she'd learned from her mother: never ask questions when the answers might make you more miserable.

"You what?"

"I had to, Jimmy. Wyatt would have tried to kick you out of the hospital."

The priest jumped up from the visitor's chair in Earl's cramped ER office and started to pace. "But to have him lead a hospital audit on pain? That's as stupid as . . . as . . . as if you put bin Laden in charge of human rights at the UN."

"Or you telling the prickly fart how to practice medicine. Why'd you pull a boneheaded play like that?"

Jimmy froze and gave Earl a withering look. "Because I won't sit at any more bedsides and try to give spiritual comfort to poor wretches who die screaming."

"You're exaggerating—"

"Goddamn it, Earl, wake up. You see something that atrocious in ER, and you'd move in with morphine, ketamine, fentanyl—whatever it takes. I can't do that. For me it's beg the nurses, who ask the residents, who don't prescribe enough, then beg them to get their staff supervisor. Even then a third of them won't budge from the guidelines, but I beg them as well anyway, and all the time the screeching goes on. I tell you, there ought to be a court for medical atrocities, just like there is for atrocities of war, and this kind of torture by omission should be made a crime. . . ." He seemed to run out of breath and simply stood there, panting as heavily as if he'd just completed one of his runs.

Earl sat stunned. He knew that crap happened, as hideously as described, and he condemned it whenever he could, but he'd never before seen it from so stark a point of view. At first he didn't know what to say. Finally he asked, "It's really getting to you?"

Jimmy nodded. "Sometimes." His eyes focused on something Earl couldn't see.

Judging from the pain reflected in the priest's gaze, Earl didn't want to see it. "You still could have come to me, Jimmy," he said softly. "Brought me patients' names and chart numbers. That's the kind of documentation that would have nailed Wyatt and others like him."

"Yeah, right. Case by case, committee by committee—it takes forever that way."

Earl exhaled long and hard. "But keep at it enough, and

even the thickest-skulled dinosaurs change their ways in the end."

"Then why didn't you do it?"

"Me?"

"Yeah. You're a physician. Nothing stopped you from stepping up with charts and patient names these last twenty-five years."

Earl bristled. "Nobody dies like that in my department. Certainly not since I've been chief."

Jimmy's eyes narrowed into a hard, unjoking glare. "And that's the trouble with you, Earl. You hide in ER."

"Hide?"

"Yes, hide. It's a domain as black and white as any in the hospital. The sicker the patients, the easier your job. Stabilize 'em, medicate 'em, and ship 'em upstairs. Don't get me wrong, you're great at it—decisive, skilled, and courageous. But one of the reasons the job suits you isn't so noble. The patients don't hang around, and you like it that way. The ones who don't make it, you can honestly tell yourself they died while you were trying everything possible. The ones who do, their pain, fear, and despair are muted by shock or postponed by drugs. The long and short of it all is that you get to keep your losses more cut-and-dried. No having to deal with the long, messy aftermath that survival involves."

"Whoa. Now wait a minute, Jimmy. I find out how people did after they left ER. Their doctors tell me—"

"I'm not talking about the clinical results or satisfying your medical curiosity."

"Jesus, Jimmy, what the hell's the matter with you?"

"What's the matter is, you can't be VP, medical and bury yourself in a mentality that has a fix for everything."

Earl leapt to his feet. "That's not fair!"

"What's fair got to do with it? You want to face a patient's lingering, share in his or her long-term agony, witness their slow settling for a fraction of a former life, then watch your *successes* as they piece together what they lost from the heart attack or stroke or car accident that derailed them."

"Damn it, Jimmy, how dare you—"

"Why, in all the years I've been here, I never once saw you up on the floors visiting with any of the people you saved."

Earl felt he'd been gut-punched.

He stood behind his desk as a tiny prickle of sweat dampened the back of his shirt despite the chill of cold air pouring over his head from a ventilation duct in the ceiling.

The black of Jimmy's eyes increased its hold on him. "If you'd had any inkling at all for that part of the game, Earl, now and then I would have found you on the wards where it plays itself out. And maybe, just maybe, when you came across wretched souls with barely days left to live, bellowing like wounded beasts, you might have acquired the same compassion for them that you found for the likes of Artie Baxter when you made sure he didn't suffer in ER."

With that, the priest released him from the tractor-beam grip of his stare, quietly opened the door, and disappeared into the darkened corridor.

The head nurse slid her glasses to the tip of her nose, peered at him, then let them drop on their silver chain. "Dr. Garnet! We don't usually see you up here."

"Here" referred to the Palliative Care Unit, or "terminus," as some of the more callous residents called it.

"Then it's about time," he answered, straining to read the woman's name tag. "Mrs. Yablonsky, would you be so kind as to grab the chart cart and accompany me as I see the patients?"

Crinkles at the corners of her eyes lessened. "See the patients?"

"Yes."

"All of them?"

"Yep."

"Now?"

He nodded.

"But why?"

"I want to check their pain medication."

The visible portion of her face corrugated itself into a frown. "You mean without their doctors knowing?"

Jesus, he'd be here all night answering her questions. "We're going to be doing an audit on pain management throughout the whole hospital. Dr. Wyatt himself will be chairing it. I thought I'd get a head start."

The far smoother foreheads of two younger nurses who had approached from behind her scrunched up in amazement.

"Dr. Wyatt knows about this?" the supervisor asked.

Earl smiled in response.

"Well, it's most peculiar. . . ." She pushed herself out of a swivel seat, surprising him with her height. With eyes nearly at the same level as his, she also possessed the big shoulders and sculpted build of someone who swam laps across Lake Erie.

While he waited for her to prepare the charts his gaze drifted along the polished, barren corridor, and he shuddered at the thought of being stuck here to die. Just park him under a tree with a nice view and a bottle of whisky when his time came.

He'd never admitted it to anyone, but deep down he hated hospitals, felt claustrophobic in them. As a patient, he'd loathe every part of surrendering to any regime that a place like St. Paul's would impose on him, especially with his butt hanging out the back of a tie-up gown.

Through windows at the far end of the unit he watched the sun as it slipped behind a column of thunderheads that had been piling up over the lake. Immediately the passageway darkened, and everything became cast in a thin yellow light. Low rumbles sounded outside, and a crackle of static interrupted the quiet music from a radio on the work counter.

"Storm's coming," said one of the younger nurses, reaching up and snapping the off button.

Only then did he hear the weak moans and wailing. Mere wisps of sound that floated out from the semidarkness of the hallway, they were the kind of noises that, once gotten used to, could easily be ignored—with the help of a radio. "Are they always crying like that?"

"Oh, this is nothing," Yablonsky said. "Sometimes they get to screaming so loud you can't hear yourself think." Oblivious to her own callousness, she never paused in pulling out charts and placing them on a pushcart.

A twist of anger turned his stomach.

In the first room they stopped in, he found an old man curled in bed, as withered and emaciated as a mummy. His skin had yellowed with jaundice, and, either comatose or sleeping soundly, he didn't respond when Yablonsky called his name or slipped the mask that had fallen off his face back into place. Earl let him be.

Next door to him lay an elderly lady in similar shape.

In the third room, a gaunt, gray-faced woman with the wisps of her remaining hair combed neatly into place sat in a chair and stared out at the approaching rain clouds. Her upper face brightened as soon as she saw him. "How nice, a new doctor."

A glance at her chart before coming in revealed her name to be Sadie Locke and that she had metastatic cancer of the breast that neither chemotherapy nor radiation could halt. As he stepped up to shake her hand and introduce himself, the sleeve of her housecoat slipped up her arm to reveal a swarm of florid red blotches where the tumor had seeded itself to her skin, and a sniff of decay floated down the back of his nose.

"I love a thunderstorm at the end of a hot summer day, don't you?" she said after assuring him she felt comfortable most days on her current drug regime. "It's so refreshing, and the air smells wonderfully clean afterward."

"Yes, I know exactly what you mean," he said. Her pleasant manner put him at ease. Normally having nothing to offer a patient but small talk made him feel awkward. "Do you have family?" he asked after a few seconds, mostly to reassure himself she knew someone who cared enough to keep her company. He couldn't imagine anything worse than being confined to a room, with no prospects of a visitor.

"Yes, one son. Donny. He owns a restaurant in Honolulu. I don't see him much, but next week he'll be here—a business trip to New York. And he taught me how to use e-mail." She pointed at a turquoise laptop sitting on her night table.

Pretty lonely, he couldn't help thinking, and tried to come up with something else to say. "Do you know the hospital chaplain, Jimmy Fitzpatrick?"

Her eyes beamed. "Father Jimmy? Of course. He's wonderful. Always says just the right thing to pick up a person's spirits."

Oh, does he now? Earl thought, still shaken by the hiding he'd received.

"Cracking jokes the way he does is wonderful," she continued, "but he can be serious when he wants to be."

"Tell me which you like best about him, jokes or serious." Maybe she could give him some pointers about the man's technique with the patients here.

"That's easy. He never wastes my time. No rubbish about doctors all at once finding a cure or me somehow getting better through a miracle. There's a relief in hearing a person tell bad news honestly and make no bones about what can't be done. It leaves him free to help me in ways he can."

"What are those?"

"Listening, talking about ordinary things, keeping me interested in the world—you know, making me feel I matter to him. Not that he's got a lot of time to do it in. There are so many others who depend on him as well."

Earl started to thank her, not much the wiser about specifics that made Jimmy so great at his job, but she laid a hand on his arm. "Know what's his real secret, now that I think about it?"

Earl waited.

"It's the way he looks you in the eye and says, 'I'm sorry you're going through this.' Twenty seconds face-to-face like that, and I feel he's given me twenty minutes."

The next dozen visits went a little quicker, but he found them no easier. Patients raised questions he couldn't answer and expressed fears he didn't know how to console.

"Why me?" some asked when he inquired about their pain.

"I'm afraid to die," others said.

Not that he hadn't heard those words thousands of times in ER. But there the confused hurly-burly of a resuscitation or the rush to line and intubate whomever he was working on allowed him to get away with brief reassurances. Here people looked him in the eye and expected his undivided attention along with a detailed response.

"I don't know what to say," he repeated over and over, bowing to a growing sense that on this ward, bullshit would be even less forgivable than his ineptness with words. "But I'm sorry for your ordeal."

Still, he pushed on with the rounds. Despite the emotional suffering he'd discovered, he began to wonder if Jimmy hadn't exaggerated his claim about patients being undermedicated, as most seemed free of physical discomfort.

Then they approached the nearest of a string of rooms where the nurses had closed the doors. The sounds he'd heard earlier emanated from here.

He quickly scanned the chart of the patient they were about to see.

Elizabeth Matthews, fifty-eight, terminal cancer of the ovary.

What had sounded like whimpering turned out to be a continuous high-pitched cry once they were inside. The lights were off and the blinds were closed, so he could barely make out her form on the bed. But he could smell the acrid, sour aroma of her sweat.

Swallowing, he drew closer, and his eyes adjusted to the dark. She lay on her side clutching her knees, curled around the point where the tumor, grown from what had once been the source of her seed, would have maximally eaten through the contents of her lower abdomen and into her pelvis. She rocked back and forth, as if her belly were a cradle to the malignancy and her hideous keening could lull its ravages to sleep.

"Mrs. Matthews?"

The piercing sound from her throat never wavered.

A movement in the corner of the room startled him. "Doctor?" a man's voice said.

Earl turned to see a tall, asthenic figure rise from a lounge chair set well back from the bed.

"I'm Elizabeth's husband." He held out his hand. "Thank you for coming."

Earl took it, touched by the simple dignity of the gesture. Either the man had nerves of steel to remain so composed in the face of his wife's suffering, or witnessing it had left him numb. "Mr. Matthews, I'm so sorry."

"Nothing's helped, Doctor. She's been this way for the last two days. The residents tell me they're giving her the maximum amounts of morphine possible. . . ."

As he talked, Earl flipped to the medication sheet and looked at the orders.

*Morphine sulfate, 5 mg sc q 4 hrs prn.*

Maximum, his ass. A medical student must have written it, copying word for word from the *Physicians' Desk Reference,* the bible of medications and their standard dosages. But Elizabeth Matthews didn't have standard pain.

He immediately felt back on his turf. "Get me ten milligrams of midazolam," he said to Yablonsky. This kind of suffering he could dispatch in seconds.

"But—"

"Now!"

One of her younger assistants darted out the door.

"When did she get her last dose of morphine?" he asked, walking over to check that Elizabeth Matthews's IV line remained functional. He opened the valve full, and it ran fine.

Yablonsky flipped to the nurses' notes. "At three this afternoon," she said, "during our usual medication rounds."

"And it's now nearly eight, five hours later. Her order says every four hours, as needed. I think we agree she needs it."

"Well, yes . . ."

"And you gave her only five milligrams?"

"Subcutaneous, as prescribed."

"You didn't request her doctor raise the dose, even though you could easily see she required more?"

"More is not what's on the chart, Doctor. Besides, we don't want her to get used to it so the drug no longer has an effect—"

"You call this an effect, Mrs. Yablonsky?" He gestured to the crumpled shape on the bed.

She fidgeted with the chart, fuming at being confronted. "No, but I—"

"What do you say we give her ten, then? And if that doesn't work, make it fifteen." He grabbed the file out of her hand and wrote the order, scrawling his signature with an angry flourish. "And once we find out how much is enough, we'll make it an IV infusion. Even street junkies know that popping narcotics under the skin doesn't hold a candle to mainlining."

Yablonsky turned scarlet all the way to the tips of her ears. "Really, Dr. Garnet, her oncologist says she could linger like this for months. She *will* grow tolerant to morphine, and—"

"Then we'll sedate her, just as I'm about to do now."

As if on cue, the young nurse who'd gone to fetch the midazolam returned and handed him a syringeful of the fast-acting sedative. He swiped the rubber portal at the side of Elizabeth's IV line with an alcohol swab, jabbed in the needle, and slowly pushed on the plunger. "Whatever it takes to make her comfortable," he continued, "*especially* if she's got months. My God, is that your policy, the longer a patient has, the longer they don't get sufficient morphine?"

Yablonsky's younger colleagues, standing behind her back, nodded tellingly.

Yablonsky snapped her head high and threw back her ample shoulders. "Of course not."

Earl wondered if she had once been an army nurse.

Elizabeth's cries lessened as he slowly injected the contents of the needle, keeping a sharp eye on the rise and fall of her chest.

Mr. Matthews walked over to the other side of the bed, leaned over, and stroked his wife's head. "It will be better now, Elizabeth. You'll get some rest." The fatigue in his voice weighted the words like rocks, but they must have fallen as gently as tears on her ears. She smiled, released her hold on her knees, and reached up to pat his hand.

A few seconds more, and she slept peacefully.

"Thank God," Mr. Matthews said, and pulled her mask from down around her neck back up over her nose. By the light from the hallway, his haggard eyes appeared gouged out by worry and exhaustion.

"Why not grab some shut-eye yourself?" Earl told him. "I promise you, she'll be fine for the night. Go home and get to bed." He put his hand on the old man's shoulder, and felt it slump in defeat. "Mrs. Yablonsky will sponge-bathe Mrs. Matthews and change her nightie and bedding." He turned to face the nurse. "And open the blinds, shall we? Let her see it's night should she wake up, right, Mrs. Yablonsky?"

She sucked in a mouthful of air. "Yes, sir."

"During the day, we'll continue to make sure they stay open and that there's natural light in here, so she'll be less confused. Agreed?"

The nurse nodded.

"And she gets her next morphine as soon as she starts to stir from the midazolam wearing off, which will be in about an hour. . . ."

As Earl rattled off his instructions, tears rippled down the haggard circles beneath Mr. Matthews's eyes to where the crescent contours of skin bunched up by the top of his mask. From there wet marks spread through the material until it grew damp enough to stick against the hollow contours of his cheeks. He reached across his wife's sleeping form and held out his hand to Earl again, except this time it trembled slightly. "Thank you," he repeated, but much more softly than before.

Earl clasped it in his as he finished outlining to Yablonsky a regime that had more to do with simple human dignity than medicine. Yet he couldn't be sure she wouldn't screw it up somehow, to put him in his place.

"Yes, Doctor," she repeated over and over.

Her sullenness worried him. "And make sure the next shift gets it right as well. I want no more problems."

She bristled, almost standing at attention. "I'm doing a double and will be here until dawn."

Resentment had probably prevented her from adding a "sir" this time. Earl pegged her former rank as at least a sergeant.

He led Mr. Matthews to the door and delivered him to one of the younger nurses with instructions to give the man a taxi voucher.

Then he and Yablonsky wrapped up the rest of the rounds in an hour, during which Earl made similar adjustments to the medications of another seven patients, who all had little more than days, if not hours, to live. Still, there'd definitely be fireworks over what he'd done here tonight. One of the seven, unfortunately, belonged to Wyatt.

Yablonsky, on the other hand, had become much less hostile by the time they returned to the nursing station. Her initial rigidity now made her seem more brittle than hard, almost fragile. Not that he could excuse the indifference he'd witnessed here, but little wonder she and her colleagues armored themselves with it, seeing people face death, day in and day out.

"Tell me, Mrs. Yablonsky—or may I call you Monica?" He sensed he might have won her over a little and that now might be the best time to get her talking, before Wyatt declared him public enemy number one.

"Of course, Doctor."

"There's something else Dr. Wyatt brought to my attention that perhaps you could help me with."

"If I can."

"He described a cluster of odd occurrences."

Immediately her body stiffened again, as if she was holding her breath in anticipation of bad news. "Clusters?"

"Yes. He said that over the last few months some of your patients were reporting near-death, out-of-body experiences."

"Oh, that!" She immediately exhaled and gave a little laugh. "Yes! It's most strange. And some of them weren't that near death."

"Do you have any ideas as to the cause?"

She shook her head. "I'd guess the effects of morphine or whatever other medication they were on. I actually looked up near-death experiences on the Internet. There's quite a lot there, you know, all about the neurotransmitters that may be behind it and what receptor sites in what part of the brain, if stimulated, will produce the experience—"

"What did Dr. Deloram think about it?" he interrupted, having no use for medicine culled off who knew what Web sites. "Didn't he come to interview some of the patients a few days ago?" Earl tried to make the question sound as innocent as possible.

Surprise deepened the wrinkles on her forehead. "You heard about that visit?" She leaned closer to him, her eyes all at once betraying the delighted eagerness of someone ready and willing to gossip. "Now there we had a really strange event. He arrived yesterday morning, pleasant as can be, took the list of patients' names, and went off to talk with them, at least the ones who are still alive. An hour later he stormed out, face so livid I thought his mask would burn off, and not so much as a word to any of us. Never did find out what made him so angry. The patients he talked to didn't know either." She leaned back and gave a little nod, as if daring him to come up with a logical explanation for such a bizarre display.

Earl asked if she could prepare the list again, intending to speak with those patients himself later. He also would ask Stewart what happened. But as he took the elevator down to the main floor, something other than near-death experiences began to bother him.

Why had Monica Yablonsky reacted so apprehensively when he first mentioned a cluster of odd occurrences, then been clearly relieved when he asked about the near-death experiences?

He walked to the front entrance, where he dumped his protective garb in the prescribed disposal bin, stepped outside, and raced through a warm summer downpour to his car.

Yet he remained preoccupied.

What kind of clusters could she have thought he meant?

# Chapter 5

Janet heard Earl's car pull into the driveway.

She threw down the Saturday edition of the *New York Herald,* wanting to swat him with it for coming home so late on a weekend. It especially galled her when politics, not patients, delayed him.

Bloated, bitchy, and mad at the man who had gotten her that way, she thought. She'd better watch it, or she'd soon come across like the wronged woman in a country-and-western song. Still, her two-hours-overdue husband had better have a damn good excuse.

Brendan looked up from where he'd been engrossed in some elaborate game on the kitchen floor involving a toy train and dump trucks. "Daddy's here," he yelled, the noise of his father's arrival finally penetrating his imaginary world. He leapt to his feet and streaked to open the back door.

She levered herself upright. God, she didn't remember being so heavy the first time. No way she'd be able to work right up to the due date lugging this one around. She also admitted to a tinge of relief at having a legitimate excuse to book off on maternity leave earlier than last time. Despite her initial resolve to never abandon her patients because of SARS, she didn't at all like some of the close calls that had been reported in the news lately involving pregnant women exposed to undetected contacts in hospitals.

"Daddy, I listened to my little brother's heart," Brendan yelled from the threshold, eyes wide with the clear blue exuberance that only a six-year-old can have. "Mommy put a radio thing on her tummy and let me hear."

Earl stepped in from the rain and swung him into the air. "She did? Wow!"

"Want to hear what it sounded like?" Without waiting for an answer, Brendan very seriously pursed his lips to make a rapid sucking and blowing sound with his breath—not a bad imitation of fetal blood flow amplified by a Doppler microphone.

Despite her annoyance, Janet had to laugh. Still, Earl should have entered the garage directly and not touched Brendan before discarding all clothing immediately into the washing machine and showering. Shortly after the outbreak they'd installed a cubicle in there just for that purpose. She'd felt paranoid doing it—Earl kept reassuring her that the precautions at work should have been enough—but the fear they might have carried the virus home on their skin or clothing stalked her every time either of them went to hug their son.

Earl glanced her way. He must have read trouble, as he just as quickly put Brendan down and said, "Well, isn't that marvelous? You're sure Mommy doesn't have a little choo-choo engine in there?"

"No, come listen yourself." He reached to pull Earl toward her. "She's been making us spaghetti, for a long time."

Earl stepped back, hands in the air. "Daddy has to go shower," and he disappeared down the basement stairs.

Five minutes later he returned dressed in jeans and a T-shirt, his dark, wet hair slicked back. He wisely stooped to first say hello to Muffy, their large standard poodle, who still considered herself the family's firstborn and Brendan one of her pups. Now twelve, the dog had taken to sleeping a lot, mainly in doorways near entrances so that any new arrivals would have to step over her rather than she having to run to them. He gave her a *kitzle* behind her ears—Janet had taught him the word shortly after they first met sixteen years ago. It meant stroking. Muffy had become an eager recipient when she joined the family, and Brendan had learned early to get his fair share too. *Kitzle* had appeared in his vocabulary almost at the same time he learned "No!"

After a few seconds with the dog, Earl got Brendan on the other side of him, and attempted a make-Janet-smile maneuver with a show of boy-dad-and-poodle funny faces. When that didn't work he led his coconspirators in a three-abreast charge to where she stood leaning against the table. Muffy jumped her first, front paws stretched shoulder high. Brendan grabbed a leg, and Earl gently slid his arms around her protruding waist, the smell of soap off him tickling her nose.

Her anger drained away. Fifteen years married, and the man could still disarm her with the old playful charm. She grabbed a nearby ladle and waved them off. "Wash your hands and set the table with knives and forks," she commanded, scowling at Earl. "Supper's late enough as it is."

He winced again. "Sorry. Something came up at the hospital."

"On a Saturday night?"

"I'll tell you when we're alone." Scooping up Brendan—"Come on, chum. You're filthy!"—he ducked out from under her blue searchlight gaze.

By 10:30 the storm had passed and the clouds abated enough for the moon to appear. Its misty light percolated through the canopy of trees in front of their house, and the grass beneath, stirred by a strong breeze, flickered between silver and shadow.

She curled up beside Earl on their living room couch, her back to his front and half listening to his explanations as to why he'd been so late.

"I won't be a widow to out-of-hours political crap on a Saturday," she interrupted, having heard all she cared to. "Not for Jimmy, Peter Wyatt, or showing up doctors who can't cut it, understood?"

"Aye, aye, Captain." He slipped an arm around her and softly nuzzled her hair with the side of his face.

"I'm serious, Earl." She looked up at him. "There are others who deserve your time." She placed his hand on her rounded stomach.

He smiled and explored her pregnant curves with his palm.

His fingers released a craving that caught her by surprise. She felt her face flush.

He continued to caress her, very slowly, in ever widening circles.

She relaxed, first letting her body mold itself against his, then beginning to follow his movements with her hips.

"Do you think your passenger would mind?" he asked after a few more minutes, their gyrations becoming more urgent.

She arched her back and lifted her arms, slipping her hands behind his neck. "Just be gentle," she whispered in his ear, drawing him to her and setting him on fire.

He reached around to the lamp and turned it off, then began to unbutton her blouse.

Afterward, in the darkness, they held each other, and he felt the cool night air flow gently over them through the open windows. Savoring the rise and fall of her breathing against his chest, he thought of all the other times like this when he'd cherished the extraordinary blessings in his life—Janet, Brendan, and now a new son on the way—but always with a glance over his shoulder. He knew from a lifetime in ER how quickly joy and love could be snatched away by fate, bad luck, or raw malice. Working emergency had ingrained it in him. While he could recount victories, the defeats, like permanent toxins in human tissue, embedded themselves the deepest and stayed with him the longest.

"Hey, you have to trust life more," Janet had told him shortly after their first encounter sixteen years ago when she'd gotten her initial glimpse of his dark take on the brutal laws of chance. "For all the victims who end up in your ER, there's thousands more who make it safely home to bed. Besides, people like us, you and me, we'll make our own luck."

Such unswerving optimism suited a woman who brought new life into the world for a living. It also counterbalanced his own daily workload of lives lost or torn apart.

Lately his tendency to think the worst had taken a new twist. Although he hadn't said anything to her yet, he worried about Janet giving birth at St. Paul's. Nobody had exposed the OB units to SARS, but it had happened in other hospitals. The culprits were usually residents who came from a ward where they'd unknowingly been around an infected patient who hadn't been diagnosed. The result was that newborns arrived only to be slapped into isolation. Only a matter of time, he kept telling himself whenever she went to work in her own department. But she knew that as well as he did, would be no less worried about it, and didn't need the extra pressure of hearing him lay it out.

He'd started to read up on home deliveries instead.

The breeze from outside picked up slightly, and he savored a sweet fragrance of nicotinia that wafted into the living room. It came from the front garden where she had planted an entire bed of the white, star-shaped flowers. Their pleasing, clean scent made him think of the lonely woman in Palliative Care who had confided how she loved the freshness in the air following a rainstorm. What was her name? Sadie Locke? Tomorrow, weather permitting, he'd have one of the orderlies take her out onto the roof garden in a wheelchair. Maybe maintenance could even spruce the area up a bit, perhaps bring in a few pallets of annuals. Janet would know what varieties might do well up there. Then patients who were strong enough could escape the walls and odors of the hospital.

He smiled and indulged in a rare moment of feeling pleased with himself. Why not? He seemed to have a knack for this VP, medical stuff. It gave him a rush of satisfaction, the prospect of having all that power and using it to do good things.

So there, Jimmy.

## Sunday, 6:00 a.m.
## Palliative Care Unit, St. Paul's Hospital

Monica Yablonsky dashed for the bedside phone. "Code blue!" she yelled, the standard order to bring a resuscitation team running to the aid of a cardiac arrest victim. "And I want the R-three in ICU or Emergency."

Not just a bunch of beginners, she added to herself, slamming down the receiver and reaching for the gray face with the staring eyes. It felt cold and rubbery. God knew when she'd died. Not recently. But with no DNR order on the chart, and given the stunt Earl Garnet had pulled last night, she'd better play this one by the book. Damn him, sticking his nose in where it didn't belong.

She plopped a pocket breathing mask over the dead woman's lips and nose, then blew.

The breath squeaked out the sides of a rubber seal that should have molded itself to the face.

Elizabeth Matthews's chest barely rose.

Monica tried again.

The same resistance blocked her effort.

Still, she had to go all out. Or would that only make her appear more guilty? Garnet would be looking ultra close at what happened here. And given his reputation for digging up shit, he'd be bound to discover the others. If he did, the nurses on the night shift would have to watch out.

She swiftly positioned her hands on the midpoint of Elizabeth Matthews's sternum and began the compressions. It felt stiff, so she applied more force to get the required inch of downward thrust that would squeeze the heart's ventricles and pump blood through the body.

Ribs snapped with a crunch under her palms.

"Shit," she muttered, easing off a bit. Still, she continued, not at all sure her efforts wouldn't make Garnet more suspicious.

\* \* \*

"We got a code, eighth floor!" Jane Simmons yelled. She turned from the phone and ran to where they kept a portable bag of airway equipment. Grabbing it, she sprinted for the door, right behind Thomas and the rest of the team. At the elevators they commandeered a car with an override key.

In less than a minute they were on the ward. Jane arrived at the patient's room to find the night supervisor, Mrs. Yablonsky, and a nursing aide administering CPR, both women red-faced from the exertion.

Out in the hallway the sounds of running feet and a familiar wobble of wheels announced the arrival of ICU residents with the crash cart. This chorus of youngsters with fear in their eyes followed Thomas through the door and swarmed the patient. Some ripped open her nightgown, while others slipped a board under her back. One of them applied well-lubed defibrillation paddles to her bony chest.

The monitor screen showed a flat line.

"I've got the airway," Jane said, shouldering Yablonsky aside and flipping off a pocket mask that the aide had been using to provide ventilation. As she worked, the sticker bearing the patient's name at the head of the bed caught her eye.

Questions flew.

"She's not a DNR?"

"When did she arrest?"

"What's her diagnosis?"

Amid a flurry of hands, additional IVs went up.

Jane tried to pry open the mouth; she found it unusually stiff but slid a curved airway into place anyway. She then connected a ventilation bag and mask to an outlet in the wall, sending a hiss of oxygen into the room. But when she applied the mask over the patient's face and squeezed, the bag remained rigid in her hand. She couldn't force air into the lungs. The woman's tongue must be blocking the way, she thought. She tried to reposition the head, but it resisted manipulation as much as the mouth had.

A pretty blond girl who had attempted to take over the chest compressions, her long hair repeatedly flopping in the way, slowed after a dozen thrusts. "This one doesn't feel right!" she said, her eyebrows bunched into a frown, but she continued to labor over the dead woman's chest.

Thomas walked over to the bed, reached through the crowd, and placed the tips of his fingers along Elizabeth Matthews's neck. "You're not producing a pulse." He signaled the young intern to step back—she'd already grown flushed from trying—and attempted a few compressions himself. A puzzled expression crept across his forehead. He stopped pumping, threw the covers entirely off, and turned the woman's body to reveal large purple blotches on her hips and the back of her shoulders. He looked up at the supervisor. "The woman's been dead four hours, minimum." He pointed to the discolorations and turned to the residents. "These markings take at least that long to appear. We call the phenomena lividity, where venous blood pools at the lowest point of the body once a person has died." His voice had slipped into the clipped tones most seniors used when teaching. He threw the bedsheet back over Matthews, allowing it to float down on her like a shroud. "A code blue never should have been called."

Yablonsky's cheeks burned red at the rebuke.

As the others cleaned up their equipment, Thomas Biggs led her to the corner of the room. "Why'd you do it?" he asked.

He may have intended their conversation to be private, but Jane easily overheard them.

A flicker of alarm shot through Mrs. Yablonsky's eyes. "I beg your pardon?" she puffed with indignation.

"Why'd you call the code? You could feel and see her as well as I did. The skin had gone cold. The lividity formed where she lay."

Mrs. Yablonsky's face flamed further, and the cords of her neck muscles tightened.

Oh, boy, thought Jane, who knew from other visits up here that the woman had a temper. And Thomas could be less than diplomatic when pointing out someone else's mistakes.

But thankfully, this morning Yablonsky seemed set on avoiding a fight. Her rigid posture relaxed a notch. "Sorry," she said, "I should have checked."

Thomas studied her, then his eyes crinkled good-naturedly as he gave her a smile. "That's okay. We can all forget something sometimes. It just surprised me. Calling a code on her"—he gestured at Matthews's body—"is a rookie move."

Yablonsky's eyes hardened.

Ah, shit! Jane thought. Now why did he have to add that? He seems set on provoking her.

The supervisor adopted a time-to-put-this-smartass-on-the-defensive look. "Oh, really? Well, I'd advise you to write it up by the book, Dr. Biggs, because Dr. Earl Garnet himself is going to be taking a big interest in her death."

The merriment in the corners of his eyes slipped a notch. "What do you mean?"

"Just what I said. Dr. Garnet will want to know what happened here, believe me."

"Why would Dr. Garnet be interested in a terminal cancer case?" he asked. The cockiness in his voice had faded a bit more.

"Because he personally doubled her morphine dose last night without her physician's knowledge."

Thomas's mask elongated as his jaw sagged in disbelief. "What made him do that?"

The other residents had started to pay attention.

"Ask the man yourself," she answered, making no attempt to lower her voice. "All I know is, he intended to jump-start some kind of audit into how we medicate pain. Well, it backfired. He'll get his audit, but now it'll be him on the hot seat."

"But surely a terminal patient's death won't be questioned." Thomas sounded more incredulous by the second.

"Oh, but it will, Dr. Biggs, because according to her doctor, she still had months to live."

"Nobody can predict that sort of thing with any certainty."

"That may be. But I advise you to write this one up without skipping any details. It's going to be gone over with a microscope, I promise you."

The ridges in Thomas's forehead thickened a little. "I see," he said.

"I should hope you all do," she added, addressing everyone in the room as if they'd all been errant schoolchildren.

The bitch! Jane thought, as wide-eyed with astonishment as everyone else at what she'd just heard. But the part that most shocked her was not that the woman had pulled a classic shift-the-focus-and-cover-your-own-behind move but that she'd done it specifically at Dr. G.'s expense. Thanks to her big mouth, rumors of his having possibly overmedicated the woman would be the talk of the hospital by breakfast. In the court of innuendo, he'd be convicted before noon. Getting out from under that kind of cloud, even if the official verdict cleared him, could be a struggle, and Yablonsky had been around long enough to know it. So why the hell would she do something so vicious?

If anyone hadn't heard about his connection to Elizabeth Matthews, Earl Garnet didn't run into them on his way to the eighth floor.

Among the groups of nurses, residents, or doctors he passed in the corridors, conversations stopped dead as he rushed by, replaced by whispers and embarrassed glances in his direction. Some he encountered avoided eye contact altogether. Even the janitors looked away. But everybody had a good gawk at him behind his back. He could feel their stares like a thousand arrows.

Thanks to small mercies, he got to ride the elevator alone. Sunday mornings, even at shift change, tended to be quieter than the start of other days. As the floors ticked by, he braced himself for the imminent confrontation with Peter Wyatt. Earl had hung up on the man rather than listen to him scream threats over the phone, but not before he'd heard a good part of what the oncologist had planned for him. For starters there'd be charges of unprofessional conduct; a motion to suspend his appointment as VP, medical; and, after confirmation of lethal morphine levels in Elizabeth Matthews's blood, an official coroner's inquiry. Wyatt then pledged to lead a push that would see Earl prosecuted by law for gross negligence at best, manslaughter at worst. And of course he'd indicated a willingness to leak every savory detail of the process to the media.

But what Earl dreaded most had nothing to do with facing Peter Wyatt.

The door slid open, and he stepped into the ward. His welcome committee stood waiting for him by the nursing station, but he focused only on the elderly man with the gaunt eyes who sat hunched in a chair, looking out the window at a dreary gray dawn.

Monica Yablonsky, her brow furrowed like a gathering storm, tried to glare at him, faltered, and fidgeted with her glasses. Two nurses whom he hadn't seen before flanked her, their expressions expectant, as if he might be there to fix the mess. Wyatt, dressed for the occasion in his three-piece churchgoing best, bolted forward like the leader of a lynch mob in a bad western.

"Shut up, Peter," Earl said before Wyatt could open his mouth. Then he walked right by him, focusing solely on the frail figure by the window. "Mr. Matthews," he said, kneeling by his side.

The old man made no reply and didn't even glance his way.

Earl hesitated, uncertain whether to take the lack of response as a refusal to speak with him, or as the paralyzing impact of grief.

"Mr. Matthews," he repeated.

"Go away, please." The wavering voice sounded hollow, as if emanating from a gourd that had had the insides gouged out.

Earl swallowed. "Mr. Matthews, I know you have every right to be angry. . . ." He trailed off, overwhelmed by how useless his words sounded. They always did when he attempted to comfort the living in the aftermath of a death, and this time he'd more than usual to account for. "I'm so sorry," he said again. He cast about for something to add, then let it be, resigned that nothing he could say would help.

In the depths of Matthews's eyes, previously so blank and lifeless, a dark glow began to burn, angry and hot. "I left her alone because you promised me she'd be all right." His voice rose barely above a whisper yet cut like steel. "From the day she got sick, that's what frightened her the most— my not being there at the end. . . ." A sob convulsed him, choking off the rest of his lament, and left him struggling to draw breath. The jagged cry that finally burst from his throat resonated loudly along the corridor. Earl imagined it penetrating the elevator shafts and extending through the morning gloom to permeate the final seconds of every patient's awakening dream. *This,* it warned, *is how much they can hurt you here.*

# Chapter 6

Thomas's silence while Jane prepared brunch became bothersome.

True, they were both worried about Dr. G. They'd talked about little else. But then he'd fallen silent, and she wondered if something else was troubling him. Had he not liked their lovemaking? Or did he find it awkward being in her new apartment?

She'd moved here just a few weeks ago, having previously shared a pad with some of her female colleagues to save money, but after two years of sorority living, she wanted the privacy of being on her own. Simple, small, but neat, the place felt cozy. She'd adorned the walls with bright travel posters from Greece, Hawaii, and the Caribbean and prints of Klee, Townsend, and Chagall paintings to make up for the lack of view—other brownstone apartment buildings and a nearby freeway. Sheer white curtains over the large windows admitted plentiful supplies of natural light while deadening the sight of neighborhood grunge. In all, not bad, especially since she'd accomplished everything on a nurse's salary. At least that's how she felt showing it to the girls from work. With Thomas, she'd wondered if her efforts might look pathetic to someone a year away from earning a doctor's income.

Not that he'd ever acted like a snob. If he had, she would have dropped him in an instant, having no time for superficial losers of that sort. Her doubts about his reaction had more to do with something quite profound in him that had taken her a while to find out. From what he'd told her of his background—farm people much like her own, his mother also a widow to whom he sent money—he seemed grounded in the same values of hard work and responsibility to family that she'd been raised to cherish. But bit by bit, usually when he lay in her arms after they made love, he also revealed how much he'd detested the harsh circumstances he and his mother endured after his father died. She slowly discovered that under his easy southern charm there burned a resolve to never again let anyone he loved fall victim to poverty. So she didn't know exactly how he'd react to her modest new home—be comfortable in it, as she hoped, or be constantly thinking he should upgrade her to a better one?

Not that he had such a great apartment himself: top floor, contemporary furnishings, but a view of Buffalo's city hall, a stumpy thirty-story building lined with narrow, pointy windows intended as a tribute to Art Deco. Too bad it resembled a circumcised penis covered with shiny scales. "Obviously this neighborhood's well beyond my meager budget, thank God," she frequently teased him. Good thing he found her jokes about it as funny as she did.

But none of that had to do with why she'd been hesitant to invite him over. Since they'd first become lovers, their desire for each other blatantly mutual, the nights she spent with him had always been on his turf, at his invitation. Changing the equation worried her. Would he feel pushed now that she could ask him? Since they were still new enough to each other that reading his moods sometimes proved a challenge, she let things stay the way they were for the first few weeks. Until yesterday. By then she reached a so-what-if-he-feels-pressure state of mind, fed up playing Daisy Mae to his Li'l Abner. He might be a hotshot in ER and a rescuer ready to snatch her from abject poverty, but when it came to romance, did all Tennessee men need women to take the lead? The good thing about Thomas in that department, once she pointed him in the right direction, was that he made it well worth her while.

"Why so quiet?" she asked, flipping the eggs.

He looked up from where he'd been sitting cross-legged on the floor and leafing through the Sunday *New York Herald*. Having often seen it lying around his place, she'd bought a copy on the way home from the hospital, fantasizing about them reading it together afterward, lounging in bathrobes, sharing interesting articles, comfortable with each other's company. She'd had it waiting for him when he arrived, along with a glass of freshly squeezed orange juice, and herself, fresh out of the shower. As she hoped, the paper ended up tossed in a corner, the drink remained untouched, and he'd quenched his thirst for her.

But as attentive as he'd been in bed, and as passionately as he swore to protect Dr. G., he seemed distracted afterward.

"Sorry, Jane, but I still can't get what happened this morning out of my head—that Yablonsky, accusing Dr. Garnet out loud the way she did. And why would he be up on Palliative Care giving out morphine in the first place? Whatever the reason, I think she may be making big trouble for him."

He echoed her own fears. "Yeah, I found her really out of line too. She must have known the others would spread the word." And boy, did they. By the time she'd come off duty, the whole hospital had been nattering about how Dr. Earl Garnet overdosed a patient. She angrily threw a handful of grated cheese on top of the half-cooked eggs and folded it in. "In fact, maybe someone should ask her why she acted so quickly to shift blame onto him. What's she got to hide?"

"Nothing, probably. Just doesn't want to be tagged for bad stuff on her watch and isn't above causing a good man a truckful of trouble in the process. At least that's my guess."

"But to insinuate he'd overdosed her like she did—that totally sucks. It can't be true!"

"You'd think not." He got up from where he sat, found her cutlery drawer, and began to lay out the appropriate utensils. "But I'm afraid that won't stop the gossip from causing him a lot of grief, especially because he's so good."

She knew what he meant. Even the few years she'd been there, it had become obvious to her there were two camps at

St. Paul's when it came to Dr. G.: the ones who loved him—generally the deep end of the talent pool—and the lesser lights, who bitterly resented his competence. Unfortunately, the latter outnumbered the former. Not that he helped his own cause with them. Though he struggled to deal with fools diplomatically, anyone whose stupidity endangered a patient quickly felt the lash of his temper. Those who had would all too gladly see him fall on his face; some might even line up behind Yablonsky to make sure he got blamed for whatever had happened to Elizabeth Matthews. "Can you help him?" she asked Thomas.

He removed a pair of coffee mugs from their hooks on the underside of the cupboard and poured them each a cup from the old-fashioned percolator she'd brought from her mother's kitchen in Grand Forks. "How?"

"I don't know. Point out that the patient would have died anyway?"

As they sat down to breakfast, continuing to share ideas about ways to protect Earl Garnet, Jane observed how Thomas appeared to be making himself at home. Her concerns about his coming here vanished, and she felt silly over having been worried in the first place. Like a friggin' schoolgirl, she chided herself again, happy to be in love.

But they came up blank again as far as a remedy for Dr. G.'s problem.

When she'd arrived fresh out of nursing school, Earl Garnet had told Jane on her first shift with him that she had the nerve and steady hands to be a great ER nurse. Tough as she'd found her rookie year, those words had kept her going. She sensed his pride in her, and under his protective wing Emergency eventually became a place where she felt not only fully confident but also as if she'd found her forte in life, that one special, exciting, worthwhile pursuit where she could excel over all else. So she'd come to care about him as much as she would her own father, were he still alive. "You can't think of anything we can do for him?" she asked, watching Thomas dig enthusiastically into the breakfast she'd prepared. The sight pleased her. "How about the fact there've been other patients without DNR orders who arrested in Palliative Care?"

He paused, his fork halfway to his mouth. "How do you mean?"

"It's not the first time the arrest team's been called up there during night shift."

"So?"

"So maybe this patient's death that Yablonsky is trying to blame on Dr. G. is simply part of the normal pattern."

"Pattern?"

"Yeah. That sometimes people die before they're expected to. And come to think of it, haven't there been more codes than usual up there lately?"

"I don't know. I haven't counted," said Thomas.

"Just seems to me there has."

"How can you tell? With this crazy backup system we have, I'm chasing all over the hospital some nights. All the R-threes do—whenever a junior resident gets scared and feels out of his or her depth."

"I know. But a run up there with the cart, even when I don't go myself—that's the kind of thing you notice. Every time it happens, I groan and wonder which doctor it was who didn't have the guts to discuss DNR orders with whoever the luckless patient is. Know what I mean?"

Thomas nodded, his fork remaining in midair. "Yeah . . . Maybe there is something I can do after all."

"What?"

His bearded face broke into that easy grin of his. "I can't tell you yet, not until I check something out." He gave her a mischievous wink and took another mouthful.

"Thomas!" She put down her utensils, having barely touched her own food. "Quit being so mysterious." His teasing ways had attracted her from the beginning as well. He had the confident air of a man with an inside track on how life worked, and in particular he possessed a knack for rooting out the juicier aspects of hospital life. She slid off her stool onto his lap, allowing her robe to fall open. "Now you 'fess up what you know," she said, slipping her arms around his neck.

"I'm not being mysterious." He gave her another wink. "Just careful. The last thing Dr. Garnet needs right now is more rumors."

"Rumors about what?"

"Palliative Care."

"You've heard something about Palliative Care?" She felt a guilty pleasure discovering the indiscretions of others at work. Who had slept with whom, which doctors or nurses screwed up, and even the occasional big-time crimes, such as sexual abuse or fraud. While the revelations appalled her, they kindled a smug confidence that she'd never make such a mess of her own life. She also felt flattered that Thomas trusted her enough to share in such unspeakable tidbits.

He reached around her, took a slice of bread, folded it in half, and proceeded to mop up the remains of onions, green peppers, and ham on his plate. "Not heard. Seen." He took a mouthful and chewed it carefully, all the while smiling at her. It was clear he knew full well he had her curiosity at the boiling point.

"Thomas!"

"Okay, okay. I don't know if you're right about the number of codes being up, but this morning isn't the first time I've been called up there to try to resuscitate someone found dead in bed. How about you?"

She shrugged. "Sometimes, I guess. But since I'm not always the one who goes, it could be happening more often. Why?"

"I want to check the records, but it seems to me that during the night shift, most codes on that ward have been around dawn, like this morning's. That means they discovered the bodies as they made their final rounds before the end of shift. Maybe Yablonsky's so hot to blame this death on Garnet because her nurses aren't keeping a close enough eye on the patients overnight."

"You're saying—"

He silenced her with a finger to her lips as he wolfed down his last bite, then slipped both hands gently inside her robe and began to caress her hips. Eyes sparkling and full of mischief, he glanced up to see if she approved.

She replied with a soft kiss.

"You could be right about this woman's death being part of a bigger pattern," he continued, speaking quietly while sliding the palms of his hands up her back, "one that has more to do with inadequate nursing surveillance than anything Dr. Garnet did."

"Now that *is* useful," she said, kissing him again, but not so gently this time.

"When did you give her the first ten-milligram dose of morphine?" Earl asked Monica Yablonsky, gesturing to the sheeted body that still remained on the bed. He'd insisted she accompany him into Elizabeth Matthews's room, as if the dead woman's presence might hold the nurse more accountable. Peter Wyatt had gone down to the labs, worried that the weekend technicians might not grant the determination of a blood morphine level on a corpse the priority he thought it deserved.

"An hour after the midazolam," she replied, "as you ordered."

"I *ordered* it to be administered the moment the midazolam started to wear off, which would have been approximately an hour later."

Monica Yablonsky wearily brought her gloved hands to her head and massaged her temples, theoretically contaminating herself, depending where the gloves had touched before coming in the room. Earl said nothing—that kind of unthinking gesture happening all over the hospital a hundred times a day—but some part of his brain registered that the battle to rid St. Paul's of SARS might already be a lost cause.

"That's what I meant," she said. "Mrs. Matthews received the morphine when she started to wake up."

"Yet the medication sheet lists the time as nine p.m. exactly. Mighty punctual of the lady, starting to rouse herself exactly on the hour."

"Are you insinuating—"

"I'm insisting you level with me about every detail of what happened here last night, down to the minute. Now when did you observe her coming around before administering the morphine?"

She drew her lips into a thin line and let out a long breath, making clear her exasperation. "Probably more like nine-ten."

"And afterward?"

"What do you mean?"

"Did you check on her?"

"Yes! Repeatedly. The larger dose worried me. And since you'd sent her husband home, I kept a close eye on her myself." Her disapproval of his having removed Mr. Matthews from the scene, thereby making it necessary for her to increase her own vigilance, hung heavily in the air.

"And?"

"She remained stable."

"Vitals and respiration normal?"

"Yes, as written on the patient's chart."

Check night nursing notes on any floor and the majority will have respirations listed as sixteen a minute, the average rate for adults who are awake, even though most people slow their breathing to twelve when they're asleep. The reason? A lot of caregivers, including doctors, never bother to count the actual number as long as they can eyeball that a person appears to be moving air in and out with no difficulty. "It says sixteen every time," Earl said, lowering his voice to a whisper. "How do you explain that?"

She flushed, yet didn't speak, having been around long enough to know exactly what he meant and to accept she'd been caught out on the point rather than argue about it.

"Obviously, whatever the rate," he continued, "the rise and fall of her chest seemed sufficiently vigorous that you didn't think the morphine had suppressed her breathing."

"No."

He looked back at the chart. "It says here you gave her the second injection at one a.m."

She swallowed, then nodded.

"Again, she started to moan at the top of the hour? The woman must have had a clock in her brain."

The skin around Yablonsky's eyes grew taut, purse-stringing her gaze into an angry stare. "All right. The morphine wore off sometime after midnight, but by then I had only two other nurses and an aide to help me—cutbacks you know—and we had to stay with some of the other patients you also medicated who were much nearer death." She didn't add, "Thanks to your injections," but her nasty scowl said as much.

"So you let her cry again. How long before you finally got to her?"

She drew in a long breath. "One-thirty." Her matter-of-fact tone held no admission of culpability for anything.

"Yet she had strong vitals, seemed no worse for wear from the first dose?"

"Her vitals were the same as before. And for your information, she'd fallen back to sleep. I remember thinking that the stronger dose hadn't worn off completely and maybe she didn't need the second shot just then, but went ahead with it anyway, given how she'd been screaming not half an hour earlier and you'd insisted we stay ahead of the pain." She'd resorted to pronouncing each word carefully and with perfect poise, as if speaking correctly could make what she'd done sound just fine.

Still, the plausibility of her explanation made him think that he'd probably gotten the truth from her. "And when did you next check her?"

Monica's face reddened to an even deeper shade of crimson.

"Let me guess," Earl said, feeling the pit of his stomach clench into a ball of muscle.

The taut defiance around her eyes slipped away, and, stealing a glance at the shrouded form, she seemed to age in front of him. "Six a.m.," she said, her voice reduced to a dry croak.

Jenny Fraser, chief of laboratories, had tracked Earl down in his office, where he'd retreated to think things over. "I have to warn you, Earl, Wyatt's riding my technician's ass for these results, but I heard what happened and wanted to get them to you first."

"That bad, are they?"

She gave a strained, tinny laugh. A small woman known for wearing pearls to a job that dealt with bodily fluids and slices of human anatomy, she also had a reputation for delivering bad news with the delicacy of a shark attack.

He braced himself.

"Unless the autopsy shows some catastrophic surprise, the cause of death will be morphine intoxication." Her slow cadence gave each word equal importance; it was a common technique used by clinical teachers in the belief it helped even the dimmest resident get the point. Except Jenny carried the practice over to talking with staff. "Her levels were double the normal therapeutic range."

"Shit."

"In your favor, her previous liver and renal tests showed normal function, so she should have theoretically been able to handle what you gave her, and no one could fault you for not thinking otherwise."

He knew all that, he thought as she continued to report her findings, had seen it in Elizabeth's chart before ever ordering the morphine. The truth was, Jenny couldn't provide the answers he needed now, such as how Elizabeth had survived the initial dose but not the second. How the first dose had worn off long enough to leave Elizabeth screaming with pain again, yet she'd managed to fall asleep before the second injection.

"Thanks, Jenny. I appreciate the heads-up," he said when she'd finished summarizing her take on the lab report.

After he put down the phone, a branching, cold logic took over his thinking, forking in various directions, and pointing to answers he didn't like.

He made a quick call to the operator, who connected him with the weekend nursing supervisor, Mrs. Louise Quint, as much a seasoned veteran at St. Paul's as himself. Like Earl, she harbored no illusions about the ruthlessness of hospital politics.

"Earl!" she said, her voice as hearty as ever. "I hear you're in the shithouse again. Just when I thought you finally got to the top of the crap pile. So much for my hopes the good guys might win a few for a change."

"Afraid so, Lou."

"What can I do to help?"

"I think Elizabeth Matthews may have gotten her dose of morphine twice."

"What!"

"You heard me."

"Why would you think that?"

"Because after midnight she woke up crying with pain again, the initial dose I ordered having worn off. Once she got like that, according to her husband, she couldn't rest. Yet around one she stopped crying, and Monica Yablonsky found her asleep when she finally went to check on her at one-thirty."

"So?"

"Apparently the staff had a busy night, especially during the time in question. I figure one of the other nurses might have given Matthews her injection after she first started to cry out, between midnight and one, but didn't sign it off in the order book or tell Yablonsky. Around one-thirty, when Yablonsky freed herself up from the other patients, she could have unwittingly given a second dose. Now they're both covering up."

"Jesus," she said, "that's pretty far-fetched." But Quint didn't dismiss the possibility outright. "Stay by the phone. I'm on it."

An hour later she called him back. "If one of my nurses gave an extra dose of morphine, they got it out of a private supply, because there's not a vial missing in the whole hospital." Her tone, now icy, made it clear that she considered the matter closed.

Every floor had a locked narcotics cupboard that required a pair of keys to open it, just like launching a nuclear missile, and the staff counted the vials at the start of every shift. Then they repeated the ritual on signing out, logging the ones they'd dispensed while on duty.

Not a foolproof system, but it uncovered mistakes, and to beat it took planning.

"They could have already replaced the vial they used?" he suggested, hoping she might not slam the door completely on his scenario. He'd need as many allies with open minds as he could muster to counter what Wyatt had in store for him.

"They'd have had to move awfully fast. And again, where would they acquire a substitute identical to the ones the hospital uses if not from the stores themselves? As far as I'm concerned, the whole notion's a nonstarter."

Unless they'd stolen it previously, he thought. Unfortunately, he hadn't a shred of evidence to be making such serious charges.

"Earl, I'd have gone to the wall for you if you had a case," Mrs. Quint added, her tone somber, "even against my own girls." Half her "girls" were pushing sixty, but she'd called them that from the days when they were rookies together, as if choosing not to notice they'd all aged, herself included. "But without proof, I fully expect you won't be repeating your allegations against them, even hypothetically."

Tough, blunt, and putting him on notice—he'd expected nothing less from her. "Thanks, Lou, for what you did."

He replaced the receiver in its cradle.

And felt very alone.

He'd no choice now but to await the outcome of an autopsy. As VP, medical, he could push to get the postmortem done quickly, but solving the mystery of Elizabeth Matthews's death at the cellular level took time. His authority couldn't hurry the process of preparing thin slices of her vital tissues on glass slides, marinating them for a required number of hours in a sequence of solutions to color their various structural features, then examining them under a microscope one by one. His fate would be in limbo for at least a week or two.

Then odds were that the official cause of death would simply echo what everyone already suspected, including him: morphine intoxication.

And Wyatt would move in for the kill.

Yet the politics of it hardly mattered, compared to what preoccupied him most about the whole affair.

If someone had overdosed Elizabeth Matthews, whoever did it had come prepared.

## Sunday, July 6, 11:52 p.m.
## Palliative Care, St. Paul's Hospital

Sadie Locke had had a good day.

Thanks to that nice Dr. Garnet, she'd spent several hours enjoying the evening air sitting out on the roof of the west wing. It felt cool against her face, despite having to still wear her mask. He'd insisted on that, explaining that other patients would soon be allowed to make excursions there and they had to keep the area free of contamination, just like any other part of the hospital. The rest was great. A perimeter of potted trees rustling in the breeze reminded her of the parks where she'd watched Donny play near her home in Lackawanna, a former railway town south of Buffalo. Later, as the sun dropped lower over Lake Erie, birds gathered in the branches above her head, mistaking the pretend forest among all the concrete for the real thing. They'd darted happily from branch to branch, oblivious to the artificiality of it all, filling the air with evening song. Along the lake's edge in the distance, the brick chimneys of deserted factories that hadn't belched smoke since the days when she'd been a young mother now attracted black swirling clouds of starlings above their orifices. At some unseen signal, they reared by the thousands into the dusky sky, then swooped inside, as if those towering columns had sucked them back down to their last flittering dark speck.

Now, after all that excitement, she couldn't sleep. The night noises of the hospital startled her awake whenever she drifted off, and an overhead air vent exhaled polar air that washed over her head with the chilling effect of ice water. Footfalls in the hallway as families on deathwatch came and went to the other rooms disturbed her further—not so much the sound, but what it evoked: the inevitable approach of that day when the steps would come for her. She thanked God Donny would return while she still had the strength for a few good hours, perhaps sit out on that roof with him. She'd like to pass an afternoon chatting about how much fun they'd had together when he'd been little and his father had been full of hope that his own dream, Lucky Locke's, would be the best restaurant in town.

She felt around in the darkness for the plastic cup of water that the nurses had left on the night table and, finding it, took a sip.

She wanted one more chance to tell Donny how much joy he'd given his father. Otherwise she feared he would only remember the man who'd slowly withdrawn into sadness, overwhelmed by the ordinariness of what Lucky Locke's ultimately became—a dreary lunch counter that sucked eighteen hours a day from him for over twenty years until he died.

She took another sip.

God willing, she would talk more frankly than ever with Donny now, hold nothing back, make sure he understood how his own achievement must be soothing to his father's dear departed soul. Especially the name Lucky Locke Two. That had been a nice gesture on Donny's part.

A third sip.

Before the cancer tied her more and more to treatments

at home, she'd visited Hawaii several times and seen the restaurant. It stood in a grove of palm trees on a street with a lot of *k*'s in the name that she could never remember, like a lot of Hawaiian words. Of course, any more trips there would be impossible.

A figure darkened her doorway.

She sat up.

"You awake, Sadie?" said a familiar voice.

"Father Jimmy. You're late tonight." The chaplain never failed to drop in to see if she'd fallen asleep yet, having learned of her insomnia shortly after her arrival.

He walked over and sat on the end of her bed as usual. In the half-light from the corridor, she saw that his eyes were more drawn and tired than ever.

"Thinking of Donny again?" he asked.

She smiled. He always knew. "I miss him so. And want to see him while I still can . . . before I . . ." She nodded toward the corridor where the latest visitors shuffled by, also garbed in protective gear, their muted voices already funereal.

He patted her hand and said the reassuring things he always did, but he seemed distant.

"How are you, Father? You're not your usual chipper self tonight."

"Me? Oh, thank you for asking. I'm fine—just tired after yesterday's big race. Did I tell you our Flying Angels won?"

"Yes. When you were here last night."

"Did I? Oh, sorry. I'm getting forgetful. And boastful, it appears, judging by my going on about our win. Pride goes before the fall."

"Depends on what you're proud of, Father. I'd say it's permissible to let your light shine in the matter of raising money for the hospital." She'd hoped to get a chuckle from him, but no such luck. "And you were right about that Dr. Earl Garnet. Remember I told you about his paying me a visit?" she continued, trying a different tack.

"Oh?"

"A first-rate man. He came by here again today and arranged

for me to sit out on a lovely roof garden. He looked almost as tired as you, Father, yet took the time. I hope you don't mind, but he also seemed a bit down, so I said that you thought the world of him. That cheered him a bit. He laughed and said you'd put him up to coming on the ward in the first place." She'd hoped that after hearing one of the many small ways he had made a difference to her and others, Father Jimmy might relax a little. The tension around his eyes made it obvious that he needed someone to cheer *him* up once in a while.

Instead he cringed. She also noticed that, side-lit from the hallway, his normally youthful skin looked puffy in the shadows.

He must really have had a hard day, she thought, after they'd said good night.

She next awoke to the sound of running feet and the wobble of fast-turning wheels that she immediately recognized, and dreaded.

Another one unprepared to die.

As much as she wanted to see Donny again, she'd signed the DNR form when the nurses first presented it to her. Otherwise, when her time came, they might resuscitate her, and she'd have to meet death twice or more. Once would be enough, thank you very much.

She lay there, listening to the whump of the paddles as they delivered their shocks of electricity and the hushed, clipped voices of the team as they called it, then the telltale quiet.

Rarely they'd rush back out of the ward, pushing the bed, pumping breath into a ghastly-faced man or woman who would then linger on tubes, IVs, and a respirator in what must be a living purgatory. More commonly, the team quietly returned downstairs with their cart, and it would be the sobs of the family, if there were any present, that broke the stillness. Afterward the staff would lead them away, green-shrouded figures escorting the family members slowly in a ghostly procession. Finally, the sheeted form would be wheeled out.

The thought of herself eventually ending up in a refrigerated morgue with a lot of other corpses gave Sadie the creeps, and she tried not to think about it.

Outside her window a rind of gray light had eaten into the night sky along the eastern horizon. She turned to her bed table and did what she always did when the resuscitation team came calling: marked a tiny cross on her calendar and said a prayer for the victim, however the body left the floor.

# Chapter 7

I leaned back on the chair and pretended to enjoy the heat of the noonday sun on my face. But fear had become my cancer. Always present, it ate away at me day and night.

There were moments when I forgot. Awakening from sleep, I could still surface to the promise of a new day with a peace of mind that belonged to the time before I'd killed. Then the memories would sweep through me, and I would sink beneath the weight of my secret, knowing I could never escape its chains, never redeem myself. But as soon as I started to play my part, I would be okay.

Until I thought of Earl Garnet being on my trail.

Like all good physicians, he had an obsessive nature when it came to solving clinical problems. But if he sensed something wrong—lab mistakes, errors in judgment, incompetent technique—watch out. It was almost as if he took screw-ups like that personally. He was forever lecturing about how they caused avoidable injuries that the culprits could have prevented, and just about everyone at St. Paul's knew he would consider such failures a betrayal of those who had entrusted their lives to his domain in ER. I don't think he consciously aggrandized himself with that way of thinking. It was more an attitude that he'd be damned if anything would go wrong on his watch. None of that bothered me as long as he'd con-

**105**

fined himself and his scrutiny to his own department. But now that he'd expanded his territory . . .

Panic at the thought of capture spread through me like rot. And for the millionth time I silently railed at having been fool enough to think I could get away with it, that I'd be so clever and outsmart them all.

But I'd had this plan, this technique, my ability to wall off what I didn't want to be or feel, I would remind myself. I'd perfected it trying to separate me from her pain, her scars. Except back then I'd learned it too late—I hadn't gotten the barricades up in time to keep her anger from becoming mine. But now, with the trick down pat, I had a cloak to wrap around myself between murders and make me invisible, an entity able to move about like a ghost. Or to paraphrase the philosopher, I don't think, therefore I am not. If Garnet or anyone else ever did realize that a killer had been at work, they'd be after someone who'd vanished, ceased to exist. At least that was what I told myself until I lapsed and thought about what I'd done, like now.

A slow, cold chill shuddered through me despite the heat and extra clothing, and I broke into a clammy sweat.

Shit! If only I'd never started. Or quit at the first death. No one would have known. But instead I pushed on, certain that Algreave had been a fluke, that I could still pull the rest through their sessions. Now I'd no choice but to continue, just to stay clear of the living death of being buried in a prison cell forever or, worse, awaiting execution.

Through half-closed eyes I watched Garnet lounging in a seat nearby, and a surge of resentment grabbed me by the throat. Leave it to old Goody Two-shoes Earl, making this into a roof garden for staff and patients. Rumor had it that he'd arranged for the greenery to be on permanent loan, or at least until the snow flew in the fall. What a fucking god he'd become around here!

My bitterness toward him and his good works surprised me. But why should it? After all, I'd condemned myself to seeing him across a moral divide, the man's inherent decency a luxury I would never again enjoy. Little wonder I envied *and* hated him for it.

The warmth of my mask and gown grew sweltering, my skin hot and sticky. Nevertheless, I stayed put, glancing around the rest of the area.

A gaunt-eyed woman whose few remaining wisps of hair floated on the breeze like gossamer sat nearby in a wheelchair parked under one of the potted trees. Perfect place for her, I thought.

From a distance of ten yards I could make out the telltale red stripe on her wristband that Palliative Care attached to signal a DNR case. She also had the necessary IV, probably because chemo or radiotherapy had left her unable to drink and eat adequately. Yet she didn't seem gorked. Now and then a nurse or orderly paused to say hello and chat for a while.

That's the kind I would have to select from now on. People who still had their marbles, but for whom there'd be no code when the nurses found them after I'd finished the session. I could no longer allow my subjects to survive and spread tales of near-death experiences. They might recall one detail too many and give me away. At least DNRs meant there'd be no resuscitation team to raise suspicious questions about too many people dying before their time. I doubted their doctors would raise questions either. That would entail an admission their prognoses had been wrong. Or maybe they'd be so grateful for the empty beds they wouldn't entertain many second thoughts about how they had become available.

I continued to study her.

At one point I overheard a snatch of a person's greeting. "Hello, Sadie . . ."

I'd need at least a dozen more subjects. Out of them I might get a couple of usable tapes—so many had turned out garbled. But added to the few other good ones I'd managed to record, that could finally be enough to convince everyone. Just the same, the added risks of being discovered scared me shitless. I still had no idea whom I'd seen prowling around

Friday night or why the person had been there. No telling when that one might show up again. And since Garnet had decided to stick his nose into the business of that ward, he posed the biggest obstacle of all to my pulling off more undetected sessions.

So how would I get around him?

Until now Palliative Care had been a place where no one thought twice when a person died. Doctors hardly ever ordered autopsies, and family, in their heart of hearts, were secretly relieved at their loved one's passing. In other words, my perfect hunting ground.

And it still could be, despite talk of audits and the bad luck that Earl had taken a particular interest in the place. Because the new VP, medical, fastidious as he might be, had also created his own problems. With a little help, those difficulties might prove useful in several ways. At the very least they should keep him distracted. If they didn't . . .

I looked at Janet, who lay sprawled on a lawn chair nearby, her protective wear outlining the swell of her stomach.

I dreaded what it might be necessary to do. But a personal tragedy to anguish over—that would sidetrack Garnet.

My own loss once more exerted its iron grip on me, stirring a rage that wouldn't die, not since all those years ago when my world fell apart. The hesitation I'd felt vanished.

I would make it appear accidental. After all, pregnancy could still be a risky business.


## 1:07 p.m.

Not too bad, Earl thought, surveying the inner corridors of his department.

The line of stretchers in the hallway, once a temporary measure to handle the occasional overflow but now an all too permanent fixture, stood empty, and the modest volume of chatter told him that his staff had the rest of the place under control.

He ducked into the nursing station, and J.S. looked up from where she leaned against the counter riffling through a magazine. "Hi, Dr. G."

"Finally, a bit of rest for the wicked, I see."

"It's about time," she said with a wink, and returned to flipping pages.

He spotted Thomas huddled in a corner with the rest of the residents conducting an impromptu Q&A session. The man had the knack of all good ER teachers, knowing to seize spare moments whenever he could and turn them into mini seminars.

Earl waited for a pause in the proceedings, then signaled him to one side. "If you need me, I'll be in Pathology. They're doing a case I want to see."

Thomas's eyes seemed to draw a bead on him. "The Matthews woman?"

Earl nodded. "I saw in the chart you answered the resus call. If it's not too busy here, you could join me—"

"Thanks, Dr. Garnet, but this bunch is pretty green." Thomas gestured with an extended thumb toward the members of his group as they continued an animated and somewhat misinformed discussion about the proper technique for pelvic exams. The corners of his eyes crinkled. "As you can hear, I'd better stay with them." He chuckled, hesitated a second, then glanced right and left, as if making sure no one stood within earshot.

Inadvertently Earl did the same.

All clear, apart from J.S.

"There's something you should know about Palliative Care that might help," Thomas said in an only slightly hushed voice. Her presence didn't seem to bother him.

"Oh?"

The resident proceeded to tell him about a pattern, a concentration of codes that occurred on that ward just before dawn.

Earl didn't find it all that surprising. Even on nonterminal floors overnight supervision could be notoriously lax, and patients were occasionally found dead in bed having obviously died hours before. Sometimes it got so bad that residents referred to morning rounds as a body search. He nevertheless thanked Thomas for the information, touched by his concern, and headed downstairs to the pathology department.

He approached the autopsy suite and pushed through a door marked ABSOLUTELY NO ADMITTANCE. The thin, high-pitched whine of a rotary bone saw set his back teeth on edge, and Len Gardner, a man of medium build even when swathed in full protective gear, looked up as the steel blade bit into one of Elizabeth Matthews's ribs. He'd already made a sweeping Y cut of her overlying skin, having sliced it open with a scalpel from beneath her collarbones down the sternum and all the way to her pubis.

"Hi, Earl," he greeted him, as casually as if they were meeting to have lunch. "I thought I'd better do this one myself."

At St. Paul's Len had a reputation as the man who would not be chief. One of the most gifted pathologists in Buffalo, yet having no time for the political niceties that accompanied such appointments, he'd steadfastly refused the honor of heading his department. He also, more than anyone, knew all the dirty secrets about who got it wrong when it came to diagnostic and therapeutic mistakes at St. Paul's. Since Len made it his personal mission to bluntly confront doctors with their errors, Earl suspected he went out of his way to remain unpopular as added insurance against ever getting stuck with an administrative title. Maybe he should have taken Len for a role model. "Thanks. I'm glad you're here," Earl told him, and meant it. Above all, Len would be scrupulously honest.

"My pleasure." He went to work on another rib.

Earl leaned back against the counter where a row of open Tupperware containers half filled with formaldehyde stood ready to receive Elizabeth's major organs. The fumes wafted up his nose, then tingled the back of his throat despite the double mask and a noisy overhead hood designed to suck out such noxious odors. Farther along, racks of test tubes, each one aligned at attention, awaited the more fluid specimens: blood, urine, stomach contents, even her cerebrospinal fluid, the liquid that bathed the brain. These Len would send to the biochemistry lab for a determination of their morphine levels.

Earl turned back to the body and studied Elizabeth Matthews's face. Under the glare of the overhead surgical lamp, it resembled a shiny wax likeness, not flesh at all. He wished he could say she finally looked peaceful, but her features remained taut, accenting the bones beneath, and her mouth, pulled into a grimace, seemed about to emit that thin, piercing cry he couldn't get out of his head.

## 2:30 p.m.

The nausea hit without warning.

Ripping off her mask, Jane barely made it to the toilet before her stomach muscles started to undulate like a belly dancer's. Her entire lunch hurled into the porcelain bowl as if shot from a fire hose.

She nearly fainted from the force of it, and had to support herself with both hands on the tank.

Then she felt fine.

What the hell? she thought, and waited a few more minutes to be sure.

As she stood there swaying, a crazy, impossible notion crossed her mind.

No, it must have been the tuna salad they'd served in the cafeteria.

She quickly flushed the evidence and returned to the nursing station.

**3:35 p.m.**

ICU at St. Paul's and casinos had a lot in common, Earl had once joked. Both had no windows, making it impossible to tell night from day. Both had luminescent screens that beeped and flashed fluorescent numbers for winners and losers 24/7. And with both, all results were final.

Carrying a beige folder stuffed with papers, he walked the length of the dimly lit room, past curtained-off cubicles where bags of IV medication and banks of machines kept the hospital's sickest patients from shuffling off this mortal coil. At least that's how it seemed when Stewart ran the show. With his skills he could blur the lines between life and death more than any other intensivist on staff. A few people clucked their tongues and accused him of playing God, but not many. And most of them wouldn't have anyone else if their time to be a guest here turned up.

Earl had recognized Stewart's passion for critical care when they had been residents together at New York City Hospital. Back then Stewart's determination to combine clinical research with practical training showed in his choice of electives. He spent them with a fledgling group of physician-scientists dedicated to evaluating what treatment protocols worked best for an array of life-threatening conditions in ICU. After completing his specialty requirements, he accepted a faculty position at both the hospital and university, eventually becoming director of that same group, only to abandon them a few years later in 1989.

Out of the blue he'd called Earl and asked if there were any openings at St. Paul's. Aware of Stewart's impressive publication record, and having received a stack of sterling recommendations for him from NYCH, Earl pitched him to the credentials committee at St. Paul's. They immediately snapped him up.

But Earl had never fully understood why a man with such a narcissistic appetite to be recognized for his genius would make the jump from the Big Apple to a place like Buffalo.

"Pollution," Stewart had told him at the time.

Earl approached a row of four brightly lit glass chambers that stood along the end wall and instinctively grew wary. They were negative-pressure isolation units, designed to house patients with serious airborne infections. Any time the door opened, air rushed in, the idea being to prevent deadly microbes from floating back into the rest of the hospital where staff and patients could inhale them into their lungs. Up until three months ago, the rooms almost always had a vacancy. Today, every bed held a SARS victim.

He drew closer.

Through the window of the nearest compartment he watched a team of green-clad figures wearing both goggles and full plastic visors. They worked feverishly on a muscular, ebony-skinned man who had fought similar battles shoulder to shoulder with Earl in ER but now struggled for his own life. Teddy Burns had been a respiratory technician at St. Paul's for over twenty years. Just weeks ago the two had joked how neither of them was getting enough sleep, and they'd shared bragging rights over who had the bigger circles under his eyes.

"Too damn proud to let the ship sink—that's us in a nutshell," Teddy had said with a wink, and rushed off.

Now those same dark, deep-set eyes desperately searched the masked faces who towered above him. Teddy's chest heaved as he bucked the tube his rescuers had inserted down his throat to hook him up on a respirator. His gaze found Earl's, and the creases in his face furrowed, angrily funneling in on the outrage that protruded from his mouth, as if ending up like one of his past patients meant the ultimate indignity.

Earl shuddered and placed the palm of his gloved hand against the pane separating them, hoping that Teddy would see it as a gesture of wishing him well.

But Teddy looked away instead, seemingly in disgust that such niceties would be offered in the midst of his agony.

Stewart Deloram, recognizable from the others by black eyebrows that were equally as unruly as his hair and which no protective gear could hide, expertly inserted a clear plastic tube between Teddy's left ribs.

It instantly filled with a foamy, pink fluid.

Kir royale, Earl thought, remembering Teddy's own unique turn of phrase to describe bloody pleural exudates when he taught medical students. Its presence meant the virus had attacked the lining of his lungs.

And a quick glance at his biochemistry results posted on the windows told Earl the infection had also damaged his liver, kidney, and muscle tissue.

Multisystem failure.

The faces of two teenage sons whom Teddy had so proudly brought to work from time to time flashed to mind, and Earl's stomach gave a sickening lurch.

Stewart emerged minutes later, having discarded his outer layer of contaminated gear just inside the airtight door, then immediately double-gowned, double-gloved, and masked himself again, including shoe and hair covers.

So many steps, so easy to miss one, Earl thought.

After nurses and doctors in Toronto started getting infected, mostly in ER and ICU despite wearing full protective gear, he and Stewart had sat side by side in each other's units, trying to figure out what extra precautions might prevent the same thing from happening at St. Paul's.

"You look like a pair of Georgia crackers sittin' on the veranda," Thomas had teased them, exaggerating his southern drawl.

Earl had laughed, then fired back, "And I suppose guys from Tennessee never pulled up a couple of chairs on a porch?"

"Ah, but we call them deep thinkers."

"Well, sit yourself down, Mr. Deep Thinker, and help us out."

Within fifteen minutes the three of them had identified a half dozen obvious breeches, from masks being improperly tied to people scratching their heads or raising their goggles and rubbing their eyes. Around infected patients during airway procedures—the spray zone, they called it—one cough and the virus could land on hair, eyewear, shoes, anywhere. If staff took off their gloves first before removing head and footwear, or if they retied a lace before taking off their gloves and then went home and pulled off their shoes, or did any of a number of variations of the same scenario, the SARS virus could end up on their fingers.

"Then it's pick your nose and die," Thomas had drawled, driving the point home to anyone who disputed the possibility. The phrase became their watchword in a campaign to heighten people's vigilance against contaminating themselves.

Teddy Burns had been the latest proof that they hadn't done enough.

"What are his chances?" Earl asked when Stewart finished changing.

The weariness in Stewart's gaze trebled. "I don't know." He pulled Teddy's chart from a wall slot beside the test result sheets and flipped to the progress notes. "Did you hear the latest rumors out of the CDC?" he asked while scribbling a few lines to describe what he'd done. "That intensive care and emergency staff will have to wear Stryker suits all the time?"

Earl's heart sank. Critical care workers across North America had been dreading it might come to that.

Stewart was referring to the outfits with self-contained oxygen supplies that personnel in level four virology labs or investigators at the hot zone site of a virulent outbreak would wear. "Space suits," the residents called them. The thought of ending up in one as a part of the new normal for ER left Earl feeling defeated. Gloves and masks created barriers that were distancing enough, but at least he could still speak to those under his care, allay their fears with the sound of his true voice. But to confront already frightened patients while dressed like something out of a science fiction movie and talk to them with the muffled tones of a voice coming through a completely enclosed hood—that tore it, stripped the final human touches from the profession he loved. People like Teddy Burns would die in total isolation, barely able to see, feel, or hear the ones taking care of them.

Earl hesitated, not sure this would be the best time to bring up his own problem.

"Out with it, Earl," Stewart said, but didn't look up. "What do you want?"

"I need a favor about the Matthews case."

Stewart's pen stopped in midstroke. "Oh?"

"Yeah. I just came from her post. The gross showed tumor as expected and no surprises." He handed over the folder. "These are the morphine levels found in her blood, and the resuscitation team's observations, including an estimated time of death. The rest are lab reports, nursing notes, the times of the injections and the doses. Plus her height and weight."

"So?"

"I want you to calculate backward and figure out the dose she must have received before she died." Complex formulas existed in obscure pharmacology references involving the metabolic breakdown rate and body dispersion quotients for just about every drug in the world. They made the exercise possible, and Stewart read that kind of thing as light reading.

"Wait a minute. You figure someone gave her more than what you prescribed?"

"In a word, yeah."

His eyes narrowed, suspicion displacing fatigue. "Why are you asking me to figure it out? You could do it yourself."

"And Wyatt would immediately demand an independent opinion. He's lit a fire under pathology to have the slides ready early next week, plus scheduled death rounds for the day after. In other words, he's hot to nail me. I need you in my corner on this."

Stewart continued to scrutinize Earl, his brow unfurling slightly. "Yes, of course. I'd be glad to help you out. But who do you suspect screwed up? I've pissed off too many people at St. Paul's already not to check out whom I'll offend this time."

Earl told him his theory about the nurses and the double dose.

Stewart's forehead relaxed the rest of the way. "Count on me."

Evidently Yablonsky and company weren't on his don't-mess-with list.

"But what if I don't get the results you expect?" he asked.

"Then I'm probably screwed." Earl got up to leave, then added, "Oh, by the way, I heard about some other peculiar goings-on up there that I've been meaning to ask you about."

The frown returned.

"Wyatt told me some patients have been complaining they'd had near-death experiences, and when his nurses asked you to look into it—"

"That was bogus!"

"Bogus?"

A flush spread over Stewart's face from under his mask. "Yes. The ones I talked to no more had a near-death experience than you or I."

"I don't understand."

"I told Wyatt it probably resulted from all the media reports my work has generated. The power of suggestion, combined with all those drugs they're on, can make for some pretty potent dreams."

"But Wyatt said that after interviewing some of the patients you accused him of trying to set you up."

His color deepened. "Well, that's not exactly true. . . ."

"And according to the nurses, you stormed off the ward mad as hell."

"Mad? Not at all. Annoyed, maybe, that they'd wasted my time, making me check out crap reports."

Earl's curiosity grew. Stewart never minimized a slight or perceived wrong, yet here he seemed intent on portraying whatever happened up there as inconsequential. "Explain crap."

"The accounts were made up. Trust me, I've analyzed

enough true experiences to know the components common to the real thing. These just weren't authentic."

For a man who always had at least ten reasons to support an opinion, and in any discussion would usually machine-gun Earl with them, "Trust me" sounded positively evasive. "Look, I'm not blaming you for anything, Stewart. It's just if you found something screwy going on in Wyatt's department, I want to know about it."

Stewart's ears became glowing red half shells. He took a breath, then exhaled slowly, practicing one of the many self-control techniques Earl knew he'd tried to learn over the years. "Okay, I first got a little steamed and figured Wyatt and the nurses had primed their patients to try to dupe me into believing a bunch of trumped-up accounts."

"Dupe you? Why the hell would they want to do that?"

The pupils of his eyes flared wide with anger. "To discredit me and my work." He leaned forward, continuing to speak with a hushed urgency that Earl found uncomfortable. "You see, if I fell for it and incorporated those stories as part of my research cases, then they could expose what happened, and it'd be ammo for all those who say my publications aren't real science."

Lord help him. "Stewart, for what conceivable reason would Wyatt and a floor full of Palliative Care nurses even want to do such a thing, let alone go to all that trouble? And how do you figure they got the patients to cooperate?"

Stewart took another protracted breath. "Well, I had to admit afterward that that part didn't make sense."

Thank God, Earl thought, grateful to see that a flicker of reason had once again prevailed, however barely.

A layperson might label Stewart paranoid. Earl knew better. He read him as someone bright enough to scan twelve steps ahead of everybody else and see possible scenarios that might mean very real trouble. A great asset in ICU, but a little hard to take in everyday life. What distinguished him from a truly crazy person? He could admit later, although it took a little encouragement, that perhaps his predictions, when they were based on his social exchanges with people, weren't all that probable. Stewart appeared to have once more cleared that hurdle as far as Wyatt was concerned, but Earl still sensed that he was holding something back. "You haven't explained why you thought the accounts were bogus," he said, trying not to sound confrontational.

The flush receded. "I just knew, that's all. Pattern recognition. Hey, some things aren't quantifiable."

Bullshit! Stewart could and would quantify anything remotely to do with his research, including how to recognize bogus data. But in an attempt to render him less defensive, not more, Earl nodded and took another tack. "So you don't think Wyatt is up to anything. Believe me, it might help my situation if I had something on the guy."

Stewart immediately relaxed. He sank back in his chair, his high color returning the rest of the way toward normal, and cocked a bushy eyebrow as if Earl were the crazy one now. "I meant only that the idea of Wyatt recruiting patients and nurses to discredit me didn't make sense. But don't think he wouldn't sabotage another researcher's work, even outside his field. That hothead's so bitter about losing the limelight, he can't stand to see anybody else step into it." Stewart raised his head a little, as if posing for a profile shot. "Especially when that person is as controversial as I am."

## 4:00 p.m.

All researchers were crazy.

Every one of them secretly believed that his or her work in whatever little corner of the scientific world, however obscure, deserved a Nobel prize. Lifelong feuds, suits, countersuits, allegations of plagiarism, fraud, and the theft of data, suicides, murders—all committed over impugned reputations. The high drama of behind-the-scenes passions remained legend, and this in a profession supposedly dedicated to the cool practice of objective reason.

And Stewart carried that fire in spades, Earl thought, steaming into the elevator. He just wished he could keep St. Paul's free of it.

Some VP, medicals, he knew, spent half their workweek pulling prima donnas from each other's throat. Stewart's wacky story hadn't made sense, but if it had even a speck of truth to it, he'd better check it out and nip in the bud whatever was developing between Stewart and Wyatt. One thing was for certain—Stewart had been hiding something. Earl felt that in his bones.

The ride to the eighth floor took five minutes this time. Small groups of masked patients dressed in robes and pushing their portable IV stands tottered off at each stop, insisting loudly to each other that they should file a complaint about all the waiting they'd had to do in physio that afternoon. He thought nothing of it until he remembered that part of his new position meant he'd be the one who would ultimately answer to them.

Monica Yablonsky stiffened as he approached her desk, and she started to fidget with her glasses again.

"Mrs. Yablonsky, I want to see that list you were to prepare for me, the one Dr. Deloram used when he came here to interview patients who'd reported—"

"I know the one you mean, Dr. Garnet." She drew herself into a parade square stance, erect, as if ready for inspection. "Except I'm afraid it won't do you much good."

"Why?"

Her eyes avoided his. "There were only five names to begin with."

"Then I'll talk to those five."

"But you can't."

"And why not?"

"Three of them already died. The other two are comatose."

**4:25 p.m.**

Medical Records hadn't picked up the files of the deceased to store them in the archives yet, so he'd looked at them on the spot.

Two of the dead had been DNRs, not expected to survive much longer. The third had rallied last week and had been slated to go home for a few days. A code had been called for her. None of the clinical notes for any of them indicated a thing out of the ordinary in their deaths, except that all three had been discovered pulseless and not breathing just before dawn.

As for the two people in a coma, it took little more than a cursory glance at their recent lab results to see they'd been in bad shape to begin with, both having started the slide toward metabolic meltdown that often accompanies cancer patients in decline. Nobody found it unusual that they couldn't be roused as the nurses passed out breakfast trays that morning.

He returned the dossiers to Yablonsky's care without comment. She'd hovered about him as he'd glanced through them, appearing as uneasy about him going over the five cases as she had with his questioning her about Elizabeth Matthews's death. Let her sweat, he thought, figuring it might trip her up if she had something to hide. Because if his instincts and math were right, somebody sure did.

"The nurses who reported the near-death experiences—I'd like a list of their names," he told her.

She swallowed. "That might take a few days."

"I want it in twenty-four hours."

He rode to the ground floor at the back of the elevator, scowling. No physician liked coincidences, especially when it came to explaining matters of life and death. People died when and where they did for specific reasons. Failure to know those reasons meant he'd missed something until proven otherwise. Yet here he had five patients able to talk with Stewart Deloram on Friday who were unable to talk to anyone by Monday.

Unusual? Maybe not, he tried to tell himself, all at once following a talent he'd honed to a fine edge over the years: to play devil's advocate with his instincts. People died every day on a terminal ward. And those expected to pass on soon might have slipped into comas last night. Certainly the outcome for any of the five patients in question, taken individually, wouldn't raise suspicions. Natural causes could explain each one. Hell, if he tried to make a case otherwise, Wyatt could accuse him of dreaming up conspiracy theories to divert attention away from the Matthews inquiry. Still . . .

He went directly to his office and sat down at his computer. Using his newfound powers as VP, medical, he entered the codes that let him access the records of all departments. He pulled up Palliative Care, intending to see how many other people had died up there overnight and whether the three deaths were part of a larger than usual number. Not that that would mean much in itself. Some days were simply bloodier than others. Nevertheless, it would be interesting to know.

As a quick way to find out, he looked up discharges for Palliative Care this morning. There were six.

Was that a lot? He had no idea. He clicked up the average number for other mornings over the last few months and got 2.7.

"So there were three-point-four more bodies than usual," he muttered, impatient with how absurd statistics could seem at times. He also bet there were other days when the count would be just as high, and sure enough, when he requested a tally, he found that at least a dozen times in the last twelve weeks the morning dead had numbered six or more.

Yet three deaths and two patients slipping into a coma continued to disturb him because of the odds.

If he'd done the multiplication right, out of the hundred patients in Palliative Care, the chances that this would happen to the five Stewart talked to, all other things being equal, were one in nine trillion.

Which meant someone must have had a hand in their outcome.

But of course all things were never equal with a ward full of cancer patients. These five might have been closer to death than Wyatt thought, and maybe Stewart, in his perpetual readiness to take affront, had been wrong about their near-death accounts being bogus. They could have actually experienced what they reported because each of them really was about to die, and their deterioration was only nature taking its course.

In terms of probability that made far more sense than scenarios suggesting foul play.

He began to feel sheepish about his initial reaction. Perhaps he'd let his imagination get the better of him. Having arrived on the floor convinced that Stewart had been hiding something, and unclear what Wyatt might be up to, if anything, he'd failed to coolly consider all the possibilities. What a dumb-ass medical-student move. He didn't usually jump to conclusions like that. Of course, his already being suspicious of Yablonsky didn't help matters any, having primed him to think the worst.

But he damn well would insist that Stewart level with him about what exactly he'd thought was bogus when he talked with the five patients. And if even a hint turned up that Wyatt had tried to undermine Stewart's or any other researcher's credibility, he'd nail his hide. Whoa, there he went, leaping ahead of himself again. Better yank his urge to be in everybody's business back under control. Otherwise there'd be no end to the nastiness he might find. He'd taken the position of VP, medical to make his job of running ER easier, not to replace it with chasing down hospital shenanigans full-time.

He sat in the stillness of his office and felt the place weigh on him. Eight hundred beds, eight hundred souls, and if he weren't careful, every one of them would land a problem in his lap. And to think that just two days ago Jimmy had accused him of being too little involved with the rest of St. Paul's. Earl wondered if the real danger wasn't that he might get too entangled and be sucked dry. Because when he sensed something wrong, he couldn't let it slide.

But it was one thing to let the workings of an ER consume him. The tenacity that drove him not to quit on a patient took hold when trouble hit. His reflex as an ER physician was to leap on a problem the way he would a bleeder, well before it got out of hand. Yet he took the challenges in stride and inevitably, one way or another, found solutions. It all happened on a scale that never threatened to overpower him.

He leaned back in his chair and regarded the spartan furnishings—a steel-gray standard hospital-issue desk, two simple chrome chairs covered in black Naugahyde for visitors, a solitary potted plant that somehow survived the closed space and poor light from a grime-coated window the size of a cafeteria tray—and chuckled. The hospital CEO had offered him surroundings "much more suitable" to his new position, but he'd declined the upgrade, having always found it an advantage to demand sacrifice and best efforts from people if he himself worked out of an austere setting. The trick now would be to keep his perception of what needed fixing just as free of clutter.

He'd have to compartmentalize like never before, carefully choose his causes, and forget about charging off on wild hunches.

Keep everything at scale.

As for Yablonsky, well, he'd deal with her at death rounds.

Except something about her bothered him. She had definitely been edgy as he looked through those five files. Of course, just being around him could make her nervous, especially if his double-dose theory regarding Matthews was true. Yet . . .

Another event niggled at him—her reaction to the word *cluster* the evening before Matthews's death.

In a medical context doctors used it frequently, referring to a grouping of any unusual incidents or diseases, even symptoms and signs. So it had an unpleasant connotation to begin with, but not one that should have upset an experienced nurse. Unless . . .

He knew one context in which the term *cluster* carried a resonance that gave him a chill.

He dialed the nursing station and asked for Dr. Biggs. "Hello, Thomas. I wonder if you could go to our teaching files and dig out an article for me. It's one of the epidemiologic chestnuts on CPR in the *New England Journal* that I present to the residents every year, so you'll probably remember it." A lot of nurses would too, including Monica Yablonsky. The nursing director had asked him to give sessions about it with her staff on several occasions.

"Sure. What's the title?"

" 'Mysterious Clusters of Deaths in Hospitals.' "

Earl hung up and returned to checking discharge statistics for Palliative Care, going a lot farther back than three months.

Jane Simmons bought the kit at a pharmacy far from her apartment where no one knew her. She needn't have gone to the trouble. The salesgirl didn't so much as look up during the purchase.

In the privacy of her bathroom, she applied the drop of urine and waited.

In one minute she'd know.

Reruns of the last six weeks tumbled through her mind.

She'd missed before. Rather, it had come late a few times, by as much as two weeks. She'd assumed that this time she'd skipped a cycle altogether but that her period would arrive any day now. She'd been so careful to use the foam with her diaphragm and insist he wear a condom. It never occurred to her that they could have messed up. "The problem arrives when you forget," Dr. Graceton had reassured her in recommending the switch after the damn pill kept causing nausea, even after many tries on different types and dosages.

But there had been times in the middle of the night when she woke with him entering her again. God help her, she loved yielding to him in that half-asleep state. Even then she remained aware enough to feel he'd put on protection, and the diaphragm would still be in place from when they'd made love hours earlier, then fallen asleep in each other's arms.

The trouble was she hadn't added more foam.

Thirty seconds.

She looked out the open door at the rest of her apartment. It didn't seem so bright anymore. The paintings she'd chosen for color rather than any specific artist looked drab and cheap, every bit the pathetic imitations they were. Strange how baubles meant to comfort lost their luster when real trouble hit.

Ten seconds.

She felt so stupid sitting there on the tile floor, her future in the hands of a reagent to detect the chemistry of an embryo implanted in her womb. It would be six weeks old now, little more than a ball of cells, but the tissue already beginning to differentiate into what would become brain, heart, and skin. She hugged her knees and began to rock slightly, the way she had as a little girl whenever something worried her.

Such little problems then: homework, what boy would or wouldn't talk to her, exams. Even her worries an hour ago now seemed insignificant: paying bills, what groceries to get. All little stuff. Her only big concern had been what would happen to Dr. G. That still mattered.

Shit, what would he think of her now? And Dr. Graceton. She'd been so kind, taking her on as a new patient—doubtless because Dr. G. had spoken to her.

Or her mother. She'd been ecstatically proud to have a daughter who would be the first woman in the family to have a profession, as opposed to her own lifetime of waiting on tables at the local Denny's, double shifts galore after Dad died.

Now this.

And how would Arliss, her little brother, take it? They'd planned to escape Grand Forks together. First she'd get out through nursing, then he'd follow, and she'd help with the money for his college tuition. He'd been crazy about animals since they got their first puppy, and he dreamed of becoming a vet. If she stopped work, his future crashed as well.

And most of all, what would Thomas think?

Or would she tell anyone? She could just get rid of it privately, with no one she cared about the wiser.

She stared at the indicator dot.

It turned blue as a newborn's eyes.

# Chapter 8

Dr. Paul Hurst threw down the article Earl had shown him. "But they're supposed to die. It's a terminal ward."

"I still thought you should know."

"On the basis of . . . what did you say? A fall in average length of stay from twenty-seven days to twenty-four about three months ago, and a point-five increase in the number of deaths reported each morning? That's infinitesimal."

"Not exactly. It's a rise of fourteen deaths a month, all of them occurring at night. And three months before that there had been a similar change, an increase of about eleven deaths a month, again mainly at night. In the previous years, the rate appeared to hold steady, about three-point-three deaths a day, and only half of them on that shift."

Hurst rolled his eyes at the ceiling. "Will you listen to yourself? You sound like my stockbroker pitching nonexistent returns. Besides, it could be that patients are admitted at a later stage of the disease these days and therefore die sooner once they're here. Hell, it sounds like something you should applaud, a reduced length of stay and more efficient use of beds. You spearheaded that trend everywhere else in the hospital to keep ER from getting overcrowded. Why not in Palliative Care?"

Most doctors were comfortable with inevitable death, considering it as natural as life, but Earl had never heard one of his profession suggest it be celebrated as part of efficient bed use. The majority were aware enough of their own mortality not to be so callous. However, there were exceptions.

Paul Hurst, originally a general surgeon, had had his first heart attack in his mid-forties and had looked ashen ever since. That had been twenty years ago. At the time he stopped practicing medicine and assumed the post of VP, medical, having made the dubious calculation that hospital politics would be less stressful than the OR.

It hadn't worked out that way.

Earl had become his enemy a decade ago by exposing an accounting scandal Hurst had attempted to cover up. In the aftermath Hurst had tried to get Earl fired more than once, and failed.

But during the last few years, once Hurst had succeeded in getting what he'd been after all along, to be CEO of St. Paul's, a watchful state of quiet had existed between the two men. Not a truce exactly, but more an admission that Earl Garnet gave as good as he got—that had been the consensus of those who followed hospital power games the same way they did baseball.

Their pronouncement had given Earl no small amount of satisfaction.

"Sure, it could be later admissions," he conceded, picking up the *New England Journal* article and shoving it back at Hurst. "I just want to make sure we haven't got our own angel of death up there taking it on herself to ease their suffering."

The report had made national headlines in the mid-eighties. It appeared after a case in New York City where police charged a nurse with poisoning children on a pediatric ward with intravenous digoxin, yet a court of law found her innocent. A group of epidemiologists subsequently looked at several hospitals with clusters of unexplained cardiopulmonary arrests; their goal was to provide a tool that would prevent such wrongful accusations in the future or, in the case of actual foul play, more accurately pinpoint the culprit. For each of the institutions they examined, they plotted all such mysterious occurrences against the work schedule of the nurses who'd had access to the patients; in several instances they found a particular nurse who had been on duty when most of the deaths occurred. The results led to the successful prosecution of four serial killers, one of whom had been active in two states. Ever since, any unexplained rise in a hospital's mortality rate had administrators nervously eyeing their nursing rosters.

Hurst grabbed the article from him and tapped the opening paragraph with his gloved hand. Even enclosed in latex, his surgeon's fingers matched the rest of him—long and thin. "I suggest you take another look at the criteria for what you're insinuating." He peered over the top of stylishly small eyeglasses with wire frames and read, " 'Suspicions should be raised only when clusters of deaths and cardiopulmonary arrests occur that are either unexpected in timing or inconsistent with a patient's previous clinical course.' " He broke off and again threw the paper back on his massive mahogany desk. "You haven't shown any of that."

"I intend to check further."

"Oh, Jesus!" He reached up as if to rub his eyes, then, as if the sight of the gloves made him think otherwise, made a pyramid with his fingers in front of his mask.

Earl had watched this gesture at hundreds of meetings over the years, albeit without the protective gear. It usually preceded Hurst making a calculated move to undercut anyone who dared oppose him. He braced for what his longtime opponent would say next. As he waited, the incongruity of two men completely garbed in OR wear amid the luxurious setting of a wood-paneled room, inch-thick broadloom, and floral-covered antique chairs that any museum would die for made the moment surreal.

"You know, Earl," Hurst began, his voice uncharacteristically weary, "despite our former differences, I welcomed your appointment as VP, medical, even spoke on your behalf to the board."

A chill ran through Earl. When Hurst started to butter

someone up, look out. "Yeah, right," he said with a sarcastic laugh, to serve notice he wouldn't be fooled.

"No, I'm serious. You care about this old place as much as I do. We just sometimes differ on what's best for it."

Really? That would be because you're a control freak who cares a little too much about St. Paul's and much too little about patients, Earl quipped to himself, keeping his mouth shut.

"And I couldn't think of a tougher team than you and me to get St. Paul's through this SARS mess. So what do you say we bury the hatchet and fight the real enemy together?" He stood, reached across the cluttered broad expanse of the desk, and held out his hand.

Earl hadn't expected the gesture. He looked at the waiting palm as if regarding a venomous snake.

"Come on, Earl. It's the right thing to do, and you know it. You're the most brilliant, hardheaded son of a bitch I ever went up against. There's no telling what we could accomplish by working together."

Earl made the shake, though tentatively.

"Now, about this business in Palliative Care. Let me ask you something: would you be so ready to investigate the place if you weren't the doctor involved in the Matthews case?"

Earl immediately went back on the defensive, feeling suckered. "Now wait a minute, this isn't about me trying to save my ass."

"Just give me an honest answer. That's all I ask. Would you press ahead, or wait and see what happens at death rounds?"

Earl hesitated, taken by the earnestness in Hurst's voice, yet not sure that the man wouldn't try to snooker him.

"Come on now. The evidence of clusters isn't that strong. And you know the effect that kind of inquiry would have on the nurses. Do you really want to distract them like that now, when the slightest lapse in the SARS protocol could be a death sentence?"

Earl hesitated, then reluctantly conceded that Hurst had a point. "No, I guess I'd wait."

"Good. Then I'll see you at death rounds. How's Janet doing, by the way? Planning to work until the last minute, same as last time?"

"She's fine," he replied, feeling as uneasy with the old man's new friendliness as he ever had with their previous snarling matches.

### 6:50 p.m.

The pathology lab occupied a cul-de-sac in the subbasement that had to be the oldest, most out-of-the-way part of the hospital. Though the facilities themselves had been renovated, the passageway leading to them hadn't. Residents called it "the tunnel." Even the lighting belonged to another era. Naked bulbs in green metal shades provided cones of yellow illumination at fifty-foot intervals while the spaces in between remained in relative darkness.

Janet Graceton hurried along the poorly lit corridor. The faint yet unmistakable aroma of decomposition emanated from the heavy wooden door to the morgue. She paid the scent little heed, being more aware, as always, of the plexus of pipes and cobwebs that ran the length of the ceiling not a foot above her head. She'd never seen the spiders that made their home up there, but more than once she'd wondered how they survived where no other insects flew or crawled. What did they eat? She refused to believe the lore handed down through generations of technicians—that scraps from the dissecting tables provided the necessary nutrition and that the resident arachnids had achieved the size of bread-and-butter plates. But inevitably, each time she walked through here on her way toward the pathology labs, scurrying noises from those darker recesses sounded all too close, and she picked up the pace.

Farther on, the autopsy suites stood empty with their doors

open, the stainless-steel tables gleaming and ready for business. Here the pungent odors of chemical preservatives lingered in the air, easily breaching her mask. The sting that spread along the lining of her nose brought on a case of watery eyes.

Next were several large rooms lined with workbenches, their silver surfaces also spotlessly shiny. On them stood dozens of microscopes, stacks of flat, wide cases containing rows of glass slides, and innumerable racks loaded with bottles of reagents or stains in colors that rivaled those of Brendan's first-grade art class.

The people who used all these tools to make diseased tissues and cells yield up their secrets had long since left for the day.

She walked up to the door with Len Gardner's name on the opaque glass and knocked.

No answer.

She'd had a pass card to his premises for years, always needing to slip in after hours to pick up path reports. Using it now, Janet entered the anteroom where his secretary normally worked. She had also done what sensible folks did in the evening: gone home to her family. At least Janet presumed so, having delivered all three of the woman's children, two girls and a boy. Their pictures adorned an otherwise empty desk. The sight of them set off a pang for her own son, and for the ten millionth time she grappled with her anxiety over being an absent mother. From the beginning she'd refused to try to rationalize her guilt. The only explanation that mattered she owed to Brendan, and while words might comfort adults, the sole language that soothed his psyche involved the feel of her arms and the sound of her voice as she held him.

She crossed to the inner door and knocked again.

Still no answer.

She opened it a crack and peeked in. Not that she expected to find Len, but he'd promised to leave her a pathology report on one of her patients. The woman waited upstairs with her husband to know if her ovarian cancer had spread beyond what Janet had been able to remove.

Among the clutter of papers she saw an envelope with her name on it propped against a stack of files.

She ripped it open, scanned the contents, and knew that the woman would be dead in six months.

She walked back out to the deserted corridor and slumped against the wall.

Nothing loomed heavier than the task of saying, "I'm sorry, but the news is bad." She steeled herself, preparing to give the support required from her, yet dreaded the moment when, as soon as she walked in the room, the couple's last hopes would shatter against the look in her eye. She'd never learned to mask that dark gaze. It inevitably emerged when it came time to pass a death sentence.

Her unborn son stirred in her and delivered a sharp kick, a reminder of his presence, as if she'd needed any. By this time of day, her belly pulled so heavily on her that she felt it had doubled in weight and size. But such a cherished load to carry and a lifetime of working with thousands of other pregnant women didn't lessen the wonder of it any. She'd pretty well decided to take maternity leave much earlier this time. Why not? She could be with Brendan more, and when he came home from school they could make plans together for his new little brother. They'd also enjoy evenings and weekends uninterrupted like never before in his young life. Hell, why not give him that—

An odd popping noise and the tinkle of falling glass interrupted her thoughts. The sounds had come from the far end of the tunnel, near the elevators. As she looked along the islands of light, she realized that that section of the corridor had fallen into complete darkness.

Had a lightbulb blown down there?

She heard more glass break, but heavier, like that of a jar or bottle, and this smash had some force behind it.

What the hell?

She pushed off from where she'd been leaning. "Hello? Is

somebody there?" She peered toward the distant murk but could see no one.

Yet a soft brushing shuffle no louder than a whisper echoed out of the darkness. Paper shoe covers on the floor? She couldn't be sure. "I said, is someone there?"

In the distance the door to a lit stairwell swung open and a silhouetted figure left the basement.

"Hey!"

The door closed behind, leaving her alone once more.

Somebody must have knocked something over in the dark, somebody who shouldn't have been down here in the first place, judging by their quick exit. No matter. She'd advise maintenance to clean up the broken glass before anyone got cut.

She started toward the elevators, hoping there'd be enough light to see her way once she got that far.

She'd walked well past the wooden door to the morgue, her mind focused on what she'd say to her patient, when she noticed a peculiar yet familiar odor that hadn't been there when she came in. Mildly irritating at first, it soon penetrated her nose and seared the back of her throat.

That's awful, she thought, and pressed her mask to her face, hoping to block out the fumes.

But the irritation continued, and her eyes began to burn.

She squinted into the darkness ahead, wondering if she could make the elevator. Probably. She couldn't see it directly, but the soft glow of the button looked to be about fifty feet away. Hold her breath and run for it, she decided.

After a few strides she immediately felt worse. What had that idiot spilled? She knew the storerooms down here contained no end of toxic liquids. The fluids that preserved organs and tissues in death were lethal to them in life, and any woman working down here who got pregnant went on immediate leave.

The button seemed to be only thirty feet away. Should she go back? She sprinted faster. Hell, ten seconds more and she could be out of here. All she had to do was hold her breath a bit longer.

As she ran, her free hand outstretched, she tried to remember where she'd smelled this before. It had a medicinal aroma, so strong she could practically taste it, and a cool, bitter sensation on her tongue. So familiar, yet—

Oh, my God!

Now she remembered it from her med school days—when they'd done basic lab experiments on white rats and anesthetized them with chloroform!

Jesus Christ, she thought, her head rapidly growing woozy. What felt like an ice cream headache began to set itself up in her temples.

She tried to stop and turn back but skidded, no longer finding any traction. At first she thought it must be the paper coverings on her shoes, but then noticed the floor glistening in the half-light, covered with fluid. At the same instant particles of glass crunched under her soles. She'd blundered into the middle of the spill.

Like a cartoon character trying to reverse direction, she ended up running on the spot; then, losing her balance, she fell heavily on her hands and knees. She cried out, and her lungs emptied, but she struggled not to breathe in. A stinging pain pierced her palms, and patterns of crimson spread under the latex of her gloves like petals. *My hands!* she thought, they being as precious to a surgeon as to a pianist. She instinctively flexed her fingers, verifying no tendons were cut, despite feeling about to faint more from trying to hold her breath than breathing in the anesthetic. The sparkling fragments that had sliced into her skin glittered up at her. She'd pull them out later.

Chloroform, like ether, had extreme volatility, vaporized rapidly, and practically poured into the bloodstream when inhaled into the lungs. Which meant if she didn't get out of this puddle, ground zero for the fumes, she'd be sleeping in it. And so would the baby.

She unsteadily got back on her feet, blood now dripping

from the perforations in her gloves, and, in a wide stance as if walking on ice, began to teeter back toward the offices she'd just left.

Once there, the fumes wouldn't be too bad. She'd call for help on the phone. Just don't breathe in. Only a few seconds more.

She feared most for the baby. A single exposure to chloroform, if it reached high enough concentrations in his blood, could harm the kidneys and liver.

She felt a wave of nausea.

Oh, God, no. The stuff had definitely hit her circulation. That meant it would be in his.

The floor felt less slippery, and she started to run toward where it should be safe. But it surprised her at how concentrated the fumes still were as they continued to burn her eyes, the inside of her nose, the back of her throat. The guy must have dropped a gallon of the liquid.

Her vision began to dim.

No, she mustn't pass out.

She staggered.

She had to make the nearest door.

The heavy wooden monstrosity seemed to hang at the center of a black funnel. It had an electric lock, like all the doors in pathology. Would her card work?

She fished it out of her pocket, inserted it into the slot, and pulled the stainless-steel handle, which reminded her of the one on her mother's old refrigerator.

It opened.

Cold air flowed over her and she gasped it into her lungs.

The ubiquitous fumes that had followed her down the hall filled her chest as well, and she felt as if she'd inhaled fire.

Her head swam.

She managed a step forward, into the morgue, and marveled at her silver breath while she sank to her knees and slid into darkness.

But she could still hear.

A loud click sounded behind her.

Just like her mother's fridge door when it swung shut.

## 7:00 p.m.

Earl glanced at his watch and swore. He'd planned to be out of here a half hour ago. But when he returned from Hurst's office, a dozen files awaited him on his desk along with a note from Michael Popovitch.

*Can you believe this shit?* it had said.

And no, he could not.

In each case a resident had committed what could have been a major error—in all, five missed fractures, three unrecognized pneumonias, four failures to correctly interpret an abnormal electrocardiogram. Fortunately, Michael had caught them all in time.

July jitters. Earl signed off on the twelve incident reports. But in the morning he'd ask Thomas to set up appropriate teaching seminars and patch up the holes in the newcomers' knowledge base.

He reached for the phone and called home, expecting to hear a very impatient Janet wanting him there pronto.

The housekeeper said she hadn't heard from her.

Strange.

"Hi, Daddy," Brendan said when she put him on. "When are you going to be here?"

"Twenty minutes."

"Promise?"

"Promise."

Janet must have gotten stuck in the case room. He dialed the extension, knowing it by heart.

"Sorry, Dr. Garnet. She's not here. Haven't seen her in hours."

He called the operator.

"We've been paging her for the last twenty minutes, Dr. Garnet. One of her patients is expecting her up on the floor."

Very strange.

"Do you want us to have her call you if we reach her?" the operator asked.

"Yes, please."

Now where could she be?

He got up from his chair, stretched, and grabbed his brief-case. Maybe she'd already started to drive home, though he doubted she'd forget a patient.

Nevertheless, he dialed her cellular.

"The person you have dialed is unable to come to the phone—"

He hung up. The recording meant she still had it turned off and probably hadn't left the hospital yet.

Well, no point in them both hanging around here.

He switched the light off and left his office. God, his back and legs felt tired. The burden of being hot and cooped up in double layers of clothing all day while breathing stale air through a mask took its toll physically.

"Any sign of Michael?" he asked, poking his head into the nursing station on his way out. He wanted to thank his astute friend for saving the day twelve times over.

No one had seen him for about an hour.

"Christ, everyone's doing a disappearing act," he muttered.

Earl found him in his office, scowling over what, from a distance, looked like a death certificate. "Hey, Michael, go home. Enough paperwork. Your wife and son are far more important." Donna, a fun lady five years older than he, and Terry, a dynamo kid six months younger than Brendan, were the anchor to this man who could be so obsessed with work. He doted on both of them.

Michael's eyes creased at the corners, the effect of what must have been an attempt to smile, but his morose gaze made a liar out of it. He also not very subtly slid his arm over the top of the paper he'd been filling out.

"Are you okay, Michael?"

"Sure. What's up?"

"You don't look okay."

"Nothing a little more sleep won't cure."

He sounded as convincing as one of their street junkie regulars promising to go straight.

Earl studied him. Michael had steadfastly denied anything was wrong, no matter how often Earl asked. Whatever had been getting him down lately, Michael either kept it to himself or blamed it on the additional stress of the SARS epidemic. Which of course it could be. Except Earl knew his friend would rather have a root canal than admit to a personal problem. Like most doctors, while inviting everyone to bring him their sick and needy, he viewed asking for help as his own defeat.

"Christ, Michael, will you cut the crap and tell me what's wrong?"

"What are you talking about?"

"Oh, Jesus."

"Jesus?"

"Goddamn it, you are one stubborn idiot. Oh, and by the way, thanks for saving the department from the first-year residents, for about the millionth time."

Michael's eyes creased at the corners again, a bit more convincingly this time, and a chuckle rumbled out of his barrel chest. "You're welcome."

"But like they say in the song, 'You got to tell somebody.'"

Michael picked up a book and threatened to throw it at him.

"Okay, okay!" Earl closed the door and hurried out the triage entrance. What could be wrong with Michael? Had he reached his limit to seeing human beings reduced to flesh, blood, and a wet mess? That tipping point crept up on all doctors who worked the pit, one case at a time. Earl had counseled enough former colleagues through it to know. But burnout victims possessed a haunted look, as if they couldn't shut out the images of what they'd witnessed and were consumed by them. Michael had something else, a wariness about him, a watchfulness, as if on the lookout for something. And why would he conceal what he'd been writing on a death certificate?

At the exit Earl peeled off his protective gear, dumped it in the disposal bin, and stepped outside, where a cool summer breeze carried the fresh scent of open water from Lake Erie. The usual release of having shed pounds of sweaty clothing flooded through him. It felt as if he'd burst free of a dead skin.

He wheeled his car out of the lot and saw Janet's green Mazda convertible, a vintage 1990 model that she drove during the summer, still resting in its spot. A surge of disappointment destroyed his brief euphoria. Not for the first time he raged against the tyranny of obstetrics, but, long resigned to it and determined that Brendan would have at least one parent to tuck him in tonight, he sped toward home.

The cold woke her.

She forced herself to blink, but the absolute darkness remained.

She fought to crawl out of the sleep that still had a hold on her.

No change. Everything remained as black as if her eyelids were clamped shut.

Except they felt open. She also became aware that her head ached, and an acrid burning at the back of her throat made her want to gag.

The chloroform!

Plus something else.

Smells flooded through her head, and she remembered.

She leapt to her feet, swayed heavily, and immediately regretted the sudden move. Reaching into the darkness, hoping to find a place to lean on, her left hand landed on the wooden contours of an open mouth, nose, and cheeks, easily recognizable to the touch under the crinkling plastic of a body bag.

"Shit!" she yelled, but held on to the face to stop from tumbling into something worse.

The spiraling in her head settled, and she turned toward the corpse, intending to feel her way along the shelf it rested on until she reached the door.

How long had she been in here? And why did the stench of chloroform remain so strong? It seemed to be making her woozy afresh, yet the morgue door should have kept much of it out—

The fall!

She'd soaked her protective clothing in the stuff. The cooler temperature in here must have slowed the evaporation enough that there weren't the fumes to keep her unconscious, but she'd have to strip and shower, wash the volatile fluid off her entirely, or the baby might—

The urgency of getting out overwhelmed her.

Bodies be damned. She palpated herself past the top of what felt like a skull with its crown cut open, crossed over a gap, found a pair of feet, and worked up the legs. The torso, neck, and head led her to another pair of feet.

She stopped.

It couldn't be this far to the door. She must have headed deeper into the locker. Muttering more curses and trying to take shallow breaths, she reversed course and worked her way back over the dubious landmarks.

In seconds she reached a wall.

A step left and she felt the door frame. A second later she found the handle and pressed down.

It didn't budge.

Shit!

She tried again.

Nothing.

How could it be locked?

She threw all her weight behind it.

Same result.

This can't be happening, she told herself, trying to remain calm, growing colder by the second, and the contents of her skull once more looping through sickening swirls of an anesthetic haze. Any meat locker she'd ever been in had a round metal disc that released the door, to prevent anyone from being trapped inside. Surely it couldn't be different here. But feeling around, she found no metal disc or any other escape mechanism.

She stood back and forced herself to settle down, trying to think clearly. Hard to do with a mind still half sodden in chloroform. First she had to get rid of the fumes. And find a light.

More waves of nausea swept up to the base of her tongue.

Take care of the fumes first.

She shed her outer gown, blouse, and skirt, throwing them toward the inner recesses of the long, narrow room, figuring the farther away the better. Finding her underclothing to be dry, she quickly pulled her slip over her shoulders and balled it up over her mask, instantly cutting the noxious scent in half.

Now for light.

With her free hand she rapidly patted down the walls where the switch ought to be, but found nothing.

Must be just missing it, she thought, and, dropping her slip, used two hands, methodically sliding them over the surface, checking a square foot at a time.

But immediately the fumes in that closed space began to work on her nose, eyes, and head again.

Time to get rid of that chloroform wick once and for all. Bunching up her slip as before, she went down on her hands and knees and felt her way along the floor toward the rear of the chamber until she came to her discarded clothing. She then stood up, reached sideways to where she figured the nearest body lay, and inched toward it, her hand outstretched.

Her fingers brushed against the plastic cover and made a rustling sound. She pressed down and felt the telltale struts of a rib cage against her palm. She palpated her way toward the head, past the jagged ends of bones where the sternum had been sawed out, and found the tab of the zipper for the body bag. Pulling it open, she released a swell of the sickeningly sweet decay that, until now, had been but a lingering background odor. The legacy of all the sugar in a body's juices, she thought, trying to objectify the odor by breaking down the science of it, a mind game she sometimes used in the case room to lessen the impact of any foul stench. She also swallowed a lot, her usual technique to keep from throwing up, and stuffed the soaked clothing inside. "Sorry," she said to her unwitting host before yanking the tab closed. It sounded like shutting the front flap on Brendan's play tent.

By the time she worked her way back to the door, she could breathe without using her slip as a filter, and she resumed her search for the switch.

She'd almost given up hope when her hand slid over a flat, slightly raised rectangle. But it had no protruding toggle, which is why she must have passed over it initially. "Please work," she muttered, and pressed it with her fingers. It pivoted slightly, and light flooded the room.

The racks of glistening gray forms in semiopaque body bags, their features partly visible, almost made her prefer the darkness.

No time to be squeamish, she told herself, and returned to the door, searching for some kind of release mechanism.

She saw it in an instant. Not the disc she'd been looking for. Another electronic lock with a slot for her card.

The card she'd left in the outside slot.

The first real flickers of panic began to stir in the pit of her stomach.

If a card is forgotten in a lock at St. Paul's, the security system deactivates the magnetic strip after a few minutes and seals the mechanism to ensure that no unauthorized person who happens on the scene can get in or acquire a functioning key.

The frigid air grew clammy, and a pressure built inside the center of her chest, expanding outward until she thought it would burst.

She couldn't end up stuck here. Not her. Not Dr. Janet Graceton, thirty-five weeks pregnant. No way she'd end up freezing to death in the goddamn morgue of her own hospital.

Yet unless she came up with something soon, that's exactly where things were headed.

She started to shiver.

A phone! Check for a phone. She'd left her cellular in her car, as always, but maybe they had a wall unit somewhere behind one of these racks, for people stupid enough to get locked in.

A quick search found none.

But at the back of the room she spotted what looked like a thermostat. If she jacked up the temperature, would an alarm sound somewhere? On closer inspection, the device seemed only to monitor the degrees, and she could see no way to reset it. Still, somewhere, there might be an alert should the room get too warm.

Whipping off her mask, she used it along with her slip to create an insulated nest around the device. Then, cupping her hands to her mouth, she blew into it. The digital readout jumped ten degrees.

She kept blowing, watching the numbers bounce up and down with each breath, until she felt light-headed again, this time from hyperventilating. As for being out of her mask, she doubted anyone in here would sneeze or cough on her anytime soon.

She frantically continued to exhale, determined to succeed, driven more to save her unborn son than herself.

Her pale swollen abdomen, in which he lay, glistened with moisture in the cold.

And her fury built at the idiot who did this to her . . . to him.

"That asshole knew," she kept saying, muttering aloud to keep her teeth from chattering. "Heard me yell, yet just ran off. If I get out of here, so help me, whoever it is will pay."

**7:45 p.m.**

Susanne Roberts met Earl at the ambulance entrance to ER, handing him a full set of protective clothing. "Mrs. Quint and I smelled the fumes as we were coming down the elevator from a nursing department meeting. She said it reminded her of ether, from the old days, when she'd worked summers in her hometown hospital as a candy striper."

"And you're sure Janet's okay?" he asked, hurriedly pulling on the surgical wear.

"Apart from being as furious as I've ever seen her. She insists whoever dropped the jar deliberately left her down there."

His innards, already knotted, yanked themselves tighter.

"She did sustain some superficial cuts on her palms, though the trail of blood she left and the handprint on the morgue door probably saved her life. . . ."

He pulled on gloves and rushed through the triage area, tying his mask as Susanne continued to explain. He'd gotten her phone call about ten minutes after arriving home. The return trip had taken seven, plus a ten-second tirade at the cop who'd pulled him over, then provided an escort the rest of the way, siren blazing.

He heard Janet the second they entered the inner doors.

"I'm fine, damn it!"

He arrived in a resuscitation room full of people, at the center of which his wife sat on a stretcher, arms defiantly crossed, eyes flashing over the top of her mask, and raising holy hell when anyone tried to touch her.

He relaxed a notch and took in the rest of the scene.

Susanne must have paged everyone she could think of. The inner circle clustered around Janet included an anesthetist and three staff obstetricians, one of them packing up a portable Doppler machine. Outside this group stood Stewart Deloram and Michael. Next was a ring of residents, all offering to draw blood or run batteries of tests, their usual response when they hadn't a clue what to do. To his credit,

Thomas stood quietly behind this bunch and attempted to rein in their well-meant enthusiasm. Even Paul Hurst had showed up. He hovered nearby, his gloved fingers held in a pyramid tapping nervously against his mask. Probably afraid of bad publicity, Earl thought, pushing through the crowd.

She saw him. "Earl! Thank God. Now tell these people to let me out of here."

"Of course," he said, grabbing her outstretched hand. "As soon as the doctors looking after you say it's okay."

Immediately the residents fell silent, his authority over them well established. Looks of relief swept through the eyes of her colleagues. Michael gave him a wink, and the anesthetist's shoulders relaxed. At last, they all seemed to say, an adult to take charge. Even Stewart approved, giving a covert thumbs-up signal.

But not Janet. "What are you talking about, Earl Garnet? The Doppler's fine, and I am not staying in this place another second. Now you just tell everyone that we're going home."

"Michael's the doctor in charge, love." He spoke as firmly as he dared, knowing the real reason she sounded so unreasonable. He could always tell when something really scared her, because she started issuing instructions, as if through them she could regain control of a world that frightened her. Threaten her child, and she'd damn well order a whole hospital of doctors to obey her bidding. "Then we'll go, I promise," he added. To further reassure her, he interlaced his latex-covered fingers in hers and squeezed gently, mindful of her cuts.

She glared at him defiantly.

He smiled, knowing she couldn't see it, but hoping his eyes would transmit the message. "Hey, I'm not leaving here without you, trust me," he whispered, leaning closer and touching his forehead to hers.

The darkness in Janet's eyes softened. "All right, I'll be good," she said, her voice a notch lower, but still at a strained pitch.

"Attagirl, Janet," he heard Michael say, and his portly

friend stepped up beside her, eyes clearly indicative of a smile. "I'd say you're probably right that there's nothing wrong," he continued, not making the mistake of talking to Earl as if she weren't in the room. His voice resonated with the warmth and encouragement he usually gave to people under his care. Nor was there so much as a trace of the forlornness in his eyes that Earl had seen earlier. "You would have been unconscious a lot longer if your passing out had been the result of chloroform. So I think we can safely conclude you fainted, the consequence of a vasovagal response due to holding your breath."

He referred to how refusing to breathe can slow the heart rate, causing both the blood pressure and the breath holder to drop like a rock.

"Exactly, Michael," she said, "so let me out of here."

"Okay, but why not let me draw one blood test, just to document no significant chloroform levels?"

She studied him. "But won't it have worn off?"

"If there's not even a trace, then you had no significant exposure. If we do pick up a level, however low, we know approximately what time you inhaled it, and can calculate an estimate of what must have been the maximum concentration in your circulation. Either way, it's more reassuring to know, right?"

Only if it's good news, Earl thought. Still, Michael had a point.

Janet seemed to consider his equation as well. "Okay, but just that one test." She scanned her audience of residents. "And no offense, but you lot are a little too eager with the needles. I'd like Michael to do the honors." She held out her arm like a princess expecting a kiss on the hand.

The corners of his eyes corrugated into even deeper smile lines, and he reached for a tourniquet. "Is everyone agreed that's all we do?" he asked, eyeing the anesthetist and the trio of obstetricians.

They all nodded.

Good old Michael, thorough as always, with just the right touch to get everyone to do his bidding.

"But wait," Stewart said. "She could have liver or renal damage, or both, and there's no telling about the fetus—"

"I'm sure that won't be a factor if there's no significant blood levels of chloroform," Earl said. Then he curtly took Stewart by the elbow and led him away from the stretcher. "What the hell's the matter with you?" Earl whispered once they were out of range for her to hear. He felt furious at the man for his insensitivity. "We all know the risks, especially Janet. She's already worried shitless without you spelling out worst-case scenarios. Are you trying to frighten her to death?"

Stewart's eyebrows shot toward his frizzy black hairline, which no cap in the world was apparently able to contain. His stare grew incredulous, as if he truly didn't understand the fuss. "Hey, no need to take my head off. I'm just trying to be helpful, for fuck's sake." He jerked his arm away from Earl's grip and strode out of the room.

Earl resisted the urge to run after him, not sure he wouldn't throttle the jerk for being so clueless and definitely in no mood to initiate the placating that might avoid a lifetime grudge. It was pointless either way, he decided, fed up with Stewart's petulance at the moment. Besides, nothing could sway that stubborn temperament until it cooled off. He'd deal with Stewart tomorrow. Maybe by then he could also get a clearer story about the business with Wyatt's patients.

"Can I have a word with you, Earl?" Hurst said as he glided up beside him, took his elbow, and led the way to a back corner. The glassy smoothness of the CEO's tone chilled the air. "This insistence of Janet's that whoever dropped the bottle of chloroform knowingly left her in danger," he began, facing away from her. "Can you not persuade her to consider the event only an accident? You and I already agree, everyone is scared enough of SARS. We don't want rumors there may be someone running around maliciously endangering the lives of—"

"My wife is the most cool-headed, most fearless, and least hysterical person I know," Earl interrupted, his tone low and cold, his temper, already primed by Stewart, nearing a boil. He leaned closer to Hurst's ear. "If she says someone knowingly left her in danger, then that's what we're dealing with, understand? That means there won't be any sweep-it-under-the-rug cover-up. What's more, if I find the creep, neither you nor the rest of the staff will need to worry about that person doing more harm anytime soon."

Hurst arched a gray eyebrow at him. "Really, Earl, I would have expected a more balanced, mature response. I suggest you need practice in learning to see the big picture."

Earl switched to Hurst's other ear, as if performing an unconsummated French greeting. "Paul, let's just say I feel about someone trying to hurt Janet the way you do about someone trying to hurt this hospital."

Hurst staggered back a step. "I see," he said, and creased his forehead. "Yes, of course you would—"

"Janet!" Len Gardner barged into the room, one of the strings of his mask trailing out behind him, the whole thing threatening to come undone. "What's this I hear about someone trying to chloroform you near the morgue?"

Hurst visibly stiffened but didn't turn around, remaining outwardly calm with his hands clasped behind his back, the way a host might carry himself upon hearing guests becoming unruly at a cocktail party.

Earl brusquely signaled the pathologist to fasten the ties properly. Goddamn it, he of all people should know better.

"Len," Janet answered. "Just the man I wanted to question. What have you got chloroform down there for, anyway? And who the hell would be carrying a jug of the stuff around?"

"That's what is so weird." Len's authoritative voice began to hush surrounding conversations and command everyone's attention. "We hardly use the stuff anymore, just to make Carnoy's solution to speed up tissue fixation. Even then, no one would ever need the whole jar."

He and Janet continued to speculate about the bizarre sequence of events, all to the rapt attention of the three main gossip groups in St. Paul's: residents, nurses, and doctors.

"You see," Hurst said, pupils boring into Earl's, "this kind of sensationalism won't come to any good." He shook his head in a show of sad disapproval, as if he held Earl personally responsible for the conversation unfolding behind him, and turned to leave.

Only then could Earl see that the long fingers of the surgeon's right hand had curled into a fist.

## Tuesday, July 8, 2:30 a.m.
## Palliative Care, St. Paul's Hospital

Sadie Locke started and sat up.

"Father Jimmy?"

She'd been lying with her eyes closed, waiting for his visit, when she heard the rustle of clothing.

No answer.

A shadow by her door moved.

"Sorry, wrong room," whispered a voice.

The shape retreated to the hallway.

# Chapter 9

"Thick as a fold of flesh on a pachyderm's ass," Thomas Biggs grumbled, his Tennessee twang cutting the gloom like a buzz saw. He squinted upward as gray tendrils engulfed the upper floors of St. Paul's. A fog bank had bulged off Lake Erie to lean on the downtown core.

Earl shivered in the clammy air. Screening at the hospital entrance progressed more slowly than usual, and chatter among the troops remained muted.

They were an army that had woken to the news their lines had once more been breached. Morning broadcasts reported thirty new cases of possible SARS and three more deaths, all of them identified on a ward in a rehabilitation hospital not three blocks away. The zinger that had this crowd so subdued was that the seminal case involved a woman who'd had hip surgery at St. Paul's, and she must have contracted the virus from an unknown carrier on staff here.

At his urging, Janet had agreed to take the day off, though Earl admitted nothing seemed wrong with her. If anything, her ready acceptance to stay home concerned him. It meant she'd been more shaken by what happened than he realized.

"Any idea who the carrier is yet?" Earl asked when it came his turn to be screened.

"No," the nurse answered, her voice having retreated to the high-pitched, thin tones that are a giveaway of taut vocal cords.

152

He took a good look at her, at least what remained visible above the mask.

Brown eyes, young and scared, met his, then she looked away, probably embarrassed that he'd seen her fear.

In ER, as usual following a SARS scare implicating St. Paul's, the morning rush of walk-ins hadn't appeared, and the waiting room stood empty.

"A good day to check supplies," Susanne said. She believed the best antidote to anxiety over each new outbreak lay in keeping busy. "How's Janet?"

"She took the day off."

"Really?"

"Yeah."

"Wow. Is she okay?"

"I think so, at least physically."

Susanne frowned at him. "Why don't you bug out and spend the day with her at home?" She gestured toward the triage desk, where J.S. sat, unoccupied and staring off into space. "There's certainly not much happening here."

She had a point. "I just might do that. Thanks, Susanne." Meantime he had a few things to prepare for next week's death rounds, but that could wait. First he checked with Michael, however.

"Go home," the man said when he learned Janet hadn't come into work. "I can handle things here." He glanced over to where Thomas had gathered the other residents to start morning rounds. "Especially with Dr. Biggs to keep me smart."

The young man from Tennessee looked up. "Thank you, Dr. Popovitch. If you'll put that in writing, I'll apply for a position here next year."

"Anytime," Michael said without hesitation.

"That goes for me too," Earl added, not having heard him express an interest in coming on staff before. "Are you serious?"

"You bet. I like it here. Your department's great. The hospital, the university, and the academic environment for research are perfect for what I see myself doing. The city's not too big and has lots of green spaces, plus being by the lake is terrific. And for a boy from the hills of Tennessee, the mountains an hour's drive south are just like home."

Earl walked over and slapped Thomas on the back. "Well, that helps fix what started as a crappy day." He also noted that every nurse in the room nodded approvingly. "And you evidently got the vote that really counts."

Susanne leaned over and whispered, "Now go home. Tell Janet that you're a gift from all of us."

He grinned. "Hey, take it easy, or I'll think you want to get rid of me."

"Perceptive," Susanne said as she headed into the medication cupboard.

On his way past triage he winked and said, "Kicked out of my own department, J.S. What do you think of that?"

He expected her usual playful response. Instead she started and looked at him as if she hadn't caught what he'd said. In fact, above the mask, she was a little pale. "Are you okay?"

"I'm fine, Dr. G."

"Sure?"

"Of course." She straightened in her chair. "Hey, I'm a triage nurse. Who should know better than me if I'm all right?"

"Of course." He let her be, but on his way to the elevators, he couldn't help but think he should have checked her out more carefully.

Carriers.

The possibility set his stomach churning in high gear.


## 7:25 a.m.

Intensive care swarmed with its usual rush of morning activities. Patients here were an eclectic enough group with such a variety of multiple problems that they attracted consults from just about every type of specialist in existence. Cardiologists, neurologists, immunologists, oncologists, internists—they all huddled in small groups at the end of one bed after another and took turns pronouncing on the state of the particular system where their expertise lay. Mercifully many recipients of this attention were too sedated to hear or care. But the sentient ones wore puzzled expressions as sage-looking professors introduced themselves, then proceeded to discuss hearts, brains, white cell responses, tumors, and metabolic abnormalities as if these were entities to be considered on their own, objects of interest that happened to be located in the body of whoever occupied the cubicle. True professionals, they at least attempted to mask their glee at each discovery, managing to be no more noisy than excited shoppers at a mall.

Earl ignored them all and walked directly to the nursing station. He came up behind Stewart Deloram, who sat rummaging through a lost-and-found drawer. "Anybody see my goddamned keys? I seem to have lost them again."

Every nurse within hearing distance rolled her eyes toward the ceiling. Earl heard at least three of them mutter something about the need for idiot strings. The guy could keep track of every molecule in a patient's biochemistry, but personal belongings were another matter.

Stewart turned, caught sight of him, and jumped to his feet. "Earl! I intended to come and see you." He blurted out the words with an urgent sincerity that sounded odd coming from him.

"Pardon?" Earl had half expected a fight.

"I wanted to say I'm sorry for not realizing what Janet must have been thinking and feeling. I can be such a dolt about that sort of thing."

Well, well, Earl thought.

"I'll go to the case room and apologize to her in person, as soon as I get the ward settled—"

"She's at home, Stewart."

The thick black eyebrows arched like warring caterpillars. "What?"

"She decided to take it easy today."

"Oh."

"I think she's okay physically. Luckily, the blood levels for chloroform came back virtually negative, so we doubt the baby had a significant exposure. But the deliberateness of what happened really upset her."

"Shit, I hope I didn't add to that."

"No, no, I'm sure that's forgotten. I'm here to discuss something else with you. Let's find a quiet corner."

They moved to an area behind a large curved console of monitors. The quantified parameters of life—blood pressures, pulses, the forces of cardiac contractions, oxygen saturations, respiratory rates—squiggled and jiggled in a dance of fluorescent green readouts.

"I went to interview the patients you spoke with on Peter Wyatt's ward, the ones who reported the near-death experiences that you called bogus."

"What?" His eyes widened, the way an animal's would if it were taken by surprise.

"Down, boy. If Wyatt had started a vendetta against you, I wanted to know, so as to put an end to it before anything got out of hand."

Stewart remained unappeased, his expression suspended between incredulity and fury.

"But since you visited with them last Friday, they have all either died or slipped into a coma."

Incredulity won.

"They what?"

"You heard me. Dead, or near dead."

"My God."

"Did they strike you as being that ill when you saw them?"

"Well, I don't know. I wasn't evaluating them medically...."

He seemed genuinely stunned by the news, but also to be fishing around for answers.

"Come on, Stewart, you don't need a full workup to sense people are near the end. It looked to me they were in bad shape on their charts, but of course nothing beats seeing them firsthand. Would you have guessed these people were about to die or go unconscious?"

"You mean you didn't talk to a single one of them?"

Earl felt Stewart hadn't heard the question. "No, I didn't. Now answer what I asked."

"Yes, they were ill," he said decisively, his puzzled expression unwinding to neutral. "None of them was going to survive more than a few days."

"Really?"

"Yeah, really."

An icy cold began to gnaw at the pit of Earl's stomach. "So it doesn't surprise you, three dead, two comatose."

"Not at all." Stewart's expression grew suspicious again. "What are you getting at?"

"You seemed pretty astounded at first."

He sat up straighter, threw his shoulders back, and raised his chin a notch. "Only that you went to question them yourself. But I guess I should thank you for that, considering you appear to be looking out for my interests against Wyatt's."

"St. Paul's interests, actually."

"I don't understand."

"I think you do." Earl turned to leave, in no mood to be stonewalled—he had other ways to find out what he wanted—when inadvertently he glanced toward the isolation chambers at the end of the room. Three were ablaze with light, the nurses busily attending to the patients within. But the one where Teddy Burns had struggled to breathe yesterday loomed dark and empty.

Stewart saw him staring at the glass cubicle. "Yeah, it sucks," he said and gestured helplessly at the heavens with both hands. Whatever else he'd been pretending about, his voice resonated with a blend of anger and remorse that couldn't be faked. "He arrested last night. I couldn't save him."

Earl slumped against the wall of the elevator all the way up to the eighth floor. As VP, medical, he would be the one to arrange a memorial for Teddy. He tried out what he would say.

*I recall all the times we struggled side by side to restore the breath of life to the already dead. . . .*

He couldn't finish. The disgust on the man's face as he'd struggled to breathe when no one could help him overwhelmed such treacle.

Earl stopped by the nursing station in Palliative Care and asked the woman in charge, a tiny person with big Elton John glasses, if Monica Yablonsky had left him a list of all her colleagues who'd reported a patient having a near-death experience.

She hadn't.

"Then would you do it, please?" he asked.

She looked at him curiously, shrugged, and made a note of the request.

It was probably better not to deal with Monica Yablonsky anyway, he thought, pressing the button to summon the elevator back. The less he had to confront her, the better his chance to quietly discover what had transpired up here without setting off alarm bells. However much Hurst had infuriated him, what the manipulative old bastard had said about how distractions could be lethal still made sense. And this morning's headlines underlined that everyone must stay focused on the minutest detail of how to protect against the infection. Worst of all, even that might not be enough. Teddy Burns had never been able to tell the SARS control committee what slip cost him his life.

The elevator arrived.

He didn't get in, wanting a quiet place to clear his head.

The roof garden. It ought to be deserted on a day like this.

Minutes later, stepping out into the fog, he might have been on a mountain ledge. Buffalo itself lay completely obscured, and the sounds of the city came to him as if out of a gray dream. Only the potted trees defined his floating world. As he walked their perimeter, droplets of moisture in the air felt cool on his forehead.

But nothing could soothe his churning gut.

Stewart had seemed relieved those patients couldn't repeat what they'd said about their near-death experiences. And it wouldn't be an exaggeration to say that, for a few seconds at least, he'd also acted genuinely surprised to hear they had ended up dead or comatose.

Which meant what?

For one, he probably hadn't really thought they were on the brink of death when he first saw them just last week.

Yet why would he not simply say so, instead of suddenly insisting they'd been at death's door, no doubt about it?

Earl looked back at the hospital. The surrounding murk had reduced it to little more than a smudge in the distance.

A real house of secrets, he thought.

But if he could persuade the nurses in Palliative Care to recount the specifics of their patients' near-death encounters, perhaps he could figure out what Stewart seemed so intent on hiding.

And he would also take a closer look at the broader workings of Palliative Care—surreptitiously, of course—as soon as he could find a way to do it. Because if Yablonsky and her crew had killed Elizabeth Matthews with an accidental overdose, he intended to make damn sure they hadn't covered up clusters of anything else.

As for whoever had pulled that numskull move on Janet last night, he'd go after that piece of work with a vengeance. Serve notice that this VP, medical would track the idiot down. Ask around if any witnesses saw somebody in the stairwell at that time. Check in particular if they noticed an aroma of chloroform off his or her clothes. Let everyone know they had a new sheriff in town. Nothing subtle about it. The person's running out on Janet had been criminal.

A rain, thin as needles, began to fall.

He remained where he stood, reluctant to reenter the oppressive confines of the building.

And let his mind fleetingly dredge up the unthinkable.

What if smashing the chloroform bottle had been deliberate?

Immediately he rebelled.

Of course not. Why the hell even think such nonsense? No one in their right mind would do that, not to Janet, not to anyone. The person would be a maniac. God, Hurst would be right to give him shit for allowing such thoughts into his head.

Definitely time to get out of here. He pulled out his cellular and dialed home.

"Hi," he said when Janet answered. "I'll be there in twenty minutes. My department gave me the day off."

She chuckled, low and throaty. "You mean they threw you out. Susanne already called to tell me so that I'd reel you in should you change your mind and try to hang around the hospital."

He liked low and throaty. "So we have the house to ourselves?"

"We have the house to ourselves."

No birds, he thought as he headed toward the door, realizing he hadn't heard a chirp the whole time he'd been outside. They must have had the sense to ground themselves for the day too.

Jane Simmons appreciated that Susanne kept her busy. Otherwise, with nothing to do, the self-interrogation started up again.

Should she return home?

Tell Thomas?

Have the baby?

Give it up?

Worse?

The questions that rampaged through her head and the choices they offered seemed so alien, she felt they must belong to some other woman, not her.

So she counted catheters, needles, oxygen masks, suturing kits, and IV packs. Then she sorted equipment trays, filled out order forms, and requisitioned what they needed. Anything not to think of herself.

And occasionally she saw patients, the ones scared and desperate enough to overcome their fear of SARS and come in.

Some of them too late.

A fifty-five-year-old math professor with a stroke arrived an hour past the time when clot-busting drugs could have cleared the blockage and saved his speech.

A forty-five-year-old policeman came in with recurrent chest pain well beyond the limit for rescuing injured cardiac muscle.

A thirty-year-old woman with abdominal pain had ignored her stomachache long enough for it to deteriorate into a perforated appendix that left her septic, in shock, and clinging to life.

Jane even abandoned her professional detachment and allowed herself to sincerely despair over these unfortunates, using the bleakness of their futures to trivialize her own misery.

And it worked. Sort of. For a half hour now and then.

At two thirty in the afternoon, there once more being a lull in the action, she hurried into a utility closet, intent on doing more inventory.

And surprised Father Jimmy going through a cupboard.

"Ah, Jane," he said, "just the person I need. Could you find me a urine cup? I'm due for my annual physical, and the doctor always wants an offering."

Startled to see him in here and not in the mood for company, she quickly found what he wanted.

"And about that other little favor I asked you?" He grabbed his earlobe. "I took the liberty of checking with Susanne. She said fine, and that it might be a good idea if we get the job done today, you having so few customers."

Not now, she thought, wanting only to be alone and lose herself in mindless tasks. "Well actually, Father, I'm supposed to be compiling a list of supplies—"

"That's something I can give you a hand with. And if I can

call you Jane, will you drop the 'Father'? The name's Jimmy, Jimmy Fitzpatrick. Now what's first?"

Oh, brother! He could be so disarming, yet she still didn't want company right now. "It's not necessary—"

"Nonsense."

"Listen, why don't I do your ear—"

"Not until I help you with your work. You look as if you could use a bit of a hand today." He leaned forward, arched his brows three times, Groucho Marx style, and widened his eyes in a clown stare. "Peaked, I'd say, definitely peaked, or I'm not the doctor I thought I was. Wait a minute, I'm not a doctor."

She laughed.

His expression reverted to normal. "Seriously, Jane, are you okay?"

*Be careful,* she told herself. He could be very perceptive. "Of course. Why shouldn't I be?"

"Because you're a little green around the gills, and your eyes haven't their usual spark."

Before she knew it, he'd removed a glove and gently laid his bare palm across her forehead.

"No temperature. That's good."

His hand had a nice warmth to it.

"So what's the matter?" He turned to the counter, where he retrieved another glove from a box and proceeded to pull it on. "You're definitely not your buoyant self."

"Hold on, Fa—I mean Jimmy." She grabbed him by the wrist and led him toward the sink. "You wash first. That's all we need, the hospital chaplain coming down sick, thanks to my forehead. You've no idea how many sick people it's been near."

"Yes, ma'am," he said with a laugh, and began to do exactly as told. "But now you 'fess up. We don't want the pierced angel of ER falling ill either."

She smiled and at the same time felt wary. "Just tired, is all."

He gave her a sideways glance. Pulling on a fresh pair of

gloves, he took her hands between his and fixed her with a stare that penetrated every layer of her masquerade. "Jane, I've been spotting troubled people all my life. Now, you need either a doctor or a friend or both, but I'm not leaving until you level with me."

She'd barely slept last night. This morning when she'd overheard Thomas indicate he might stay on at St. Paul's, a surge of elation had swept her hopes high. *He must intend us to be together,* she'd thought, then wondered, *But if that's the case, why didn't he tell me first?*

Danger, mood change ahead, she'd warned herself, and sure enough, she'd rocketed to the verge of tears. A few minutes later she managed to slam on the brakes and act calm when Dr. G. asked if she felt okay.

The wild ride had continued the rest of the day, and the more her shift wore on, the lonelier she felt. Still, she'd at least won her battle to appear cheery.

Until now.

Father Jimmy's insistence that she open up to him crumpled something inside her chest. She again refused to cry but balled her hands into fists and pulled them out of his. Then she turned away from him, wanting to disappear, feeling ashamed.

"Hey, J.S., what's happened? Tell me. I can help you through it. Come on now, don't expect to be rid of me until you do."

His voice acquired a new urgency and seemed to come from all around her. She felt oddly safe within it, as if his words created a protective sphere where nothing could hurt her. She stopped listening to the meaning of what he said and let just the sound of his talking soothe her. Then she felt his hands take her by the shoulders and gently bring her around until they stood eye to eye. She could see her face reflected in his pupils, and it came as a shock that his concern for her would be so intense.

"I'm sorry, Jimmy," she said, also puzzled by the impact his presence had on her. For a second she'd seen a man, not a priest.

As if sensing her discomfort, he immediately released his hold on her. The guy must be used to women reacting to him that way, she thought, embarrassed at herself.

"What in God's name has made you so miserable?" he asked, his voice soft. "Or should I say who? I'm frankly surprised you'd let anything or anyone best you like this."

Despite the quiet of his words, they stung her. He must have guessed about Thomas. And he'd probably seen enough stupid small-town girls who'd gotten into trouble to pick up on her new problem. Except she damn well wasn't going to admit to him what she'd done, become another victim he had to take care of.

Victim!

The word had a sting to it as well. For the first time since that accursed blue dot had changed her life, she felt angry. What a weepy, dreary idiot she'd let herself become. For as long as she could remember, it had been her style not to cry, to tough out better than the boys whatever hurt her. Never play the helpless girl—she had carried that motto into her teenage years with a cocky pride that gave substance to her hard exterior. It had gotten her out of Grand Forks, through nursing school, and into St. Paul's ER, so it shouldn't fail her now.

Well, if nothing else, he'd created a resolve in her to handle her own predicament. "Nothing I care to discuss right now," she said, firmly putting a distance between him and whatever had happened just now.

His eyes regained their usual playfulness. "Now that sounds a little more like the spunky J.S. I know." He tactfully handed her a box of tissues and, as if nothing substantial had happened, suggested he wait for her in one of the procedure rooms. "To get my nerve up for the operation," he added, and left her alone.

He'd also known she needed time to compose herself, and had managed to withdraw without embarrassing either of them. That took style.

A sense of calm settled through her. It felt like the return of an old friend who'd been away. She liked the feeling. It made her comfortable with herself and filled her again with a quiet confidence that had faded away recently, almost without her realizing it. Yes, she loved Thomas. And yes, she carried his baby. And yes, he could be a clueless asshole about whether they would be together even beyond this year.

The serenity with which she could admit that jolted her. She also realized any decision about the baby would be hers. Just knew this. Couldn't say how or why, but knew, the way she knew her heart beat and her lungs breathed. In that instance the child became a life, not just part of her body. And for a moment she felt liberated from all the worry or regrets that had poured through her in the last twenty hours, freed even from the burden of trying to second-guess how to please Thomas. She'd choose what would be best for her and her progeny, period.

Yet she still felt whipsawed by everything, all in the wake of Father Jimmy's question. Or had it been a challenge? What he'd said had certainly put her through a sea change.

Using a mirror over the sink, she fixed her eyes and worried that if Dr. G. and now Father Jimmy could notice something was wrong through them, then Susanne and the others in ER wouldn't be far behind. But the stare that gazed back at her seemed steady enough. Suitable for public consumption, at least, she decided, and took an ice cube from the medication refrigerator, chose a large enough bore needle, and grabbed a test tube with a rubber cap to use as a backstop. Picking up the paper on which she'd kept a tally of the supplies they'd counted, she headed for the treatment room.

As she worked on Father Jimmy, he chatted about growing up in Chicago with an Irish cop for a dad. "I was the youngest of four boys, and my mother, second-generation Greek, ruled us all, including Dad, with an iron hand. . . ."

She found herself relaxing as he talked solely of himself, since it took the focus off her. She suspected he intended it that way. "Why did you become a priest?" she asked at one point.

"Good question. My brothers all became doctors, and Dad wanted none of us to have anything to do with being a cop. Since he dealt with the realm of right and wrong, and my brothers had the physical side of human nature sewn up, the soul seemed ideal terrain for me to occupy."

She laughed and did the jab.

He never so much as flinched. "But I'm not actually a priest yet, despite everyone around here thinking of me as one and calling me 'Father.' Did my seminary studies in Rome, two years philosophy, three theology, then a master's in hospital administration, and am currently doing my Ph.D. in pastoral services. While I'm a full-fledged chaplain, the actual vows are a few years off yet."

"Sounds as long as med school," she said, compressing the site of the puncture to stop the blood.

"I'll say it is, except I find philosophy and human thought more intriguing than learning how all the nerves and muscles work."

Minutes later Jimmy Fitzpatrick walked away wearing a shiny but small gold ring in his right ear.

As Jane cleaned up, Susanne stuck her head through the door. "I must say, you're looking better."

"Me? I didn't know I'd been looking worse."

"You know what I mean. You didn't seem to be yourself."

"So I'm told."

"Father Jimmy have something to do with cheering you up? He's out in the nursing station, showing off your handiwork. Like a kid, he is, telling everyone who'll listen, 'J.S. is a marvel. Didn't feel a thing.' "

Jane smiled. "He's something, all right. And yeah, he really knows—" She almost said "how to treat women" but thought it not proper.

"Knows what?" Susanne asked, tidying up the counter.

"Really knows people and the right things to say to them."

Susanne stopped midway through tossing the used gauze into a biohazard container. "You like him?"

Jane continued to wash her hands. "Sure. Doesn't everybody?"

Susanne watched her a few seconds more. "You know what's interesting about Father Jimmy? His mother."

"He told me about her. Sounds like quite a lady."

"Did he mention her father was a priest?"

Jane stopped in midscrub. "What?"

Susanne scanned the counter for anything they'd missed and picked up the piece of paper that listed the totals for the supplies. "Yeah. He served in what's called the Eastern Orthodox Church, at least the Greek Archdiocese of it. There the priests can marry, as long as it's before they're ordained. Jimmy explained it to us once, at one of the ER parties."

"I didn't know."

"Same goes for Father Jimmy. Because of his mother's connection, he's received permission to be ordained in the Greek Orthodox Archdiocese. He doesn't make a big deal about it, so as to avoid confusing the patients. 'Being a hospital chaplain,' he once told me, 'is about spiritual comfort, not religion or what church I belong to.' I guess understanding that is what makes him so good with all sorts of people."

"Yes, I see."

To anyone listening, Susanne's easy chatter would sound no different than the usual running conversations coworkers often engage in during down times. Except Jane knew that her boss detested gossip, and that for her to say anything about anybody's personal life, there had to be a good reason.

Susanne held out the paper she'd picked up. "What room is this inventory list for?"

Jane refocused on matters at hand. "Oh, that's from the supply room beside resus. I did it to keep busy."

Susanne shook her head. "I hate to tell you, but I did the place this morning. And you must have miscounted the syringes." She handed over the list, tapping where Jane had totaled the ten-cc size.

"What's wrong with it? That's the count I got."

Susanne frowned. "Do you mind checking with me again?"

"Not at all."

Five minutes later they'd confirmed Jane's numbers were correct.

Susanne's frown deepened. "Shit!"

Jane couldn't remember her ever using the word. "What's the matter?"

"This morning I got fifty more than you did."

"Maybe you lost track? It's easy enough to do. Besides, how can you remember so exactly what you got?"

Susanne sighed. "Keep this under your hat, but I've been keeping a close watch on syringes that size."

"Why?"

"Because I think someone's stealing them."

"What?"

Jane spent the next fifteen minutes quietly verifying that none of the other nurses had grabbed a handful of needles from the storeroom to replenish one of the many bins they kept them in, ready to grab on the fly. As she worked, her mind wandered back to Susanne's unusually candid remarks about Father Jimmy and why she felt Jane should know that he could marry.

A crude attempt at matchmaking? No, that would go totally against Susanne's own fastidious insistence on privacy. Besides, she already knew about Thomas and seemed to approve. So what then?

"Because I didn't want you to feel uncomfortable about finding him attractive," Susanne explained when Jane asked her.

"But I didn't find him attractive."

Susanne laughed. "Then that would make you the only woman in the department who hasn't."

"But—"

"Relax. He's never indicated a willingness to date anyone he works with. But let's just say men and women give out subliminal signals about their sexuality in spite of themselves. On that front he's liable to seem as available as the next man. This is why I think he let the rest of us know he can have a woman in his life, so none of us would feel guilty about normal chemistry and an innocent, unspiritual 'what-if' or two. In anyone else, I'd call that kind of thinking the height of conceit. But with him, I figure it's just his way of keeping unnecessary tensions out of an already charged work space."

"Well, he needn't worry about me," Jane insisted, still not willing to admit she'd had her own moment of attraction to him. But finding out that he hadn't been sworn to celibacy somehow helped her feel a little less weird about what happened.

"Now how about my needle count?"

Jane shook her head. "No sign of the missing fifty."

Minutes before the end of her shift at three, a half dozen ambulances arrived within minutes of each other.

"Figures," she muttered, running into the supply room to find more IV bags. Grabbing them, she noticed that Father Jimmy had forgotten his specimen cup on the counter. Odd, it being what he'd come for in the first place.

## That night, 11:45 p.m.

I let myself in the basement door and closed it softly behind me.

A piercing squeak in a hinge sounded inches from my ear, and I froze, listening for any response upstairs.

Standing in pitch darkness, I heard the soft purr of a freezer somewhere nearby, but otherwise the muffled silence of being belowground remained intact.

Then a slight creak came from the floorboards above my head.

The dog?

I held my breath not daring to move.

Nothing else stirred.

I strained to hear the telltale click of her claws on wood or linoleum.

Still nothing.

The freezer clicked off.

Now absolute quiet reigned.

I exhaled through my mouth, careful to make no noise at all, still alert for a hint of anything stirring, man or beast.

The house seemed reassuringly dead.

I snapped on a penlight and tiptoed to the foot of the stairs leading up to the kitchen, then paused.

The steady dry click of an electric clock ticking off the minutes came somewhere on the ground floor. Otherwise, the rest of the house remained as hushed as the basement.

I'd have to be extra careful if I didn't want to wake the dog.

I sat down on the cement floor and played my light around the room, looking for what I'd need, checking the diameter of the pipes overhead, and fine-tuning my plan.

Yes, this would work well.

Very well indeed.

## Wednesday, July 9, 1:30 a.m.

Janet rose, unable to sleep, and pulled on her housecoat. She heard Muffy stir in the dark at the foot of the bed, then the soft sound of her paws hitting the carpet. The dog would routinely accompany her to the door when she left on a delivery, and be waiting there on her return. Earl, having trained himself to sleep through such nocturnal excursions a lifetime ago, didn't so much as vary his breathing.

Their bedroom remained pitch-black, the usual glow from the streetlamps unable to penetrate a fog thick as silt.

She went down to the kitchen, made herself a mug of hot chocolate, and curled up on the living room couch. Despite the murk outside, she cranked open a window and let the sweet scent of her nicotinia bed waft through the darkness.

Muffy came up and gave her a puzzled look. After receiving a reassuring *kitzle* behind the ear, she plopped on top of Janet's feet and emitted a little groan.

"You getting stiff, old girl?" Janet said, working her toes into the dog's woolly coat.

A long canine sigh greeted her effort.

She'd decided. Not only would she stop work, but her leave would begin as soon as she could farm out her patients.

She tried to tell herself what had happened at the hospital last night didn't affect her, that her body had been telling her for weeks to slow down, that this pregnancy would be different, demand she rest more. And now she finally found the common sense to listen.

But something had changed. Her nothing-stops-me bravado wore a little thin in the face of what could have been if Susanne hadn't set the rescue in motion.

Remembering the iciness of the morgue, she shivered and clasped her cup with both hands so its warmth would flow into her.

A chill completely separate from the night air remained.

Hunching up inside her robe, she adjusted some throw cushions at her back in a vain attempt to get comfortable, and received a kick from within for her trouble.

"Sorry, little man," she murmured. Knowing her voice would sound like talking underwater to him, she started to hum. The random notes evolved into the tune for "Puff the Magic Dragon." His movements settled, and she giggled. "In another five weeks you'll hear your momma's real singing voice. That'll be a shocker."

He gave her another little nudge.

"Let you sleep, right?" she whispered, and quietly resumed the song, this time with words.

He settled again and stayed quiet.

Her thoughts drifted.

To Brendan, whose young eyes had ignited with delight when he found Mommy and Daddy at home after school. She would give him more of those days with her. Many, many more.

She stretched and rested the nape of her neck against the top of the sofa, savoring images of all the fun they'd have—setting up his old crib, preparing the tiny bedding, digging out all the stuffed animals that he still loved but carefully hid away so his six-year-old friends wouldn't see them when they came to play.

Smiling, she also experienced a hint of relief. For once he could be her little boy, she'd be his mom, and there wouldn't be the demands of an obstetrical practice competing for her attention. Maybe, she thought, just maybe, she'd be able to create a magic interlude for him, an oasis where he could store up on all he'd missed from not having her around. "Yeah, right," she said aloud, having counseled enough mothers through the demands of career and kids to recognize a guilt fantasy when she conjured one up for herself. Still, she liked the idea. A couple of months stretched like a lifetime for a six-year-old. Not that he didn't already feel safe, confident, and loved. But you can't ever have too much of that stuff, she thought, then laughed out loud.

Muffy raised her head and looked up at her.

"I've become exactly like my own mother," Janet told her. "Now, *she* was a woman who knew how to make you feel loved. Drove me and my two brothers crazy, never missing an opportunity to give us a big smooch."

Muffy put her head back down, not at all interested.

Of course Brendan could react the same way as her brothers, Janet thought, and find that Mommy turned into a big, embarrassing bore when she hung around him all the time. Wouldn't that be a kick in the head.

She took another sip.

As for Earl, he'd be relieved to get her out of the hospital. He was so fastidious about tiptoeing around the question, never intruding on her right to make the decision, but his studied neutrality practically shrieked, "Get the hell out of there, woman!" What's more, the lovable goof would actually believe he'd been the epitome of a noninterfering husband.

But she damn well intended to interfere with *him*. She'd known when he became VP, medical that the combination of his instinct to sniff out crap and a complete inability to let shit slide would suck him into a ton of trouble sooner or later. Yet she'd encouraged him to take the job. Not just because he'd be miserable under the kind of hotshot MBAs that ran hospitals these days, but because the work would take him out of ER now and then. She knew he needed the rush of extreme medicine, the exhilaration of "raising the dead," as some of them called it, but as magnificent as he'd become at it, that addictive allure sometimes frightened her. What of the day he couldn't do it anymore, once he flamed out like a lot of his colleagues? They'd been equally exhilarated by the job, but past triumphs didn't save them when they ultimately stayed on one year too many. That's why people in the business calling emergency "the pit" seemed so apt. It eventually consumed all who worked there.

She'd decided the best to be hoped for with Earl would be to slow the process down a bit, maybe buy time to wean him off what had become like oxygen to him. A new challenge with fresh demands seemed just the ticket. But the expanded responsibilities appeared to be engaging him quicker and more than she ever predicted. Between their lovely romantic interlude earlier in the day and Brendan coming home from school, she'd listened with unease as he explained why recent clusters of deaths in Palliative Care troubled him. Since his suspicions ranged from a nurse playing an angel of death to Stewart Deloram covering up stories of near-death experiences, and the five patients who might have shed some light on the matter were conveniently dead or in a coma, this problem meant exactly the sort of trouble that would eat at her husband. She'd lived with his doggedness long enough to know he wouldn't back off until he either proved or disproved his worst imaginings. She also knew to never attempt to divert him head-on. And most sobering of all, she'd learned to trust his damned uncanny instinct to read patterns where others saw only a maze of unrelated events. Because more often than not, whenever he sensed rot and dug after it, he found exactly that.

But he hadn't a clue of what he needed most now—a sidekick. Someone to carry out all that rooting around he felt so compelled to do himself, but who could fly below the radar of Hurst or Wyatt. Those two, if they guessed what he'd be stirring up, would make his life a living hell, and by extension, hers and Brendan's. Earl in battle mode meant having Hamlet in the house, he became so preoccupied. Worse, if he had stumbled onto foul play, a backlash from an angel of death who felt threatened could be bloody dangerous.

Yes, she'd make a good sidekick, one with time to spare during her son's school hours and who also had her own authority to quietly snoop through nursing work schedules and death records. She would be just the perfect answer to keep him out of trouble. And if the focus of her inquiry should stray a little outside her usual realm of obstetrics, who the hell would know? Best of all, if by some slim chance she found he'd been on a wild-goose chase, they could all relax.

But first she'd have to convince her Lone Ranger to accept his new Tonto. Being brighter than most people around him, he had an infuriating yet deeply ingrained propensity to solve a problem, even in ER, by barging ahead on his own. Well, maybe she could make him want to barge after his wife for help.

She drained her mug and stared outside.

The fog had lifted slightly, thinning into tendrils that reached out of the darkness and curled through the light of the streetlamps, tentatively exploring the muted glow with a cautious touch. Then a breeze caught the swirls, and they languidly drifted away, joining more of their kind to swim through the night like bad dreams.

# Chapter 10

Three days later,
Saturday, July 12, 12:45 a.m.
Palliative Care, St. Paul's Hospital

Earl pressed back into the darkness.

He had seen something move through the shadows at the far end of the hall.

His muscles ached as if someone had winched them tight, and he shifted his weight for the hundredth time since he'd sneaked into the room nearly an hour ago.

Yet he kept his gaze locked on the black recesses where a person could hide.

And waited.

He'd initially felt foolish coming here at all. But his idea about a cluster study hadn't yielded much so far. At least Janet hadn't found any obvious patterns in the duty rosters and mortality figures, but they had a ways to go.

The job had turned out to be huge, and thank God he'd been smart enough to ask for her help. The idea had come to him out of the blue while they were having breakfast a few days ago. Not only did it give him a big edge in processing a ton of data, the project turned out to be exactly the carrot that convinced Janet to take an early pregnancy leave. Best of all, she thought it was her own decision. Funny how things just turned out sometimes.

Too bad their results weren't as obliging.

No one nurse had worked significantly greater numbers of

shifts that corresponded to patient deaths than anybody else, and Monica Yablonsky's record seemed least suspicious of all. From what they'd looked at to date, she stayed on after evenings to work a double no more frequently than once a week.

"So maybe Hurst got it right. Patients are simply being admitted sicker and dying sooner," Janet had said last night, almost hopefully, even though they still had months of data to check.

Or a self-appointed angel of mercy could have anticipated a classic cluster investigation, then dispatched her victims when she wasn't on duty, he'd thought. So he set out to see how easily anyone could get in here and move about with no one the wiser. He also realized this line of thinking bore a striking similarity to that of the hard-core conspiracy nuts who turned up in ER occasionally. But he figured his being aware of the likeness mitigated against total lunacy. Unless Janet found out, in which case he'd plead complete insanity.

Coming up the back staircase unobserved had been no problem. He'd calculated that no one would be there after midnight, as might someone intent on committing a mercy killing.

When he'd reached the eighth floor, he hesitated in front of the door. If he pulled it open, light would spill into the corridor on the other side, and any nurse who might be there could spot it. He stepped over to a triple set of wall switches and flicked them off, casting himself into near darkness. The pale glow of the illumination from landings below barely reached this level. Shouldn't attract much attention now, he thought, and turned the handle.

He'd managed to slip all the way up to his destination, the empty room where he now stood, but he could just as easily have stepped into any door and done as he pleased with any patient on the floor. And he still hadn't seen a single nurse, just heard their radio and them chatting in their workstation near the elevators. Judging from the relaxed tone of their voices and occasional laughter, they remained as indifferent to the lowing cries that floated through the hallway as when he'd visited last Saturday evening.

He found the noises impossible to ignore. They permeated the air with a forlorn sadness yet had the same soft urgency that went with the sounds of making love.

The longer he stood in the doorway listening, the angrier he grew. Having proved that any fool could waltz onto the ward, he felt an urge to stick around and see for himself how long these alleged caregivers would let men and women lie unattended in their last hours. While he'd skin his own staff alive if they ever allowed anyone to suffer like this in ER, the bunch up here did worse than fail to treat pain. Their indifference conveyed a message tantamount to telling someone in his or her final moments, "You don't matter, not even so much as for us to hold your hand while you die."

By God, he would give these so-called nightingales thirty more minutes in which to hang themselves. He'd keep watch while holding the door open with the toe of his shoe so he could personally attest that not one of them had taken the trouble to check on their charges during his time here. Then he'd nail them.

At least that had been his plan until he'd seen the figure that now galvanized his attention.

The person glided from doorway to doorway, coming ever closer, faceless as a ghost. Yet light from the distant workstation caught the shape's eyes, causing them to glitter in the blackness.

Earl shivered, certain they were looking right at him. He slowly withdrew his foot and smoothly closed the door until only a crack remained for him to see through.

The figure crossed the hall and, moving faster, reached forward as if to come in the room.

Holy shit! Earl thought, and leapt backward, then continued his retreat, tiptoeing in reverse toward the bathroom. He'd barely made it inside when the door he'd just left swung open without a sound and the intruder stood silhouetted against the dark grayness of the corridor. Earl froze where he stood, hoping the inkier interior of the small space would conceal him.

The person entered, restrained the door from swinging closed too fast, walked over to the blinds, and used the cord to open the slats. An orange glow from the sodium lamps outside the window immediately lined the entire room with tiger stripes.

The intruder then turned, looked at the bare mattress, and seemed to be surprised, going dead still, as if transfixed by the naked emptiness of it.

The hammering of Earl's heart so filled his head, he imagined the sound must be as loud as drumming on a hollow log. *This must be the killer nurse!* he thought on pure impulse, and got ready to pounce, until he saw his own reflection in a mirror that hung opposite the washroom where he stood. The lateral bands of light and darkness on his cap, mask, and gown lit him up like a mummy, and he wouldn't get a step into the room before his target spotted him. The pause also allowed him to consider a more rational explanation: what if it was simply someone here by mistake?

Not daring to breathe, he slowly raised his right arm, intending to find a light switch and snap it on. He figured the surprise would cause the interloper to bolt, but not before Earl got a good look at her, or him. With all the shadows and the unisex nature of protective wear, he couldn't tell which.

Except his reaching movement showed in the mirror.

The figure stiffened, twirled, and charged him.

Earl took the brunt of the hit in his chest and, caught off balance, felt himself lifted by a firm shoulder, then rammed into the tile wall behind his back. The blow turned his lungs into a pair of bellows, his breath left him in a roar, and a white light exploded behind his eyes. He crumpled to the floor, fighting a tumbling sensation inside his head and struggling to keep himself from spiraling down a deep, dark hole.

But the blackness around him poured into his brain, and the high-pitched squeak of someone running on linoleum in crepe soles filled his ears. Like birds cheeping, he thought. Whoever it is mustn't be wearing paper booties.

"Would you be tellin' us what the devil you were doing here?"

Jimmy's alarmed voice penetrated Earl's skull like a drill bit. He opened his eyes to the brilliance of a ceiling light and saw the priest, flanked by two nurses, hovering over him. He moved to get up and found himself lying on the bare mattress. "Did you get him?"

"Get whom?"

Earl glanced at his watch. He couldn't have been unconscious for more than a few minutes. "The person who sandbagged me."

"I didn't see anyone—I just found you like this when I dropped in to say my usual good night to Sadie." He looked around at the two nurses. "Where is she, by the way?"

"I gave her a weekend pass," Earl said, managing to sit at the side of the bed. His head and back hurt like hell, even when he breathed. "Her son from Honolulu showed up a day early. As a surprise, he hired a private nurse and opened up the family home so he and Sadie could stay there a few days. When she couldn't reach Wyatt, and the residents didn't want to make the decision, she didn't know who else to call."

"But then what are *you* doing here?" The priest's tone continued to sound strained.

Earl looked past Jimmy and up at the nurses. The overhead light pierced his brain with the splitting force of a migraine. "With Sadie's room empty, I decided to conduct a spot check—see how often the night staff attended to their patients. Believe me, ladies, you failed to impress!" Not the whole truth, but enough to explain his presence. As his own thoughts raced to explain the intruder, he wasn't about to confess the far darker suspicions that had brought him here.

They reacted with predictable indignation.

"Why, how can you say such a thing?"

"We treat these people as if they were our parents."

Then pity poor Mom and Dad, Earl thought. "Tell me, were any of the nurses away on break during the last twenty minutes?"

They looked surprised.

The younger of the two had freckles to match the wisps of brown hair that protruded from under her surgery cap. "No! Hey, what do you want to know for?" Her voice still came across in a petulant whine. "You saying one of our people knocked you down?"

He ignored her question. "What about orderlies? Would any of them have reason to come in here now?"

"Of course not," the older woman replied, working a wad of gum under her mask with the sass of a street hustler. "We stripped Sadie's bed when she left. It will be made up just before she returns Sunday night." ·

"Cleaners?"

"At this time of night?" the younger one asked. Her eyes said, Gimme a break.

He looked over to the night table. It contained a calendar, photos of a tanned young man whom he assumed to be Donny, and assorted pencils. He pulled open a drawer, finding only a Bible, tissues, and writing paper. "Did she keep jewelry or anything else that someone would want to steal?"

"Probably took it with her," the chewer said. "After all, she knows there won't be many more times she'll get to wear it."

Earl gritted his teeth at the coldness of the remark.

"What about residents coming here to use an empty bed for a quickie?" the younger one said, sharpening her words with a twist of insolence. "Why don't you suspect them?"

"Residents?"

"Yeah, the cheapo kind that won't spring for a motel—you get my drift. You think that doesn't happen?"

Of course he knew it did. Except would someone waiting for a cheap grope react so violently to being discovered?

He'd about had it with the sullen resentment from these two, and pointed to the one with the freckles. "Get hold of security. Tell them to look for a person without shoe coverings." It would likely be a useless exercise. There were bins all over the hospital with supplies of protective wear. His assailant had probably pulled on a new pair within a minute of leaving the floor.

"Why would someone take off his or her paper boots?" she asked.

Jimmy did a Fred Astaire shuffle, his feet sliding easily on the floor. "For traction." He still sounded tense.

She nodded and left.

Earl got up off the bed, and Jimmy moved to help him.

"Thanks." He grabbed the man's arm for support as his head did a few twirls around the room. The wooziness persisted, and he sat back down.

"Maybe I should be takin' you down to your own ER and let them check you out?"

He must really be unnerved by what happened, Earl thought. The Irish lilt appeared only when he kidded around or got shaken to the core. "No, I'll be fine. I couldn't have been out more than five minutes, tops. Anything under twenty doesn't usually even warrant a CT." Not exactly true, but close enough to get him out of here. He wanted his own bed.

"Maybe we should ask how you got in here, Father," the one with the gum asked, her tone more sour than ever. "We didn't see you come in. Hardly ever do." She looked over to Earl. "Or is it only the lower ranks who make good suspects?"

Jimmy's eyes flared like stoked embers.

Earl leapt to his feet. "That tears it—" A sudden swirl inside his skull sat him down again. He steadied his head in his hands, only to watch in disbelief as Jimmy leaned toward her, his hands up like a prizefighter's but open, not clenched, fingers spread wide and pointed right at her.

"Ya don't see me because ya never take your noses out of your coffee cups or your minds off whatever important chatter constantly fills your heads. If so, you might not only catch me walkin' by, but actually hear what's all around you." He directed his fingers skyward. The muted wailing ebbed and surged the way it always did, steady as a distant sea. "If you listened, actually listened to what you've become deaf to, just maybe you'd be finding it in your hearts to comfort a tormented soul or two as they slip away, alone and afraid."

She recoiled, eyes wide with surprise. "Now wait a minute—"

"Because if you don't"—he moved a step closer—"when it's your turn, every one of those tormented souls will be circling, waiting for you at St. Peter's gate, ready to testify as to your good works and send you down."

She flushed as crimson as if scorched by a sunburn. "How dare you threaten—"

"Threaten? Oh, no, my dear. It's called old-time preachin'—puttin' the fear of the Lord into a miserable sinner to save her soul." His eyes crinkled into the accompaniment to a smile, but their flash was as hard as diamonds.

She chewed her wad of gum a few more times, appeared to roll it from one side of her mouth to the other, then retreated to the hallway.

"God forgive me, but she needed tellin'," Jimmy said, his jaw so bulging with tension it made his mask look a size too small.

"No doubt about it," said Earl. But he'd never seen the man so steamed.

Jimmy feigned a double take. "Well, what a difference a week makes. To think just last Saturday you were tellin' me to ease up on my fight with Wyatt and his crew. Now you're cheerin' me on."

His lilt had definitely acquired an edge. Earl tried to chuckle, hoping to lower the tension a notch, but the sound came out dry and cheerless.

The fire in Jimmy's eyes died, and he let out a loud sigh. "Sorry, Earl. I guess I'm on a hair trigger as much as everyone else these days."

Earl shrugged. "It's understandable."

"I also can't help thinking that if I hadn't goaded you into coming up here last Saturday, you wouldn't be in the mess—"

"Hey, I needed to see what goes on."

"I sure didn't mean you to get obsessed by it and go sneaking around the place at all hours."

"I'm not obsessed."

"And look what happened tonight. You could have been badly hurt. For God's sake, play it smart. There's probably nothing more to this than you interrupted a bit of petty larceny. If we know the nursing is slack up here, so must the thieves in our little community."

"Play it smart?"

"Yeah. Play it smart. We all have big enough problems to deal with as it is. Let security take care of creeps who would sneak into rooms and steal stuff from little old ladies. I'm serious about this, Earl."

It sounded like good advice.

"Maybe Sadie herself would have an idea who it could be," Jimmy added, "if she noticed anyone taking too close an interest in her stuff."

Maybe.

Except Jimmy didn't know that the creep sneaking around tonight could be killing patients. From the size it might have been anyone. Even a woman, come to think of it. Certainly Monica Yablonsky had the physique to knock him on his can. As for males, so did that bulldog Wyatt if he was involved. Even Stewart might have done it because of whatever he might be trying to keep secret up here. Or most troubling of all, it could be a person he didn't know, a cipher among the four thousand people who worked at St. Paul's and were not doctors, his or her motive totally unknown.

He shivered.

A search vast enough to discover someone like that would be hopeless. Better this attacker turn out to be just some small-time crook after all.

He declined Jimmy's offer of help and made it outside to his car by himself.

As he unlocked the door, his brain spun into overdrive, unable to shake the idea that what had happened tonight was somehow connected to the unexplained deaths on that floor. And the possible suspects expanded anywhere from those who might be on some twisted mission, seeing themselves destined to put cancer patients out of their misery, to anyone who'd stop at nothing to cover up a scandal. Anyone from Hurst on high to God knew who down low. Nor could he keep the nightmare scenario from popping up again, that it could be anyone and the motive anything.

Faces flashed through his head. He couldn't shut them out.

Friends, colleagues, anybody the least bit zealous about euthanasia in the past, pro or con, came to mind, even . . . No, that went too damn far. Time to go home and get some sleep.

A few deep breaths of the cool night air slowed the maelstrom in his head. But an image played repeatedly in his thoughts during the drive home, then recurred later that night, during his dreams.

In it a shrouded figure with glittering eyes hovered over Sadie Locke's bed, reaching for her.

# Chapter 11

The dreams came at the end of sleep this time.

Sometimes I stood at the top of the stairs and called down to her.

No answer.

No lights on in the basement either.

Yet I'd definitely heard a noise down there.

Other times I walked along the corridor leading to his office.

The lights were dim.

As I drew closer I heard the sound of water running. Lots of water. Like someone filling up a bathtub.

Except there should be no such thing down here.

Or the dream would begin with no hint where it would ultimately take me. It could start in the middle of a sunny day at a park with green grass, cool caressing breezes, and warmth under the blaze of orange and yellow leaves. Or were those clues as well? Had it been sunny that day? Did we go to the park? I couldn't remember. But yes, the season would be fall. Not that I recalled seeing the colors of the foliage. I knew because of the date, November 9, 1989—a date that had become lodged in my head like a bullet, a day the world changed for the better but my universe collapsed.

Was that why he'd chosen that day—to make sure no one would ever forget the anniversary?

Maybe.

Or perhaps our imminent visit had precipitated the choice—he couldn't face us—and he simply took advantage of a coincidence of history, a time when everybody else would be glued to the television and wouldn't interrupt.

Sometimes the points of view got changed about, and I would be inside Jerome's head, forced to experience how alone he must have felt in those desperate yet methodical moments.

And then I'd be back at the beginning again, dreading but not precisely knowing the events to come.

But no matter how or where they started, all the dreams led me to the same spot and all ended the same way.

I stood in darkness, listening to the cascade of water on the other side of the door. There were also strains of barely audible music. The dripping from my shoe when I took a step made me realize that a puddle had spilled under the threshold to form around my feet.

I called out again.

No answer.

I tried the handle.

Unlocked.

I turned it and pushed.

It swung open, and the sound of the streaming torrents trebled in volume. I could also recognize the song now.

"Hello?" I raised my voice to be heard above the din and peered into the semiblackness of the laboratory.

Still no response.

The digital readouts on the equipment, fluorescent green and fire red, cast a neon glow that shimmered on the surface of the flooded floor. At the middle, like an inverted fountain, a huge cascade of water spouted from what must have been a broken pipe in the ceiling. The spray caught enough illumination to glitter like a downpour of emerald and ruby sparkles, but something dark and solid hung in its center.

I should have just turned and left, gone for a maintenance man.

But that dark shape drew me forward.

As I stepped closer, it became a human form, like someone standing under a shower, head slumped forward and shoulders rounded to receive the full force of the stream-ing water on the neck and upper back. Nearer still, I felt droplets from the spray as it cascaded off the top of the per-son's crown, creating a domed effect. Knowing I shouldn't, I ducked inside the watery cupola and looked up to see a down-turned face looking at me. Its wet skin reflected the ambient light, making it seem coated in a sheen of olive and purplish paint. The eyes bulged as if he were enraged, his cheeks were bloated to the bursting point, and a tongue swollen to the girth of a Polish sausage hung twisted from the side of his mouth.

I screamed and woke in a sweat.

For an instant I felt the relief that always flooded through me when I escaped the nightmare.

But dawn slashed across my eyes, a light shredded by the horizontal blinds, and reminded me of the old woman's room.

And Garnet's ambush.

The never-ending dread of getting caught settled in for another day. I could hardly escape it anymore. Even in my other self, it would leech through from time to time, which meant someone might spot that I'm scared and get suspi-cious.

Shit.

At least Earl hadn't recognized me; if he had, the police would already be at the door.

But what the hell had he been doing there? And how did he know to get the old lady to safety? Could he be on to everything, could he have figured it all out? Christ, he might even have been the creeper on the ward last week.

My skin grew clammy again, adding to the sour aroma from the already damp sheets. I threw them off in disgust, retreated to the shower, and turned the cold water on full. The blast of icy needles overrode my runaway thoughts and helped me focus, not that that offered much comfort. As I tried to rein in my worst fears and sort out pure imaginings from fact, a few gnawing realizations shoved everything else into the shadows.

Whoever had been the figure in the hallway, it didn't change the fact that Garnet had been skulking around last night. And whatever reason Garnet had had to move the old lady out and keep watch in her room, he now knew for certain that she'd been in danger. Which meant he'd be more watchful than ever up there, and there'd be no delaying or diverting him until he got at the truth.

The trouble would be, which truth? *The one I planned for him to discover, or the reality behind it? But false leads might not fool the likes of Earl.* All the pieces in their entirety were there to be found, and he definitely had the smarts not only to find them but also to fit them into place.

*Time to accelerate the plan.*

## Sunday, July 13, 6:10 p.m.

"Sit down, Thomas." Jane felt eerily calm and totally in charge. She'd had a sense of complete control all weekend, first refusing to see him, then instructing him to show up at her apartment. That he'd arrived twenty minutes early only enhanced her heady my-way-or-the-doorway attitude.

He didn't stretch out on her living room rug as he usually did while waiting for supper, but took one of the upholstered chairs, which seemed a size too small, making him bend like a half-folded lawn chair.

The sight of him made her giggle.

He immediately smiled. "Well, that's better. God, I thought you had bad news, it felt so serious in here."

She said nothing.

Immediately he leaned forward, his features funneling into a pointed look of concern. "What's up, J.S.?"

She never really liked how he'd appropriated Dr. G.'s nickname for her. It felt like an intrusion on something private she shared with a special friend.

She studied Thomas's sleek, sturdy frame and lean, bearded face, thinking how his appearance had fed her schoolgirl ideal of a Tennessee woodsman, hard as an oak ax handle, yet still more boy than man. Well, time to grow him up. See what he could make of himself.

"I'm pregnant."

He appeared to stop breathing.

The seconds crept by in discreet silence, as if trying not to eavesdrop.

"Thomas, did you hear me?"

"Jesus, Jane, give me a moment. That's quite a shock."

"Really? Uh, how many times have we made love? A hundred, maybe? And do you remember putting on a new condom each time we sampled seconds? Look, I may have been as lax as you, but we were a team in this one. Do me a favor and spare me the surprise." The impatience she felt surprised her. But what the hell, let it rip. She'd no time for bullshit. Not now.

He gaped up at her as if she were a stranger.

She put a hand on his head, running her fingers through his hair. "Forget kind lies, Thomas. I need to know. Do you want your baby and to be a daddy, or not?" Her voice sounded serene despite the abruptness of her words.

His jaw slipped another notch.

"And I won't beg, damn it. If you don't want to share the child, you're out of here, and I get a lawyer."

He seemed to fold up a little more in his chair.

Think only of the baby, she reminded herself, and the freedom exhilarated her, liberated her in a dozen ways. From Mom's inevitable disappointment in her, from the disapproval of all Grand Forks, from the clucking tongues at St. Paul's—their hold on her slipped like chains to the ground. Second-guessing and hesitation about what to do vanished. Work? She'd keep her job as long as possible. Where to go? She'd stay here in her apartment. Whom to count on for no shit about how she ought to have been more careful? Her little brother, Arliss.

Decisions and answers flew into place—snap, snap, snap. She felt weightless.

Thomas stared up at her in absolute awe.

His expression fueled her exuberance over having taken charge.

"I've never seen you this way," he said, sounding totally incredulous. "You're . . . you're . . . radiant."

It's the hormones, stupid, she wanted to say, but didn't. Yet her silence caused a weight to tug on the middle of her chest, as if she'd allowed him to snag her in flight and pull her back toward the ground.

"I mean it, Jane. You're absolutely glowing." He got to his feet, walked to where she stood, and put his arms around her.

She resisted. "No. Tell me what you want."

"I love you."

"Yeah, right. How about the child?"

He grinned. "I'd be proud to be a daddy with you."

She watched his eyes dilate as fully as she'd ever seen, even in lovemaking. But from desire? Not this time. He looked more as if he'd been caught in the middle of telling a joke and a bomb had gone off.

Her scrutiny must have made him feel defensive. "What?" he said, his grin widening.

"Proud?"

"Yeah, proud. I'm surprised but proud." He grinned wider still, seeming to warm to the word he'd chosen, and lowered his head to kiss her.

She ducked out from under his lips and held him at arm's length. "Proud!" she said, as if she found the term repulsive.

All at once he looked even less sure of himself.

It made her want to attack harder. "What the hell does *proud* mean? You intend to put a notch on your . . . your . . . well, your whatever, because you knocked me up?"

The pupils pulsed bigger than ever, then narrowed to pinpoints.

She'd only seen people's eyes do that in a strobe light.

He mouthed air a few times, but no words came out.

Her impatience hit the stratosphere. "Well, here's a news flash, buddy. I'm not your or anyone else's trophy." She knew somewhere in her head that her behavior had careened from bitchy to totally unreasonable and back. Yet as he flinched under her onslaught, she loved it.

"Shit, Jane, I'm sorry—"

"So am I."

"But don't be so angry."

"Why not? I feel angry."

"But—"

"But what? Speak up, Thomas."

To her astonishment, a nervous chuckle bubbled out of him. He tried to stifle it, but instead he broke into a loud, rolling guffaw that rumbled from deep within his chest. "You're a real firecracker tonight," he managed to say, and knelt in front of her. "Forgive me, beat me, scold me, but I am delighted, proud, happy, surprised, eager, ecstatic—stop me if I get the right word—to be the father of your child."

All her anger melted away.

He held out his arms to her, beckoning with that damned seductive grin of his.

She lunged, knocking him on his back, and pinned him under her, then straddled his chest, her knees on his arms. "So you want to be a dad?"

"I want to be a dad."

"And you want me?"

" I love you."

"You want to love, hold, and obey?"

"Oh, yeah. Especially the obey part. Or you kill me, right?"

"Right!"

She felt jubilant, as if she'd won a great victory, stood up to the fates, spat in their eye, seized the brass ring, and cliché of all clichés, done it all her way.

And gotten herself a sexy woodsman from Tennessee to boot.

Just like Daisy Mae.

## Monday, July 14, 9:30 p.m.

Earl leaned back in his study chair and let the speed dial of his cellular ring through to Michael's house. The man would have to run the department during death rounds tomorrow and needed a heads-up. Should the anticipated fireworks take place, it could be a long session.

"Hello?" Donna answered with the throaty slur of someone who's been asleep.

"Donna, it's Earl. Did I wake you? Sorry. I wanted to speak with Michael. I thought you guys would be up." They were one of the last holdouts in his age bracket who stayed up to watch the eleven o'clock news.

"But he's in ER this evening."

Oh, shit. "Of course, how stupid of me. I can't keep up with the schedule anymore," he said quickly, wanting to get off the line. "I'll call him there. You get back to sleep. Good night." He hung up before she could say anything.

He'd made other calls over the years to the homes of staff members only to be told by a puzzled spouse that the person should be in ER. And he always played the absentminded professor, claiming to have forgotten the schedule. But he could no more forget what shifts he'd assigned to people than his own phone number. Everyone had their regular slots. They knew them; he knew them. An ER physician's life revolved around the damn schedule: who gets what vacations, who works Christmas, who does New Year's Eve. There's no steadier headache for a chief than making sure every hour of every day of every year is covered. Michael didn't do Monday evenings. So unless he had pulled a last-minute switch with someone—not a total impossibility—he had lied to Donna about where he'd gone.

Catching someone out always cost Earl. He didn't like knowing the personal problems of people he worked with. But trouble at home often translated into trouble at work. So he kept a close eye on the men and women whose secret lives he'd unintentionally discovered. But to find it out about his friend, colleague, and acting chief of the department meant worry on all three fronts and having to walk on eggshells at a whole new level.

Please let me be wrong about this one, he thought, ringing ER. "Hi, it's Dr. Garnet. Who's on call tonight?"

"Dr. Green and Dr. Kradic," said the clerk, naming the two veterans who had manned the shift for years. "Do you wish to speak to one of them?"

"Actually, I wondered if anyone saw Michael. Maybe he's working in his office?"

"One moment. I'll check."

He took a deep breath and watched the trees outside his window toss in the wind as yet another storm threatened. Their leafy branches swept back and forth in front of the streetlamps, covering and uncovering the lights in a frenzied semaphore.

"I'm sorry, Dr. Garnet, but no one's seen him."

## Tuesday, July 15, 7:00 a.m.
## Pathology Conference Room,
## St. Paul's Hospital

The remains of Elizabeth Matthews lay in open Tupperware containers arranged end to end along the length of a massive polished oak table. Earl scanned her ocher-colored liver, a pair of charcoal-tinted smoker's lungs, two glistening gray kidneys, and a maroon heart coated with yellow fat, the four cardiac chambers sliced open like the inner compartments of a large red pepper. A separate tray displayed the pièce de résistance: an amorphous knobby-shaped mass of pearl-colored tumor that had penetrated the ovaries and uterus, reducing much of the structures to an unrecognizable reddish brown mush. The final two specimens, a coil of bowel and the halves of her brain, were parked to one side, too anticlimactic for comparison.

Pre-SARS, the aroma of fresh coffee would partly cut the

acrid fumes at these sessions, but not anymore. Nothing was served at morning rounds these days. Signs posted throughout the hospital read NO EATING ON THE JOB, and cartoons of people raising their masks to gobble down donuts bore stamps of big red circles with lines slashed through them. Most found this new form of prohibition harder to take than the clampdown on cigarettes. Smokers were a minority. Restrictions on food left *everyone* hungry, in caffeine withdrawal, and snarly as hell.

Even so, death rounds remained popular with staff and trainees. A pathologist's knife spared nobody in exposing the final diagnosis and laid bare the mistakes of all, from the loftiest chief to the lowliest student. The combined prospect of picking up teaching pearls and witnessing the great equalizer of a public stripping-down usually packed them in.

Except today Earl had invoked his powers as VP, medical and limited participation to the players directly involved in the case. What he had in mind required them and only them, not a general audience. Hurst had gladly gone along with the ruling, never even questioned it, always eager to keep anything controversial as secret as possible, SARS or no SARS. And it still wasn't clear if Mr. Matthews would launch a lawsuit.

Earl looked around at the invited guests.

On this side of the table Thomas Biggs sprawled in a chair a few spaces away. Dressed in a crisp white coat, he sleepily inspected the open containers from under drooping eyelids, the aftereffect of a recent string of night calls.

Beside him Jimmy sat upright and alert, leaning forward and raring to go, but wearing a king-sized frown, obviously baffled at why he'd been included.

Everyone else had chosen to sit opposite Earl, face-off style.

Midpoint in the lineup, Paul Hurst formed his graceful fingers into an elongated triangle and absently beat a tattoo with them on the front of his mask.

His sister, Madelaine Hurst, director and chief of all

things to do with nursing at St. Paul's, occupied the place at his right side. No surprise there. She always took that position, either oblivious of or indifferent to its symbolic right-hand-man implication. An asthenic woman with austere gray eyes, and known to protect her domain as fiercely as her brother defended the hospital, she clamped her steel gaze on Earl. It felt cold and hard as shackles.

Next to her sat Mrs. Quint, seemingly relaxed, her expression a thousandfold more congenial than her boss's. Earlier she'd even wished Earl good morning. But her corpulent figure exuded an air of authority, and as acting supervisor at the time of the incident, she'd be defending her "girls" just as vigorously as Madelaine Hurst would.

The most openly hostile pair, Peter Wyatt and Monica Yablonsky, glared at him in unison from the far end of the table. Having placed themselves near the large, wall-mounted video screen that would be used for the upcoming presentation, they'd picked the prime spot to make sure everyone else would witness their show of disapproval.

Predictable, Earl thought.

Stewart Deloram, however, surprised him. He'd positioned himself at Paul Hurst's left elbow and, with surprising charm, cozied up to him from the minute they sat down together, chatting breezily while studiously avoiding eye contact with Earl.

Now what could that be all about?

Len Gardner, habitually occupying the oversized chair at the other end of the table, rose to his feet. "We might as well begin," he said, and with a touch of a finger to his laptop computer, the wall-mounted screen sprang to life. A swirl of pink lines and blue dots appeared, the primal color scheme pathologists use when staining body tissues so that they will be visible under a microscope. This particular pattern, wavy mauve strands reminiscent of a van Gogh, were woven beneath an array of tiny purple dots worthy of a Monet. Together they depicted normal uterine muscle lined with disintegrated mucosa.

Len clicked through a series of such images—the strands of muscle and sheets of mucosa appearing successively more shredded—to document the tumor's relentless progress. "Invasion by increments," he described it, "destroying Elizabeth Matthews's reproductive system cell by cell."

Earl recalled the ghastly distortions on the woman's wan face as she'd endured what they were seeing.

As the demonstration continued, Stewart occasionally whispered something in Hurst's ear and pointed to the screen, seemingly adding his own spin to the narrative. He still hadn't looked in Earl's direction.

Len moved on to pictures that confirmed the cancer hadn't yet disseminated throughout the rest of her body, flicking through shots of the other vital organs and showing them to be free of any metastatic spread. "Certainly her neoplasm had not reached a stage such that it would be incompatible with life," he emphasized.

Laying down his laser pointer, he removed the tumor from its container and, sticking here and there with a steel stylet as long as a knitting needle, demonstrated in macroscopic terms the assault on Elizabeth Matthews's womb.

"Any questions?" he asked when finished.

No takers.

Earl often worried how voyeuristic and sicko these sessions would seem to the outsider. Yet they remained at the heart of learning medicine, exposing the profession's victories and errors with a certainty that no other part of the discipline could provide. Should they ever suffer the ax of public outrage because the media exposed them to lay scrutiny, doctors wouldn't be flying blind, but it would be as if they'd lost an eye.

Len gestured to Stewart. "Dr. Deloram has volunteered to present and interpret the biochemistry of the case, including the postmortem drug screens."

"Thanks, Len." Stewart stood up, and with a click of a remote, a slide projector mounted on a steel table began to whir noisily. A few more clicks, and its carousel advanced with a loud rattle. Pushing another button, he caused a movie screen to descend from the ceiling and come to a stop above the video monitor.

It's a wonder he didn't play the theme from *2001,* Earl thought.

Enlarged charts of lab values sprang into focus on the white surface.

"As you can see, aside from a raised calcium level, the result of the tumor having eaten into the bones of her pelvis," Stewart began, "the hematological and biochemical values remained mostly normal until the time of death. In other words, as Dr. Gardner has so elegantly demonstrated, multiple organ failure had not yet become part of the picture." More numbers flicked by. "Specifically, I draw your attention to the patient's normal liver and kidney function, since this will have a bearing on our ruling about the cause of death." He turned to address the nurses. "You no doubt recall that morphine is broken down in the liver and excreted in the kidney. After looking at these standard values, a physician might reasonably conclude the patient ought to have been able to metabolize a dosage increase of the magnitude Dr. Garnet ordered, especially since previously prescribed amounts of the narcotic hadn't treated the woman's pain."

He paused and cast a glance at each of the women, eyebrows raised like a mime telegraphing that he expected a response.

Mrs. Quint gave a reluctant nod of agreement.

Madelaine Hurst simply stared back at him, unwilling to yield up so much as a blink.

Monica Yablonsky had the startled look of deer blinded by a poacher's light. She started to fidget with her glasses.

Attaboy, Stewart, Earl thought. So far so good.

"And I take it that all present are aware of the sequence of events leading up to this woman's demise," Stewart continued, "Dr. Garnet's doubling of her morphine dose, the times that the nurses administrated it, and the patient's vital signs throughout?"

Nobody indicated otherwise.

"Fine. Now while a lethal level of morphine undoubtedly killed this woman, the source of that toxic concentration is not at all clear."

*What?*

"The amount present in her blood at the time of death might indicate that approximately double the amount Dr. Garnet prescribed may have been administered to the patient, but this explanation isn't that certain."

Wait a minute. What's this "not all that clear" and "isn't that certain" crap?

"A fall in blood pressure could have resulted in a delayed uptake of the first injection that had been given around nine that evening. Later, should the pressure recover and the uptake of the drug into the patient's bloodstream return to normal, both the remnants of that shot and the entirety of the second dose would enter the circulation simultaneously, leading to the toxic levels that killed her."

No! Wrong! Wrong! Wrong!

"Even though the nursing records indicate no such fluctuations in her vitals," Stewart continued in a fluid, singsong delivery more appropriate to a travelogue than a death review, "they might have come and gone undetected. And to reiterate Dr. Gardner's findings that the woman's cancer, while undoubtedly painful, had not yet brought her near death, it's a known fact that morphine itself can drop a patient's blood pressure. So we are left with two possible scenarios: either someone doubled the second injection, or undetected fluctuations in blood pressure led to a delay in the absorption of the first, leading to an accumulation of the two shots."

Earl leapt to his feet. "What the hell are you talking about?"

Stewart sat down and studied the table between them.

"That's garbage, Stewart, and you know it."

Stewart said nothing, still avoiding eye contact, but Earl saw the black of his pupils grow wider.

Like a variation on Pinocchio's nose, the lying son of a bitch. "Why are you doing this, Stewart?"

"Doing what?"

"You know damn well. All that 'fluctuating pressure' bullshit." But Earl had already guessed the reason: to provide a scenario that could give Hurst an out. Not a good one with legs, but enough to confound the findings and keep the table from reaching a definitive conclusion. Then the whole mess would end in limbo, and he'd avoid a public scandal.

"Patients fluctuate wildly near death," Stewart said with a shrug. "They can be nearly comatose one day and rally the next, the improvement there for no more apparent reason than a need to say good-bye, and it all happens with no change in their metabolic numbers. It's a part of cancer we don't understand, almost as if bad humors were at work—"

"Level with me, you son of a bitch." Earl nearly grabbed him by the collar.

"How can you be sure it isn't so?" Paul Hurst said, maintaining his finger pyramid as he looked up at Earl. His voice remained as calm as a pond locked in ice. "Actually, both scenarios seem reasonable to me. Do you have proof to support one over the other?"

"There were never any serious dips in Matthews's blood pressure, not that night, not ever," Earl said, controlling his anger.

"Not recorded, no. But without continuous monitoring, how can you say for sure?"

"It's unlikely as hell, and you know it." He turned to Len. "Do you agree with this?"

The pathologist's scowl said it all. "Of course not. No way shock had anything to do with this woman's death. Stewart, this is a crock."

"Hey," the intensivist said, locking eyes with him, "I'm just laying out all the possibilities. You guys decide which one's most probable." He sounded miserable.

"You were told to pull this stunt, weren't you?" Earl said.

"I might have expected as much from some." He gestured toward the Hursts. "But you?"

Stewart shook his head as if denying the accusation and finally looked directly at Earl. The pitiful gloom in his eyes admitted everything. "Don't you understand? A hung jury here gets you off the hook too," he said, as if that justified what he'd done. "This way neither you nor the nurse can be officially cited for negligence. The matter dies."

Paul squinted imperiously over the top of his bifocals at Len. "Of course, as a former surgeon I know enough never to go against the pathologist as far as cause of death is concerned. Morphine overdose, right? There we are in agreement?"

"Yes. But I repeat, shock did not play a role in that overdose."

"And the minutes will record your opinion. As for the rest, we'll just have to agree to disagree on this one."

His arrogance took Earl's breath away. In a court of law he'd never get away with such a bald-faced attempt to distort the facts. But death rounds had no legal status. Touted as a sacred crucible of final clinical truths, nothing guarded its integrity but good faith between physicians.

The constriction in Earl's gut coiled even tighter. He looked over at Yablonsky. She blanched and began to use her glasses as worry beads.

"Do you have anything to say, Monica?" he asked. "This leaves you much more out on a limb than it does me, and you know it."

Jimmy shot him a disapproving glance, as if to tell him to cut his losses and run.

Madelaine Hurst hunched forward, and her brow acquired the sharp-edged contours of a hawk's. "Now see here, Dr. Garnet—"

"I'm waiting for an answer, Monica," he said, ignoring them both.

Paul Hurst leaned closer to his sister. His normally colorless skin became dusky gray, the change suffusing up his temples, across his forehead, and down from under his mask to his neck like creeping smoke. "Garnet, we agreed not to discuss this—"

"I agreed to wait and hear the pathology reports before I took any action, not to cover them up."

"You can't be serious, throwing the hospital into a tumult at a time when—"

"What tumult? That's why I restricted this gathering to the people most directly involved. I'm betting someone in this room knows the truth about Elizabeth Matthews's death and the deaths of other patients on this ward. We can get at it, here and now, behind closed doors."

"You still aren't seeing the bigger picture."

"Oh, no?" He pointed at Yablonsky. "The bigger picture is that she tried to shift the blame for this patient's death onto me. And my chief resident, Thomas Biggs, tells me there's also been a rise in the number of people who die on the ward but are discovered only in the early morning. Clearly no one is keeping close watch during the night. A few days ago I witnessed that for myself, and our hospital chaplain, Jimmy Fitzpatrick, will back me up. Not only could I sneak onto the ward, but some other intruder came prowling around as well. I don't think we can ignore events like that, can we, Paul, what with a rise in the mortality rate and the possibility that Elizabeth Matthews's death might be part of a cluster—"

"No!" shrieked Monica Yablonsky, her eyes wide with fright. "I won't be your scapegoat." Her voice soared into the high, thin register that jangles the human ear and makes dogs howl. "I won't!"

Bingo! Earl thought. This was shaping up to be a "You can't handle the truth" moment.

Despite working on the numbers all weekend, even with Janet's help, Earl hadn't been able to conclude whether the statistics really indicated a cluster of suspicious deaths. He certainly hadn't been able to incriminate Yablonsky in anything specific. Nor could he tell whether his assailant had played a role in it all. But he'd come here to squeeze Yablonsky, because all her anxiety told him she knew something about what had been going on, and this in itself gave her good cause to be afraid.

Why? Ever since that groundbreaking article in the *New England Journal,* it was the nurses whom investigators went after when patients died and the reason wasn't clear. She'd know that, and it would scare her, whether she'd accidentally overdosed a single patient and lied about it, or done much worse, or hadn't done anything herself but covered up for the real culprit. Earl intended to rattle her enough that she'd drop her guard and let slip her secret, whatever it might be.

At least, that had been his plan, and it seemed to be working.

But then Jimmy sprang to her side, his arms protectively around her shoulders. "For the love of God, Earl, back off!"

Mrs. Quint quickly walked over to join them. "Monica, calm down," she said, rubbing her underling's back the way she would a child's. Her voice, no louder than usual, but ice smooth, rang out like a command.

Monica looked desperately from her to Jimmy and back again. "Calm down? It's not you he's after."

Madelaine turned on her brother. "Paul, stop this disgraceful attack on the good name of a fine nurse."

"Garnet!" Peter Wyatt roared, getting to his feet like some smoldering volcano rising from the sea. "I'm formally charging you with making libelous comments against my department."

"And I'm suspending your authority as VP, medical," Hurst chimed in, as if singing a duet with Wyatt, "pending a hearing into charges of unprofessional conduct."

Earl ignored them all and kept his sights on Yablonsky. "How about it, Monica? Stop lying now or I'll go to the police, and this business will finish you—"

"No!" Her voice once more cracked into soprano territory. "I won't be hung out to dry!"

"That's enough, Monica!" Madelaine Hurst's glare launched a thousand scalpels at her. "The subject's closed."

Monica's eyes flashed a counterstrike. "No, it's not closed.

Not by a long shot." She swung back to face Earl, her pupils so dilated with fright that they squeezed her irises into thin brown rims. "Dr. Garnet, you wanted to know what the patients who reported a near-death experience told their nurses?"

Stewart sat bolt upright.

"That's right," Earl answered evenly. "Apparently no supervisor, including you, could find a single nurse who remembered anything."

"Because they were told to keep quiet—"

"Shut up, Monica," Madelaine Hurst shrieked.

"I won't, not when he's talking about clusters of unexplained deaths and hinting at allegations of murder." As she spoke, she trained her eyes only on Earl, as if forming a corridor that linked them together and excluded everyone else.

"Go on," he urged.

"Monica!"

"Some of the girls who heard those near-death stories found one particular detail doubly peculiar."

"What?"

"Damn it, Monica, I order you to stop."

"Patients didn't just claim they'd seen lights, tunnels, lost loved ones, or themselves floating above their bodies—all that standard stuff." She rattled off the usual catalog of near-death experiences with the contempt of someone who considered such matters to be utter nonsense.

Paul shot to his feet, toppling his chair backward. "Continue and you'll be suspended permanently, Mrs. Yablonsky." He spoke through clenched teeth.

Earl leaned over the table toward her. "No, you won't. Trust me. Talk now, Monica, and nobody can touch you, not even me. What's said in this forum has automatic immunity." He hadn't lied. Anything stated at death rounds could not be subpoenaed in a court of law. The rule had been intended to protect doctors from legal action if they honestly admitted their mistakes so that the rest of the staff could learn from them. But whether the law would protect Monica from a CEO and a nursing supervisor, he had no idea.

Monica must have believed it could. "A lot of the patients said that someone kept whispering questions at them throughout the whole ordeal," she said, never taking her eyes off him.

"Questions?"

"Yeah. Had they seen God? Were they looking down on themselves? What did heaven look like? Crazy stuff."

"You're kidding."

She retrieved a tissue from her pocket and dabbed her eyes, careful not to touch them with her gloved fingers. "I swear, it's the truth."

Earl felt he'd stepped into an elevator and dropped too fast.

Why should he believe her? This might merely be another attempt to throw suspicion on someone else. But the story sounded too bizarre for her to have made it up, and pieces of the puzzle snapped into place, giving an answer he didn't want.

Reluctantly he looked over at Stewart.

The man's pupils grew to the size of quarters.

Oh, my God, Earl thought, his insides plummeting further. "This is what made you say the reports were bogus?" he said, sounding incredulous despite knowing he'd stumbled on the truth.

Stewart's forehead began to glisten under the overhead lights, the effect of a sudden sheen of sweat. "No, honest—"

"Don't lie to me, Stewart!"

"I'm not. I mean, it's not what you think. Please, Earl, you have to believe me—"

"Of course he's lying about it," Monica said, "to protect his ass!" Fury propelled her voice down to its deepest registers, stripping it raw, and the words scraped against the back of her throat. "Who else around here wanted to talk with the dead?"

## Department of Clinical Research, subbasement, St. Paul's Hospital

"I swear to you, Earl, I didn't do anything wrong." Stewart's voice shook. He rose from his desk, fluttering his gloved hands here and there, his fingers as tremulous as wings. A lifetime of data on resuscitation outcomes and volumes of scientific papers about critical care towered about him in stacks. Except now the piles seemed about to fall in on him as he cowered at their center, shot up with fear, eyes as jumpy and desperate as any junkie's.

Earl leaned against the closed door and watched with clinical fascination as Stewart spun and turned, until the sight of him falling apart turned repugnant.

As the meeting had disintegrated into confusion, Stewart had fled death rounds, his eyes straining so far to the side toward his accuser that they nearly disappeared into their sockets. Earl had chased after him to his cubbyhole office.

"You lied to me," he said to Stewart.

"Yes, I know, but only about what those patients told me. I knew if word of that got around, people would react exactly the way everyone else at the table did—think that I had something to do with it." He spoke in short, rapid spurts, alternating between a whimper and a bellow. "All it takes is a whiff of shit to finish you off as a researcher in this game. And I've made more than my share of enemies, believe me, though as far as I can see it's for no reason other than envy."

How about on account of insufferable conceit? Earl thought.

"Oh, there'll be plenty of volunteers to mount a whisper campaign against me," Stewart continued, then blanched whiter still. "Oh, God! My funding, it'll dry up overnight—"

"What, specifically, were you afraid these whisperers would say?" Earl interrupted. He tried hard to sound sympathetic, to keep him talking, but found it difficult.

Stewart reacted with an impatient wave. "You know very well. That I'd badgered dying patients without getting their consent." He expanded his restless movements and started to pace. But in a ten-foot cubicle he still ended up turning in circles. "That I precipitated the near-death state to get more material to publish. That I went after immediate accounts of the experience rather than retellings, to silence critics of my original work. All of it crap, but clever enough to do damage."

Earl shuddered from the creeping realization that just as he didn't know for certain whether Stewart would be capable of something so appalling, neither could he dismiss the possibility. With increased foreboding, he asked, "And how might these so-called accusers explain you could pull such a thing off?"

Stewart immediately came to a standstill, looked at Earl, and went so white around the eyes, he seemed about to faint. He laid a hand on his desk as if to steady himself, and slowly sat down again. "You think I did it too, don't you?"

Come across as an ally, Earl told himself. He also sized up Stewart's physique, wondering again if he could have been the man who attacked him. Hard to tell, he thought. Despite spending most of his hours in the darkness of ICU, Deloram had managed to keep reasonably trim. He also had the height and the breadth of shoulders to fit the bill.

"Jesus, Earl," Stewart continued, "you of all people have to believe me. And it could be anyone trying to set me up—"

The ring of his phone cut him off.

"Hello?" he answered. His forehead grew fire red and his skin glistened with sweat again. "No, there's nothing to it," he said to the caller on the other end of the line. "Just some negligent nurse who's trying to blame everyone else. . . ."

His coloring deepened, and his knuckles glowed white under the latex as he tightened his grip on the receiver.

Obviously somebody at death rounds had talked, and word had gotten out. Probably Yablonsky. It fit her style.

"She even tried to incriminate Earl Garnet. I guess it's my turn now. Who knows, maybe next it will be yours." He laughed far too loud and long. "No problem," he cried. His desperate cheeriness set Earl's teeth on edge. In ER, that sound usually accompanied a chilling smile and signaled a person who might go home, open the medicine cabinet, and start counting out pills.

As Stewart continued to reassure his caller, a laptop on his desk began to chime, announcing the arrival of separate e-mails. The noise continued, like a slot machine paying off, and the dread in his eyes deepened at each sound. Still, he managed another pumped-up laugh and gaily suggested, "Let's have lunch sometime soon. Do you like Mexican?"

He hung up and clasped his head in both hands as if he were afraid it would fall off. "This is going to ruin me!" he said, his voice quivering on the edge of a sob. He looked up at Earl with the agonized stare of a man who didn't quite comprehend why his world seemed to be crumbling around him. "I swear, in all my years of research, I never, ever breached a single ethical protocol."

Earl struggled for something to say, but the phone rang again, once more bailing him out of an embarrassing silence.

Stewart frowned, hesitated, then picked it up and repeated the same bravura performance he'd put on minutes earlier, except this time he offered to buy dinner and suggested Chinese.

When he hung up, Earl asked, "Was the show you put on at death rounds about Matthews your idea, or did Hurst approach you?"

He didn't answer, choosing instead to peer at the tropical fish that languidly swam across the screen of his computer.

"Stewart?"

He took a deep breath, as if he were a diver about to take a plunge. "I approached Hurst to warn him that there might be strange stories floating around Palliative Care about near-death experiences that wouldn't do St. Paul's, or me, any good. Up until then, near as I could determine, any nurse who reported the patients' experiences to a doctor or supervisor had been told they had to be hallucinations and not to take them seriously. But I still wanted to make sure no one said anything to implicate me. He promised to silence any such insinuations, but suggested I also put an end to your poking around and stirring up trouble on the ward by making the Matthews inquiry end in a draw. That would be good for St. Paul's, and with no clear wrongdoing, he said, you wouldn't have cause to investigate any further, which would reduce the chances of you also turning up the near-death stories, which would be good for me."

"You were that naive?"

"I was that desperate."

Earl said nothing.

The phone interrupted them again.

Earl watched as he sweated through another frayed showing of high spirits—eyeballs bulging with fear, squirming in his seat, rattling off yet more futile reassurances, his free hand ceaselessly searching for a place to light.

As if babbling frantic lies to a few people could save him, Earl mused. Not in the age of the Internet. After a lifetime of scientific toil, he would be pilloried around the globe with a push of a key.

Stewart issued yet another invitation, jovially suggesting drinks at a nearby Italian bistro this time, then hung up the phone and pulled the cord out of the jack. "Fuck 'em!" he muttered in a bleak attempt at defiance.

Earl lost patience with the bullshit. "What's next, Stewart? You buy me off with a cup of coffee and breakfast? You can't schmooze your way out of this mess by plying everyone who hears about it with food and booze."

Stewart shot out from behind his desk and in two strides stood nose to nose with him. "How can you be as stupid as the rest of those idiots to believe I had something to do with those patients?"

"I don't know what to believe just yet."

"Well, smarten up, damn it. You of all people should realize that none of this mess rings true. Ask yourself why I'd be so idiotic as to risk my career in some clumsy scam to fabricate data about near-death experiences. I mean, it'd be like pointing a finger at myself. Let's get real here."

"You don't get it, do you, Stewart?"

"Get what?"

"Whether or not you committed ethical hanky-panky as a scientist isn't the big question here."

"Oh, no?"

"No. It's whether you'd kill three people and slip two others into a coma to prevent them from saying you did."

Stewart turned crimson again, and up this close, Earl could see the individual beads of sweat that filled his pores.

"You bastard!" he said, his voice guttural, as if gathering phlegm from the back of his throat to spit in his face. "Get out! Get the fuck out of my office."

# Chapter 12

Thomas spotted him the minute Earl entered the ER. "Dr. Garnet!" he called out, and excused himself from a woman who clutched a gauze pad soaked with blood to the palm of her hand. A couple of medical students, circling nearby in hopes of picking up a suturing job, eagerly moved in to fill the void.

"Walk with me," Earl told him, keeping a brisk pace toward his office at the back of the department.

"About death rounds—"

"Sorry, I'm in no mood to discuss that goddamn meltdown, and officially it's out of my hands."

"But that's why I wanted to talk to you. If I could help in any way, check things out on the QT, the sort of stuff you might not be able to do since Hurst suspended—"

"It won't be necessary." Earl was in no mood for an overly earnest resident in his way right now, however well-meaning Thomas might be. He had his own plan. "Thanks anyway."

Thomas continued to trot beside him. "I just thought . . . well . . . what Hurst did to you sucks, sir. You, and this hospital, deserve better. And how else can we get to the bottom of what's going on?"

Earl straight-armed the door leading to the administration wing and strode on through. "Look, I appreciate the offer, Thomas, but I'm not going to involve house staff in cleaning up a hospital mess. The academic requirements of the R-three program are plenty enough to fill your time."

Thomas stuck at his side. "But that's what I mean, sir. I've got to write a research paper as part of my curriculum. Why couldn't it be on clusters of unexplained deaths?"

Earl slowed his pace. "Why, that's . . ." He didn't know what to say.

"Think of it. The topic is legitimate, exciting, and I hope intriguing enough to get me published so I can pursue more research with my ER work. The result might also provide the key to what's going on in Palliative Care. The beauty of it is that no one, Dr. Hurst included, would know. Who on staff pays attention to a resident doing a project? At this point we don't have to tell a soul what it's about. I could sit at a computer or in medical records, look at anything I wanted, and no one would even notice, let alone get nervous."

Interesting, Earl thought. So far Janet had done exactly that without anybody being the wiser. But she still had another three months of data to check, and with Hurst bound to be on the lookout for an end run, it might become more difficult for her to continue undetected. Hell, she'd be the first one he'd keep watch on. A resident, on the other hand, just might fly under his radar. Thomas could pull charts from all over the hospital as a subterfuge to keep anyone in records from realizing that he'd zeroed in on Palliative Care.

"Let's talk about it," he said, and continued toward his office. He unlocked his door, threw himself into his high-backed chair, and gestured Thomas to take a visitor's seat. "You'd check everything you plan to do with me first?" he asked.

Thomas quickly sat and leaned forward, his arms on Earl's desk. "Absolutely."

"And you'd have to keep this totally confidential. Tell no one, understand. You heard about the run-in I had early Saturday morning? I don't want whoever decked me coming after you."

"Understood. Not a word."

Earl switched on his computer. "And as your director, I'd have the final say over what we publish."

He looked puzzled. "Sure, except you wouldn't cover up anything we found, would you?"

"I'm saying we stick to the definite stuff—a classic cluster study, correlating times of death with staffing coverage. What has no place anywhere, let alone in a scientific paper, is unsubstantiated, poisonous insinuations like the one Yablonsky threw at Stewart this morning."

Thomas recoiled as if he'd been slapped. "Don't tell me you think he's innocent?"

"I don't like lynchings," Earl continued, ignoring the question. "That's exactly what the person who blabbed about the proceedings this morning did, probably Yablonsky, and the wolves are already tearing Stewart apart." As he talked, he clicked up a popular search engine for medical topics. "I just came from his office. It's not a pretty sight, seeing a man have his reputation shredded. Especially if it's not deserved. Might as well skin him alive."

"My God. From the way you tore into him, I thought you agreed with her—"

"Oh, I know he lied to try to keep what those patients said from becoming public knowledge. But that's a long way from actually staging some conversation from beyond the grave. And he forced me to ask the one question anyone with half a brain would want to answer before rushing to judge him." He paused, allowing Thomas a moment to get the point, and continued to scan the offerings on the Web page he'd selected.

The resident frowned at him.

"Come on. Why would Stewart pull something so bush league that pointed so obviously at his own work? Ah—and then there's this." He pivoted the computer screen so they could both see it. Large black letters proclaimed THE KETAMINE-INDUCED NEAR-DEATH EXPERIENCE.

"Holy shit," Thomas said, wide-eyed.

"Before all the trouble started, Monica Yablonsky mentioned in passing that this sort of stuff could be found on the

Internet. I didn't think anything of it at the time," Earl said, scanning the summary.

Thomas hunched toward the screen and joined him in reading it.

It seemed to be a legitimate paper that described how a team of scientists had induced classic near-death experiences in some subjects using IV ketamine. Everything could be explained by chemistry. Earl knew the intended pharmaceutical action of the drug as an anesthetic, having used it in ER. But what the article highlighted—how ketamine blocked the neurotransmitter glutamate at certain areas of the brain, called N-methyl-D-aspartate (NMDA) receptor sites, and caused subjects to report seeing bright lights, rushing through tunnels, rising above their bodies, and meeting lost loved ones—went into more detail than he'd seen before. When those same symptoms arrived following a shot in an emergency procedure, Earl simply called them side effects.

"It's a fucking how-to manual," Thomas said, reading alongside him. "And Monica Yablonsky told you about it?"

"Yes, when I first asked her about the reports from Wyatt's patients."

"So you think she could be involved after all?"

"In the near-death stuff? I don't know. Why would she be, unless using ketamine might be connected to some mercy-killing spree she's been part of? But then why would she badger people to describe what they see? And if we're dealing with mercy killings, why are patients left alive to talk about it?"

Thomas sank back in his chair, and frowned in silence. "Everything you say . . . it's all pretty vague, isn't it?"

"Not really."

"How so?"

"There's someone prowling around the ward with a set of shoulders on him that could stop a truck. Nothing vague about that at all."

"Shit!"

"What?"

"Stewart Deloram has a good set of shoulders."

Earl sighed. "And every reason not to shoot patients full of IV ketamine."

"I hope so, because he's been a great teacher, and I don't want him to be in trouble, except . . ."

"Except it's hard to be sure of someone once suspicions about them are let loose."

"Yeah. I mean, even now I'm wondering, how do we know a guy like Stewart didn't count on people thinking that he'd never do anything so obvious. Being a little too clever is something he might try, except it backfired on him."

"Maybe." Earl decided not to even mention his worst suspicion, that Stewart might have silenced five patients to avoid the type of scandal that now consumed him. Thomas would really find it hard to believe in Stewart if he heard that one. "We could speculate all day," he said instead, and stood up to end the meeting. "But your study will put some real probables on the table."

Thomas slowly rose to his feet, seeming almost reluctant to leave. "In a way, I'm afraid of what we might find. Finger-pointing can get ugly."

"Leaving a killer at large would be worse," Earl replied, hoping Thomas could remain objective despite a sense of loyalty to Stewart.

The young man nodded, but the eager spark he'd had in his eye at the start of their talk had faded. Probably hadn't put faces on the people they might end up going after when he first offered to help.

"Now, Janet has already done some of the work you'll need," Earl continued. "Of course, it'll save time if she shows you her results, but not in the hospital. Seeing you two huddled together might tip Hurst off."

Thomas's eyebrows arched. "Dr. Graceton's already been doing a cluster study?"

"Obviously our secret held," Earl said, once more pleased with himself for having had the sense to recruit his wife's aid. "So how about dropping over to our house for dinner this evening? You can review her material safely enough there. Until now she's covered only the staff in Palliative Care, but it looks as if we'll have to go beyond them and check the whole hospital. And she can continue to process the data you collect. It'll take the two of you to track everyone we need—nurses, doctors, residents, orderlies, and porters, including who entered the hospital after hours when they weren't on duty."

"But—"

"You see, key card access leaves a computerized record. Of course, I'll have to call in a few favors to get into those databases."

"Yeah, but—"

"So we'll talk more tonight," he said, determined to keep him speechless so that they wouldn't start arguing in circles again, guessing who did what to whom. "And bring your appetite. Janet's the best cook in Buffalo—"

"Dr. Garnet, I'm sorry, but I've been trying to tell you, I already have a dinner engagement tonight."

Feeling sheepish, Earl invited him for tomorrow evening.

## 5:55 p.m.
## Palliative Care

Sadie Locke had left Dr. Earl Garnet a message requesting to see him.

Sitting on the side of the bed, picking her way through a dinner tray that held several bowls of different-colored mush, she looked at her reflection in the mirror. I'm definitely better for my weekend at home with Donny, she thought. The pallor of her face had picked up a coppery tinge of tan, and her eyes sparkled, a change that only family and love could evoke.

She looked at her watch. Dr. Garnet had said he'd be here before six.

"Hi, Mrs. Locke," said his now familiar voice from the doorway. "Don't let me interrupt your dinner. . . ."

"Dr. Garnet! Come in, come in." She pushed the meal aside and waved him closer. "The nurses told me you had some excitement here after I left."

He chuckled. "Afraid so."

"Are you all right?"

"My back still twinges after an hour in a chair, and if I turn my neck too quickly, I get a reminder of what happened. Other than that, I'm fine. Now, what can I do for you?"

She motioned him closer still. "It's what I can do for you," she said in a whisper. "I may have seen the person who knocked you out."

"Oh?"

"Yes. Someone tried to come in here in the wee hours of last Tuesday morning, but I scared off whoever it was."

"What!"

"Well, not scared so much as surprised. The individual apparently didn't think I'd be awake."

"What happened?" He sat beside her on the bed.

"I heard someone come in, and thought it might be Father Jimmy—the dear man always drops by, no matter how late his day goes—but saw this form. It was too dark to see his eyes—"

"It couldn't have been one of the nurses?"

"Don't think so. Too big."

"Man or woman?"

"Couldn't tell. Too dark."

"Did he or she say anything?"

"Just that it was the wrong room."

"What about the voice? Might you recognize it?"

"No. The person spoke in a whisper." Her wisps of hair stood up like Dairy Queen curls, and her eyes flashed with pleasure from telling what she knew.

Yet the story troubled Earl. If the visit on Saturday morning had been a second attempt to get in the room, then theories about someone looking for an empty bed for a quickie

with a nurse, or even an attempt to rob the old lady's belongings while she'd been on a weekend pass, went out the window. He wanted to ask her if she had any reason to think
someone would want to do her harm, but first, he thought, it
was better to reassure her. "Sadie, I want you to know it won't
happen again. You may have noticed that I've posted a security guard in the hallway."

"Yes." She leaned her head toward his in a conspiratorial
gesture. "That's how I knew you took what happened seriously and would want to know about the Tuesday visit." A
curt nod punctuated the claim.

More excited than afraid, he thought with a grin. "Okay,
then here's what I need to know. Any enemies?"

Her eyes widened in delight. "Me?" She sounded hon-
ored, as if someone thinking she could matter enough to be
the target of who knew what was high praise indeed. Back
went her head and out came a hoot of laughter. "Go on!" She
waved a hand at him, the way one fends off flattery while enjoying it to the hilt.

He asked her a few more questions, not so much because
he thought she could tell him anything else, but to feed the
relief most patients got from being part of something bigger
than their disease. As they talked, his gaze roamed over the
same simple belongings on her nightstand that he'd seen before, and once more his eyes fell on her calendar. Yet this
time he noticed she'd marked about a quarter of the days
with crosses, occasionally two and three at a time. Looking
for a way to wrap up their conversation—Janet wanted him
home on time this evening—he changed the topic. "Are those
the visits Father Jimmy paid you?" he said, pointing at the
markings.

"Oh, no. He's here almost every night. Those are the times
some pitiable soul tries to pass on but gets jumped on by that
team of young doctors with the squeaky cart. Why people
here can't at least slip away without all that fuss, I'll never
understand."

Earl noticed the DNR bracelet on her own wrist. She certainly had a point, he thought, but said nothing. Still, the large number of crosses disturbed him.

## 11:07 p.m.

Stewart stepped inside the entrance to his house, closed the door, and slumped against it. If only he could just as easily bar the outside world from his life, not allow it to rampage through and trample everything, he thought. Except it already had.

He looked around at his marble entranceway, its polished gray surface softened in the dim glow of recessed lighting. Tonight it looked like a mausoleum, but a well-furnished one. A rosewood end table supported a small brass lamp with a green shade. It funneled a golden spot on the mail his housekeeper had placed there for him. Usually the sight of letters waiting for his attention had an uplifting effect—the prospect of reading the latest news from admiring colleagues was one of the pleasures he savored at the end of a marathon day. Not anymore.

From the dimly lit living room to his left came the quiet strains of Mozart. His stereo was programmed to come on at the same time as the lights so he wouldn't return to a silent, dark home—the ruse of a man who'd allowed his personal life to become stripped bare by work. This clever tactic now struck him as pathetic, and underscored the emptiness of the place.

Tocco came running down the stairs from where she'd been sleeping on his bed, black coat gleaming, brown eyes full of warmth, and pink tongue ready to slurp him a kiss. The Labrador retriever, big as a bear cub, greeted him the same way she had every night for the last ten years.

It didn't comfort him at all.

Couldn't.

Maybe never would again.

He dropped his briefcase and walked in a trance through

the tasteful arrangements of antique chairs, a pair of sofas, more end tables with brass lamps, all chosen by a hired decorator, to where he had a wet bar in a recessed corner.

He never drank. At parties club soda would be his choice of beverage. "ICU may call," he told any host who tried to ply him with liquor. The truth was that he didn't like the taste. Never had, not even at beer parties in med school.

Nevertheless, he poured himself a tumbler of brandy and downed it the way he would some foul medicine.

It burned his stomach. Little wonder, with nothing to eat all day.

Tocco pushed her snout under his free hand and turned her head so he'd have an ear to rub.

He poured himself another drink, wandered into the dining room, and slumped at a table made of Brazilian mahogany that could seat twelve but rarely did. Then he got up and, leaning against a matching hutch filled with seldom used fine china, admired his little-seen collection of wall tapestries, each one a van Gogh re-creation.

Still restless, he abandoned his untouched drink on the polished wood and entered a kitchen that had every appliance known to chefs, but a refrigerator with little more than staples and the freezer filled with gourmet frozen meals. As he stared at the selection, feeling less like eating than before, Tocco walked up to the cupboard that held her dog biscuits and wagged her tail expectantly.

He walked over, pulled a few from the bag, and threw them at her feet. She plopped down, captured the nearest one between her paws, and gnawed happily on its upright end, oblivious to the collapse of her master's world.

He strolled through a swinging door to a den with a plasma screen the size of a billboard and a thirty-speaker theater center. A stack of overdue DVDs lay on the floor. At the top of the heap, Vittorio De Sica's *The Bicycle Thief* teetered precariously, ready to fall to the floor.

He ended up back in the entranceway, sank to the marble floor, and proceeded to add up the score.

The first dozen calls had been more of the "Is it true?" crap that he'd fielded with Garnet there.

And he'd danced the same I'm-all-right, it's-all-a-big-misunderstanding jive, but knew he'd ended up conning no one.

Next the ones who had already made up their minds signed in.

"It's not just you. All the research money is drying up," they lied apologetically. "Of course you'll be the first to be funded again once the economy improves. . . ."

They'd stripped ten million dollars' worth of pending grants from him in less than two hours, and he knew he'd never get that kind of cash again. His fall had been extra steep because so many wanted to punish—no, make that eviscerate him.

Tocco wandered out of the kitchen, spiraled three times before plopping down, and contentedly gave herself a bath, as if her master sprawled in the middle of the foyer floor were no big thing.

Grateful for the one living creature that hadn't judged him today, he reached over and rubbed the ear he'd ignored earlier.

She immediately tried to give his hand a kiss.

He thought of the men and women who'd dissed him today. He remembered their goofy, want-to-be-around-a-winner expressions when they threw endowments at him and felt it a privilege to do so, not the sour faces that he had imagined went with the cold, dismissive tones they'd subjected him to over the last twelve hours. It reminded him of the discrepancy between how the eternal whines of disappointment from his ex-wives differed from the eagerness with which they'd once said "I do."

But the loss of control over his domain at work panicked him the most. His ability to command respect and make others do his bidding had slipped through his fingers like water.

He got up and glanced to the coatrack where Tocco's leash usually hung. It wasn't there.

He wandered down to the basement, to check the hook where the housekeeper sometimes left it.

Tocco followed, wagging her tail in anticipation of a walk.

He eyed the water pipes and saw the face that had haunted him since 1989.

Purple, swollen, and twisted, the image of it lurked at the core of his memory, always ready to intrude without warning, triggered by the slightest of associations. It could happen while he presented a paper, listened to accolades from younger colleagues, even appeared once in the middle of an interview on *Oprah*. Like an avenging ghost, it haunted him, particularly the bulging eyes. Their black scrutiny bored through his pupils and, like probes, activated what no anatomist could find—the convoluted cerebral coils of gray and white matter that housed conscience. Because that cold lifeless stare forced him to relive his treachery, admit to the innuendos and whispered lies that had been the ruin of the phantom who looked on him so accusingly. His only sure respite from the curse? When a case consumed him in ICU.

He ran back upstairs, Tocco whining at his heels. When he went out the front door without her, she barked her disappointment.

He rocketed his car out of the driveway and sped toward the hospital.

ICU, he thought. He'd be okay there.

## Wednesday, July 16, 2:33 a.m.

Jane Simmons awoke in her bed with a cry on her lips, pain ripping through her abdomen.

"Christ!" she moaned, grabbing her stomach and curling into a ball. "Thomas!"

Then she remembered. He'd gone back to ER to relieve the resident who'd replaced him for a few hours. Since the Sunday revelation, much to her pleasure, he'd adjusted his schedule so that they could have dinner together the last three evenings.

Another cramp hit, twisting her intestines as if they were caught in a wringer. "Jesus!" she groaned, curling tighter. Must be something they'd eaten. Tonight she had picked up fresh snapper. It had looked fine, and she'd cooked it thoroughly. But she'd also made potato salad, so it could have been the mayonnaise. Nothing else would have done it. They'd drunk only fresh fruit punch—no alcohol, of course. He'd brought back lemons and grapefruit this time, enough for a pitcherful.

"A toast," she'd said, insisting the third supper in a row on using the champagne glasses kept for special occasions.

"Shucks, here's how we do it in Tennessee," he'd joked, and took a big swig directly from the jug as he usually did, just to tease her.

"Grand Forks too, but only behind the barn," she'd tossed back, and she chugged it with him, slug for slug, determined not to be outdone, but then insisted they fill the glasses to the brim and toast each other in proper style, raising them to each other, to the baby—

"Oh, my God!" she screamed.

Another surge, this one stronger than the others, gripped her like giant hands tearing her in two. Between her thighs she felt slippery, warm, and sticky. Her hand instinctively flew to her groin, and a flow of hot fluid coursed between her fingers.

"God, no," she whimpered, reaching for the light switch and bracing for what she'd see.

Nothing could have prepared her.

A circular red stain between her legs kept spreading, from beneath her hips to below her knees. With each surge of pain another swell of blood gushed from her vagina. In the middle of it all lay the crimson detritus of what had been her baby.

She let out a cry, reached toward it, then restrained herself.

More waves of pain jackknifed her into the fetal position again, and the periphery of her vision grew dark.

Head reeling, she uncoiled enough to reach the phone and tried to punch in 911. Her fingers slid off the keys from all the blood.

Michael Popovitch stepped outside the ER's exit door and loosened his mask. The cool night, still moist from rain an hour earlier, smelled sweet. He stayed near the changing area—"limbo," as the residents called it, the zone between the safety of the outside world and the infected realm of the hospital. He always figured that this was where the battle would be won or lost. Sooner or later, despite all the precautions, someone would carry the virus into the street, take it home, spread it to family, to friends, to everyone.

He drew a deep breath and, freed from the stuffy confines of his mask, enjoyed the heady freshness of inhaling air unencumbered as much as he'd once savored the rush of nicotine from his smoking days. A faint sound like a wheeze rose and fell in the distance, then repeated itself, rising and falling as regular as breathing.

An ambulance on its way in.

Five minutes out, he judged, sound carrying far through the city when it slept.

He leaned against the wall and looked up at the stars. Patches of twinkling silver had opened amidst traces of clouds that still lingered overhead. Probably would be clear tomorrow. Rather than sleep off his shift, he'd take Terry and Donna to the beach.

It might be a good break for the three of them.

The quarrels between himself and Donna couldn't be good for the kid. They didn't throw things or physically hurt each other, but tension filled the house, thick and as smothering as a pillow to the face.

He remembered those kinds of times between his own parents. Hadn't scarred him, he figured. But they'd made him unhappy. The big difference was that his mom and dad had known how to end them. Unless he quit ER, the trouble between him and Donna would go on for as long as SARS lasted, which could be forever.

Sometimes she wouldn't even sleep with him. She cringed every time he picked up Terry, and found every excuse she could to take the kid to her mother's. And each time news broke of another nurse or doctor coming down with it, she looked at him as if he were a murderer.

He could leave St. Paul's, go to a place that hadn't been infected yet. But it wouldn't be that simple. SARS could pop up anywhere. Probably would. And besides, if whoever replaced him here got involved with his files, they'd see what he'd been doing—

The door bashed open, startling him out of his thoughts.

"Dr. Popovitch!" Thomas Biggs said, breathless as he leaned out the opening. "We just got a heads-up from an ambulance. They're bringing us a woman in shock, big time, from a miscarriage."

Michael pushed off from the wall. The wail sounded much louder now, approaching faster than he estimated. They must be really gunning it. "You got everything ready inside?"

Thomas nodded.

Michael felt his heart quicken, the way it did from the first day he stepped into ER and the sirens drew closer. The only thing that had changed was that he'd learned to channel the adrenaline, stream it through his head to clear his thoughts and sharpen his reflexes. He entered a zone where he would react without doubts, second-guessing, or hesitation, a purity of moment he found only in the pit. As that telltale wail swelled louder, the stiller he grew.

Thomas, like all rookies, fidgeted with increasing restlessness but stayed outside.

As they stood waiting, a familiar dark Mercedes pulled into the doctors' parking lot, and Stewart Deloram got out.

"What's *he* doing here?" Thomas muttered. "Anyone who took the pasting he did should be at home hiding under his bed."

"Then you don't know Stewart," Michael replied, and waved at him.

Stewart saw them, then looked over his shoulder in the direction of the howling siren, so close now the shriek had set up a slight vibration in Michael's ear.

"Waiting for something special?" Stewart called, heading toward the other side of the ambulance bay and the door designated for people entering the hospital.

"Woman in shock," Michael said, "from a possible miscarriage."

Stewart used his card to open the lock. "Mind if I help?" He reached inside the entranceway and pulled a clean gown off a cart stacked with protective wear.

"It's an OB case," Thomas said, fixing his eyes on the oil-stained asphalt that separated them. His tone of voice hinted that Stewart should mind his own business.

Needless to say, the resident had already passed judgment on the man.

"Posse justice, Thomas?" Michael murmured. "Nobody innocent until proven guilty anymore?"

At first Thomas said nothing. Then he murmured, "I want him to be just what he's always seemed. But I don't know if I can trust that anymore."

"Understandable," Michael said in as low a voice as possible without it becoming a whisper, "but you learned a lot from him. Doesn't he at least deserve the benefit of a doubt?"

"You think he's innocent?"

"I think he's worked too many years at my side saving lives for me to turn on him now." Besides, Michael thought, he'd have at least one friend at St. Paul's when his own moment of reckoning arrived. "Glad to have you, Stewart," he called out loudly, all the while looking directly at Thomas. "After all, shock is shock, right?" he added in a loud voice.

The young resident lifted his eyebrows in a show of disapproval but kept silent as the ambulance roared into the hospital driveway, its siren dying to a deep-throated growl.

* * *

Jane lay shivering on the stretcher while faces bobbed above her like windblown balloons.

"Femorals in!"

"Type and cross six units—no, ten!"

"Two units, type O, up and running."

The voices came at her from the other end of a long tunnel. They sounded frantic. Always did, when one of their own came in, she thought.

"Still pouring blood."

"Systolic's down to eighty."

"Where's OB?"

Cold flowed through her.

The IV lines they'd jabbed into her arms, legs, and neck stung.

The catheter someone had rammed up her bladder filled her with a phantom urge to pee that she couldn't relieve.

And the pain in her belly pummeled her with the brute force of fists.

Not even Popovitch and Deloram had a moment to comfort her as they yelled orders and spoke excitedly to one another. That really made her afraid.

It also pissed her off. How dare they reduce her to a slew of pressure readings, blood counts, and chemistry parameters? And why should Deloram be here anyway? "Looking for a few words from the near-dead, Stewart?" she murmured, feeling strangely uninhibited and defiant enough to use his first name.

He started, his dark brows curling in amazement.

"Just kidding," she said. "At least now you noticed me."

"You sure you want me working on you?"

"Damn right, but don't you be thinking of your own problems. And quit staring at me as if I were already a ghost."

A muffled chuckle came from behind his mask. "You're something, Jane."

"How bad?"

"Hey, don't worry. I'm not about to let one of the few people around here who's still talking to me slip away."

Michael Popovitch appeared above her, a lab report in his hand. "You sure you don't take aspirin or blood thinners?" he asked.

"No." Her reply sounded like a moan.

"Bleeding problems?"

"None."

The pain returned. All at once she wanted Dr. G.

And Thomas. He continued to dart here and there, anxiety blazing out of his eyes. "Hang on, Jane," he whispered each time he came close enough to say anything. She thought of how they'd made love only hours earlier, and suddenly she'd never felt more naked.

*Talk to me, damn it! Leave the numbers, tests, and needles to the others. Just hold my hand.*

She started to spiral downward, her head lurching in a nauseating, off-center spin.

*Oh, God, I'm going.*

"Beta subunit's positive," a female voice called out, echoing through the room as if on a loudspeaker.

She didn't recognize it.

"Definitely got herself pregnant."

*Bitch!* Jane wanted to scream.

"Why's she still bleeding so much?" one of the residents asked.

"Retained placenta," Thomas said with the forced coolness he used when trying to sound calm and professorial. "We have to do a D and C, clean out her womb . . ."

Another flash of anger slowed her plunge into darkness, even buoyed her up. She wanted to grab him by what got her pregnant in the first place, and twist. Then she heard a woman's voice from out in the hallway that sounded as welcome as a distant bugle cry heralding the cavalry riding to the rescue.

"Okay, what have you got for me on my last night of call—my God, J.S."

Dr. Graceton came into view above her and leaned in close, grabbing her hand with a reassuring squeeze. "Okay, I need straight talk here," she whispered. "How long since the start of your last cycle?"

"Nearly two months." Her mouth felt full of cotton and didn't let her enunciate properly.

"Are you on any meds?"

"No."

Dr. Graceton leaned closer

"Did you try and abort yourself? Take something like RU-486 from Europe?"

"No, nothing—" She broke off with a cry as her uterus seized into another contraction.

Dr. Graceton frowned. "Sorry, J.S., but I have to ask."

"No, we decided to keep the baby."

"Oh, I see." Her frown deepened. "Then did you take anything by accident?"

"I don't think so."

"Do you use anti-inflammatories?"

"Sometimes, but—"

"Arthrotec or Cytotec?"

She shook her head, recognizing the names of drugs containing misoprostol, an analog of prostaglandin intended to block the ulcer-producing effect of arthritis medication. It also caused the cervix to open. She'd seen a number of women in ER who'd miscarried because they'd made the mistake of taking the pills Janet had just referred to. "No, nothing like that."

Dr. Graceton glanced over at Popovitch. "Any other lab results back?"

He'd just cranked up the bottom of the bed to autotransfuse her with blood from her legs. The strain around his eyes drained the skin of color and made it seem as if he should lie down and do the same for himself. "Hey, Dr. Popovitch, lighten the mood," Jane told him with as much firmness as she could muster. "You're scaring me."

He looked down at her and must have tried to smile, because the lines at the corners of his eyes shifted slightly. "Sorry, Jane. Hey, I guess I always rely on you for that." He glanced back over to Dr. Graceton. "Biochem's okay. But even without the rest of the results, I can tell you right now her coagulation's off. She's hardly forming any clots."

"Then let's give her fresh frozen plasma," Janet said with an impatient flip of the hand, implying a no-brainer. She referred to blood that had not been separated yet into its individual components and would boost clotting factor as well as red cells.

He fired J.S. a wink. "Already thawing in the microwave, my dear."

His W. C. Fields imitation made her smile. It had always gotten a few chuckles and relaxed everyone as they worked. "That's better," she told him.

Stewart raced up to the table with a printout in his hand. "I got the other results," he said.

They huddled around it as if sharing a newspaper, and threw out the alphabet soup of acronyms used to describe bleeding disorders.

"DIC?" Thomas said.

*Oh, God!* Jane recognized that one. DIC was a dreaded complication in hemorrhagic shock—the acronym stood for disseminated intravascular coagulopathy and meant that she'd used up all her clotting factors with excessive coagulation throughout her blood vessels, even where she didn't need it. Bottom line, her chance of survival would be fifty-fifty. Plus the treatment had always struck her as desperately insane. They'd give her heparin to slow her clotting even more, in the hope this would spare the few factors she had left and allow them to work at the site of the hemorrhage. Not many of her patients with the same problem had survived. "I'm going to die," she murmured, or had she just thought it?

No one seemed to hear.

Dr. Graceton grabbed the report. "What are you talking about, Thomas? Of course it's not DIC. Only her INR is elevated. Platelets and PTT are fine."

*More alphabet soup.*

"Yeah, watch what you're saying," Michael added. "You'll frighten our J.S. to death."

"I taught you better than that, Thomas," Stewart piped in, his frizzy eyebrows lifting in indignation.

Thomas acted stunned. "Oh, right," he said. "Stupid call."

*They're lying to protect me.*

The *bing* of the microwave sounded, and in seconds the nurses added more maroon IV bags to the ones flowing into her, except these felt warm in her veins from the recent thawing. The rest of her remained cold to the core. She started to slip away again. "I'm going," she cried.

"No, you're not," Janet told her in a firm voice.

But she plummeted into free fall, and her womb seized in another contraction.

The other three moved out of earshot, where they continued to chatter and gesticulate.

"Pressure's down to sixty-five," someone yelled.

Thomas appeared at her side and grabbed her hand. "Hang on, Jane. I love you," he whispered in her ear.

*Finally,* she thought dazedly.

He dashed from view and returned with a needle to take another blood test.

*Jesus.* She felt furious at him again.

Janet reappeared back at her side. "We're heading to the OR now!"

Everyone scrambled frantically to pile what they'd need for the trip onto the bed—monitors, oxygen tanks, IV poles.

"Give her an IV shot of phytonadione," Stewart ordered.

Jane knew that stuff—it was another name for vitamin K. In ER they used it to reverse the effects of Coumadin, a drug that thins the blood by interfering with the role vitamin K and other components play in normal clot formation. "But I've never taken Coumadin in my life—"

"Relax," he interrupted. "You were probably born with low prothrombin levels. That mimics a Coumadin overdose on testing, and phytonadione will shore up the effectiveness of the bit you have. People deficient in it often don't find out until a time like this. Do you normally bleed a lot when you cut yourself?"

"I don't know if I'd say that."

"How about your periods? Are they heavy?"

"Sometimes, but—"

"Hi, J.S.," said another familiar voice, putting an end to Deloram's annoying questions. Then a gloved hand, warm even through the latex, grabbed hers.

"Hey, Jimmy," she replied, her own words sounding like a distant echo. "Tell me this isn't a professional call."

His eyes crinkled at the corners. "No, I'm here just as a friend."

"I need a friend."

"Then I'm your guy."

"You're sure, now that I've practically got a scarlet A on my forehead?"

His grip on her hand tightened. "Hey, enough of that. We'll soon be having coffee together as usual."

Just twelve hours ago they'd been sharing a pot of tea in the lunchroom set aside for ER staff.

"And when you're better, I want a match to this." He flicked his earring with a gloved fingertip. "You've no idea what a hit it makes me with the old ladies in Geriatrics."

She tried to grin at him. No one had given her a mask. He might be the last person on earth to see her smile.

Janet leaned in close again. "Okay, here's the score. In the OR I'll do a D and C, and once the plasma kicks in, the bleeding will stop. Bottom line, you're not going to die, and there will be more babies."

Shivering, she felt her head swim again. "Sure hope so."

"And if these ER cowboys are finished spearing you," Janet continued, but much louder, "perhaps we could get the lady a blanket?"

She started to lose consciousness, and tightened her grip on Jimmy's hand, but he couldn't hold her out of the darkness.

# Chapter 13

Janet dashed through the corridor, guiding the stretcher around corners, the race a deadly earnest repeat of what they'd done in jest through the streets of Buffalo two Saturdays ago.

Even Jimmy helped, setting intravenous bottles swaying in the turns as he muscled their precious cargo along.

Stewart Deloram adjusted IV rates on the run.

Janet continued to utter a steady stream of comforting words—reassuring J.S. that all would be well, that they'd beaten these odds many, many times before, that this would soon be little more than an unpleasant memory. But she couldn't be sure her patient even heard, and she estimated they had ten minutes to stop the flow of blood or J.S. would die.

They commandeered an elevator and seconds later were met by a team of nurses and an anesthetist who ushered them into an OR.

The bleeding continued.

Changing, scrubbing, then redonning sterile gowns, gloves, and masks cost more precious minutes.

"Pressure's down to sixty-two," called out one of the OB nurses.

Stewart rushed to open up the IVs as wide as they'd go.

Jimmy hustled back to J.S.'s side. No stranger to keeping out of the way, he hovered discreetly by her head, holding her hand and talking quietly to her, until a nod from the anesthetist indicated she'd finally been put under. He then stepped back into a corner, apparently determined to stay and observe, his dark eyes glistening.

Janet recognized in them what she'd never seen him show before: fear.

My God, he's in love with her, she thought.

"Ready for you, Doctor," said the anesthetist, his voice clipped and urgent. "Pressure's falling, sixty over zip." He had the requisite wisps of gray hair sticking out from under his cap to tell her she hadn't pulled a rookie.

The nurses secured J.S.'s legs in stirrups and positioned an OR stool adjusted for Janet's height between them. Taking her seat, Janet prepared to do the definitive treatment—scrape any pieces of afterbirth off the inner lining of the uterus. With nothing left in the way, the organ could clamp down tight on itself and tamponade the bleeding sites, like pressure on a cut.

The os of the cervix hung open, pouring blood, and tissue trailed out its orifice, debris caught in a stream.

"Suction," she ordered.

Catheters drained everything away with the sound a straw makes at the bottom of a milk shake, and the crimson flow receded.

Janet quickly inserted a dilator to widen the passage, then went into the vault with a curette to clean out any remaining material.

"Still sixty over zip, and pulse climbing to one sixty. You may not have much time." The anesthetist spoke the grim warning with glacial cool.

"Keep calling out the readings." She retrieved only small amounts of tissue, yet blood continued to pour over her hands, warm and fluid with not a clot in sight.

Definitely something wrong with her coagulation.

"Any repeat on the INR?" she asked.

"Still high, but the rest is okay," Stewart replied. In other words, low prothrombin remained the problem, not the more horrific DIC, at least so far.

He continued to work frantically with the IVs—replacing

spent packets of red cells and plasma, binding the new ones in pneumatic cuffs that accelerated their flow, hanging up more liters of saline to pour in as much volume as possible— all to keep her circulation from collapsing completely. The dread in his eyes said, *I'm losing!*

"Fifty-five over zip."

Janet finished raking the curette over the inner uterine wall and pulled out the last segments of the afterbirth, none of it enough to explain such a copious hemorrhage. There should have been some improvement by now.

Unless . . .

"BP down to fifty, pulse is still high . . . one fifty-five . . . one sixty . . ."

She'd soon arrest.

A cold sweat crept up Janet's back.

Either the coagulation problem hadn't corrected at all, or in doing the curettage, she'd shoved the instrument right through the uterine wall and opened up a new bleed. Pliant enough to expand and accommodate the size of a baby, the tissue is delicate, and a curette could penetrate it without her ever feeling the pop of the metal tip punching all the way through. She'd never made the mistake before, but shit happens when you least want it.

She'd have to go in and check.

"A number eleven scalpel," she ordered, removing the curette. "Prepare for a laparotomy and a repair of a possible uterine puncture."

She heard the indrawn breaths as everyone's pupils pulsed wider, but nobody said a word. From now on she'd be the only one to speak.

The nurse at her side snapped a pointed blade onto a stainless-steel handle and laid it flat in her outstretched hand.

Her colleagues shoved the additional instrument trays they'd need into easy reach and whipped off the sterile covers. One of them quickly prepped the area she'd be cutting.

Stewart slid a nail-sized needle under J.S.'s collarbone and into her subclavian vein to start a sixth IV.

"Get ready to tamponade the incision with gauze, and give me suction, plenty of it."

In a single move Janet made a four-inch horizontal slice through the skin into a yellow layer of subcutaneous fat, following along the top of the pelvis, the so-called bikini cut. Immediately the trench filled with blood, but the nurses' fingers pulled the edges apart and pressed folded white gauze into the incision, soaking up the flow as fast as it appeared.

In a second pass she cut deeper, parting the yellow globules where she'd left off down to the glistening white fascia that lined the abdominal muscle. Across this layer she made a third sweep with just the tip of her blade, and the diaphanous sheet sprang open, permitting strands of maroon-bellied muscle to bulge out. Handing back the scalpel, she quickly separated them with her fingers, working around the catheters that noisily sucked out the blood, making her way down to the pearl-gray membrane that lined the pelvic cavity. Without needing to be asked, two nurses assumed the task of holding the tissue apart with small stainless-steel claws as she went.

Once she'd cleared enough space, a third nurse slapped a pair of pointed tweezers into Janet's left hand and surgical scissors into her right. Using the former to snag the membrane, she lifted it enough to make a tiny tent and snipped another four-inch opening.

Retracting the edges with her fingers, she brought the dark maroon surface of the pear-shaped uterus into view. Gleaming like new, it lay in a blood-free bed of ligaments and ocher-colored membranes.

Perhaps she hadn't perforated it after all. To be sure, she delicately explored the slippery contours with her fingertips, checking for any tiny holes.

None.

She watched it for leakage.

Crimson seepage from severed vessels in the skin flowed into the space, but nothing else. The exterior remained intact, giving the appearance of a womb as ready to receive and grow life as always.

But from its interior the unrelenting flow persisted, silently coursing out between J.S.'s legs to spatter noisily into the most recent steel basin the nurses had placed there.

After the rush of activity, Janet felt overwhelmed with helplessness. She'd reached the limit of what she could do.

More vitamin K wouldn't help. It took hours to work.

Removing the uterus would produce more hemorrhages.

The sole hope for survival rested with the fresh frozen plasma—if the clotting factors kicked in soon enough.

She prepared herself for the hardest task a surgeon had to endure: to stand by and let time decide life or death.

"Pressure?"

"Fifty-five," the anesthetist reported, his voice as ice-smooth as ever.

No one else said a word.

In the silence, each squeeze of the ventilation bag seemed to become louder.

The tiny intervals between the rapid stream of beeps from the heart monitor grew so infinitesimal that the noise approached a continuous scream.

And the spatter of blood filling yet another basin ran steady as a faucet.

One of the nurses emptied it and recorded the amount.

Others counted the blood-soaked gauzes that lay in foot-high piles on the surrounding trays, estimating each to hold a twenty-cc loss. J.S.'s heart would either find enough volume of blood to pump or collapse in on itself, empty. And even if she continued to have a pulse, whether the rest of her vital organs—brain, kidneys, liver—could scavenge enough molecules of oxygen from the sparse circulation to survive intact, Janet had no idea.

With nothing to do but wait, she drew on raw nerve honed by years of experience to just stand there, outwardly calm but seething inside, suffocated under a sense of dread that she'd lost J.S.

Then she thought of Jimmy and what he must be going through.

When she glanced in his direction, he remained as still as a sentinel, yet gave her a nod, as if to say it would be all right.

J.S. went into full cardiac arrest at 4:10 a.m.

Stewart cracked open her chest, slid his gloved hand into the cavity, and did open-heart massage.

As he worked, the bleeding slowly subsided.

Because she's dying, Janet told herself.

Nearly five minutes later the anesthetist said, "You're getting a good pulse."

Thirty seconds after that the heart resumed pumping on its own, coming back to life in Stewart's hand.

As Jane's pressure climbed, everyone waited for the bleeding to resume.

It didn't.


## Later that same morning, 7:30 a.m.
## The roof garden, St. Paul's Hospital

"I tell you, Earl, he was terrific," Janet said, throwing her arm around Stewart's shoulders. "Absolutely terrific."

The man reddened, but the corners of his eyes betrayed a smile. "Janet's the one who called the shots," he said, unusually muted in the face of praise.

Falling to the status of pariah and then reclaiming the mantle of hero in less than a day can have that effect on a person, even a resident prima donna, Earl thought, not exactly comfortable with Janet heaping such unqualified accolades on a man who still had a lot to answer for.

Stewart seemed uneasy as well, having difficulty looking him in the eye.

The sounds of morning traffic floated up from the street below, and overhead an azure sky stretched out over Lake Erie to where water and air became indistinguishable and the horizon disappeared in a blue haze. The coming day would be a scorcher, and as at the start of most shifts since the roof garden opened, a lot of staff had gathered here to talk and savor the coolness while it lasted. While some still gave Stewart a stink-eye scowl, many of the nurses who'd done the same yesterday now came up to him and said, "Thanks for saving her."

As for J.S., she lay in ICU, still unconscious, but, with her vitals stable and blood chemistry normal, expected to recover. Even the problematic INR had returned to a reasonable level, probably thanks to the vitamin K. The hematologists would be keeping an eye on it. "Thank God she'll be okay," Earl said to Stewart, his tone guardedly neutral. "Who got her pregnant?" he then asked, wanting to shift the conversation.

Janet's eyes sparkled. "You're going to love this. As soon as his shift in ER ended, Thomas Biggs showed up at her bedside, attentive as hell. Looks like you had a discreet romance under your nose."

"Thomas?"

"That's right. Surprised me too. For a moment, I even thought it might have been Jimmy, the way he stuck to her—"

"Well, if you'll excuse me, I'm going home," Stewart interrupted, sounding tired as he unfolded his tall frame from the bench. "At least now I ought to be able to sleep."

"You deserve it," Janet said warmly, giving his arm a squeeze.

"You're awfully friendly with him," Earl said after he'd left. He hadn't had a chance to talk with Janet privately since the events at death rounds yesterday morning.

"You believe what that Monica Yablonsky's saying?" she asked, the skeptical arch of her voice and eyebrows making her own opinion clear.

"I'm not sure."

"Only not sure? Come on!"

"Well, I agree that he wouldn't be so stupid as to rig a bunch of near-death experiences."

"But?"

"Even if he had nothing to do with that, I don't know how far he'd go to try and prevent that story from coming out."

Janet frowned. "You mean to say you think he knocked off the patients who reported those stories?"

"It's a terrible thought, but . . . yes."

"Jeez!" She looked out over the lake, her blue eyes darkening, growing as deep and faraway as the distant water. "I know he can sure get prickly over what people say about him, almost paranoid at times." She shook her head. "But to actually silence people, cause them to die or slip into comas . . . that's a hell of a leap." She exhaled hard, inflating her mask around her cheeks. "But the trouble with thinking the worst about someone is that once you start, it's hard to stop."

"Tell me about it. Better yet, tell me I'm wrong."

She breathed out a second time, hard, as if doing her breathing exercises in preparation for labor. "I can't say I don't know what you mean. Stewart has always been a difficult read. And if anyone could tweak a patient over the edge without leaving a trace, he's got the skills." A shudder passed through her. "As wonderful as what he pulled off with J.S. might be, it always kind of scared me, seeing how he throws himself into a case on the brink. There's a desperation to it. Oh, I know anyone in our business who's really good has to be obsessive about getting all the details right—we all are— but I don't think I realized before just how consumed he is by what he does. It's like he hides in it. But would he kill to protect his right to play God?" She again shook her head. "I just don't know."

Earl felt more uneasy than ever. Part of him had hoped she would dismiss his concerns about Stewart. Time to once more change the topic. "What about supper tonight? Remember, I invited Thomas over. Are you going to be up for working on stats with him?"

She arched her back into a stretch and gave a big yawn. "He already told me to expect him."

Earl felt a flash of annoyance. "Really? You look exhausted."

"Don't worry. After I look in on a few patients, I'll sign out and go home to bed. Brendan will get another surprise treat when he comes back from school and finds me there, and we'll make the meal together."

"From what you said, I would have thought Thomas might want to be with J.S."

"There's that too. But seems he's more determined than ever to discover what's going on in Palliative Care. I got the impression he'd totally changed his mind about Stewart and wants to help clear his name, all because Stewart saved J.S. Ain't love grand?"

Earl frowned. "Wait a minute. He can't turn this into some damn personal crusade."

Janet got up to leave. "Don't worry. I'll keep Thomas in line. Besides, I already explained to him that a profile on Stewart's presence in the hospital wouldn't work. Trouble with a guy who has no life is that he's always here, so a cluster study on him wouldn't be valid."

Earl had an idea. "It might be if you look at when he's not here."

"What?"

Minutes later he stood leaning over her shoulder as she sat in front of her office computer screen and clicked up some of the Palliative Care statistics they'd been scrutinizing the last few days. "Locate the initial numbers that showed the first jump in the mortality rate six months ago, then go to the second increase, last April, just after the SARS outbreak," he told her.

She brought them up on the screen. The first three columns showed a rise of eleven deaths a month that held steady, and the last three indicated the second increase of fourteen patients a month.

"Now break down the data so we see it by the week."

Six big columns of figures became twenty-six shorter

lists. Within any given month, the numbers held steady week to week.

"Now," he said, "you remember those media junkets Stewart went off on?"

"Oh, my God, yes."

"One was at the beginning of the year. Believe me, I remember, because ER is always hell without his help."

"Then let's see. . . ." She clicked up the mortality figures in Palliative Care for that period and broke them down according to days.

Sure enough, while Stewart had been in New York, Chicago, and LA gabbing with Connie, Larry, Letterman, Oprah, and Jay, the numbers of people dying in Palliative Care held more or less steady at the then new high of 25.6 patients a week, or 3.6 per twenty-four hours.

"At least we can forget about him having anything directly to do with the first overall rise," she said.

Earl thought a moment. "It doesn't rule out the possibility that he had an accomplice, and it sheds no light at all on whether he had anything to do with silencing five patients a few days ago."

## 7:56 a.m.
## ICU, St. Paul's Hospital

Jane Simmons felt the darkness. It pressed into her nose, into her mouth, and down her throat, suffocating her the way black earth would if someone had buried her alive.

In a panic, she clawed her way to the surface, back aboveground, until a hand grabbed hers and pulled her toward the light. "Jimmy?" she tried to say, opening her eyes, but choked on what felt like a hose down her throat.

Thomas's dark brown gaze greeted her. "Hi, love," he said, his voice very soft. "Welcome back."

For an instant the sight of him confused her, and the beeping sounds from behind her head, though familiar, seemed totally out of place. It took a second more to realize she had a half dozen IVs sticking into her, a tube in the left part of her chest, and a respirator hooked up to her lungs.

Then she remembered.

The pain, the blood, ER . . . Jimmy holding her hand. His had been the last voice she'd heard. It felt odd to come to and find Thomas in his place.

Nevertheless, she was glad to see him.

"Jimmy had to leave but said he'd be back," he told her. Undoing his mask, he leaned over to give her a kiss. "The important thing is, you're doing fantastic and are going to be fine. Dr. Deloram found it amazing, but he thinks they'll get you off the respirator and extubate you by this afternoon. That's a powerful set of lungs you have."

His breath smelled of toothpaste. Glancing at the drawn curtains around her cubicle as his lips pressed on her cheek, she could tell by the powder blue color that they were in ICU. Obviously he'd gotten over his being barely able to look at her in ER. *You aren't afraid of someone catching us?* she wanted to ask him, surprised at the intensity of her sudden annoyance with his behavior.

He must have sensed her anger, because he pulled back and studied her, a puzzled look creeping onto his face, only to be dispelled in the flash of a smile. "Hey, I wasn't about to stay away at a time like this, so our secret's out. But who cares? I've been silly about that. Now I want to shout from the rooftops that I love you."

*Too little, too late,* she would have said if she could, just to make the goof suffer. Even Daisy Mae had her limits.

Then she felt empty inside.

Probably all the drugs they'd given her and everything she'd been through.

He squeezed her hand.

She tried to smile in return, a tough feat around a tube, and drifted back to sleep.

**8:35 a.m.**

Before SARS hit, at the start of each day Earl had routinely sipped a cappuccino in the privacy of his office and glanced through the morning's *New York Herald.*

Thanks to his own rules that banned the removal of masks anywhere in ER but the designated lunchroom, he had only the paper now. Without a hit of caffeine to propel him through the headlines, more often than not he leaned back in his chair and stared at his window, the opaque light a reminder that sun and fresh air still existed.

What Janet had said about Stewart hiding in his work bugged him. She hadn't revealed anything the whole hospital didn't already know, but what could be dismissed for over a decade as the quirk of a gifted physician, as long as he performed his daily high-wire act in ICU, had become a flaw demanding a harder look.

Hiding from what? Earl wondered.

An old evasion suggested where the answer might lie.

He leaned forward, picked up his phone, and dialed a 212 exchange that had branded itself on his brain nearly three decades ago.

"New York City Hospital."

"Yes, I wonder if I could speak to the director of clinical research."

"That would be Dr. Cheryl Branagh. One moment please."

The name didn't ring any bells. Good, he thought. NYCH and he had history, big time. He'd probably get further with someone who didn't know him.

Ten minutes later, after talking with a dozen secretaries, an officious female voice said, "Dr. Branagh here."

"Dr. Branagh, my name is Earl Garnet. I'm calling from St. Paul's—"

"I know who you are, Dr. Garnet. There's hardly anyone around here who doesn't. You turned this place inside out a few years back."

Oh, boy, Earl thought. She was referring to a nest of dark

secrets he'd uncovered at NYCH while investigating the death of a former classmate. "Uh, yes, well, this is entirely another matter—"

Her hearty chuckle interrupted him. "Hey, it needed doing. That makes you a good guy in my book. How can I help today?"

Well, that's a break, he thought. "I don't know if you can. This involves ancient history as well, and has to be kept completely confidential."

"Now I *am* intrigued."

"We may have a problem with one of our staff members. He's a clinical researcher who came to us in eighty-nine, highly regarded, but I never got a good answer from him as to why he left NYCH."

"You're talking about Stewart."

"Yes. Do you know him?"

That chuckle again.

He liked the sound of it. She came across as open, friendly, straightforward, and cooperative.

"You might say that. I was his second wife."

Oh, Jesus.

More chuckling. "Hey, it took him five years to drive me crazy. Of course, two people working in the same lab should never have married in the first place, but I'm surprised you've lasted this long with him. What's he done?"

Earl wondered if there were ethical proprieties to discussing a physician under investigation with that physician's ex-wife.

After a second's consideration, he decided no, not if he didn't reveal anything, and she did all the talking. "What I need to know is why he left NYCH in the first place. I mean, his credentials were good, but he's always been rather evasive about it, and I wondered if anything irregular had happened there."

No chuckles rolled across the line this time, only the sound of her breathing.

"Look, if you don't feel comfortable talking about this," he said, "perhaps I should speak with someone else."

"It's not that. I may be his ex, but I don't want to hurt him. Is he in trouble?"

Earl weighed his answer. "In a word, yes."

"And what's your part in it?"

"I'm trying to find out if he deserves the trouble he's in."

"Is this to do with some of the chatter I saw on the Internet yesterday about his near-death research? There are rumors going around that he may have been staging events with patients."

"That's part of what I want to find out."

More breathing.

"I know your reputation," she said after a few seconds, "and not just from recent events here. Stewart spoke about you before he left. We were already divorced, yet the guy had no one else to confide in. By then I'd stopped being mad at him all the time, at least enough to feel sorry for him, and we had a young daughter. So for her sake we tried to be civil."

Earl remembered a dark-haired teenage girl who had shown up in Buffalo a few times. Stewart had proudly introduced her around the hospital, but then the visits seemed to peter out. "Yes, I think I met her. Very pretty."

The woman let out an industrial-strength sigh. "I'm not surprised you never heard what happened in eighty-nine. Both the hospital and the medical school hushed it up." She sighed again, the sound more leaden than before, almost closer to a moan.

Earl leaned back in his chair and said nothing. The art of medicine is first and foremost to get people to tell you what's wrong, even when it's painful for them to do so, and his years in ER had made him good at it. He could tell when to prod and when to just listen. Over the phone, unable to see a face, he couldn't be as certain, but what he'd heard conveyed the kind of heavy-layered regret over long-lost dreams that could build up forever. In other words, she might be ripe to unburden herself.

"He left NYCH because a colleague of ours, Jerome Wilcher, committed suicide, and Stewart blamed himself." Another deep breath sounded, ingoing this time. "I wish I could say unjustly so, but I can't. They'd been longtime rivals in the department, and both were after the position of chairman. In the lab, they were equally brilliant, but Stewart outmaneuvered Jerome politically, a combination of being smarter, faster, and more ruthless at that game.

"Also, rumors began to circulate about the integrity of Jerome's experimental data. No hard accusations, just whispers—yet you know how devastating that can be to a scientist's credibility. Jerome had been in charge of research trials at academic centers all over the United States—visited them repeatedly—yet one by one they revoked his appointments and grants. After Stewart became chairman, Jerome lodged several formal complaints against him with the dean, claiming sabotage, but got nowhere. He published less and less, until in the fall of eighty-nine they found him swinging from the water pipes in his lab."

"Good God!"

"In a way, he finally got his accusations against Stewart to stick. Though nobody could prove anything, the dean didn't want Stewart around, in case the story leaked to the press. In exchange for a voluntary resignation, glowing letters of reference would be provided to anyplace that was interested in him."

Son of a bitch. "Is that when you took over the department?" Earl sounded more angry than he intended. But even though it had happened long ago, he despised the kind of smarmy moves by which hospitals passed their problem staff on to other unsuspecting institutions. Would it have changed his own recommendation that St. Paul's take the man? Maybe not. But he didn't like being lied to, not by Stewart, not by a whole administration, and especially not by his alma mater. What made his resentment feel so fresh? That kind of game still went on today, particularly at teaching hospitals, where they valued academic reputations more than truth.

"Down, boy," she said. "Not only didn't I benefit, but I got tarred by his brush, despite the divorce and the fact I'd been publishing before we ever met. They couldn't kick me out, but they made it clear with pointed hints that I could also leave. Nobody likes seeing faces around that remind everyone of how dirty their own research games got. But you know how it is in a center like NYCH: publish enough, and eventually anything can be forgiven, including having married the wrong man. I've been chair for five years."

"Sorry, I didn't mean to take what happened out on you."

"Don't worry. That's all water under a long-ago bridge."

If you say so, he thought, still getting the distinct impression he'd probed old scars that could still hurt. "Why didn't you leave?"

"The best reason in the world—Carol, the daughter you met. A teenager in high school with friends doesn't want to move away."

He couldn't think of anything else to ask and was ready to say good-bye when she added, "I don't think he could do what they're suggesting on the Internet."

"Pardon?"

"Tamper with data."

"Oh? Why?"

"He may be a son of a bitch when it comes to people, but science is like a religion to him. He wouldn't desecrate it."

She had a point. But his original question remained: would Stewart commit murder to save his reputation within that religion? Then, knowing the passions involved, Earl wondered what someone close to a wrongfully disgraced researcher might be willing to do. "This Jerome Wilcher—did he have any family?"

"All I ever knew about him is that he'd been divorced almost a decade earlier—apparently the guy was a womanizer—and his ex-wife didn't come to the funeral. No surprise there. She took him to the cleaners and, from what I heard, kept coming back for more, to the point that he apparently started hiding his assets. They never had kids, his parents were dead, and he had no siblings. There were a few red-eyed women at the service, and from the suspicious way they were eyeing each other I figured they might all have been his former girlfriends. Word had it that one of them actually went home after the service and tried to hang herself as well."

This time Earl remained silent, letting what she had said percolate.

"Why? You thinking somebody set Stewart up, avenging the way he sabotaged Jerome?" she asked after a few seconds.

"It crossed my mind."

"After all these years? I doubt it. Jerome could be an excessively self-obsessed, compulsive scientist, like so many of our breed. Heroes in the lab, losers in the real world, and especially lousy at marriage. However much Jerome's women missed him at the time, nobody I can think of would still care about him that much."

"That's harsh."

"You're probably more acquainted with the crossovers in the research game, the ones who treat people in addition to rats, like Stewart. They have a smattering of human graces. The purists, like Jerome, wilt in sunlight."

"The one who tried to hang herself—you wouldn't happen to remember her name?"

"Sorry."

He thanked her, gave her his numbers—including the private line at home for after hours, suggesting she call him if anything more about Stewart's past came to mind—and hung up.

The thought of someone close to Jerome Wilcher seeking revenge and setting up Stewart still resonated with him, mostly because he hoped it might be true. What a clean and simple way to get Stewart out from under his current trouble. As nasty as he might be, he remained an asset at St. Paul's, whatever had happened at NYCH fourteen years ago. And despite his impossible personality, Earl liked the guy, even wanted the best for him. Because over and above his being a clinical genius, the man still practiced medicine with the same fire in the belly that all doctors start out with but which few keep alive, even the brilliant ones. In that, Earl considered him a kindred spirit.

But as Cheryl Branagh had said, who would feel passionate enough to avenge Jerome Wilcher fourteen years after his death? The woman who'd tried to kill herself over him? No question her feelings were strong at the time, but for that emotion to have persisted until now would seem highly unlikely. One of the other several girlfriends? Even less of a chance. Once they found out about each other they would have been more apt to hate him, not seek revenge for his death. So who else? He'd no immediate family. But sometimes *distant* relatives could have strong feelings about blood connections.

On a whim he typed the name Wilcher into the staff registry.

Nothing.

What about patients with that name?

He clicked to the admissions page, but no Wilchers were in the hospital at the moment.

Perhaps previously?

According to the patient directory, there never had been.

He dug out the Buffalo phone book to find there weren't any listed in the whole city. A rare name, he thought.

Could there be an avenger with a different name? That he would never find. Oh, well, it had been wishful thinking anyway, and certainly not logical. He'd heard of revenge being a dish best served cold, but to wait fourteen years—

A tap on the door interrupted him.

"Dr. Garnet?" a woman's voice said.

"Yes?"

Even though she wore a mask he recognized her tanned, round face and the corners of eyes that crinkled like fine leather as she stepped into his office.

"Mrs. Baxter," he said without hesitation. Sometimes the person that death left behind stuck with him more than the one it took. Yet something had changed around her eyes. The swollen ripeness of fresh grief had withered into dark hollows, probably due to the aridity of being cried out and the loss of her husband having sunk in. "Come, sit down," he said, rising to his feet. "What can I do for you?"

She stepped over to the chair opposite him. When she settled in, it seemed far too big for her.

"How are you doing?"

Most people at this stage just said, "Fine," and rushed to tell him what they wanted, being in no state to let feelings interfere with the endless paperwork that went with death.

But she hesitated, and he knew he would get a truthful answer.

"It's hard," she said. "Really hard."

She looked down at her hands, and the silence created a divide between him and her.

"I have to say you were magnificent at your husband's side when he died," he said, attempting to close it. "The kind of strength and self-control it took to say good-bye the way you did is rare."

"I loved him." She spoke without looking up.

The silence settled in again.

"Do you have family here?"

"Oh, yes. My sister."

"Children?"

"No. We never . . ." Her eyes glistened, but no tears fell. "In a way, it's a blessing. What could be harder than to tell a little boy or girl why Daddy's gone, right? Hell, I can barely take care of myself."

Earl nodded sympathetically, having heard the same rationale a thousand times from childless survivors. Inside he would invariably wince and once more thank the fates for the joy of having Brendan and his soon-to-arrive little brother as part of his life with Janet. He would endure any pain for having had that treasure.

"And of course there's no one who explains to me why my husband's gone," she added, her lids narrowing like gun slits. "I mean, there's a lot of assholes left walking around out there. Why'd it have to be him?"

Her glare dared him to try and give an answer.

He shook his head and, gesturing skyward with his palms, referred her question to the heavens.

She sighed as if to say, Spare me the fools. "I do appreciate what you did for Artie, and your kindness toward me," she added, as if that at least compensated in part for his current failing to tell her what she needed to know.

"I wish I could have helped him more."

She reached inside her handbag and pulled out a business envelope bearing the logo of a well-known insurance company. "I'm sorry to bother you with these. Dr. Popovitch filled out the initial forms, but he's not here, and they just require a confirmation of his initial report. Do you mind?"

He hated insurance papers. Most of the time the questions attempted to derail the claim and demanded irrelevant details that had more to do with filling in squares than providing an informed medical opinion as to the cause of death. And if the doctor who'd actually handled the case happened to be off duty when the family showed up with the documents, a frequent occurrence, Michael, bless his soul, had mostly taken over the mind-numbing chore. But occasionally one still got through to Earl. "Sure, I'd be glad to," he said, taking the papers out of her hand.

"Thanks. You don't know what a relief it is getting them out of the way. I thought there might be trouble, and Lord knows I need the money. But Dr. Popovitch assured me everything should go through fine. And thank God. It's a terrible thing to say, but that policy's the only good investment Artie made since the bubble popped."

He got the message. She expected him to be as helpful as Michael had been. He started to skim through what he'd written.

Five minutes later he wished he hadn't.

\* \* \*

"Michael, we have to talk."

Earl had phoned him at home the instant Mrs. Baxter left his office.

"Jesus, Earl, can't it wait? You know I just got off a shift from hell."

"I just had an interesting conversation with Artie Baxter's widow about insurance papers."

Silence reigned supreme.

"Where?" Michael asked after a few seconds.

Earl thought of the nearest place outside the hospital to get a cup of coffee. "The Horseshoe Bar."

A copper haze from the morning rush hour lingered over Buffalo, staining the previously blue sky a color of rust. He made the ten-minute walk in five, despite the temperature having already climbed past the predicted high. Ducking inside a front door of smoked glass to the dark air-conditioned interior provided welcome relief. A former hangout for gangs and druggies, the place had mellowed into a respectable watering hole where many of the staff and medical residents gathered for a beer after work. The change had been helped along by a makeover with mirrors, plants, and several coats of dark green paint, but no amount of interior decorating could erase Earl's memory of the kids whom he'd pronounced dead after they'd OD'd here.

Over the last three months the management, in another adjustment to the times, had started to serve an early-bird breakfast, taking advantage of hospital staff determined to avoid the designated eating areas of a SARS environment. That crowd would be long gone to work, he'd figured.

His eyes adjusted to the dark. Sure enough, most of the tables and booths stood empty, and a long chrome-trimmed bar, gleaming under the neon glow of a large, red-script Budweiser sign, wouldn't open until the lunch rush arrived a few hours from now. But the aroma of fresh coffee filled the air.

He chose a corner table and had downed two cups by the time Michael slid into the seat opposite him.

"So what's the deal?" Earl said without ceremony.

"Artie Baxter died of a cardiac arrest. You were there. That's what it says on the form."

"You didn't mention the fact he came in unconscious from hypoglycemia."

"That's not the cause of death."

"It's the cause of the cause, Michael. Don't kid around with me."

He shrugged. "That could be one opinion."

"Well, here's another. That story of his, that he took his normal dose of insulin, then got too busy to eat, stank like three-day-old fish. I think he deliberately tried to check out, using insulin. As to why, I don't know for sure, but I bet you do. Mrs. Baxter is pretty forthright about Artie's lousy investment skills. So what happened? He became suicidal after getting in over his head with the stock market? And you hid that little fact so a pretty young widow could still collect his insurance?"

Michael's expression hardened. "Her being pretty had nothing to do with it."

"Oh, yeah? Then where were you Monday night? Not ER, where Donna said you'd be." On the fly, he decided to take a big leap, in the hope of provoking an outburst of truth. "What's going on, Michael? You into consoling widows?"

Michael's face reddened until it resembled a beet with a beard. "If you weren't my friend . . ." He clenched his fist. "Just stay out of this, Earl. It's not what you think."

"Then change my thinking."

Michael exhaled, the way he'd done in his smoking days, as if intent on expelling the last traces of air in his lungs. His fingers uncoiled. "She needed the money. It's not her fault her husband tried to check out. And he did have chest pain that he ignored, like a lot of men we see who don't make it, and *they* still get the insurance. So where's the harm?"

"It's fraud. If that company asks to see the original chart—"

"They'll see my note that describes exactly what happened in ER. An insulin-dependent diabetic male arrives comatose, receives glucose, wakes up, arrests, and dies. Wife says he'd been complaining for days of chest pain that he blamed on indigestion—amen. And not a fraudulent statement anywhere."

"What if they ask you why you didn't mention the coma on the insurance claim? And if they also read the nurses' notes, they'll see that cockamamie story of his about the insulin. Just because you didn't spell it out doesn't mean they won't put it together, just like we did."

"Bullshit. Once they get a doctor's signature, they never ask for nursing notes unless they suspect something's not kosher."

"What do you mean never? You've done this before?"

"Of course not."

But he'd taken a second too long in answering.

"Have you ever had an insurance company challenge your ruling on a cause of death, let alone go so far as to demand nurses' notes for corroboration?" he asked, barely skipping a beat.

No, he hadn't. But Earl couldn't shake the feeling of being fed a lie.

"And don't tell me you never fudged a form," Michael continued. "Left out a detail that might have torpedoed a claim, stood over a corpse that had tobacco-stained fingers and ticked the 'don't know' box in answer to the question 'Has patient smoked in the last year?' "

Again Earl couldn't disagree. Every doctor knew the drill: don't outright lie, but don't hand the adjusters an outright gift either. What made this case dirty was the blatancy of the omission and if the doctor got any favors in return.

Michael stood up to leave. "So we're square?" he said, as if the matter were closed. "Now I'm going home to sleep."

Earl decided to try a more delicate approach. "You look as if you haven't had a good rest in months, Michael. Something's been eating you up—has been for a while now—and don't tell me again that it's just that you're tired or worried about SARS. Even when we get together for dinner or take the kids out somewhere, there are moments when you get a look in your eyes that's a million miles away. Hell, I've even seen Terry looking at you funny, wondering what's wrong. And you wouldn't have come all the way down here if this thing with Artie Baxter's insurance form was as innocent as you claim. So let's cut the bullshit. I want to know what's going on."

His friend leaned on the back of the chair he'd just vacated and towered over Earl. "You know, I liked you better when you were just chief of ER and mad at everyone else who ran the place."

"This place? The Horseshoe?"

Michael laughed. The smile looked good on him, and for a few seconds the craggy landscape of his face softened. Then he leaned closer, grinned wider, and his expression hardened. "Since they made you VP, medical, you've been getting in more trouble than ever. Oh, excuse me, make that suspended VP, medical."

"This isn't about me, Michael."

His grin vanished. "It sure is. Because I'm betting my good friend Earl won't go around making accusations about me and widows that would upset the hell out of my wife. And for my good friend's information, SARS *is* why I'm losing sleep. It's wrecking the shit out of my marriage. Donna's so scared I'll bring it home to Terry, she's thinking of moving to her mother's with him. So I'm also counting on my good friend to give his long-trusted pal Michael the benefit of the doubt and not pry into matters that are best left alone. Now I'm going back home to bed." He started toward the door.

"Michael, damn it, you can't do this to me." Earl threw a few dollars on the table and ran after him. "Tell me what the hell you've gotten into—"

Michael spun around and jabbed an index finger that felt like an iron pipe into Earl's chest. "Something that needs doing, understand! For God's sake, harness that righteous bloodhound streak of yours and quit fucking with the good guys!"

Stung, Earl took a step back. "The good guys?"

"Yeah. The ones whom you've seen fit to rag lately. Stewart, now me, even Father Jimmy."

"Jimmy told you that?"

Michael nodded. "Trust me, you don't want to pursue any of it."

"What the hell are you talking about?"

He opened his mouth to reply, seemed to think better of it, and turned toward the exit, walking stiffly, his shoulders rigid. At the blackened doors he paused and peered back at Earl. "Just remember, we're all trying to do our best." Transient as a blink, the bulky posture of Michael's upper body bunched up and reminded Earl of an animal, hunched over and about to charge, warning off an intruder. It looked so out of character that Michael might have been some stranger standing there. Then he was gone.

# Chapter 14

I had only allowed myself to remember the dream while alone.

It helped keep me invisible.

That would be more critical than ever now.

Because the dream had changed.

I walked into the lab as usual.

The water sprayed down from the broken pipes.

But when I looked up at his face, the swollen tongue lashed to and fro, angry as a trapped snake. The engorged lips pulled back in a swollen leer. The black orifice mouthed, "Do it!"

Death rounds had been the tipping point—my stage perfectly set.

If I acted quickly now, with everyone primed, they'd all draw the logical conclusion.

One, two, three, and I'd be free.

First the suicide.

Then Graceton. My perfect dry run had left no doubt about her fate.

And finally, if grief didn't stop Garnet, I'd do it myself.

And everybody would be fooled.

One, two, three . . .

The little ditty kept running through my head as I prepared the chloroform, then gathered up what else I'd need for the night's work.

## Wednesday, July 16, 4:40 p.m.

Stewart woke with a start, only to hear a loud roll of thunder slowly die out.

Outside his bedroom window a gray fog thick as flannel cut the light and made it seem dusk, but a glance at the glowing figures on his digital alarm clock surprised him. An afternoon storm must have blown in, he thought, getting up to close the windows. But the air, much cooler now, held a pleasant scent that reminded him of fresh laundry, so he left everything open.

More thunder rumbled not too far off.

"Tocco," he called, surprised the dog hadn't stayed by his bed. She hated storms and stuck as close to him as possible whenever they occurred. If alone in the house, she'd head into the basement, and he'd find her there when he came home, huddled in the darkest nook she could find.

He pulled on his clothes and headed downstairs, his feet still bare. "Tocco, come here, girl."

Sleep had helped him. And having saved Jane Simmons. His stock had soared so much with the nurses for that one that maybe he'd have a chance to ride out Yablonsky's accusations. At least at St. Paul's.

His enemies on the Web were another matter.

His mood immediately darkened.

In that forum he'd be held guilty until he could prove himself innocent. Even then, he might never be good enough again for the kind of grant money he used to get. Awarded on merit, it could be denied on a whim. He'd have to convince everyone that crone Yablonsky had concocted the whole thing, tried to use him as a handy scapegoat to cover up her own incompetence. "Or worse," as Earl had put it.

"Tocco!" he called, entering the kitchen. His basement door yawned open as he usually left it, so she could have the run of the house. "Come on up, girl. Suppertime."

He expected to hear the click of her nails on the linoleum-covered steps and the jingle of her collar tags.

Nothing.

"Tocco?"

He flicked on the light switch near the cellar steps.

The darkness below remained.

Bulb must be burnt out, he thought.

"Come here, Tocco," he called out, and started down. The small basement windows, even with the gloom outside, would allow him enough light to see by. She must have really been scared by the thunder.

He reached the bottom of the stairs, certain she'd come out of hiding and greet him.

No dog.

What the hell? he thought, feeling his way through the semidarkness toward one of the spots she often curled up in.

A tiny rectangular window in his laundry room admitted a thin, almost yellow glow as the late afternoon sun penetrated layers of fog blanketing the city. In a far corner lay a shadow darker than the rest.

That's when he caught the first whiff of chloroform.

## 5:45 p.m.

The steady rumbling chased everyone else inside, but Earl stayed put. The luminous haze of the mist suggested the storm clouds were thinning out. Even if they didn't go for a brisk paddle as planned, it would be as good a place as any to talk with Jimmy alone. One thing was for certain: he wasn't about to let the priest cancel.

He stood on the worn wooden boardwalk of an area called the basin, a harbor where some of Buffalo's more affluent boaters moored their yachts. Less ostentatious sailors kept smaller craft on nearby racks. That's where Jimmy stored his sixteen-footer.

As he waited, Earl found himself carried back to a time in medical school when he and his roommate, Jack MacGregor, would seek relief from their studies by launching paper airplanes from the roof of their apartment building. They would craft various weird shapes and give them stabilizers and lift vents; though some nosedived to the street below, others would rise in the air, catch a breeze, and sail out of sight. The model that went the farthest and highest, no matter how wonky-looking, won.

Jack had always been the more daring of the two in this venture. "Your trouble, Garnet, is not allowing yourself to think outside the box," he'd accused more than once, and with reason. Medicine required pattern recognition, and that meant disciplining one's thoughts to symptoms and signs that were mired in evidence-based facts. The convention gave science its reliability but kept imaginations in check.

So Earl made himself remember those days with Jack whenever he faced a seemingly insolvable problem. Ideas, he'd realized, were often like those crazy paper planes. No matter how silly or bizarre they seemed at first, every now and then one would soar above all the others, usually to his complete surprise, and provide the answer that had eluded him.

The late Jack MacGregor—he'd died over five years ago saving Earl's life—must be proud of him now. Ever since his talk with Stewart's ex-wife and the bizarre confrontation with Michael, Earl's imagination had gone into overdrive with out-of-the-box ideas.

How could he help but look at Stewart's dilemma in a different light? If the man had had a hand in destroying another researcher's life, as odious as that might be, more and more his claim of being set up took on a different resonance.

Michael definitely required a new take, whatever he'd gotten himself into.

And since Jimmy had seen fit to label both of them "the good guys," maybe he could also explain what they were up to.

He glanced at his watch. The priest should have been here twenty minutes ago. He'd been dodging Earl the whole day, claiming to be busy. But Earl had finally cornered him with the suggestion they use Jimmy's daily hour of exercise as a chance to talk, something they'd often done in the past. Jimmy then proposed that they take out the canoe.

Just when Earl figured he'd been stood up, he heard footsteps approach, and a dark shape became visible in the yellow mist.

"We go out there with a storm threatenin'," said a lilting voice, "the good Lord is likely to zot us for our stupidity."

"We can just take a walk instead, Jimmy." No way you're evading me any longer, he added to himself.

"Only if we pick up the pace. After a day like mine, I need to run."

Earl groaned. He'd slipped into shorts, sneakers, and a T-shirt, anticipating a workout on the water, but jogging, especially in a city of smog, never held much appeal, let alone made sense. But what the hell. Once wouldn't kill him. "Lead the way."

They took off along a pedestrian path that curved through a grassy area surrounded by trees, but beyond that, the mist prevented Earl from seeing exactly where they were.

"So what did you want to talk about?" Jimmy asked, breathing as easily as if they were standing still.

Although Earl found the pace a bit more of an effort than Jimmy, biking, swimming, and racing around the yard with Brendan had kept him in reasonable shape. "I had an odd run-in with Michael this morning over a rather selective way he'd filled out Artie Baxter's insurance form. You remember the case?"

"I'll never forget it. What do you mean by 'selective'?"

"No mention of anything that might raise questions about the widow getting the check."

"I thought death from a heart attack would be a straightforward claim."

"Not when falling comatose from too much insulin might have been a factor."

The priest increased the pace. "What are you suggesting?"

"Artie may have deliberately taken too much."

"But you can't be sure."

"No."

"Then Michael did the right thing. Why give the insurance company an out not to pay?"

"I'd normally agree, Jimmy, except this time it seemed a bit too obvious."

"How?"

"A bunch of reasons. One, whenever you have any kind of physical stress—and from what Artie's wife said, he'd been suffering unstable angina for days—blood sugar usually rises in a diabetic. For Artie to make himself fall into a hypoglycemic coma, he would have had to do more than skip breakfast after his regular morning insulin. He would have had to have taken more than usual."

"But if his sugars were high, wouldn't an increase be called for?"

"Yeah, but experienced diabetics can tell when they're slipping into a coma. I just don't see Artie ignoring the symptoms of hypoglycemia."

"And you would have put that down on paper?"

The path tilted upward into an all-encompassing gloom, the momentary hint that the fog would disperse anytime soon vanishing like a false promise. "Probably not. But I wouldn't have gone so much out of my way to make it seem I'd never even thought of it. No physician worth his salt could look at Artie's file and claim that. Not that I would have spelled out my suspicions either, but there are ways to state them subtly. For instance, Michael could have noted that on questioning, the patient 'claimed' to have taken only the regular dose. Then it's the adjuster's problem to put two and two together, or not."

"And that game makes it all right? Sounds like covering your ass to me. And abandoning the widow to the mercies of the company."

"It's how we do it yet stay legal, Jimmy. And it still works. An agent may call and ask outright if I'm willing to say the patient committed suicide, and I'll say no one could claim that for certain, and eventually they pay up."

"Just the kind of hassle a grieving family needs."

Earl ignored the jibe. "Look, if it were just the Artie Baxter case, I would have let it go. But what really bothered me is that something's obviously been eating at Michael recently. One look at the guy says he's worried—"

"It's called SARS, Earl. Look around you. Everybody's scared shitless these days."

The image of Michael's hurt expression when he'd blurted out how the outbreak had caused problems between Donna and him made Earl wince. He hadn't realized the couple had been having such a hard time coping. "Maybe. But to be precise, he also reamed me out for, if you'll pardon my literal rendition of what he said, 'fucking up the good guys lately'— namely, you, himself, and Stewart—and practically begged me to keep my nose out of his business."

Jimmy responded by yet again picking up speed. "So the guy's stressed and he overreacted. Don't make a big deal of it."

"Do you think I'm acting like an asshole and getting in the way of the good guys?"

Jimmy started to laugh. "You want a professional opinion from a chaplain, or something more personal?"

Earl strained to keep up. Sweat had already soaked through his clothing despite the temperature having dropped with the afternoon showers. "What I want to know, Jimmy, is if you've had a talk with him like you did with me, and coaxed him into the service of some greater good, such as making certain that suitably deserving widows and orphans collect money from insurance companies without any troublesome questions or delays."

"I'd think that would be the job of any responsible doctor toward a patient."

"I know you, Jimmy. In another age you'd have been a swashbuckler, a musketeer, a wielder of the sword of justice in a fight for the downtrodden, beholden only to the laws of God."

"Sounds like my kind of guy. What's wrong with that?"

"What's wrong is that you might not be above tweaking man-made regulations, especially if they stood in the way of a righteous cause."

"I believe these days we call that civil disobedience, and a noble activity it is. But no, I've not led Michael astray. Now are you goin' to start running, or is hobblin' along like this as fast as an old man like yourself can do?" He pulled away into the gray haze until his form had no more substance than smoke.

How flippant would he be if he knew Michael might be taking favors from the damsels in distress? Earl wondered, and dug harder. He managed to accelerate up the slope and pull abreast again. "What about Stewart?"

"What about him?"

"You heard Yablonsky's accusation. Do you know if he's been up to anything in Palliative Care?"

"You're not serious."

"Something's going on up there. Increased death rates don't lie."

"They're supposed to die."

"You sound like Hurst."

"Now don't be gettin' nasty with me."

"Then what's going on, Jimmy?"

"Did you ever talk to any of the patients you brought back from a cardiac arrest?"

"Sure, sometimes."

"What did they tell you they remembered?"

"Sometimes nothing. Others gave the usual story of rising above their bodies, a bright light at the end of a tunnel . . ."

"And what do you make of those stories, Earl?"

"If you mean do I think they're proof of an afterlife, I'm afraid not."

"Neither do I. I made a point of reading up on it. Interesting how neurologists think it's got to do with neurotransmitters, certain parts of the brain being stimulated or losing the blood supply to the outside of the retina first, and the optic nerve last, creating the image of a dark tunnel with a bright light at the end. But there are some stories that can't be explained by chemicals, physiology, or anatomy. Did any of the patients you talked to ever tell you about the dark man?"

"What?"

"The dark man. A person dressed in black hovering around the end of their bed."

Earl chuckled. "No."

"You wouldn't laugh if they had, yet I'm not surprised they didn't. It's not in any of the published accounts either, not even Stewart's, though I suspect when researchers refer to subjects who report frightening images, had those descriptions been specific, the dark man would be as common to near-death as lights and tunnels. But people don't feel comfortable in getting too detailed about that sort of thing unless it's with chaplains, figuring we're bound by belief to be sympathetic, not scoff at it."

"What do they see exactly? A guy in a black hood with a scythe?"

"The figure usually wears loose-fitting clothes, always black, and the face is mainly in shadow. Except for the eyes. They're all too visible and have an icy vastness to them that people feel sucked into when he comes closer. At the same time they feel their skin burning hot."

"Ischemia," Earl muttered.

"What?"

"The burning feeling is from ischemia. The lack of blood in muscle and skin results in a buildup of metabolic acids. They burn like fire." Exactly the way my legs are now, he nearly added, but until the priest came up with a few more answers he didn't want Jimmy to know how easy it would be to leave him behind.

"Maybe you're right about the heat, but nothing explains the fear. Everybody who reported seeing the dark man seemed more terrified at the prospect of him waiting for them the next time than they were of dying."

"Don't tell me you believe there's something to tales like that. And what the hell do they have to do with Stewart?"

"I'm just suggesting that people who venture near death and return can find the experience very traumatic. The accounts from Palliative Care about someone badgering patients as they hovered on the brink may be a variation of the dark man encounters. The last thing I'd do is try to link Stewart to them."

Jimmy's words silenced Earl. Perhaps they were meant to. Because if the priest had done his homework, he'd know that Earl had had his own encounter with near death seven years ago. He still tried to avoid thinking about it. Certainly the memory of it remained traumatic. But no dark man had awaited him. Instead he'd felt death as a dilutent, as if he were being thinned out, like a drop of water returning to the ocean. And as Jimmy had said, he seldom wanted to talk about it. Maybe that's what didn't make sense. "But how could it be the dark man, Jimmy, with so many patients suddenly willing to tell the nurses about him?"

The priest answered by pulling ahead.

Earl thought, Aha! Got him, and tried to keep up.

But in a hundred paces the fire in his lower legs spread to his thighs and the inside of his lungs.

He slowed and came to a stop. The scuff of Jimmy's shoes on the gravel underfoot faded into the distance.

"You can't avoid me forever about Stewart, Jimmy," he shouted after him. "And if you have recruited Michael on some quest, I think he's out of his depth."

"Relax, Earl." The words floated back to him like a message out of the ether.

Earl caught his breath and started to walk back along the path toward St. Paul's. The muffled traffic noises on the freeway came at him from the front, and a guttural roll of thunder originating far out over the lake rumbled up behind him.

Either Jimmy really had no idea what Michael and Stewart were up to or he'd become a hell of a good actor. Or maybe Earl hadn't a clue as to what was going on, had gotten it all wrong in the first place, and had been the one who'd swum out of his depth.

Ten minutes later he passed the smoked-glass entrance to the Horseshoe Bar and Grill. Up ahead the bulk of St. Paul's loomed in the thick gray smog, a giant hive of tiny lights. For an instant he felt overwhelmed at the sight. Who could really know all the enigmas of the place? A big teaching hospital held more human emotions per cubic foot of air than any edifice on earth. Always at the core were the patients—they numbered eight hundred here—their thoughts closer to their own mortality than ever before, yet they came and went, changing every ten days on average, each set of newcomers bringing a whole host of different dreams and fears. Then there were the healers. In addition to laboring over their charges, they lugged around the personal baggage of ambitions and desires, everything from a need to do good works, find love, and win the wealth of success, to far less noble pursuits—right down to settling old scores, nursing slights, or exacting revenge, usually in petty little ways, but sometimes on a more serious scale. Most agendas focused on the mundane issues of life, such as putting food on the table and how to get laid Saturday night, but they were legion in number and sometimes led to their own league of trouble. Who broke which rules to satisfy what appetites? There often could be no way of telling, and through all that complexity, he'd no more chance to see the thread of a single coherent motive than to track the purpose of an individual ant in a swarming nest.

So was it Stewart's lethal cover-up or the work of a saboteur? Michael's noble service to needy women or the exploitation of them? Jimmy's undue influence on either man, or just a good priest doing his job? The answers might never come to light. And if he was on the wrong track altogether, God knew what other secrets might remain hidden forever. No wonder Hurst preferred to hide the nasty side of things. With such an impenetrable matrix to help cloak everything, odds were he could get away with it.

And now SARS underlined the whole kit and caboodle with the issue of survival.

As he drew closer to the blurred dark shape of St. Paul's, it appeared to expand through the charcoal-seeped air and spread outward, towering over where he walked.

For a second he had the illusion it reared defiant before his growing sense of helplessness, a leviathan set to devour him whole.

## 6:45 p.m.

Windows rattled with each thunderclap, and the count between a flash and the boom narrowed to three. Drops of rain the size of marbles pelted the roof and walls with the force of hailstones.

"I'm sure everyone's lying to me—first Stewart, then Michael, and now Jimmy."

"Sit down, Earl, and have a drink," Janet ordered, presiding over an array of pots on the stove. The aroma of teriyaki chicken, fried eggplant, and grilled peppers filled the air.

At her side, perched on a stool and wearing an apron with MOMMY'S LITTLE HELPER emblazoned across the front, Brendan wielded a wooden spoon with the authority of a royal mace. "Yes, go have a drink, Daddy."

"Ordered out of the kitchen again," he muttered, and went to the liquor cabinet.

"With good reason," Janet called after him. "Your mother never taught you how to cook."

" 'Never taught me how to cook,' " he mimicked, filling a glass with ice and pouring himself a Black Russian, the one hard liquor concoction he actually enjoyed. Except he used more Kahlua than vodka, soothing a sweet tooth more than any love for alcohol.

"Not like me, huh, Mommy?" Brendan chimed in.

"You, my love, will be a thoroughly modern man when it comes to culinary skills, and some lucky woman will thank me for educating you."

Earl chuckled, and wandered back into their domain,

swirling the ice in his tumbler with his finger as a swizzle stick.

While some doctors golfed or played tennis for recreation, Janet cooked. Her ideal getaway involved uninterrupted hours over a woodstove at their log home beside an isolated mountain lake south of Buffalo.

She sent Brendan upstairs to clean up his room. "In case our guest wants to see your budding train collection," she explained.

"Oh, yeah!" he said, his train set far higher on the scale of what would interest company than food.

"Now sit over there." She directed Earl to the far corner of their breakfast nook. "And tell me what's got you so riled."

He took a sip of his drink and enjoyed the cool burn it made on the way to his stomach. "Well, it started with an interesting call I made to NYCH this morning. . . ."

Stewart's legs ached from standing on his toes.

The storm had struck with force, rumbling the house to its foundations and making it impossible for anyone to hear his screams. Even without the thunder and teeming rain, it would be unlikely that all the yelling in the world would reach the ears of a passerby. These old dwellings had foundations like fortresses.

The soft vinyl cover of the stool under his feet sank with his weight. Anytime his muscles faltered, if he even began to buckle at the knees and go down on his soles, the noose tightened.

"Pretty woman," Roy Orbison sang, the voice sounding tinny on the small tape deck, the same as it had that night when he'd found Jerome's body.

Why had the man played it?

To muffle the sounds he'd make dying, one of the cops had said casually, as if this were knowledge every person should have at hand, in case . . .

Stewart forced himself to think of something else, anything to keep terror at bay and his mind off the agony in his legs. He must manage to stand until someone came for him.

His thoughts whipped backward in time.

The door to the lab had been open. "Somebody must have already walked in on him but left him hanging," he told the police. "Perhaps the person heard Jerome dying despite the music."

Nobody had cared.

Stewart's muscles tightened, yanking him back to the present. As spasms shot through them, he sagged, tightening the loop another notch. With his wrists handcuffed behind his back, he'd no chance of loosening them to free himself however much he struggled. But links of the chain were long enough that the fingers of one hand could circle the wrist of the other—consistent with a pair he could have snapped on himself. That little detail must be for the cops.

"Pretty woman . . ."

Orbison launched into yet another chorus. The damn recording must be a fucking loop.

He teetered, let out another strangled yell, then regained his balance.

And again thought of that night, everyone in the hospital glued to the television, watching the reports out of Berlin. It had always haunted him, indelibly clear in his head—Thursday, November 9, 1989, the day the wall fell.

They'd all agreed that Jerome had seemed depressed for months.

Some wondered if he had picked that evening to make sure the date would stand out and forever haunt those who'd driven him to his death. Others figured the ever-practical scientist had seized on a chance moment of opportunity, choosing a supper hour with everyone transfixed by newscasts so nobody would interrupt him.

Whatever the intent, Stewart couldn't hear the word *wall, Berlin,* or even *Germany* without a flashback hurtling him into that lab and leaving him staring up at the limp body.

Another cramp gripped the sole of Stewart's foot, the right one this time.

He screamed, but the loop around his neck garbled the sound, reducing it to a gurgle.

He lost his balance again and swayed, fighting to recover.

Each drawn breath became a coarse rasp, and every expiration produced a rattling wheeze. His face throbbed as the venous blood engorged his skin, and the periphery of his vision darkened, encroached on by a night that had nothing to do with the slow creep of dusk through his basement window.

He listened, trying to hear some clue whether his soundless killer remained in the shadows, just beyond where he could see. At first he'd thought there were two of them, that he'd heard their voices, like whispers through the din of a rushing noise inside his head. But then he sensed only one, someone behind him. Now he couldn't be sure anyone stood there at all.

"Please! I don't deserve this," he cried. It came out a squawk.

His mute sentinel remained silent.

Or had left.

The coldness of that empty quiet sent his panic skyrocketing.

*Just hold on. Somebody will come. It's not too late. Still no permanent damage done. As long as they loosen the loop soon, my throat will heal,* he tried to convince himself.

But the only person with a key, his cleaning woman, wouldn't be here until morning. And he seldom had visitors, never encouraged them, preferring the people in his life to be part of his work, where he could use his authority over them to control how close they got. The only ones he invited over willingly were residents, for journal clubs, because even on social occasions there was no lack of clarity about his being their superior.

His only hope of rescue lay with his killer.

"I shouldn't have to die!" he attempted to yell, unable to

accept that he'd been abandoned. A croaking noise seemed to originate inside his skull, and nothing but the rushing sound, loud as an express train, filled his ears. He nevertheless continued to spit out words, intelligible only in his mind, like someone with a stroke.

"Who are you? Why do this to me?" If he found he knew the person, understood the reasons, he'd know how to explain that there'd been a terrible mistake.

The last thing he remembered before a gloved hand had grabbed him from behind and rammed chloroformed gauze into his face had been the fumes. He'd turned only enough to glimpse a shadowy form before everything went black. He came to already bound and suspended from the overhead iron pipe, Tocco's leash looped around his neck. The powerful arms that locked him in their grip and held him up until his own legs could bear his weight were muscular, but he couldn't see the face.

"What are you doing?" he'd mumbled at first, still floating up from the no-man's-land of being anesthetized. "If Tocco's dead, goddamn you, I'm calling the police."

Then the realization he stood on a makeshift gallows had catapulted him awake.

Indifferent as an executioner, the person at his back had partially supported him until he stood entirely alone, straining up on his toes, winning some slack in the braided strap that choked off his air.

All to the tune of "Pretty Woman."

The present cramp in his right foot eased.

But the leash had again cinched tighter.

That's why the person had used it, why Jerome had used one, why so many did—handy, strong, effective.

His once magnificent brain began to plod for want of oxygen. He'd no means of measuring time or knowing how long he'd been dangling there. Questions that he might have reasoned through and disposed of in seconds grew impenetrable to his crippled flow of thought.

Who would do this to him? Jerome's wife? He couldn't remember her name, nor even recall her face. No, she'd dumped the man years before, hadn't even bothered to attend his funeral, didn't care enough.

He strained higher on his toes.

But why would anyone else who cared so much about Jerome have waited until now?

He felt his eyes bulge. He flexed his feet to push higher still. *Goddamn it,* he thought. *This is a lynching.*

Could it be the work of a more recent enemy? One who knew about what had happened at NYCH, yet wanted to get rid of him for another reason altogether? Somebody determined to make it look like he'd chosen suicide over being discovered as a fraud? Someone who'd set up a scene to make it appear he'd copied Jerome Wilcher, the man he'd discredited so many years before?

He lost strength in his legs, and the leash choked him harder.

Like a man inebriated, Stewart could still snatch seconds of clarity from a progressive swoon into darkness, enough to know that this scenario definitely widened the field as to who might have done him in.

Everyone who hated his guts.

He sucked in air as if inhaling it through a straw. Soon his windpipe would be squeezed smaller still, and his brain would shut down, seize, and die for lack of oxygen. He'd see for himself the greatest riddle that had preoccupied him these last few years. Would there be a tunnel, the bright light, and loved ones?

His thoughts began to shatter and drift apart. He fought to hold them together, but it felt like trying to make jagged shapes fit alongside each other.

What loved ones?

His daughter had stopped visiting years ago.

Two wives no longer saw fit to even talk to him.

Colleagues admired his skills, but who liked him besides Garnet? And even Earl suspected him of murder.

All he had were legions of grateful patients whose lives he'd saved.

Not the same thing at all.

"Who are you?" he shrieked again, outraged he wouldn't know his killer or the reason why he'd been targeted for murder.

This time spittle rather than noise bubbled out his lips.

He again pushed up on his toes and recovered some slack. With the arrival of more blood to the brain, his desperation to live revived. New terrors raced through his head, insane panic driving his thoughts at high speed with the frantic, illogical, futile clarity that visits a man about to die.

*"Are you there? Tell me why you did this,"* he sobbed, not realizing he no longer made a sound. *"Is it punishment for Jerome? Yes, that's it, isn't it? All the reminders are to make me think of the poor man's last agony. Yes. Please, let it be punishment. Because that means you must still be here in the basement. Because what good would punishment be without someone to witness it and see the torment? And there still might be time for me to explain, make you take pity and cut me down. You see,"* he tried to say, *"I hadn't meant Jerome to kill himself. . . ."*

He became faint. His vision closed in around the edges again, but this time it was as if he were inside a black hood and someone were pulling it shut with a drawstring.

*No! No hood! This needn't be. Not an execution.*

The pain in his legs trebled.

And he felt himself get an erection.

He could explain that too.

Something to do with the blood supply being cut off to a certain level of the spine.

But he couldn't remember the specifics.

All from insufficient oxygen.

A new panic blasted through his delirium.

His lifetime of medical knowledge, his skill to bring people back from death, would slip away into oblivion, cell by cell, memory by memory.

*That's my legacy, my entire worth.*

This time both his legs curled into spasm.

The noose cinched tighter and crushed his larynx.

No more breath.

The darkness swept it all away.

No white light.

No loved one.

No peaceful floating above himself.

Only inexorable pain.

And one last thought: end it fast.

Except . . .

He wouldn't kick away the stool to let his full weight hurry the process.

He'd simply allow himself to sag and prolong the agony.

Something a suicide wouldn't do.

Something someone smart enough might notice and figure out.

Earl, for instance . . .

# Chapter 15

**That same evening, 8:27 p.m.**

"Damn," Janet said.

It had been the fifth time Earl heard the word coming from their study where she and Thomas were working.

Sounded like they weren't getting very far, he thought, putting away the last of the dishes from dinner.

Brendan steadied a stack of bowls under his chin and carried them toward their proper cupboard. "Is that the beaver kind of dam or the bad kind?" he asked, managing to set his load up on the counter, where it teetered precariously. Then he hoisted himself up beside them.

Earl tried not to smile. "Beavers."

"How do you know?"

"Because I do."

"How?"

"Just do. Now it's up to bed."

The familiar routine—bath, teeth, pajamas, story—unwound at its usual slow pace. Earl savored each step of it, the ritual having become an oasis for him at the end of each day.

Half an hour later he joined Janet and Thomas in the study only to hear her again mutter, "Damn."

"No correlations?"

"Not so far," she said. "But I'm trying a new approach."

He saw a printout of the *New England Journal* cluster

study lying on the floor beside her chair and absently picked it up.

"I expanded the search to include the whole hospital," Janet continued, gesturing at the NO MATCHES FOUND message on her screen with one of Brendan's pencils. A tiny figure of Big Bird clung to the eraser end. "We thought we could save time by checking each staff category for a home run—namely, anyone who'd been on duty for eighty percent of the deaths in Palliative Care."

Earl saw in the article where she'd circled that number, it being the magic threshold in most cases where the study technique had actually unmasked serial killers.

She slumped back in her chair. "But I've checked every type of worker at St. Paul's I can think of—nurses, doctors, residents, orderlies, porters, cleaners, nursing aides, lab technicians, even secretaries and security guards. Who am I missing?"

"Visitors?" Earl said, resigned to the limits of a cluster study.

Her frown deepened. "Then we're out of luck."

"And pastoral services."

She threw him a give-me-a-break glower. "Stop it." She hadn't liked his voicing suspicions about Jimmy.

"Dr. Garnet, you mentioned using the computer record of electronic keys," Thomas said, "to see who accessed the hospital after hours, when they weren't on duty?"

"Yeah, but I haven't had time to set that up yet," Earl replied, flipping through the article. Finally he reached the section that stressed: *Suspicions should be raised only when clusters of deaths and cardiopulmonary arrests occur that are either unexpected in timing or inconsistent with a patient's previous clinical course.*

Janet turned to Thomas and began to explain Earl's previous concern that another way someone could foil a cluster study would be to work with an accomplice.

The resident listened intently.

Earl barely paid attention. The words *unexpected in timing or inconsistent with a patient's previous clinical course* had jolted his memory, and the image of a dying woman's calendar, carefully marked with crosses, popped to mind. Crosses that marked the deaths of patients who had not been declared DNR. In other words, patients who, for the most part, were probably thought to have sufficient time left that the matter could be decided later. Their deaths, though anticipated, might have been unexpected in timing.

"Wait a minute," he said, and moved to the keyboard. As chief of ER, he still had access to all cardiac arrest statistics, since his staff responded to calls from the floors. He punched in the key words to pull up a list of all the code blues at St. Paul's from midnight to dawn in the last six months and organized them by date on a bar graph. "The trouble is, we've been looking at overall death statistics. But in front of our noses there's been a simple way to separate them into two groups—those who died when they were expected to, and those who went a bit prematurely." As the computer worked, he told them about Sadie Locke's calendar.

The image that appeared on the screen stunned him.

Above January, February, and March, the incidence of codes called in Palliative Care seemed practically nonexistent. But over April, May, and June, three tall columns, like black towers of equal height, indicated the arrest team had been summoned about fourteen times each month.

"Well, look at that," Janet murmured at his side.

Thomas leaned forward. "Wow!"

The odds were zero that so many patients not yet designated DNR would go into cardiac arrest before their expected time by pure chance. Someone had selected them for death.

After chasing vague trends and trying to make mere fractions of patients add up to something concrete, the stark, solid pattern gave Earl a hell of a sense of accomplishment. Now not even Hurst would be able to deny that they had a killer at work.

Except he hadn't a clue who or why.

"Any comments or ideas?" he asked, assuming the other two had reached the same conclusion and raised the same unknowns.

The three of them studied the screen, their grim silence cocooned in the sound of rain pelting the study window.

"If someone's been killing patients for the last three months," Janet said after a minute, her voice little more than a whisper, "let's assume that that same person is also responsible for the first increase in deaths. At least then we could ask the question, Why kill only DNR patients for three months, then add patients who were not DNR to the list?"

Earl saw Thomas open his mouth as if to say something, then close it again.

"Spit it out, Thomas. All ideas are welcome."

The young man's dark complexion reddened. "I just had a rather nasty thought."

"Go ahead."

He hesitated, running a hand over his beard. "Well, what if there were something to Yablonsky's claim that someone had been pestering patients with questions about a near-death experience? No, that's too weird."

"Hey, go on."

"Well, maybe that someone tried it with patients who were more advanced in their disease but couldn't get anywhere with them. The people might have been too obtunded to reply with anything meaningful. So it would make sense, in a weirdo's way of thinking, to use people who weren't that far along, figuring they'd be able to at least speak. But our weird someone would have to manipulate these relatively more stable patients, bring them near death using drugs, say, or simulating the experience with ketamine, like in that paper you found."

Janet looked at Thomas in surprise but said nothing.

"Are you thinking of Stewart again?" Earl asked. "I thought you were all for his being innocent now."

Thomas's color deepened. "I am, but figured we need to put all ideas on the table, whatever we want personally."

Earl agreed with the part of needing to be complete. "Right you are. But you'll be glad to know there are still problems with pinning it on Stewart. He wasn't in town during a few weeks of the first jump in the mortality rate."

"But you're the one who keeps telling me that that doesn't rule out an accomplice," Janet piped in. "And there's a hideous logic to what Thomas just said that could apply to Stewart."

"And there's still the possibility someone is setting Stewart up," Earl responded.

"Then I'd advise you to check out that ex-wife of his," Janet said. She'd already voiced this suspicion twice before, first when Earl told her about Dr. Cheryl Branagh a few hours ago, and again later when he briefed Thomas.

Earl shook his head. "My instinct says no."

"Patterns are your strong point. Instinct's mine."

"Mine are good."

"They've been wrong before."

"Yours too."

It took Earl a few seconds to realize that he and Janet had slipped into the shorthand form of sparring that they, like most couples, had built up over the years. Thomas might just as well not have been in the room. "Sorry, Thomas. Rude of us," Earl said, and glanced at his watch. Only 9:05. "Look, it's not too late for a visit to Stewart's. He doesn't live that far away and might be able to shed light on who could be after him." *Especially if confronted with the name Jerome Wilcher,* he thought, seeing no need to release that tidbit to Thomas. Stewart had enough gossip to live down. "So I'm going to leave the both of you at it here—"

The sound of Janet attacking the keyboard interrupted him. The two men turned to her. "What's up?" Thomas asked.

"Maybe nothing. But I'm going to try for a home run again. This time I'm using only the list of patients who were not DNR when they died, For starters, let's see if there's a particular nurse in-house most of those times."

A single answer popped up on the screen.

The three leaned in to read it.

Earl felt his stomach knot into a fist.

"It can't be," Janet whispered.

Thomas went rigid.

It read JANE SIMMONS.

Janet braced herself against the passenger door as Thomas swerved her car around yet another corner, then accelerated toward the freeway. Already she regretted having accepted his offer to drive, but he'd insisted on going with her so they could discuss how much to tell J.S., and on getting behind the wheel himself.

"It can't be too comfortable for you these days," he'd said, patting his flat stomach to contrast it with her own.

She'd initially been grateful for his thoughtfulness, if not his lack of tact, as it was true that getting in and out of the driver's seat was more difficult with this pregnancy than she recalled it being with Brendan. But then she couldn't adjust the seat belt on the passenger side to accommodate the new girth, and ended up leaving it off. "Just don't tell my patients."

He'd followed the quickest route to the freeway and downtown but drove her peppy little car at twice the speed she would have in this weather, even if a patient fully dilated awaited her at the hospital.

"Slow down," she told him, raising her voice above the din of rain that peppered the heavy leather top of her vehicle. It sounded like they were in a tent. "J.S. isn't going anywhere."

He eased off and leaned forward to see better. The wipers barely parted the steady cascade of water that poured down the windshield.

The three of them had agreed there must be a simple explanation. But they needed to talk with J.S. and discover that reason before anyone else stumbled onto the data, because the history of cluster studies had a dark side. Effective as they were in nailing the guilty, they had also destroyed the lives of the innocent, the same persuasiveness of numbers that made them so successful also being what made them so dangerous. Whenever such studies fingered someone who happened to be around but had nothing to do with the killings, even in cases when formal charges were never laid, the accused inevitably went through a legal wringer for years before being exonerated. Often the person never worked in health care again, and sometimes lost the support of family and friends in the process.

"My worry is Yablonsky," Earl had said. "As long as she feels threatened that someone might try to blame the rise in deaths on her, she'll continue her attempts to pin them on anyone else who's handy."

"But she's already done a pretty good job at setting up Stewart," Thomas had countered, his voice tight with tension. He seemed the most shaken up by what they'd found.

Earl had scowled at him. "Maybe. But you saw how scared she was yesterday. And once everybody else starts thinking straight, they're also going to have serious doubts that Stewart would knock off patients as part of some weird near-death research. So who's to say dear Monica won't see the writing on the wall, realize she could still take the fall, and mount her own study to try to shift the blame to yet another patsy? Hell, my talking about clusters yesterday might even have given her the idea. She knows as well as anyone what kind of trap they can be, and she already has access to the ward's death records. She could be sitting at home right now, trying to tap into nursing rosters and doing the same thing we are. If J.S. pops up on her screen, she's finished."

Thomas's ruddy complexion had gone pale listening to Earl's all-too-blunt stark assessment, so much so that Janet felt obliged to give her husband a pinch on the butt to shut him up.

She also had said nothing about an even more obvious and imminent danger for J.S. The young nurse might be able to identify the real killer—she might be aware of someone else who worked the same nights as she did, someone who hadn't yet shown up on their study. That put her in danger.

Some slight slip on her part, an innocent comment about having a schedule similar to that of the actual murderer, could be a death warrant—if it wasn't already too late. When Janet had phoned ICU to check on her this evening, the supervisor reported that J.S. had received a steady stream of nurses, clerks, porters, orderlies, even interns and doctors from ER, all dropping by to wish her well. And since her endotracheal tube came out, she'd been talking to all of them.

Thank God Earl had had the good sense not to blab out that particular risk—he must have seen it as readily as she had—or the already skittery Thomas would really be climbing the walls.

She glanced sideways at him and saw that he remained hunched forward as he drove, staring straight ahead, his jaw clenched, his features ghastly as they moved in and out of the shadows between overhead streetlamps. Maybe he'd already figured it out anyway.

Back at the house Janet had insisted to both men that she be the only one to talk with J.S. tonight. "For no other reason than she's my patient, and I won't have you two descending on her, scaring her silly. Besides, I may be able to keep what she says under doctor-patient confidentiality," she told them, figuring it sounded reasonable that she'd also want to protect Jane from the police. Mostly she needed as many reasons as possible to keep Thomas away from J.S. until he calmed down. The last thing J.S. needed would be for him to pass all his anxiety on to her. "And I'm going to briefly see her tonight, warn her to watch what she says, so she doesn't incriminate herself with some off-the-cuff comment about her schedule to the likes of Monica Yablonsky." At this point she'd managed to slip her husband a private little wink. He'd fired one right back. He knew her real concern, just as she'd thought. "I should give her a post-op check anyway, so my dropping by won't seem too out of the ordinary or alarming. So why don't both of you stay here until I come back?"

Thomas had refused to wait behind.

Now as she watched him drive, the tension in his neck

and shoulders grew, subtly sculpting the shape of the muscles visible at the open collar of his white golf shirt. Definitely not in a state of mind to calm J.S.

"I have to see her alone," she reiterated for about the tenth time. "Until we know more, for her own good. Of course there's a perfectly plausible explanation for her schedule, but it may take a while to figure it out, and until then we must be careful."

He slowly turned and looked at her, a dappled yellow hue playing across his cheekbones from the rain-filtered glare of sodium lights. His eyes seemed sunken in their sockets and glittered at her through the darkness. "It's only right that I be at her side," he said, his voice a grim monotone.

She felt a chill at the flatness of it.

Earl punched redial.

"You have reached the home of Dr. Stewart—"

He slammed down the receiver.

He couldn't just stay here, pacing the floor and trying to figure out connections that didn't make sense.

The flashback of a dark form hurtling at him in the darkness increased his sense of urgency. He had to get answers before the real killer realized J.S. could identify him.

Best just go over to Stewart's house. Confront the son of a bitch face-to-face. Force him to reveal what he knew about the pattern of DNR and non-DNR deaths. Pin him down over what J.S.'s schedule might have to do with the killings. Grill him to admit who might want to get even with him for Jerome Wilcher's suicide.

He phoned Annie, their housekeeper, explained that an emergency had come up, and asked that she watch Brendan.

"Be there in five minutes, Doc."

Always willing to bail him out, bless her heart.

As he waited, he racked his brain over how J.S.'s name could have come up, but as before, got nowhere. He even considered the possibility there could have been a glitch in the program.

He went back to the computer screen and typed in his own name.

Zero correlation.

Janet's.

Same result.

He stood there, unable to think of what else to try.

Into that vacuum crept a gloomy acknowledgment. Even as the three of them had stood in this room and openly proclaimed that J.S. had to be innocent, a little stir of protest had wormed its way along the dark veins of his pessimism. In complete contrast to the way Janet's instincts could give J.S. a pass or Thomas's love could preclude his doubting her, Earl would test whether his comfortable assumptions about J.S. withstood scrutiny. It always had been his way of ordering the world—troubleshoot it and avoid nasty surprises—which meant he allowed himself to ask questions that no one else dared raise. In this case, could J.S. be someone he didn't know at all?

Annie arrived, using her own key to let herself in.

"Off you go," she said, waving him out. Then she gave Muffy a big pat and shook the rain from a soaked umbrella before folding it up. "I'm sure you've got lives to save." Though sixty, she wore her white hair in a GI cut and still had a figure that let her borrow some of Janet's dresses. She swept by him into his den to plunk herself down in front of the computer.

Muffy, having long ago decided that here was a lady who knew how to pamper a poodle, settled happily at her feet.

"I'm in the middle of a Rogue Squadron game with my grandson on the Internet and can't talk right now," Annie called over her shoulder.

"You're an angel, Annie."

She grinned and clicked open a Web page picturing a heavily armed man in a Special Forces uniform. "Oh, I know I am," she said, without so much as a glance in his direction.

Sixty seconds later he reversed out of the driveway and

started up the street, forced to lean forward, his visibility nil because of the storm. Plowing through shimmering black pools that covered the streets, his tires started to hydroplane, and his knuckles went white from holding the steering wheel against the pull.

"Christ," he muttered, regaining control.

In ten minutes he came to a stop under the black canopy of trees drooping over Stewart's driveway.

The house remained in absolute darkness.

Not at home?

Earl couldn't tell if Stewart's Mercedes was gone, the garage being closed up tight.

He got out of his van and ran for the front door.

A four-chime bell sounded inside, then died out in the answering silence.

Shit. Tocco usually barked up a storm whenever anyone came calling if she had Stewart in there with her. But leave her alone in the house and she would hide in the basement, never making a sound. Dog lovers said she knew enough to protect people, not belongings. Stewart had a slightly different take on the matter. "The mutt barks when I'm there so I'll come and protect her. Otherwise she's a scared wimp, and anyone could break in."

So maybe Tocco's silence meant Stewart had gone out again. Damn, he should have checked the hospital. Probably the guy went back to the sanctuary of ICU. He used the place the way lesser mortals found comfort in a tavern.

Lightning sent molten cracks through the black sky.

Earl hesitated about using his cell phone out here, never having seen anyone get their brain fried while making a call during a thunderstorm, but not willing to risk the remote chance of being a first. Before returning to his car, he turned the front door's ornate brass handle, figuring it a useless gesture.

The door opened.

He quickly stepped inside and pulled it closed behind him.

"Stewart!" he called out, fumbling for a light switch as he stood dripping on the marble floor of the foyer. He braced himself to feel Tocco's cool nose coming out of the darkness to give him a sniff. Although the dog was timid, it took only one meeting to be her friend for life. Whenever he'd visited before, once she recognized him, he inevitably got a good going over, probably because he carried Muffy's scent.

He found what felt like a row of rheostat dials and pressed. The overhead chandelier flooded the room with an amber glow.

No Tocco and no Stewart.

"Hello?" he called out again.

Absolute stillness.

Stewart must be out, but there was one way to be sure. Earl made his way to the kitchen, flicking switches as he went, and found the door to the garage.

The dark blue Mercedes glistened in the light streaming past him.

Out for a walk with Tocco? Could be. But back at the main entrance he'd seen Stewart's big umbrella in its stand as usual. Still, the leash didn't occupy its regular spot on a varnished pine coatrack.

So he'd wait, Earl decided. Stewart wouldn't be long in this downpour.

After ten minutes of sitting at the bottom of the spiral staircase leading to the upper floor, he figured hanging around any longer would be a waste of time.

But Stewart *must* have the dog with him, so he wouldn't have gone far, especially without an umbrella. Maybe he'd taken shelter somewhere.

He got up and went into the living room to peer out the front window, trying to catch a glimpse of the pair returning home.

The streetlights illuminated falling rain but no people or animals of any kind.

At least the downpour had started to recede. It no longer

hit the glass with the force of a fire hose, and the accompanying roar had begun to diminish.

Good. If Stewart and Tocco had holed up someplace, they ought to be back anytime now. He sat on the sill to keep watch.

Over the next few minutes the rain became a gentle patter, and quiet filled the empty house, except now he could hear what sounded like faint voices.

What the hell?

He got up and walked back into the foyer.

"Stewart," he called upstairs, wondering if he'd been in his bedroom watching television the whole time and hadn't heard he had a visitor.

No answer.

And Tocco would have barked by now.

Besides, the noise, more a distant murmur than distinguishable talking, didn't seem to be coming from there.

For a second Earl thought it might be outside, and went to the front door. When he opened it only the hiss of a gentle shower filled his ears. The voices remained at his back.

Closing up, he wandered into the interior of the house and paused where the hallway met the kitchen. The murmurings came from behind a door he thought led to the basement.

Turning the handle, he pushed. Immediately faint words floated up from the darkness below. They sounded like something on a radio or from a television. Had Stewart a den down here?

"Stewart?"

He expected a response.

Again none came.

He flicked the light switches.

The blackness remained.

A blown fuse?

He began to catch snatches of what seemed to be a conversation between two people.

"Any more pain?"

"None. It's gone. . . ."

"Do you see anything?"

"Only blackness. . . ."

The questions were whispered, the words barely loud enough to make out. The rasping replies, more audible, seemed to come from a woman. "Hello?" he called.

Still no answer.

"Look harder! Now tell me what's there."

"You're not my doctor. . . ."

"No, I'm replacing him tonight. . . ."

Definitely a television left on, or a radio.

"Just leave me be. It doesn't hurt anymore. . . ."

"Do you see anything yet?"

"Yes . . ."

He wanted to go down but needed a light and had no idea where Stewart might keep one. He stepped into the kitchen and, after a little looking, found a handheld spot on a charger in the pantry. The harsh white beam probed the thick blackness like a sword as he started down the steps with it, still listening to the voices.

"Do you sense yourself rising?"

"Leave . . . me . . . alone. . . ."

"Not until you tell me what you see. Are you looking down on us yet?"

There followed what sounded like static.

"What did you say?" the whisperer asked.

"I . . . see . . . me. . . ."

What the hell? Earl thought, and slowed to a halt halfway down the steps, unable to believe he'd heard correctly. But the conversation continued, the telltale reverberation of speakers evident now.

"What else can you make out?"

"The . . . bed . . . nightstand . . . pictures . . . all my pictures . . ."

"Is that your husband?"

"Yes . . ."

In that closed space Earl caught a whiff of a very medicinal smell that tingled the inside of his nose. A more cloying, fecal aroma joined it, causing the back of his throat to tighten. Oh, no, he thought, and started down again, the spot throwing garish shadows against the walls.

"Is he dead?"

"Yes . . ."

"Do you want to find him?"

"Yes . . ."

He rounded the bottom landing and stepped into the basement proper.

"Are you still looking down on yourself in bed?"

"Yes . . ."

"Let go. Allow yourself to float, escape the hospital, go high above the building. You must do this before you can see Frank. . . ."

He swept the lamp's beam toward the sound. A miniature cassette recorder, the kind doctors often used when they dictated clinical notes, lay on the floor not far from his feet, and the tiny, slowly turning spools glistened as they caught the light. He guided his cone of light onto a small dark mound against the wall. It became shiny black fur that stood out in stark relief against a background of gray cinder blocks. He took a step closer and saw a motionless pink tongue lolling out over white fangs like a carefully placed ribbon. Farther into the darkness something much larger loomed. By reflex, he started to breathe through his mouth, and the sounds from the tape seemed swallowed by the heavy stillness of that suspended shape.

He slowly brought his beam to it.

Stewart's swollen, purple face stared back at him, eyes protruding from their sockets, the whites crisscrossed with broken veins, the pupils so huge they seemed filled with a starless night.

# Chapter 16

"You're doing fine," Janet said. A quick check of J.S.'s vital signs and abdominal and chest incisions assured her that the young woman remained stable. Sitting on the side of the bed, Janet leaned closer to her, determined no one would listen in on what she had to say next. The curtains that ringed the cubicle from ceiling to floor and the vertical shadows caught in their folds might make the place feel as claustrophobic as a jail cell, but the easily heard conversations from all the other beds dispelled any illusions of privacy. She also chose her words carefully, so as not to frighten the girl. "How are you feeling?"

"As expected, I guess." Her voice sounded frail, as if her struggle in the OR had drained all the fight from her.

But she must be warned. "J.S., I need help with a problem that's completely unrelated to your being here. Are you up to answering a few questions?"

"My help?" She seemed incredulous that anyone would ask anything of her.

Janet nodded, already wondering if it would be better to stop.

But a sudden spark of interest in J.S.'s eyes said otherwise. "I'll try."

"You're sure?"

"Yeah. Shoot."

"I must insist this stays absolutely hush-hush."

The caution further ignited J.S.'s pale brown irises toward far warmer tones, and her black eyebrows inched upward with curiosity. "Of course."

"Have you discussed your schedule in ER with anyone recently, even casually?"

"What?" Her forehead relaxed, and she frowned, looking disappointed.

"Just answer, please. Believe me, it's important."

"My schedule? Not at all. Work's the furthest thing from my mind."

"You're sure? Not with a visitor here, or anyone else even before today?"

"Before today? You mean at work? Probably. You know how it is with nurses. People want to switch all the time. And of course we all discuss what shifts we want with Susanne. But what do you want to know for?"

"Just bear with me. Do you have any particular criteria about when you choose to work, especially at night?"

"Not really. Why?"

Janet hesitated, still not sure how much to say. Even if Jane hadn't accidentally tipped anyone off, could she identify the killer? "Have you noticed anybody who always works when you do?"

"I think I'd like to know what this is about," she said, her voice hardening.

Janet noticed the change. Had she struck a nerve? "J.S., you've heard about the trouble Dr. Deloram is in?"

"Who hasn't?"

"And you're aware he may be tied to a rise in the death rate on the Palliative Care ward."

J.S. scowled. "Yablonsky ought to be shot, spreading that kind of garbage against him. Hell, I told Thomas a week ago I thought there were more codes being called up there lately, but it's probably a function of her bad nursing, the bitch. I sure as hell don't think Dr. Deloram has anything to do with it. I mean, he helped save my life. . . ." The angry flash in her eyes extinguished itself.

Janet guessed that she'd realized the man's heroics didn't exclude him from being a killer. "Look, J.S., none of us wants him to be guilty," she whispered, "but to help him, we need evidence, not only that he didn't do it, but of who did. I won't tire you with the details now, but at least half of those deaths, if not all, were murders. So Thomas, Dr. Garnet, and I were looking at shift schedules, trying to see if any single person in the hospital had been around when people died unexpectedly in Palliative Care."

"You're doing a cluster study, like the one Dr. G. always gives a lecture about?" Her eyes sparkled with excitement, their washed-out appearance vanishing. "What a great idea! And Thomas is helping? That's wonderful." She made an effort to raise her head and sit up. "Who'd you find? Yablonsky?"

Janet gently motioned her to lie flat. "Easy, girl," she whispered, "or you'll pop a stitch. And remember—" She paused to hold a finger to her own lips. "Keep it down. No, we didn't get Yablonsky, or anyone else on the ward. So I threw the search open and ran a program on the entire nursing roster for St. Paul's."

The anticipation in J.S.'s stare sharpened. "And?"

Janet hated what she had to do. "Now, I assure you that Dr. Garnet, Thomas, and I know it's some kind of fluke, that there's no link whatsoever with anything illegal."

The young woman's eager gaze became guarded in a blink. "What is it?"

"We got your name."

J.S.'s face remained absolutely motionless, at least the part Janet could see. Yet everything changed. A grayness seeped through her eyes, covering her emotions like a lead shield, and she seemed to shrink in on herself. Even her breathing became less pronounced.

"Listen, J.S. We understand the deaths have nothing, absolutely nothing, to do with you. But somehow your schedule corresponds to the killings, and we need to know why. Most important, you need to be careful."

J.S.'s expression didn't so much as flicker. It might have been frozen in ice. But after a few seconds a subtle transformation took place, no more substantial than the play of light and shadow on her skin, yet her features became haggard again, and her eyes, already sunk deep within their sockets, appeared to retreat further into her skull. "But those kinds of associations convict someone these days," she said. With her lips hidden behind the mask, her voice seemed to float out of her head.

"Trust me, we won't even mention your name in connection with the investigation. The worry is, this killer apparently operates the same nights you're on duty."

J.S. looked dazed, as if having difficulty comprehending it all. "I see," she finally said. "You think someone I always work with is a murderer." Her words still had an eerie, disembodied sound.

"Do you know anybody who's always taking shifts when you are, and not necessarily just in nursing? It could be a clerk, a porter, a secretary, perhaps an orderly, maybe a doctor—"

"In ER we're all together one time or another," she interrupted. "Even Dr. G. would fit that criteria."

The sudden sharpness in her tone surprised Janet. It had a harsh bite. "But we're mainly talking nights," she explained, trying to mute her own intensity so as to come across less like an inquisitor. "That ought to narrow it down. Think of someone who's around more than anyone else."

J.S. said nothing, her stare far away.

Janet again second-guessed the wisdom of having even discussed the problem. "I know it's a hell of a thing to dump on you, especially now, but—"

"No, no, it's good you told me. Absolutely the right thing to do. I had to know." J.S. spoke with the singsong cadence of someone reciting a cult mantra.

Alarmed, Janet gave her a moment to collect herself, then

said, "Please understand, I'd do this all with a computer, but it could take forever and might even miss the person we're after."

J.S. didn't respond. The soft sounds of ICU at night reverberated from beyond the curtains—the hiss and pop from ventilators, murmuring voices, a steady chirp of monitors like birdsong in a forest of wires and IV tubing.

Might as well press on and try to get the answers we need as quickly as possible, Janet decided, there being no way to take back the upset now. "So any ideas who—"

"None," J.S. said, her voice at a slightly higher pitch.

Janet also noted the quickness of her reply and sensed that the interview had been terminated. "Do you want me to order you a sedative?" she asked as gently as possible, not wanting her to withdraw further. "All this is understandably upsetting."

J.S. shook her head. "I have to think. And of course I'm upset. You just asked me to imagine the worst of everyone I work with in the place where I have never been happier." She managed to bestow an angry edge to every second syllable.

Janet forced a smile and hoped it showed in her eyes. After so many months in a mask, the tiny movement against the material irritated her lips and cheeks. She reached to take J.S.'s hand, instinctively wanting to comfort her. But those same instincts told her that J.S. had thought of someone and kept back the name. "Anyone whom you come up with need never know we checked him or her out," she said, admiring the woman's natural reluctance to implicate colleagues, "provided, of course, there's been no crime committed—"

"Excuse me, Dr. Graceton!" a woman's voice called from somewhere outside the cubicle.

Janet got up and parted the curtains.

A silver-haired nurse wearing wire-rimmed spectacles, the lenses tinted a matching gray, stood at the workstation, phone in hand.

Behind her the banks of monitors recorded the progress of this evening's patients, the fluorescent green squiggles heaping beat upon beat in a steady ticker tape of rising and falling fortunes.

"Dr. Garnet's on the line," she said. "It's urgent."

## 9:45 p.m.

Had Graceton believed her?

Jane couldn't tell, never having been a good liar.

Nor was she in any shape to deal with this. Last night they'd curetted away much more than the remnants of an unborn child. She felt completely hollowed out, emptied of her spirit and cored of its strength, her courage no more substantial than an eggshell, its contents sucked dry. Yet when Graceton asked if anyone always seemed to be around, she'd found the heart to cover up for him.

His name naturally came to mind, and of course she wouldn't mention it. Couldn't. Because ever since Susanne had told her he could marry like any other man, she'd realized he'd been coming around all this time to see her. Not an oh-my-God-what-am-I-going-to-do-about-it? type of realization. Just a quiet awareness of his attraction to her that she enjoyed, savored even, both flattered by it, and comfortable that he'd never make her act on it or put pressure on her to betray Thomas. She could indulge in the pleasant boost to her ego that came with having a strong, handsome man like him drawn to her, safe in the knowledge he'd do everything necessary, including keep a certain distance, so as not to complicate her life. In return, he'd be the last person she would cause trouble for. Besides, whoever they were after, Jimmy wouldn't be the guy. He couldn't have anything to do with killing people. But if not him, then who?

During the day and earlier in the evening, dozens of nurses and colleagues had dropped by on their breaks to wish her well. As tiring as the visits were, she'd welcomed their company. Now she found herself wondering if one of them had been the murderer. She also remembered Susanne's concern over all the missing syringes. It frightened her how, in spite of her reluctance, she came up with doubts about many of the people she worked with. And if her imagination could run loose like that, someone might do the same against her, and probably would, once word of the cluster study got out. She shuddered at the prospect of a public rending. But it's only a matter of time, she thought, however much Graceton promised to protect her. Secrets didn't stay secret at St. Paul's, especially not those kind. And once suspicions about some-one took hold, they could feed on themselves and grow like a cancer. Anybody could make a case about anybody.

So should she warn Jimmy? Give him a heads-up that Dr. G., Dr. Graceton, and Thomas were comparing her schedule to others' and any matches could mean big trouble for him as well? Even without a cluster study, sooner or later it might occur to someone how often Jimmy showed up whenever she worked, day or night.

Except . . .

The image of when she had walked in and caught him going through the utility cupboard popped to mind.

Later she'd told herself that his story about the urine cup and a pending medical checkup had just been another excuse to drop around and see her, like the earring business.

Now *she* fell prey to thinking the worst.

*God, what's the matter with me?* she reprimanded herself, and felt sick at having, even for a second, allowed that there could ever be a connection. She'd certainly never told any-one, especially Susanne, about finding him in there on the af-ternoon the needles went missing. As far as anyone knew he'd dropped by to get his ear pierced, and it should stay that way. No one would be given the opportunity to twist inno-cent circumstances against the man if she could help it.

All the more reason to warn Jimmy. She could just imag-ine the argument that could be made against him if some busybody had seen him go into that utility room, thought nothing of it at the time, but, on hearing he'd been associated with the deaths, had a resurgence of memory.

She grew increasingly uneasy, and not just about his safety.

Being afraid for him had also forced her to acknowledge more than she'd wanted to about her and Jimmy. Lying there, spiked with the aftermath of fatigue, fear, and morphine, she felt the gloom of the place close in on her, adding to her sense of isolation.

She wanted to see Thomas. The nurses had told her he'd been at her side all morning, until they sent him home to sleep. But she barely remembered his being there. Now she wanted to feel the warmth of his hand and the soothing sound of his voice.

Yet her thoughts drifted back to Jimmy.

Until now she'd only admitted to herself how clearly he sought her out; she'd avoided examining too closely how she felt about him. Graceton's bombshell galvanized her out of that convenient haze. Being frightened about his safety pushed her to face the fact that she'd grown a lot fonder of him than she'd realized. Not that she'd been actively denying her feelings for him. She'd just chosen to enjoy their time together and not complicate the situation with questions.

But now she had to accept that emotions might have matured well past liking on both her and Jimmy's part. The way he'd stayed by her side all night suggested a much stronger sentiment on his side. And the strength she'd drawn from the touch of his hand holding hers, the way his words had penetrated her fear, had reached her even as she went unconscious— She pulled up, surprised at the intensity of her reactions to him. They confused her.

*Obviously I'm an emotional basket case,* she insisted to herself, trying to blame her near-death ordeal for the unexpected feelings that were ambushing her from all directions. But she couldn't evade the fact that Jimmy had affected her far more than she realized.

She heard someone approach, and gasped when Dr. Graceton stepped inside the curtains. The woman's luminous, steady gaze and warm expression from minutes ago had vanished. She looked stunned, with her eyes blank and her face as white as her mask.

"Sorry, J.S., I've got an emergency." The words came out clipped and fast. "Sedation orders are written. Get some sleep. I'll be back first thing in the morning and we can talk more then." She wheeled and headed for the exit, disappearing out the sliding door in seconds.

Something must have happened at home, Jane thought. Otherwise why would Dr. G. be the one who telephoned? Besides, last night had been her last on call for obstetrics.

A terrible possibility flew to mind, accompanied by a sense of dread that made it seem certain.

My God. Dr. G., Dr. Graceton, and Thomas were working on the cluster program tonight. They might have already matched Jimmy's schedule to mine.

She rang for a nurse.

The woman with silver glasses and matching hair listened to her request, then tried to argue that Dr. Graceton had left specific orders there were to be no more visitors.

"But I want to see the chaplain. He's not a visitor. At least let me talk to him on the phone."

The lady looked about to say no.

"Surely you wouldn't deny a patient spiritual comfort, especially not in here."

"I know he's your friend," she said, sounding annoyed, but brought her a phone anyway.

Jimmy Fitzpatrick's hand held steady as he replaced the receiver in its cradle.

He had taken the call at a patient's bedside and used the lack of privacy as an excuse for not being able to speak very long.

But he'd heard enough to set his heart racing and send himself running back to his office.

"Hey, I'm here so much, everybody thinks I work when they do," he had said to J.S. No telling if she'd bought it.

He'd known when he started it might all come down on his

head. That still didn't make him ready to be led away in handcuffs for murder. And he definitely hadn't anticipated this twist involving J.S.

He fumbled the keys as he opened the lock and shut the door behind him but didn't turn on the light. Somehow he felt less panicky in the dark. He had enough ambient glow to see from the sodium lamps over the parking lot outside his window.

He'd gotten used to working in that ambient glow.

Around him were the bookshelves that held the words he'd chosen to live by. The Bible, of course, but also the philosophers he'd studied with such enthusiasm and love. Perfect thoughts from Aristotle, pupil of Plato, teacher of Alexander the Great, first in the struggle to reconcile science, ethics, politics, and the soul. John Locke, champion of empiricism and the inherent right of man to life, liberty, and a patch of land to call his own. Jean-Paul Sartre, who liberated all individuals to the lonely burden of defining right and wrong by themselves, then condemned those same individuals to the cold ethical void of existentialism. Sartre alone probably came closest to re-creating the ice bath of freedom and responsibility that God threw Adam and Eve into when He kicked them out of Eden.

Who could read any of the great teachers from all the ages, take their writings to heart, and not become an outlaw spirit?

At least that's how he'd read his calling among the realities of today at St. Paul's. How else could a man live for the greater good, help the meek, define right, and back it up with action if he wasn't willing to step outside the law now and then? Not to be pretentious, but he saw his predicament as merely a smaller-scale version of what had always been the dilemma for philosophers, people of God, and defenders of the oppressed who dared turn beautiful thoughts into concrete acts. Whether Jesus Christ, Robin Hood, Joan of Arc, or Zorro, they were rebels all, and he would have been proud to work at their sides whatever the period. No way was he just the grandstanding swashbuckler out of his time that Earl made him out to be.

At least that's how he'd thought of himself in the heady days at the start of their plan when getting caught seemed nothing more than a vague but unlikely possibility. He'd even promised the others they would never be found out, that, if necessary, he alone would take the blame and, by standing proud for what he did, make the deeds seem courageous and noble.

His head reeled in disgust at having been so naive and reckless, forcing him to grip the side of his desk.

Whom had he been kidding?

His downfall, if it came, would be a seedy, petty event, the stuff of tabloids blaring news of yet another disgraced priest.

He ran into the bathroom and threw up.

His stomach, emptied out, clenched itself tight as a fist, and he staggered back to his desk where he collapsed into his chair.

He could still get away with everything if he acted fast.

In the minimal light he pulled out the lower right drawer where he kept his prayer shawl, folded and ready for use. He lifted it out.

Next he withdrew a small mahogany box lined with purple velvet that held his holy oils and pyx, a circular container for consecrated wafers. He laid the kit unopened beside his shawl.

Reaching back into the drawer, he removed the false bottom in its recesses. There lay the syringes he'd stolen from ER. Beside them stood two vials of morphine, one provided by Stewart, the other by Michael.

### 9:55 p.m.

Janet had told Thomas to wait for her in the doctor's lounge. She found him there with mask off and sipping tea. He'd made an entire pot, and alongside it on a low magazine table sat a mug with cream already added, exactly the way he'd seen her take it after dinner hours earlier.

When she came closer, he jumped to his feet, eyes wide with alarm. "My God, are you all right? Is J.S. okay?"

"She's fine, other than scared and worried. I ordered sedation, and you must let her sleep. But there's other bad news—"

"What did she say?"

"What we expected. She hasn't a clue how her schedule could match the killings. And when I asked her if anyone always seemed to be around during her shifts, the denial came a little too quickly for my liking. Probably afraid to get a friend in trouble, so tomorrow see if you can get her to talk."

"I'll go see her right now." He started to get up.

Janet put a restraining hand on his chest. "Whoa! I just had the nurses sedate her, remember. She's safe enough until morning."

He hesitated, then said, "Here, sit down," and motioned her to an overstuffed, leather lounge chair.

The decor in here hadn't changed since Reagan had been president, and maroon must have been a popular color back then. Even on a good day the furnishings jangled her eyes.

"And drink this. You look as though you could use it." He poured the steaming brown liquid to the mug's brim, gave the mix a stir, and handed it to her. "Now what's the other bad news?"

She pulled down her mask and took a sip, savoring the warmth as it traveled to her stomach. "It's about Stewart," she began, and described how Earl had discovered his body.

Thomas's face fell slack in disbelief.

Having to tell the story left her feeling leaden.

"He hung himself?" Thomas said when she'd finished, his voice as incredulous as his saggy-eyed expression.

She nodded. As the misery of Stewart's death sunk in, displacing her initial shock, she took another sip of tea. It tasted even more mellow than the first. "They found a tape playing at the scene that sounded like recorded interviews of people in a near-death state," she continued. "Some of them included the patient's name, so it will be easy to compare them to our list of suspicious deaths. But the interviewer is whispering the whole time. While we can presume Stewart is the one asking questions, they won't be able to verify it. Apparently, according to the detectives, a whisper can't be matched the way speaking voices are."

Thomas sank back where he sat and regarded the ceiling, slowly shaking his head.

"If all that isn't weird enough," she went on, "the first quarter of the tape is of Roy Orbison singing 'Pretty Woman.' Nobody can even hazard a guess what that's about."

Up came his head, an expression of dismay on his face. " 'Pretty Woman?' "

"And get this. They found a small bottle of chloroform. The cops think he used it to put his dog to death, then made a noose with the animal's leash for himself."

He leaned forward. "Wait a minute. You're saying Stewart had been the guy in the hospital subbasement who left you there—"

"Stewart left no explanations. All they discovered in the form of a suicide note were two words written on his personal computer: 'I'm sorry.' The machine had conveniently been left on sleep mode so it came to life as soon as one of the cops touched the keyboard." She paused and took several more swallows from her mug. The familiar comfort smoothed away the tightness in her gut.

"But it seems as if everything Yablonsky accused him of turned out to be true," Thomas said, his voice quiet, as if he was thinking aloud.

Janet shook her head. "Not according to Earl."

"What?"

"Come on, Thomas. Where's your healthy sense of skepticism? Every good clinician has one."

"I don't understand."

"It's all too neat. Everything, from the tapes to the chloroform to the hanging."

"The hanging?"

"Yeah. Apparently a researcher in New York hung himself exactly the same way fourteen years ago, and Stewart may have had a hand in what drove him to it."

"Wait a minute. Another researcher hung himself? Who?"

Janet downed her tea. "Come on, drive me home, and I'll explain on the way. But it all stinks to high heaven—too much like a package wrapped up in a nice ribbon. And to top it all, Earl thinks Stewart left a sign to say he didn't commit suicide, but had been murdered."

Thomas's eyebrows notched a quarter inch higher. "A sign?"

"I'll tell you in the car."


## 10:10 p.m.

Neighbors began to appear in the street, huddled under umbrellas. They stood around like clumps of black mushrooms despite the storm picking up force again.

"Don't touch the body, and treat the house as a murder scene," Earl had said to the first officers who arrived over thirty minutes ago. "Above all, protect this tape." He indicated the microcassette on the floor that continued to broadcast the whispered interviews. "You'll want to check it for fingerprints," Earl said, though if this was the clever setup he thought it to be, the only prints on it would be Stewart's. Then he added, "And by using the cue numbers, we can work backward to determine when someone started it."

The eerie questions and answers floating out of the miniature speaker had brought a frown to the fresh young face of the cop who knelt down to inspect it. "What the hell am I listening to?" she asked. A blond ponytail dangled out the back of her peaked cap. The big gun on her tiny hips seemed incongruous with her cheerleader appearance.

"I'm not sure," Earl had said, but in fact he had a damn good idea.

"Get me a set of gloves," she'd ordered her partner. Minutes later, her hands appropriately garbed in latex and holding the device by a corner so as not to smudge any traces of its previous handler, she pressed stop using a ballpoint pen. After writing down the cue number and the time, she again used the pen, pressing rewind. But when she started the tape at the beginning, and they heard the familiar strains of "Pretty Woman," he'd no clue at all what to make of that.

He'd called Janet and broken the news to her, then waited in the living room as more cop cars pulled up. Some of the newly arrived officers came inside and went downstairs. Through the front window he saw others run yellow tape around the perimeter of the property. He gave a brief statement about discovering Stewart's body to the woman with the ponytail, all the time thinking she couldn't be any older than J.S.

That had been ten minutes ago.

Now he had nothing to do but watch the onlookers outside as they watched him.

Finally, at 10:20, a pair of plainclothes homicide detectives walked in and said they'd be in charge of the investigation.

The older of the two, a tall, blond woman about Janet's age, introduced herself as Detective Lazar. She wore a Burberry raincoat and carried a sadness in her eyes that most cops eventually assume. Her colleague, a man of equal height but at least ten years her junior, his perfectly coiffed black hair and square jaw suitable for a recruitment poster, stood with pen and pad in hand, ready to take notes.

Earl gave his name, led them downstairs, and proceeded to explain why he thought Stewart had been murdered.

"First, look at his feet," he began.

Though the body remained suspended enough that it seemed to be standing tiptoed, the balls of the feet were pressed a good inch into the soft vinyl surface of the stool under them. "Have you ever seen hanging victims before, Detective?"

She nodded.

Her partner did the same but found it necessary to also

flex his eyebrows in an attempt at a boy-have-I-seen-hanging-victims look.

Earl ignored him. "Then you know most end up dying slow, strangling themselves." He directed his comments only to Lazar. "They're ignorant about the benefit that a drop from a gallows provides—haven't a clue how the momentum causes the rope to mercifully snap the neck at the second cervical vertebrae and, if the victim's lucky, severs the spinal cord, bringing as near-instantaneous brain death as possible. Instead, they linger in the noose and suffer hideously. Stewart wouldn't make that mistake. If he wanted to die by hanging, he'd have launched himself at the end of a rope out a second-story window." He looked at his friend's limp body, the rumpled trousers stained with the indignity of death, and shuddered. "Never ever would he have set up something so amateurish as this. At the very least, he'd have kicked the stool away. I think he deliberately didn't do that, at the price of excruciating agony, to signal us this is not a suicide." A mix of pity, sorrow, and horror swept through him as the terror of Stewart's final moments hit home. He grimaced and grew angry. "You may be willing to render such a brave last act meaningless by ignoring it, but I'm not."

Detective Lazar studied him.

The young man furiously scribbled down notes.

Earl pegged him as a rookie, at least to the homicide business. Cops were just like medical residents. The ones who wrote everything down were the least experienced and would know squat.

"This is all very interesting conjecture, Dr. Garnet," Lazar said after a few seconds. "But presumably something else got you suspicious enough to be so skeptical. Frankly, I would have taken this as a suicide, however ineptly done. Stewart, you said his name was?"

"Dr. Stewart Deloram. Yes, there are reasons to believe someone did this to him. But they're very complicated."

"Try to keep it simple."

Her partner got ready with the pen again.

Earl took a breath. Maybe notes would be useful after all. "Well, it started over two weeks ago with the death of a terminally ill patient named Elizabeth Matthews. . . ."

## 10:43 p.m.

One moment they were talking.

Then the car lurched right and roared forward.

Janet screamed and thought the accelerator had jammed.

They went over the edge of the road and plummeted down the bank. The headlamps carved a glistening tunnel through darkness pierced with a million silver streaks of rain. At the bottom a tree trunk loomed larger, like a crosshair in a target that drew them toward itself. And while their descent happened fast, it also appeared to unfold slowly. She got both knees up in time to brace her abdomen against the crash.

## 10:53 p.m.

When Earl finished speaking, Lazar regarded him with a puzzled frown that suggested she might at least consider his version of events. "How would this someone who'd been setting Dr. Deloram up get in the house?" she asked. "There's no sign of forced entry, and nobody can pick the kind of locks he has without leaving some marks."

"Stewart always left his keys lying around in the hospital. Anyone could have grabbed them and made a copy."

She looked over toward Tocco and frowned. "Then why didn't the dog bark at the killer and wake the victim up?"

"Maybe she did and Stewart didn't hear. He'd been up all night at the hospital, so he probably slept pretty heavily. And don't you read Sherlock Holmes?"

She smiled and nodded. "You mean the dog could have known the person and therefore not barked?"

"That's right. Tocco remained friendly with people once she got to know them."

She glanced around the room, and her eyes fell on Stewart's laptop. "How'd the killer get into the victim's computer to write the suicide note, brief as it is?"

"Everyone knew he used the dog's name for the password."

"Tocco?"

"Tocco. The computer belonged to the teaching office. Stewart used it to file residency schedules, night call lists, teaching rosters for medical staff and nurses, seminar calendars, journal club articles—all kinds of stuff. And he gave everybody access so they wouldn't be bugging him for the information all the time."

She turned back toward Stewart and studied him, as if viewing a statue. "Why leave him the stool at all?"

"To make him suffer? Prolong his dying? Who knows?"

"When do you think he died?"

As the questions continued, the professional neutrality of her cop face began to say that she wanted to believe him and her inquiries, though still probing, became more a test to see if his story held up rather than an attempt to tear it apart.

After a few more minutes of interrogation, she said, "Stay put in case we need you."

He sat in the living room while people in dark blue jumpsuits with BPD emblazoned on the back began to arrive. Some pulled on latex gloves and started to poke around the house with tweezers, bagging stray hairs or anything else they found interesting. A few others brushed a fine powder onto any surface that a killer might have touched. A photographer headed toward the basement.

Enough waiting. Janet had sensed that J.S. might be shielding someone. A sample of what that someone might be capable of hung from a pipe in the basement beneath him.

He pulled out his cell phone and called the one person who probably knew as much about J.S.'s schedule as she did herself.

He had hardly ever contacted Susanne at home, even though she'd entrusted him with her unlisted number. He knew her fierce need for privacy and respected it.

"Hello?" said a woman's voice.

"It's Dr. Garnet speaking. Is Susanne there, please?"

"One moment."

He'd been aware that the woman's first name was Rachel and that she'd been Susanne's partner for ten years—but not because Susanne had told him. He'd picked up enough fragments from those few whom Susanne confided in, such as Mrs. Quint, to piece things together over the years. At first he'd found it odd that in this day and age someone as self-assured and comfortable with herself as Susanne hid her personal life. But as time went on and she still never talked about her partner at all, he began to suspect her reticence reflected a deep respect for the privacy of those she loved and it would have been the same no matter whom she lived with, man or woman.

So he had never presumed to call Rachel by her first name, staying outside the boundary of familiarity that Susanne had set up for him. Old-fashioned? Who cared? So was loyalty, courage, and guts, and Susanne had those in spades. If she needed the distance to feel comfortable, she'd get it.

"What's up?" Susanne said, coming on the phone. She sounded alarmed.

"You'd better prepare yourself. I've got bad news." He again relayed the evening's events, just as he had to Janet. The retelling didn't lessen the ghastliness of it.

She remained silent for a long while after he'd finished. Finally he heard a stuttering intake of breath. "So bright, yet so alone," she finally said, her voice breaking.

"I'm afraid there's more. And this has to stay absolutely confidential." He told her about J.S.'s schedule coinciding with the cardiac arrests in Palliative Care.

"Oh, God, no," she moaned.

"Don't for a moment think I believe it's her," he quickly added, wondering if Susanne would revisit her own take on

J.S. the way he had. It needn't be a big process to do damage. Just a hint of doubt could infringe on the easy trust there'd always been between the two. He felt angry at how such suspicions about so many had spread through him lately, like a contagion. "Since you draw up her schedule, I hoped you might have a clue if it mirrored someone else's."

"Not that I know of."

"You don't use any specific criteria for assigning her shifts, especially on nights?"

"None. She gets the same treatment as all my other nurses."

"Does she make many special requests?" People in ER were always wanting to keep this weekend or that free, or asking for specific vacation times months ahead of the desired date.

"Just the opposite. She's more likely to offer to take a night or weekend than to request to be excused from it." She paused, then added, "It's pretty public now, so I can say what I only guessed before. She seemed to like working when Thomas Biggs had a shift."

"Thomas?"

She made an attempt at a little laugh but still sounded close to tears. "Hey, as Janet is wont to say, 'Ain't love grand?' "

He felt a spark of hope. "So did you end up giving her lots of nights?" That would explain J.S. being around the times of the cardiac arrests more than anyone else.

"Not overall. Just kept her in mind for last-minute replacements, but always gave her fewer nights the next time. In the end she did no more than anyone else."

So much for that idea.

"J.S. certainly never requested I put her on the schedule just when her boyfriend would be there, if that's what you're thinking," Susanne added. "She's too good a soldier to pull anything as unprofessional as that. She worked just as many nights when he was off, more even, probably three out of four."

And so must have the killer. He'd just have to grill J.S. himself.

"I guess that means you can eliminate the residents as well," Susanne added.

"Pardon?"

"I mean, residents work one in four, and nurses take their graveyard shifts in blocks of at least a week at a time. So just by the luck of the draw, she'd be with all the house staff about the same amount of time."

"Yes, of course, no surprise there," he agreed, but privately something about one in four bothered him. Thanking her, he hung up, and immediately called home.

Annie answered.

"No sign of Janet yet?"

"None. But don't worry. I'll stay as late as you like. By the way, you got a message."

"Oh?"

"A Dr. Cheryl Branagh in New York. Said it wasn't urgent, but she'd gotten some information for you, and you could call her at home before ten tonight, or tomorrow morning."

He glanced at his watch. It was 10:55.

Damn. He thanked Annie, took down the home number Branagh had left, and tried now anyway. He'd have to break the news of Stewart's death to her. And if she'd found out anything connecting him to Jerome Wilcher, the police should hear about it as soon as possible.

"You have reached the residence of Dr. Cheryl Branagh. I cannot take your call right now. . . ."

He left a message.

He next called Janet's cellular number.

She had it shut off.

*Must still be in the hospital,* he thought. But he'd been under the impression she intended to sedate J.S., then leave, and not tell her about Stewart.

He called ICU.

"Dr. Graceton left here over an hour ago, Dr. Garnet," the nurse whom he'd spoken with earlier told him, "shortly after she talked with you."

He started to get a bad feeling.

A rotten night for driving, terrible visibility, some jerk traveling too fast—his tendency to conjure up worst-case scenarios kicked into action. Despite Janet's efforts to lighten him up, at his core he nurtured pessimism. The business of ER demanded it. In the pit his ability to read a situation and anticipate what could go wrong saved lives. In private life, it made him hard to live with. He reined in his anxiety. She and Thomas would be taking their time driving in the storm. And she may have sat him down to tell him about Stewart before they left the hospital. Working through that kind of bad news could take time. "How's Miss Simmons?" he asked.

"J.S.? She's fine. I found her dozing and turned out her light. She'd asked to see Father Jimmy, but it looks like whatever had been bothering her can wait until morning."

"Father Jimmy?"

"Yes. She spoke to him on the phone just after Janet left, then told us he'd be paying her a visit."

He didn't know what to make of that. Probably shouldn't even try to read anything into it. The kid could simply be frightened. No surprise there either, considering all she'd just been through. And since she and Jimmy were friends, it would be only natural she call him.

Still, he didn't exactly trust Jimmy these days. And come to think of it, he could be considered someone who saw a lot of her at work. Maybe Janet's suspicion of his being secretly in love with J.S. hadn't been off the mark. But then he saw a lot of everyone in ER, constantly dropping by the way he did.

"Did you want to know anything else, Dr. Garnet?" the nurse said, pulling him out of his thoughts.

"No. Just keep a close eye on her."

He cut the connection, got up, and began to pace, unable to sit still any longer.

"Can I go now?" he asked Detective Lazar.

"We need your prints," she said. "It won't be long."

**11:15 p.m.**

Jane Simmons started awake. Her nurse must have turned off the night-light because she found herself in darkness. It took a few seconds to realize someone stood in the shadows at the end of the bed.

"Jimmy?" she whispered.

"Hey, J.S.," he answered, very softly. "Sorry to be so late, but I had business to take care of. And I was just going to leave. You obviously need to sleep."

"Come here." She held out her hand to him. "What I need is that we talk."

He came out of the shadow and sat on the side of the bed. She could see his face in the green glow from her monitors. His hair looked shiny, as if recently wet. But the unnatural color of the illumination highlighted every fold and hollow above his mask, rendering him gaunt, and the laugh lines around his eyes, normally so ready to deepen with his smile, splayed toward his temples like claws.

"Oh, no." The words escaped her as involuntary and inaudible as a sharply drawn breath. In that instant she knew that disaster had struck and somehow this mess involved him. Simultaneous flashes of pity, sorrow, fear, and love packed themselves into a single heartbeat, and a plummeting sensation filled her chest. The reflex to help him came as natural as her urge to put her arms around him, even without knowing what he'd done, or why. That she could learn later. For now it felt right just to reach up and pull him toward her, the instinct to protect him overwhelming all other emotions. "Have you told anyone?" she asked, not sure where even that rudimentary piece of information would lead. Whether he had or not, she'd no idea what to do. Absently she noticed the dampness of his shirt under her palms.

At first he widened his eyes in a feeble pretense of not knowing what she meant. "Told anyone what—"

"Don't lie to me, Jimmy. It's too late for that."

His eyes sank back into their hollows. "No," he said, his voice barely audible. "But how did you guess—"

She silenced him with a finger to his lips.

In Grand Forks she'd hung out with her share of bad boys. It complemented her choice to dress and act hard. Some, she had heard over the years, had gone on to be bad men. Some had fared better, especially the ones who hadn't gotten caught. She'd helped a few of them in that regard, taking charge when they'd been scared shitless of being picked up for this or that petty larceny, helping them forge an ironclad story, even claiming to have been with one or two of them when she hadn't.

So she'd had some practice in getting men out of trouble. And in forcing them to level with her. "No, you won't lie to me, or no, you haven't told anybody about whatever mess it is you're in?" Even in a whisper, her question sounded more like a command.

He took a breath, then let it escape slowly from his pursed lips. It sounded as if he were deflating. "The latter."

She felt a glimmer of relief. There would be time. She'd hear the details of what he'd done, then they could decide on a plan.

Never once did she think to be afraid of him.

# Chapter 17

Rain pelted on metal.

Her head hurt.

She also heard the rush of running water.

Cold seeped through her, insinuating itself deep into her bones, and icy liquid crept up her chest.

Her eyes flew open.

But everything remained black.

She couldn't remember what had happened.

Then a contraction seized her belly and cut her in two.

*Oh, my God, I'm in labor.*

Janet doubled over with a cry, vaguely aware she lay on her side in a cramped space with a hard irregular surface. *Where am I? How did I get here? Why can't I see?* But the brutal agony in her belly cut off all her questions.

She couldn't breathe, not even scream. The pain smothered her, shrank her world until all she sensed were the impossible forces at work in her womb.

*My baby,* she thought, forcing herself to count off the seconds, to think rationally, to mentally catalog the primitive thrust of the uterine muscles into their physiological stages, as if her ability to name what racked her could exert mastery over its hold, deaden its grip, and break its power. After a full minute, the contraction released, dropping her back into the darkness and cold, as flickers of memory tried to tell what had happened.

A crash?

And Thomas!

Where was he?

They'd been in her car together, coming back from St. Paul's.

He'd offered to drive again, promised to go much slower this time, and apologized for speeding on the trip in. "Finding J.S.'s name in the cluster search really shook me," she remembered him saying.

But the recollection remained shrouded in a haze, and her thinking came in slow, disjointed fragments. She couldn't see the time on her watch or even tell if it still worked. How long had she been in labor, let alone unconscious?

She tried to feel around her. Her hands found knobs and dials that felt like parts in the dashboard of her car, but twisted, and arranged vertically, as if tipped sideways. Everywhere were fragments of broken glass spread thick as confetti.

And water. She lay in half a foot of it.

Her brain continued to work at half speed.

Obviously they'd crashed.

But where?

She recalled pulling out from the parking lot. The rain had seemed less, but a few blocks away they found parts of the downtown core to be in complete darkness, including the expressway. The beam of their headlights barely penetrated the murk.

The storm must have come back at full force, she thought, judging by the constant din on whatever remained of her car. But water also seemed to be gushing around her. If only she could see.

"Thomas!"

No answer.

What had happened to him?

She felt above her to where the driver's seat should be. Free ends of a seat belt trailed toward her, and her fingers found the gearshift, the leather upholstery, but no Thomas.

Had he been thrown clear?

"Thomas!" She screamed louder than before.

Even if he was conscious and able to hear, the roar from the storm and whatever that rushing water might be would drown her out.

She tried to move her legs. Sore yet functional, though cramped in the crumpled shell of her car. By now she'd realized it had rolled on its side, but not all the way over. Otherwise she would have been crushed or had her neck broken, the windshield and flimsy convertible top offering no protection to a car flipped upside down. And she hadn't been able to buckle up. God, she could easily have died.

And the baby. God, what had happened to her baby? If her stomach had hit the dashboard or been compressed by the rollover, he might be injured. Reflexively she palpated her own abdomen. It hurt only slightly, not nearly as much as her head, and had no focal areas of tenderness that might mean contusions or damage to the fetus. But she had to find help, make it to a hospital where they could monitor him, check him with ultrasound, get him safely out and treat any injuries to him. A month premature, he'd need special care anyway.

She tried to extricate herself from where she'd been lying, gripping the steering wheel and the back of the driver's seat, then hoisting herself up while pushing with her feet. It felt like climbing out of a pit.

"Thomas! Help!"

Lightning split the sky, and in a flash she saw above her the driver's-side door, its glass starred with cracks but intact, the windshield on her right equally fragmented yet also in place, and she remembered something that shouldn't have been.

The right side of her head throbbed, not the front.

Crawling higher, she strained to look around, saw only darkness, and the steady sound of water streaming around her smashed vehicle became louder. But the effort left her dizzy, so much so she sank back into the passenger compartment.

Where the hell had they crashed?

She wished for yet another lightning burst to give her a chance to get a bearing.

None obliged.

*My cellular,* she thought, hands diving into her coat pockets. *I can call for help.*

Empty.

It must have fallen out as the car rolled.

She felt around for it in the darkness.

Still nothing.

Struggling again to reach the door, her fingers gripped the far edge of the driver's seat, and she pulled herself to her knees. This time her head spun so severely she thought she'd pass out. She nevertheless persisted and felt around for the handle.

Her fingers scraped over the jagged metal edges where it had been snapped off. Nothing else budged. The door was jammed shut.

Had Thomas crawled out the roof? Gone for help?

She flapped her hands behind her, touched the taut surface of the leather and explored it with her fingers. It was intact.

He must have been thrown out the door after all, but the rollover had swung it shut again. And she'd definitely landed in water. Her side of the car rested in a shallow pool.

Her brain spun through a few high-speed revolutions, and she sank back to her knees.

God, she must have really hit her head.

She couldn't recall past Thomas starting up the access road to the darkened expressway. Retrograde amnesia, they called it. Meant she'd given her noggin a good enough whump to knock off her memory for events leading up to the accident. Neurologists considered it a sign of significant head trauma.

No kidding. The throbbing that ran from her temple to her ear could have told her that. Again something concerned her about where she hurt.

She once more mustered her strength, pulled herself up, and tried to force the driver's-side door open.

It remained stuck. She couldn't even release the locks.

Nor could she unclip the front of the retractable roof from the windshield frame. The mechanism must have been twisted or jammed with the crash.

She'd nothing sharp enough to cut the leather, so she tried to rip it with her hands and punch through it with her fists, but the material proved to be too tough. She even lay back and thrust at it a few times with her legs, hoping to poke a tear.

No luck. She didn't have the strength, and the effort left her increasingly light-headed.

She twisted to try to smash out the driver's-side window, though her swollen belly would probably be an impossible squeeze through it.

She'd struck it with her shoe just as the inside of her brain revved all the way up to a death spiral. Oh, God, what's happening? she thought, feeling her heart start to race as she collapsed back into the passenger compartment.

And something clicked.

Dizzy, a fast pulse, and in labor.

Pain could cause it, but at the moment she'd no contractions.

*Not a hemorrhage,* she prayed, reaching inside her skirt to check.

From the waist down she'd been soaking wet in cold water. But between her legs the fluid felt warm to her fingers.

*Oh, God, no!*

She fought back a surge of panic, trying to tell herself it might not be blood.

Yet she now dreaded the next lightning flash for fear of what it would show.

Once more a sickening spin filled her skull, and she clutched blindly at wherever she could for support.

The dark sky detonated into a searing light, making it possible to see.

Swirls of crimson curled away from her through black water like fronds of seaweed, and small currents where the stream flowed through the car swept them away.

In an instant darkness returned, more impenetrable than ever, her eyes no longer adjusted to it.

Seconds later another contraction hit.

## Wednesday, July 18, 11:31 p.m.

There'd still been no word from Janet.

And her cellular remained off.

He'd repeatedly phoned the hospital and asked them to page her.

No response.

He'd asked them to page Thomas.

The same result.

When he'd tried to call the man at home, in case Janet had dropped him off, he reached a recording inviting the caller to try St. Paul's. The man's cell phone number produced a full minute of intermittent buzzing, until the same answering machine clicked in.

"Shit!" Earl yelled, tossing the phone into the passenger seat and gliding his van through yet another small lake that had formed across the road. Everyone else he knew justified owning a four-wheel-drive beast for family trips, luggage, kids, a nanny, or the family dog. His reason? On a bad night, he could power through anything.

Thomas's car remained parked in front of their house. Nevertheless, he dared to hope the familiar sight of Janet's green Mazda would greet him when he opened the automatic garage door.

Empty.

At least they still had power. The rest of the suburbs he'd passed through were riddled with blackouts where wires had gone down.

He stepped over Muffy as she lay inside the front entranceway, stooping to give her ears a perfunctory rub. She must have been out for a walk, because her coat, softened by the rain, had the sweet aroma of wet wool and felt young

•

again. She raised her head and slipped her tongue out for a quick comfort lick of his hand.

The dog probably sensed his fear.

He strode through the living room and headed straight for his study, where he found Annie still busy at the computer.

"Hi, Doc," she said, not looking up from a screen filled with swat soldiers and a scoreboard displaying an impressive number of kills.

"Sorry, Annie, but can you hang around? I may have to go out again."

This announcement won him a glance, and her face fell. "What's happened? You look spooked."

"I'll explain later. Right now I need my computer." He wouldn't frighten her about Janet just yet.

She vacated the chair and bustled out of the room. "I'll put on a pot of tea."

She'd a great talent for knowing when to make herself scarce.

He clicked up the cluster program and, as the machine erratically hummed to retrieve it, thought about Sadie Locke's calendar marked with crosses.

The tiny memorials, when he first saw them, had occupied about a quarter of the squares demarcating days. Not systematically one in four—he would have picked up something so recognizable on the spot—but in a distribution close enough to it that those crosses popped to mind after Susanne mentioned residents being on one in four nights. In other words, could the murders correspond to a resident's schedule? And if J.S. had been on duty in ER for 80 percent of the kills, plus seemed to be protecting someone, the obvious question became, How often had the man she most liked to work with been there?

He typed in DR. T. BIGGS.

The computer digested the command and proceeded to download the R-3 duty roster, a lengthy process that let Earl stand there and battle nausea as Janet's being overdue grew more ominous by the minute.

God help him, he'd no reason to suspect Thomas of anything sinister. The man had been his best resident in a decade. But a knack to see all possible answers to a problem, no matter how far they lay outside the box or how unsavory their implications, meant he jumped on perverse ideas the same way he might seize on an isolated clinical sign to track down a mystery illness. In fact, the unlikelihood of a piece of information attracted him, because pursuing a rogue notion made him approach the puzzle from a different angle, forcing a new perspective on it. And now, cold certain that something bad had happened to Janet, he wasn't about to spare anybody.

The screen flashed up the verdict.

Fifty percent.

Jesus Christ, what the hell did that mean? he wondered, not in any mood to be toyed with, especially by a machine.

The number seemed high. Not 80 percent like J.S., but more than what it should have been if the nights on which killings occurred were part of a completely random and unrelated pattern.

A sensation that his lungs were being sucked inside out filled his chest.

*Slow down, and don't jump to conclusions here,* he told himself. *Cluster studies only focus on opportunity.*

They totally ignored things such as motive or the personality of the perpetrator, he reminded himself, and he slowed his breathing.

Besides, there might be other explanations unrelated to Thomas. Perhaps the killer had a schedule that overlapped all the resident's on-call rosters at least half the time.

He quickly plugged as many third-year residents' names into the cluster program as he could think of. About a quarter of them got the same 50 percent Thomas had, half got 25 percent, and another quarter got 0. He'd no idea what it meant, but at least the man who had Janet with him didn't stand out alone. While that didn't totally exonerate the guy,

Earl's runaway imaginings that his protégé might be some secret fiend began to abate.

But he'd no sooner reined in his paranoia than it leapt out with another possibility.

Any one of those residents in the 50 percent group would have the opportunity to move around the hospital without raising suspicions, given the way they were called here and there to help out their juniors all the time.

*Shit! Stop it! This is over-the-top crazy.*

He brought his breathing under control again. In his mind he could even hear Janet spout her usual refrain whenever his instincts to think the worst ran amok. *There you go again,* she would say, *dreaming up nasty inklings. I swear, they pop up as insubstantial as the kernels of corn that Brendan loves to watch puff open in the microwave.*

In fact, Thomas and Janet might still arrive at the house any minute now, decrying abysmal road conditions, having broken down where their cell phones wouldn't work on account of the power outages. Then Earl would be red-faced. *Hi, Janet. Glad you're back. I've been beside myself thinking young Thomas here had done God knows what with you. Why? Oh, I also figured he'd been part of that killing spree we've been working on, and the apparent plot to blame their deaths on Stewart Deloram. Of course I haven't a clue as to his motive for committing such terrible crimes.*

He pushed away from his desk and started to pace, frustrated out of his head, desperate to take concrete action.

He sat back down, picked up the phone, and dialed Janet's cell number again.

Still turned off.

And no answer at Thomas's numbers.

The ferocity of the storm slammed the house, and rain pelleted the windows with increased fury. The sound set his nerves even more on edge.

He punched in 911. "Hello, this is Dr. Earl Garnet, chief of ER at St. Paul's. Listen, I need a favor. . . ."

By pulling rank, he managed to get a supervisor and asked

if there'd been a report of an accident on the part of the freeway or any of the side roads Janet would have used returning from St. Paul's.

"You realize this is highly irregular," she said, her irritation rasping in his ear.

"Please, my wife is over an hour late, and I'm worried sick."

He must have sounded as desperate as he felt. "One moment, Doctor, I'll check."

The receiver amplified his own breathing as he waited. When she clicked him off hold, he tensed.

"We're having a busy night, but nothing so far on the streets you gave me."

A brief surge of relief immediately gave way to more anxiety. Where the hell could she be?

"Thank you," he said, and hung up.

Should he go looking for her himself? In the storm she might have gone off the road where no one could see her. There were large tracts of parkland on either side of the freeway where that could have happened.

He glanced at his watch.

Nearly midnight.

Definitely time to head out.

But if it's not an accident . . .

He stared at the computer screen, fear swelling through him as the blood in his veins congealed with cold.

If her not coming home had to do with the killings after all, could her going to see J.S. tonight have spilled the beans? Because J.S. may have warned whomever she'd been protecting—

*Oh, God!*

He jumped up from his seat.

He never would have even considered such a thought if he hadn't already found the man's behavior suspicious. *No, that can't be,* he told himself.

But suspicious it had been.

His hand trembling, he reached toward the computer keys

and downloaded the on-duty roster for chaplains provided to ER, going back until the beginning of the year. Then, dreading what he was about to do, he typed in JAMES FITZPATRICK.

The number for him came out at 80 percent.

An icy hollow formed in his stomach.

Okay, now, that meant nothing, since Jimmy worked all the time anyway. Especially attending to his many charges at night. Some of the residents had nicknamed him the "Prince of Darkness" because of his hours. Any cluster study on this man would be ruled invalid.

But a smart killer might count on that.

What about motive? Why would someone like Jimmy want to kill patients?

"Oh, God," he repeated, this time out loud. The answer, in a word, was pain.

He called locating at the hospital. "Can you find Jimmy Fitzpatrick for me, please?"

"Believe it or not, he signed out tonight, a half hour ago. I can get you his replacement—"

"No, that won't be necessary."

He called Jimmy's cell phone number.

Turned off.

He called ICU. "Did Jimmy Fitzpatrick ever turn up to see J.S.?"

"Yes, about forty-five minutes ago."

He stiffened. "Can I speak to him?"

"Oh, he's been gone for a good half hour."

Shit. "What about J.S.? Is she all right?"

"Of course. At least, she's sleeping now, but she was fine earlier—"

"What about her vitals? She's still on the monitor?"

"I'm looking at her screens right now. Pressure, pulse, respirations—everything seems good." She sounded puzzled. "Is something wrong?"

"Just go check her yourself, will you? Make sure she can be roused."

"What?"

"Just do it."

He slammed down the receiver and fished out the card Lazar had given him. She picked up after one ring.

"My wife is missing," he said, "and it may have to do with Stewart's murder." His words seemed to come from far away.

Five minutes later he grabbed a large flashlight, left a puzzled Annie standing in the study with a teapot in her hands, and, in a fury, roared his van down the street. Buffalo's finest would only promise to inform him if Janet turned up in an accident. No APBs, no search, no watchful eye of the law on the lookout for her car being driven God knew where.

He plowed through yet another small lake, peering over the sides of the road into a sodden night, his strategy pathetically simple—scour every foot of pavement between here and St. Paul's until he found her. And if that failed, expand the hunt.

He sped up the access ramp to the expressway that led into Buffalo and saw the inky expanse spread out ahead of him. Here and there speckles of emergency lighting sparkled like phosphorescent foam on a dark sea, and in the distance the larger buildings at the downtown core shone pale blue, as if they were obelisks planted to mark a far shore. Between him and them loomed a blackness that hid twenty miles of urban clutter, parklands, and ditches. What little hope he had of finding Janet disappeared into the vastness of it, and a clamminess befitting a corpse filled the core of his bones.

# Chapter 18

She shivered nonstop.

Both shock and cold had weakened her, until she could only lie in the dark.

And her contractions came on top of each other now. She'd barely recovered from one when the next hit. There was no preparing for that pain.

Earlier, with more time in between them, she'd still tried to force the door or break open the roof. The windows were a lost cause, none of them big enough to let her through.

But escape by any route had become impossible now. She no longer possessed the strength. It took all her willpower just to stay conscious in the intervals between contractions.

This one seemed to seize her harder than all the previous ones, spreading down her abdomen and into her groin, a malignant iron fist that would burst the baby prematurely from her womb. Her scream began as an involuntary screech, then built to a howl of rage, her fury at the unnaturalness of what assaulted her and the infant exceeding even the pain. These weren't normal uterine constrictions—the gradual crescendo of compressions, the incremental forcing of the fetus against the birth canal to progressively dilate the cervix and ultimately expel a live newborn. These were violent convulsions that could crush the fragile head and limbs, compress the still vital umbilical flow of blood and oxygen, tear the life-giving membranes and sacs that surrounded him, and rupture her uterus, explode it from within, killing her and the child.

She continued to writhe, one second defiant that she would hold on, beat this, and save them both, the next overcome by despair. Yet even then she shrieked every curse she knew rather than yield to sobs.

The ripping forces inside her increased. "How dare this happen!" she roared. She'd be damned if she'd break. After all, Dr. Janet Graceton, who'd brought the benefits of modern childbirth to thousands of women, would not end up in mud and darkness dying with her infant.

At the pinnacle of her agony she remembered.

They'd been driving at a crawl along the expressway where it skirted the campus of Buffalo University, a section that cut through parklands with occasional clumps of large trees. The two of them were straining to see through the wash of an ever harder rain. Where he'd driven too fast going in, now he drove as slowly as possible, almost unnecessarily so. But she'd said nothing about it and the whole way had been explaining why Earl thought Stewart had been murdered and how she could use the cluster study to find whomever J.S. might be protecting. But when they'd come to the ravine where a shallow creek meandered through the grounds, the car had lurched forward.

"What are you doing?" she'd screamed. His foot must have jammed the accelerator, she recalled thinking.

But their speed couldn't have been more than forty when they hit the tree. The impact threw her forward, yet didn't knock her unconscious. No air bags inflated on the passenger side, not in a car of a decade ago, but the frame crumpled as it should, protecting them, and the shatterproof glass fractured into a silver mosaic before her eyes at the instant the front lights went out.

She'd sat there, stunned, hearing Thomas unclick his own seat belt.

"What happened?" she'd asked.

No answer.

She'd felt a pair of hands reach for her.

His, to help her, she'd presumed.

Until they'd grabbed her head and smashed it, repeatedly, against the side window.

## Thursday, July 17, 12:20 a.m.

Earl had tried to keep his speed down—he'd driven through car washes with more visibility—but a slower pace gave him too much time to imagine the worst. His stomach churned, and the sense of foreboding in his chest grew as big as a bowling ball for fear of what he'd find in one of the many darkened ditches or around the next slick curve. As long as he kept moving, giving himself one dark roadside pocket after another to peer into, he could keep visions of her broken body out of his head.

At the same time he couldn't stop from thinking, *This is useless, useless, useless!*

He'd made the trip toward St. Paul's in record time despite the storm, scanning the darkness across the divide for any sign of Janet's car. As that proved futile, he tried to postpone the acknowledgment that he could miss her altogether even if she was there, telling himself he'd have a proper look into the green space once he crossed over and headed back in the other direction. Bent grasses and bushes where the car went through ought to be pretty visible.

Now, already three-quarters through the return trip, he'd been forced to admit the truth that had initially overwhelmed him when he first drove onto the expressway.

If she'd skidded or been rear-ended and rolled down an embankment in the built-up districts, somebody would have already spotted her car, even with a blackout, because it would have landed in a backyard. But where gullies, tall grasses, brush, and trees lined the dark route, anyone, himself included, could easily miss such a small vehicle. And forget bent grasses and bushes showing him where the car had gone. They drooped every which way, sodden with rain.

Worse, if foul play was involved and someone had hidden

her, his odds of finding her were nil. He fought desperately not to think of that possibility at all, otherwise the things he'd seen creeps do to women swarmed through his head.

And the more he dissected his moment of insight about Jimmy, the more the whole notion fissured, one flaw cracking through it after another. Everything fell apart over motive. Why, for instance, would the priest set up Stewart and kill to do it? And sheer instinct rejected the idea that man would ever hurt Janet.

Several times Earl left his van and slid down an embankment to probe into the foliage of overgrown areas, but the rain severely cut visibility, and everything—wet leaves, stems, trunks, blades of grass—glistened like polished steel in the beam of his flashlight.

He continued to drive, soaked to the skin, sick with dread, and swallowing to keep his stomach from heaving. Up ahead he saw a pulsing glow the color of flame and soon arrived at an array of orange flashers where several hydro trucks had congregated. The white beams from a half dozen spotlights captured a group of men in hard hats who hung off a hydro pole amid a coil of wires. Wearing tangerine jumpsuits, they looked like an act out of Cirque du Soleil.

Earl pulled to a stop and got out. "Any of you guys seen an accident along here involving a green Mazda convertible?" He yelled through cupped hands to make himself heard above the rain and a loud stream of static-laced dispatches over the vehicles' radios.

"Nobody's stupid enough to be out here except you," one of the workers suspended in the air yelled back.

Nice.

A few of his mates laughed.

Clenching his fists, Earl walked up to the man who seemed to be doing the least, figuring he'd be the one in charge. "Listen, asshole, I'm looking for my wife. She's hours overdue, and right about now I'm not in the mood for jerks." He'd spoken loud enough that a few others on the ground would hear. Reaching inside his breast pocket, he retrieved a hospital card and shoved it at their boss. "That's got my cellular and the number for ER at St. Paul's, where I work. Ask for the chief. I want news if you hear of anyone who saw a green Mazda convertible, understand?"

The guy immediately frowned. In the illumination of the orange flashers, the veins on his beefy cheeks were a purple scribble, drawn by years of drink and exposure to cold. "You're chief of ER at the Saint?"

His crew also looked concerned.

Earl nodded. He'd known these bozos would respond to his pulling rank. They weren't about to piss off the person who'd be staring down at them the next time a jolt of electricity fried their hides.

The man's sour expression became unctuous. "Sure, Doc. And sorry for the crack. The boys are really stressed out tonight, with the storm and all. There's transformers blown from Cleveland to the Falls."

Earl stayed silent a moment, long enough that the smart ones in the bunch would also start to worry. Maybe the chief of ER at the Saint could hold a grudge. When he figured he'd put them all sufficiently on notice that it would be in their interest to give him a call should useful information about a green Mazda come their way, he nodded again and returned to the van.

"Good luck in finding her," one of the other men called after him.

"Don't worry, we'll keep an eye out," added another. "We expect to have the lights back on before dawn."

"And you be careful too," their boss added. He gestured toward the faint luminous shine on the horizon that marked Earl's part of town, where the lights still blazed. "Between here and there we found live wires draped across trees, the free ends dangling in midair, some not too far off the ground. Watch it in case we missed a few."

A mile farther he entered the largest expanse of parkland he'd have to check, three hundred acres of protected green spaces near the university. By now the sheets of water pouring down his windows made it impossible to see much of the asphalt in front of him, let alone the embankments on either side. He turned on his flashers and pulled over to the shoulder, parking at an angle to direct the harsh glare of his headlamps toward the meadow and its undergrowth below.

But the deluge cloaked the range. The cones of white light penetrated a few hundred feet, then got swallowed up in the dark.

Putting on the parking brake and leaving the motor running so as not to run down the battery, he picked up his flashlight and once more set out on foot.

The rain pelted his face and, having already soaked through his clothing several outings before, ran in cold rivulets down his back, chest, and stomach, pooled briefly at the waistband of his trousers, then streamed the length of his legs to end up sloshing about in his shoes. He squished with every step and slipped repeatedly on the wet grass as he descended the slope, his leather soles not at all conducive to a cross-country hike in a storm.

The air had cooled enough that his breath steamed white and luminescent in the glow outside the beam of his torch. But he didn't feel cold. The exertion quickly took care of that.

If necessary, he'd park and do this every three hundred yards, until he had walked the whole damn grounds, all the way up to where they ended at Ellicott Creek.

# Chapter 19

I knelt in the darkness, watching.

Not that I could see much.

I more listened and waited.

The rain tingled my skin, heightening my senses.

If I could just get through this, I'd be in the clear. The idea left me incredulous, heady with relief. The obsession that had infested half my life would be lifted, the chasm it created filled, the hunger sated. It had seemed so overwhelming for so long, been so entwined in my psyche like a malignant tumor, I couldn't quite believe I'd finally excised it. But by hoisting Stewart Deloram into the noose and standing him on the brink, ruined and sentenced to death by hanging, I had accomplished exactly that, and more. Because unlike Jerome, who had faced doom with a determined courage, Deloram had screamed and sobbed for pity. Had he also uttered Jerome's name and begged forgiveness in all his garbled talk? I wanted to think so. That would have amounted to a confession—an unexpected bonus—and made his execution all the more perfect.

I started to tremble, not from cold, but at the freshness of the memory.

My plan had initially been to let Deloram endure the agony of a destroyed reputation for weeks, perhaps months, maybe even take his own life, just as Jerome had. But then I realized that I couldn't afford to wait, not with that damn cluster study in the works. Still, the justice of quietly stealing up the stairs and leaving that simpering coward to die a prolonged death alone in the darkness had filled me with exactly the tranquillity I'd hoped for. It reached back through all the scars and deep into the fissure I'd felt open on that November night in 1989, and salved it closed. At this instant of healing, the spectacle of him teetering on his toes, crying and struggling to draw breath, became an epiphany, one that I knew would displace the corrosive nightmares of the past fourteen years.

I also thought of the farmhouse surrounded with gardens and green hills where the shattered woman who'd never recovered from her loss of Jerome spent most of her days, self-confined with the blinds drawn, while my aunt cared for her.

Perhaps she would finally find solace as well, now that I had ended her long wait for vengeance. But she would still insist I feed her "all the tiny details" to let her "smell, taste, see, hear, and touch" how I'd destroyed his killer. She'd always claimed her catharsis wouldn't be complete unless she experienced every stage of that retribution herself, even if through my telling of it.

I'd little time to savor the possibility. Glancing in the direction of Janet's car, even above the storm I could hear faint traces of her screams. Definitely in labor now. And the heparin would be making her bleed. I'd injected it intravenously at the site of an abrasion where no one would notice the puncture wound. Nor would anyone have reason to do toxicology studies. They'd find her bled out, the consequence of a tragic miscarriage caused by accidental trauma. Of course I'd be there to manipulate everyone's interpretation in this direction.

I fingered the tire iron that I'd removed from the trunk of the car and used to break the door handle, jam the lock, and bend the roof latch so it wouldn't release, making sure she wouldn't be going anywhere. But Garnet should soon come looking for her. Take-charge Earl wasn't one to sit at home and wait for bad news. I'd counted on it, having no option but to silence him as well. He had a talent, more than anyone, for figuring everything out, and no way would he buy that Janet died here accidentally.

It wouldn't be easy to kill him.

I raised the tire iron in my right hand and sliced down with it. A menacing whoosh cut through the rain. That would be the force of the blow it would take.

I looked up in the direction of the highway and scanned a landscape I couldn't see, imagining the slope leading down from it. Occasionally a car or truck glided by, the sound of tires and motor drowned out by the hiss of the downpour, but the running lights, floating through the night like UFOs, gave me a sense of the terrain.

No way could a man slip and kill himself here. So I'd need to stage yet another credible accident, one that would make everyone think poor Earl had died of massive head trauma while trying to save Janet. At the moment I hadn't a clue what that mishap might be.

I would also have to take Garnet by surprise.

There I had an edge.

He wouldn't arrive the cool, rational, man in control who normally commanded ER with such a heads-up, steady-handed calm. Instead he'd be frantic to find Janet and not at all cautious.

I looked toward the tree where the car first hit and could barely make it out in the darkness. Neither could I see the ground around it. Earl, however, would probably have a light. If so, he'd spot his favorite resident lying there, and he'd stop and check me. Finding me alive but unresponsive, he'd rush on down toward the car to look for Janet. It should be easy to come up behind him with the tire iron.

But then what?

After I knocked him out, how to kill him and explain it?

I still had no idea.

I looked again toward the road.

The highway remained deserted for the moment. At least no one passing would see what went on down here in the dark—another plus.

I continued to stare, imagining the terrain between the highway and where I stood, trying to conceive a way to pull this off, but drawing another blank.

I felt a stab of panic. What if I couldn't think of something in time? Garnet could be here any second.

Once started, doubts nattered through me with the speed of a computer virus, and I knew for certain that all my plans, my subterfuge would end in disaster here at this last step.

The cries from the direction of the wrecked car below grew weaker. Or had the sound of the rain swelled? Its drumming disoriented me, the sameness of the noise as ubiquitous and confusing as the lack of visual markers in the darkness. My sense of up and down came only from the hard ground beneath my feet, and I widened my stance to better keep my balance.

Time played tricks as well. As I stood there, desperate for a way to deal with Garnet, the minutes oozed by so slowly they seemed to stand still. I nearly wore out the light on my watch checking it. Maybe I'd misjudged and Earl wouldn't show.

Eventually a white glow appeared beyond a line of bushes up beside the highway as a slowly moving vehicle drove into view. The lights, front and back, defined the shape of a van. It slowed and parked at an angle, the high beams on full. To my relief, the heavy rain made it impossible to see beyond a few hundred feet into the ravine.

The interior of the cab blazed white as the driver opened his door, and I saw Garnet slide out from behind the wheel. His tall figure became a silhouette as he started down the grade, flashlight in hand.

The sight of the man who had been my teacher, who would soon die, set my heart pounding, and I began to shake.

Yet borne on that same surge of adrenaline, the scenario I needed to explain his death crept to mind.

# Chapter 20

Rain stung Earl's face.

Wet clothes clung to his skin.

But he felt only the gut-shredding, ice-water terror that he'd find Janet dead.

If he found her body at all.

Either way, the answer lay in the field ahead. If she wasn't down there, he'd no idea where else to look.

The sodden ground had already soaked his shoes up to the laces in black paste. He watched for downed wires as best he could, yet with everything so slippery, he might just as likely slide into a live one as step on it. And he'd treated enough accidental electrocutions to know that circuit breakers didn't always trip the way they were supposed to.

But his desperation to reach Janet overrode everything. Despite poor footing, he walked briskly, his flashlight providing a ghostly pale orb that wobbled over the uneven ground. Beyond this little sphere, land and sky fused into a dizzying void, and the hissing patter of rain shredded by ragged, quick strokes of his own breathing were all he could hear.

His beam caught a solitary large tree surrounded by an apron of glitter.

What the hell?

He ran toward it.

Soon his shoes crunched on fragments of broken glass. The ground was too messy to show him any tracks, but the surface of the trunk seemed abraded, and the rough bark had picked up a smear of dark green paint.

His heart leapt as he played his light in a circle. No car, but off to the left lay what looked like an elongated twist of muddy cloth.

Oh, God, he thought.

As he ran closer, he couldn't tell if its color was the beige of Janet's raincoat. A few seconds later he made out the dark hair.

Thomas!

His body lay on its side, arms above his head as if he'd been dragged there, legs akimbo. Earl knelt by the young man and felt for a pulse at his neck.

The carotid artery rose firmly, a bit fast, but strong and regular.

He leaned down and put his ear to Thomas's open mouth.

Normal breathing.

He forced one eyelid open, saw a reactive pupil, then did the same on the other side with an identical result.

A quick check of the trunk and extremities verified no external bleeding to speak of.

Just a nasty looking bruise on the side of his temple.

He must have been thrown out of the car. Whether his neck had escaped injury and the cervical spine remained intact, he couldn't tell without a proper examination. Bottom line, nobody moved him until he had a support collar.

But where was Janet?

And the car?

He desperately played the light around him.

Nothing but the flash of wet grass, leaves, and bushes glimmered back at him.

The vehicle must have continued down the slope.

"Janet!" He sprinted in the direction it would have rolled, the rain smothering his cry.

Another hundred feet, off to the right, the red wink of a brake light caught the edge of his beam. He spun toward it and saw her car on its side in the middle of the creek, the undercarriage of rods, pipes, and cylinders glinting at him like the tightly packed innards of an open abdomen.

"Janet!"

His stomach clenched down so hard that its juices surged to the back of his throat. The burning fluid made him gag. He rounded the back of the car and probed the interior with his light, clamoring up the leather roof to reach the door on the driver's side. He saw her slumped and motionless, crumpled in the passenger compartment, her legs half submerged in water red with blood.

The fear he'd contained until now exploded in his chest. He heard himself screaming her name, but his voice sounded as if from someone else far off in the darkness as he yanked at the handle.

He couldn't open it.

He scrambled up to stand astride the door and heaved on the grip with both hands.

Nothing moved.

He stomped the window.

It crisscrossed into a webbing of cracks.

He whipped off his jacket, wrapped it around his fist, and punched a small hole. Wanting to prevent pieces from falling on Janet, he reached in and slammed the pane from inside, sending showers of small, round fragments flying outward. It took several blows to clear it entirely.

But when he reached for the internal handle, he found it snapped off.

Frustration soared.

Using his flashlight, he knocked away the remnants of glass stuck around the edge of the frame and thrust himself through the opening, straining to grasp Janet.

Her head lay slumped forward on her chest so he couldn't see her eyes. But with her pallor in the light, she looked already dead.

His free hand grabbed her left arm, draped as if she were gesturing up at him, and the cold clammy surface of the skin terrified him.

"Oh, please, God, no!" He fumbled to find a pulse in her wrist.

It felt cold and lifeless.

He struggled to get closer, but wedged himself at the waist in the window frame. He propped the flashlight between the seats, and gently pulled her toward him.

"Oh, please, please, please," he whispered, sliding his fingertips into the depression where her carotid artery lay.

It fluttered like a frightened bird, the pulse weak, twice as fast as normal, but there. Definitely there.

"Janet! Janet! Janet, it's me!" He clasped her head between his hands and raised it so he could see her face. Her eyes remained closed, but she moaned, and her arms stirred, weakly shoving at his. The beam from the light cast her features in grotesque shadows, exaggerating a growing look of fear.

"It's all right, Janet. It's me, Earl," he reassured, frantic over what injuries she and the baby might have, at the same time desperate not to show it. "Everything's all right—"

Her lids shot up, her pupils flared wide, and she screamed, flailing at him with her fists.

"Janet! It's me, Earl! Earl!"

She froze. Her shimmering eyes darted in all directions, and he wondered if she could see him. "Earl?" The word floated from the depths of her chest on a long held breath.

"Yes! And now I'm going to get you out of here—"

"But the baby . . ."

"We'll take care of everything and he'll be fine."

"You don't understand." Her frail voice wafted between them, no stronger than a whisper.

The pool of blood where she lay assured him he understood all too well. "I'm going to get something to pry open the roof and get you out." He gently released his hold on her head, and started to wiggle back out the window.

"He's already here."

"What? Who's here?"

She reached down to where her clothing appeared to have balled up over her stomach, or so he thought. One by one she removed the crimson-soaked folds, and revealed a round puddle of purple and red chunks. From its center trailed a telltale maroon cord that had been crudely tied off by strips of torn cloth. It looped deeper into her lap where he saw a flash of gleaming pink flesh.

He stared at it, unable to breathe or speak.

"Meet your son," she said, looking down at the infant swaddled in his own afterbirth. The corners of her mouth flickered upward, not in a smile, but tenderness. "He's alive, but just." Her murmuring voice remained flat and as drained of emotion as her body had been of blood. "Take him first. Get him help, then come for me." She looked up at Earl, her features drawn so tightly that a suggestion of the skull beneath emerged before his eyes. She began to gather the child in her hands, about to lift him up.

Already terrified for Janet's life, Earl hung above her, the sight of the baby momentarily paralyzing him. But her stark instructions galvanized him to action. His training, as did hers, allowed no illusions about what they faced. He immediately writhed backward, struggling to extricate himself. "Oh, Janet, Janet, Janet," he breathed, his emotions a cyclone—anguish, love, despair, grief, horror—all spinning out of control.

"He tore me up on the way out. I'm still bleeding badly, and already lost a lot of blood," Janet said, her matter-of-fact tone chilling. No embellishments were necessary. They both knew she lay near death. "The way he came out, so fast, I'm sure Thomas slipped me something to precipitate labor. The easiest would have been misoprostol."

Earl froze. Though no more than halfway out the window, he couldn't have heard right. "Pardon?"

"Thomas did this to me, Earl. Crashed the car. Knocked me out. Probably also injected me with heparin, the way I'm bleeding."

Her spent monotone made what she said all the more unreal. But he didn't need to be told twice. His own paranoid ravings fueled by anxiety an hour earlier had primed him, gotten him well past the it-can't-be stage for anything she might have told him, so that her words fell into place with an authoritative clunk. "Jesus!" he said, and immediately squirmed twice as hard to extricate himself.

"He's been gone for hours—left me here to die."

"He's outside, lying on the ground. He must be playing possum, damn it—"

"What?" Even in her depleted state, her voice suddenly found strength. "Get him! For God's sake, before—" She cut herself off, eyes bulging wide, looking behind him.

No sooner had he propelled himself the rest of the way out the window than his world exploded into white.

But he could still hear Janet as she summoned new powers to scream.

I stood over Garnet's body, squinting down at him as the rain stung my eyes, watching the rise and fall of his chest. Out cold, or pretending?

Janet's scream from the interior of the car stopped abruptly, as if she'd checked herself. In the ghostly illumination of the flashlight, I saw her huddled over, rocking, and heard her murmuring something. Strange that her fury would be strong enough to rise over the roar of the storm, then she'd shut up like that.

But no one could have heard, not with the din of all this rain, I thought, glancing back toward the deserted highway. Neither would people be likely to see us if they did come along. The glare of the van's headlights continued to hit a wall of darkness well before reaching where I stood. Still, with its motor running and being lit up like that, its presence would attract the attention of passing vehicles. Better shut it down, make it appear abandoned at the roadside, as if someone had car trouble. But first . . .

Tire iron at the ready, my hand shook as I leaned over, lifted Garnet's limp wrist, and felt for a pulse.

My fingertips found the strong throb of a radial artery. Nowhere near dead. And he could be faking the unconscious bit.

Still holding my weapon in the air, in case of a miraculous

recovery, I grabbed him by the ankles and began to drag him around the rear of the car. I avoided looking in Janet's direction. The way she swayed back and forth while muttering soft, barely audible noises disturbed me more than the shriek she'd let out earlier.

As I struggled with him over the rocky streambed, my mind raced, obsessively going over the night's events, making sure that in my hastily ad-libbed plans I hadn't left any loose ends.

My initial plan had been rock solid and wasn't supposed to have ended like this. I'd gone to join Earl and Janet for dinner, confident that I could have no better choice of companions at the very time Deloram kicked and choked himself to death. Not that I should have required an alibi. Once someone discovered the body and the police ruled his dying a suicide, there would have been no official suspicion of foul play. But Garnet and Janet might have had niggling doubts about that verdict. So I wanted to stay off their radar by appearing as eager as they were to get at the bottom of things, plus, if Stewart managed to hold on for hours, be by their side at the determined time of death. And if it all worked out, they'd have no formal option but to accept that Stewart died by his own hand, nor would there be any concrete evidence to justify their continued pursuit of the cluster study. But just to be on the safe side, I'd come prepared to give them something else to worry about.

Then Graceton had blindsided me by turning up exactly what I'd been afraid J.S. would eventually realize: the correlation between her shifts and the unexpected deaths in Palliative Care. That connection could point directly at me, once someone figured out the key, and I couldn't allow it to happen.

So after dinner I'd implemented the plan that I'd originally intended to be a diversion—slipped misoprostol tablets into a steeping pot of tea with no one the wiser, the drug having no effect on me or Earl—and improvised the rest. First I insisted on driving Graceton, to keep her at my side and under my control until I could think of what else to do. Then on the way into St. Paul's the extent of the blackout and the landscape at Ellicott Creek, combined with the blind luck that she couldn't buckle up her seat belt, presented the opportunity to stage a crash that I'd survive and she wouldn't. But it was such a desperate long shot that I didn't dare attempt it without thinking everything through a bit more. Instead I tried to accompany her to J.S.'s bedside, hoping my presence would keep the woman who loved me from saying anything reckless even if she had begun to guess the truth. Then I had to back off that move in the face of Graceton's insistence that she see J.S. alone. My continued persistence on being there might in itself have aroused suspicions.

God, what a back-and-forth, seat-of-the-pants mess everything had become.

I finished tugging Garnet into position, leaving him on his back, his feet perpendicular to the undercarriage of the car, his face lined up to be crushed when I righted the vehicle. Standing over him, I began to tremble again, still frantic that having thrown everything together on the fly, I'd made a misstep that would trap me.

Finish the job, I thought, reining in my nerves, and leaned my weight against the car. The idea was to get it rocking and then pull it on top of Garnet. The Mazda looked precarious enough, sitting on its side. After it smashed his head, no one would notice he'd been knocked out first, and the cops would think he'd toppled it on himself while trying to free Janet.

I couldn't budge it.

Shit!

It must be wedged against some rocks in the streambed.

Unable to see much, I reached down into the flowing water and felt around near the submerged front tire. Several small boulders the size of soccer balls were wedged against it. I worked at one near the periphery with my fingers and felt it loosen. But this would take time.

I'd also have to erase any tracks I'd left from dragging Garnet into position. Then I'd resume my act of being knocked unconscious but thrown clear.

I checked Garnet again—nothing too clinical, just a particularly savage kick to see if he responded to pain—and got not so much as a grunt.

Setting to work with the tire iron, I pried the first rock loose. About a dozen more remained.

While trying to dislodge the rest, I obsessed on the details of what I'd done, certain that something had gone wrong.

By the time I'd retreated to the doctor's lounge, hoping J.S. would say nothing that might give me away, I began to think and act more logically. Preparing a pot of tea, I added sufficient pills to top off Graceton's dose of misoprostol, knowing that what I had in mind would work best with an unusually violent and quick labor. I also sneaked into one of the nearby utility cupboards where I stole the syringes and vials of heparin. Its fast-acting anticoagulation effect would do the job immediately, unlike the slow-acting warfarin tablets that I'd slipped into J.S.'s lemonade over a period of three days.

No choice but to use the pills with her, not just to avoid the need for an injection, but because the antidote to warfarin took hours to work, time enough for the hemorrhage to do its worst. Heparin, on the other hand, could be neutralized in minutes. But in Graceton's case, that wouldn't matter. There'd be no heading to ER and receiving an antidote for her.

And every step of the crash had gone perfectly. Having cinched my seat belt extra tight, I emerged from the impact of hitting the tree with little more than a few bruises and a sore chest from the shoulder belt. Graceton, though still conscious, ended up severely dazed and was easy to knock out. A further push of the car sent it hurtling the rest of the way to the creek.

My plan with J.S. hadn't gone as well. She could still finger me. But with her sedated for the night, I'd have time to think of a way to dispose of the problem. Maybe I wouldn't have to. Maybe I could still have her. No—it would be so risky. Before long she would figure it out. And every day I would be waiting for it to happen. Oh, God. I'd grown so fond of her, and the release she provided in bed was fantastic. I didn't want to hurt her. But the danger of keeping her around would drive me crazy.

I pried what felt like the last rock free, the lurch of the tire iron snapping my thoughts back to the present. With Earl and Janet, maybe I hadn't made any mistakes after all. Could it be? If I could just finish this, I'd have fooled everybody about everything so far. The prospect gave me a surge of strength as I leaned my back against the underframe and pushed with my legs.

I still couldn't budge it.

A quick probe around the rear tire this time revealed more rocks. I went to work on them but couldn't find the right spot with the tire iron to dislodge the first one. I went to get the flashlight.

After checking Garnet again—still unresponsive to pain— I made my way back around the other side of the car, hoisted myself up to the broken side window, and froze.

Janet looked up at me, eyes black with hatred.

But that's not what had my attention.

At her breast she held a baby soaked in the bloody remains of its afterbirth, sucking at her nipple.

I shrank back from the sight.

"Save the boy," she ordered in a flat, cold voice. "I'm as good as dead. And I know you'll kill Earl if he isn't already gone. What would it cost you to spare the child?" Her stare penetrated mine with the icy stealth of needles.

I looked away, but the image of that infant had emblazoned itself on my brain, and she continued to speak with no more expression than a corpse.

"No matter what story you cook up, someone will doubt it, and you're doomed. But if you rescue my baby, you'd be a hero, and less likely to draw suspicion."

I tried to shut the words out, but they grated through me, permeating my head and scraping the inside of my skull.

"Please!" she persisted. "I'm begging. Save his life. Who'd question a hero?"

She continued to implore me to have mercy on her son.

Definitely not what I intended.

Even if I succeeded, got away now, a new nightmare would replace the old. Visions of a blood-covered newborn and Janet's accusing stare might await me every time I closed my eyes for the rest of my days. What the hell had I accomplished?

I recoiled from the thought, fought to deny it, but broke into a sweat. I'd already experienced how the power of a dead man could possess my mind, putrefy my subconscious, and roam my dreams. Against a haunting by a dying mother and child, I would have no defenses whatsoever, because this ghost would be fueled by my own guilt, not rage against the guilt of another. I may have been able to harden myself against relatively bloodless killings, but to have actually seen the baby, heard Janet plead for its life—that wouldn't succumb so readily.

Grabbing the flashlight, I retreated from the interior of the car, turning my back on that malignant scene, and attacked the stones with a frenzy.

As I worked, I shut out her pleas and desperately tried to force my wild emotions to order.

Feelings never flowed easily through me or came freely. They either surged out of control, having to be wrangled and herded like errant beasts, or died completely until I exhumed and reanimated them, as if forcing spiritless things to life. Clinical objectivity, on the other hand, was something I naturally excelled at. In addition to serving me well in my medical career, it concealed a terrible coldness. And I'd taken that objectivity to new heights recently. Several times over the past weeks I'd argued myself in or out of killing as if the matter were merely a question of logic. So why not now? It would just be a matter of hiking objectivity to yet another level.

And I had another talent: making everybody laugh or feel

good about themselves. It deterred them from being too critical of me and protected my secret self. So I'd perfected the graces of charm and wit the way some people polished their golf game. I would only have to work the skill on a higher plane, and no one would ever begin to think I could do anything appalling to a baby.

But charm couldn't stop dreams. Even sparing the infant might not do that.

I adjusted the flashlight and reattacked the rocks with the desperation of a man digging for air.

"Thomas, I beg you, don't murder my son," Janet persisted, her voice nearly lost in the sounds of rain and the stream. Yet her words rang as clear and hard as if she'd whispered them in my ear.

At first Earl heard the rain.

Then felt it across his face like icy streamers.

He managed not to flinch when Thomas kicked him.

Let the bastard think the crack on the head still had him out cold. He needed time to subdue the twenty migraines that had set up residence in his brain.

But when he heard Janet's voice, he surfaced fast.

He cracked an eyelid just enough to catch a glimpse of Thomas off to his left hefting rocks like he was harvesting watermelons.

What was he doing?

No matter. He had to take him. Whatever his favorite resident had in mind for him and Janet, it would be terminal. He felt around with his right hand for a rock, found one the size of a five-pin bowling ball, and, with memories of Bible stories, got ready to heave it at the man's head.

But Thomas suddenly threw down the tire iron, walked around to the other side of the car, and leaned hard against the trunk, causing the whole vehicle to teeter over Earl's head.

"Holy shit!" he cried. He sat bolt upright and rolled forward just as the front and back tires hit the ground, bracketing where he'd been lying in a half foot of water.

"Earl!" Janet screamed.

"I'm okay!" he hollered, and threw his rock.

It glanced off Thomas's shoulder as the big man rounded the car and flew at him.

Earl saw the abandoned tire iron glinting in the pale light and leapt for it.

They both reached it at the same time and wrestled with it between them, like a steel taffy pull. Earl managed to hang on for the first few twists, but the younger man had much more strength and soon wrenched it out of his hands. Earl stumbled backward, ducking swipes at his head, the bar whistling past his ear.

Three times. Four times. Sooner or later it would hit.

Then, over Thomas's shoulder, he saw a row of trucks with orange flashers pull up behind his van, and a bunch of men in tangerine jumpsuits pile out.

"Help!" he screamed at the top of his lungs. "Help me!"

He ducked for the fifth and sixth time, high-stepping it backward, slipping on rocks, trying to keep his footing.

"You don't think I'm going to fall for that stupid trick, do you, Dr. G.?" Thomas asked, winding up for strike seven.

Searchlights befitting a Hollywood opening sliced through the gloom and spotlighted them both.

Thomas shielded his eyes, and his white features twisted into a look of horror that would have done Marcel Marceau proud. He began to run in the opposite direction, giving Earl a wide berth, across the stream and up the far bank, still clutching the tire iron.

Earl immediately ran to the passenger side of the car and got the door open. "Go with the baby," Janet ordered, handing him the tiny figure.

"We go together," he said, clasping the infant inside the folds of his coat. He turned to the group of figures running down from the highway. "We need help here," he yelled at them. "My wife's just had a baby. And someone get that man."

He pointed to where Biggs was disappearing up the far slope. "He tried to kill us."

A half dozen of the hydro workers reached the edge of the stream and stopped.

"I said, get him! He's going to escape," Earl yelled at them, still clutching his tiny, newborn son and kneeling beside Janet. Together they watched through the shattered front windshield as Biggs struggled up the far bank and disappeared beyond the reach of the spotlights.

"That bugger's not going anywhere," the man with the ravaged cheeks said as he ran up beside them.

Seconds after he spoke, an arc of electricity bright as the sun exploded out of the darkness where they'd last seen Biggs. At its center stood his rigid silhouette, limbs extended and quivering, hair and clothing ignited in flames. For an instant it turned him into a human lightbulb, the strands of his tissues serving as filaments of carbon, their glow strong enough to illuminate an area as big as a baseball diamond. Then the current snapped off, the effect of a circuit breaker somewhere, and as darkness returned, his blackened form collapsed to earth.

# Chapter 21

Janet's next few hours came to her in snatches.

She heard Earl yelling into a two-way radio that a hydro worker must have given him, demanding an ambulance, an incubator, and vials of protamine zinc, the antidote to heparin.

Seconds later the attendants seemed to be putting her on a stretcher.

She heard snippets of conversation about CPR and possible organ retrievals.

"Don't bring the bastard to St. Paul's!" she heard Earl snap.

The next moment she found herself in the back of a swaying vehicle, a siren rising and falling above the hiss of tires on the road and the battering of rain against the roof. Earl hovered over her, setting up portable oxygen tanks, inserting several IVs to infuse her with normal saline, and administering the first injection to counteract the hemorrhage.

"Let me hold him," she said, her voice sounding hollow to her own ears.

The rest of the way she comforted their son in a blanket, clutching him to her, refusing to surrender his tiny form back to the isolation of a plastic chamber just yet. *This may be the only time he feels me hold him,* she thought, and warned Earl off with a sharp glance when he suggested putting a line in one of the child's veins. Time enough for tubes and needles later.

They pulled up to the unloading dock and the rear doors of the vehicle flew open.

A pair of nurses she recognized from the preemie unit leapt inside, their uniforms a cliché of powder blue and baby pink. "We've got him, Dr. Graceton," the older of the two said, carefully lifting him, so little and so light, from Janet's hands to the isolette.

They transferred it onto a cart and ran off, wheeling the Plexiglas chamber between them.

*Like a miniature coffin,* Janet thought, and her insides gave a wrenching twist. "Stay with him," she ordered Earl, interrupting the string of orders he issued as his ER team rushed her into a resus room.

"I've got Janet," a familiar voice said. Michael Popovitch stepped to her side, the concern in his eyes at odds with the wrinkles of an attempted smile.

The ridges of anxiety on Earl's face rose up in surprise. "But you're not on—"

"They called me in. Now go."

"Thank you—"

"Get!"

Earl nodded, squeezed Janet's hand, and whispered to her, "I love you," then ran out the door.

"My thanks too, Michael," she said quietly. All the ER doctors were competent, but some, like Michael, held the distinction of being a physician's physician, that rare breed not afraid to take care of his own.

By the time he added red cells and fresh frozen blood to Janet's IVs, then got her to ICU, her vitals had steadied and her bleeding had started to subside.

She drifted in and out of nightmares that had her trapped back in her car, screaming at Thomas Biggs, demanding, "Why?"

Awake, she anguished about the baby. Had the violent labor injured him? Had the heparin thinned his blood? Had the combination of drug and trauma led to internal bleeding, in particular the dreaded complication of a brain hemorrhage?

Sometime before dawn she started half awake. Through barely open eyes, she saw Earl leaning over her and felt his hand, free of its glove, stroking her hair. Even in the dim glow of her night-light she could tell that his eyes were washed clear of the worry and dread from before.

He must know from the initial tests and examinations that the baby should be all right.

Her own fear released its grip, and she sank into a dreamless, exhausted sleep.

## Two days later, Saturday, July 19, 11:10 a.m. Preemie Unit, Obstetrical Department, St. Paul's Hospital

"Thomas Biggs was Jerome Wilcher's son," Earl began, settling into the chair by Janet's bed.

"His son?" She'd only just been wheeled upstairs to the obstetrical floor, where the baby could room with her. Though still wan from her ordeal, her color had improved at the prospect of holding the recently named Ryan Graceton Garnet in her arms. She kept glancing toward the door, expecting the nurses to bring him to her any second. Yet she'd also insisted that Earl tell her everything he'd learned about why Thomas Biggs had done what he did. She seemed to need an explanation, as if that would somehow make it easier to recover from the horror of her ordeal. "I thought Jerome and his wife had no children."

"Thomas's mother had been one of his mistresses."

"Really?" The revelation grabbed her full attention for a few seconds, then she resumed her watch of the door.

"Are you sure you want to hear this now?" He'd spent the last two days on the phone tracking fragments of information, then pieced it together sitting by her side in ICU while she slept. Whenever the nurses allowed, he also visited the nursery to hold the tiny, scrawny-limbed little boy with a wrinkled red face under a straight-up brush of black hair. He would watch in wonder as the miniature fingers of a doll-sized hand tentatively closed on his own gloved finger, barely able to reach halfway around it, yet exerting a titan's pull on his heart. To let the sordid, twisted story of Thomas Biggs intrude on such sacred moments seemed a sacrilege, yet it insinuated itself, each time leaving Earl weak-kneed at how closely that legacy of buried pain and obsession had touched Ryan and Janet.

She glared at him. "How the hell did you find out?"

"Through Cheryl Branagh. After my conversation with her Wednesday, she began to think that my idea of someone caring enough about Jerome Wilcher to avenge his death might not be so crazy. I made a call to the cemetery where she remembered attending the funeral, giving the caretaker a story that former colleagues wanted to include the late doctor in a hall of honor but were unable to track down any family members. The caretaker, demonstrating most people's willingness to give doctors confidential information, looked up who had been paying the maintenance for the grave. He found a Mrs. Kathleen B. Otterman, her address on a rural route somewhere in Tennessee."

"The B stood for Biggs?"

"Right. It was her maiden name—she's a divorcée. But I'd no idea of that when I first phoned. The woman herself wouldn't come on the line to talk with me, but her sister gabbed readily enough. Said Katie, as she called her, had been an invalid for years. I asked outright if they knew Thomas Biggs. 'Thomas?' she said. 'Oh, my God, what's happened?' I told her just about the electrocution, not the rest of what he'd done, letting it sound like an accident. Then I told her what hospital they'd sent him to. From the way she went to pieces, he undoubtedly meant a lot to her, and she kept saying, 'This will finally kill Katie.' "

"Is he still alive?"

"More a heart-lung preparation from what I hear. He's got spurts of brain activity that no one can really account for, enough that they won't pull the plug to chop him for parts just yet, though his kidneys and liver are spoken for."

She shuddered. "But what's the rest of the story? I mean, he'd have been what, thirteen when Jerome killed himself? And the man probably wasn't much of a dad, no? Why the hell would he go after Stewart now?"

"I've spent forty-eight hours trying to figure that out. I'm afraid all I could get were secondhand scraps of information, so it's been more filling in the gaps than anything else."

"But what about the police? Won't they—"

"The woman investigating Stewart's death, Detective Lazar, spoke with the county sheriff where Biggs's mother and aunt lived. He knew all the dirt about the family, and gave the impression most of the locals did too. According to him, Thomas's mother had still been married when she started having an affair with Jerome Wilcher. She'd worked as a technician at one of the labs he visited where they were doing research trials for one of his projects. After getting pregnant, she divorced her husband but kept her married name and raised Thomas on her own. Jerome Wilcher visited a lot but must have kept his little family a secret from his New York colleagues—probably because of that ex-wife who kept trying to clean him out financially. Thomas and his mother apparently never got much support, but at Jerome's death, they found out he'd set up a trust for Thomas's university education. Except Katie went off the deep end."

"How do you mean?"

"Once Jerome hung himself, she no longer saw any reason to be discreet, though most of the locals knew what was going on anyway. But she didn't just begin to speak openly about their long relationship. She obsessed about Jerome's death and belabored anyone who would listen with all the details about how he had been sabotaged by colleagues at NYCH. One tidbit that became common knowledge as a result of her going on all the time is that apparently Thomas discovered Jerome's body. The night he killed himself Katie and the boy were due to arrive on one of their rare trips to visit him in New York. Jerome must have been in such deep despair over the collapse of his career that by then he could no longer face them.

"And if that weren't trauma enough for Thomas, the mother went nuts afterward, first trying to hang herself in her basement at the farmhouse. Local rumor had it that she staged the event so Thomas would find her in time to cut her down. But the real damage she did him, according to the neighbors, was done over the long term. When she ran out of sympathetic people willing to listen to her ranting about how Jerome had been so heinously wronged, she unleashed it all on Thomas, feeding him a steady diatribe of hatred against those whom she held responsible for his father's death. To his credit, he moved out as soon as he could, but that wasn't until four years later, when he accessed the trust fund and got himself into a community college as far away as possible. But his mother had unquestionably done her work on him, marked him indelibly—much the way, I suppose, a terrorist might indoctrinate a son to be a suicide bomber—spooning him a daily diet of malice against the intended target."

"He went into medicine just to avenge his father?"

"I doubt that. Again relying on what the locals say, it seems he always wanted to be a doctor, just like the father he never really had—an understandable enough impulse. But his aspirations to follow in the old man's footsteps had an unmistakably morbid twist, thanks to Mama. With the smarts to have his pick of all the top schools, he chose the one where his father had been destroyed. Whether he went there with a plan in mind, to hunt down the one his mother held responsible for Jerome's death, we'll never know. But I doubt it. Otherwise, he probably would have come here straight off. Maybe he first wanted to make a mark where his father had been, and the compulsion to destroy the man who'd engineered his father's downfall only took hold later. And of course, there's the possibility his mother continued to egg him on. But again, that's all part of the story that I doubt we'll ever know."

"My God," she said, quietly, as if thinking out loud. "And he would have gotten away with it too, except for you starting to investigate Elizabeth Matthews's death."

"Yeah, he would have. And the real irony is, I don't think Thomas Biggs had anything to do with that woman's dying."

## 3:30 p.m.

Earl thought J.S. seemed worse than when he'd initially broken the news about Thomas to her. Her moods fluxed all over the place—flashed with outrage, plummeted into misery, roiled with disgust—and every one of the changes beamed at him through glistening dark eyes.

"It was an act. All a vicious act," she said the instant he stepped into her room. She'd also been transferred out of ICU that morning, the same as Janet.

"He fooled everyone, J.S.," he told her. "Me, Janet, everyone."

"But I loved a lie. What the hell does that say about me, my instincts, my trusting anyone again?"

"I think Thomas believed his own lie most of the time. Escaped into it. He couldn't have pulled off that big a charade as an act. The whole thing was complex as hell, and none of us will ever encounter the likes of it again."

"You think that makes me feel better? I loved something unreal. And in the end, the bastard tried to kill me, for no reason other than what, a dry run for his plan to make Janet miscarry?"

"Oh, he had a reason. You were smart enough to eventually see what he feared that Janet and I would see, especially if I checked the records of people using pass cards when they weren't on duty."

"How do you mean I could have found him out?"

Earl swallowed, grateful for something he could answer.

"Because he couldn't run his trials only during the nights he was on duty—not enough time—and because he didn't want you to know he was sneaking back into the hospital other nights, he did it only when you were safely at work, and not apt to want to spend the night with him."

She blushed. "It wasn't that often."

"Well, he couldn't risk you even phoning him in the middle of the night and wanting to know where he was. If you realized the killer worked only when you were safely in ER, you might catch on."

"But I didn't." She seemed as disgusted with herself as ever.

"Oh, I bet you had doubts but dismissed them. Look at those," Earl persisted, determined to dig up some evidence that might make her see she hadn't been totally naive. "They'd prove your instincts weren't all that bad, if only you trusted them enough."

She didn't respond, still looking morose, then all at once cocked her head at him. "What do you mean?"

"I mean, quit beating yourself up. You probably weren't as completely fooled by him as I was. Take that business about the pass cards. He kept asking if I had started to check them yet. I didn't think much of it then, but now I realize that he'd been making sure I hadn't started yet. And there was other sneaky stuff I didn't twig to, such as how he ingratiated himself into our cluster study. His apparent enthusiasm to be part of it seemed in keeping with what an ambitious resident might want, but of course he was only out to keep an eye on how close we were getting to the truth. And now I recognize all the clever little ways he raised doubts about Stewart while apparently trying to champion him. But at the time, no way. He even got me and everyone else to want him on staff. So don't think you were alone in getting taken in."

"Nobody got taken quite the way I did."

He struggled to come up with a reply but flushed instead.

The defiance in her gaze died. "Sorry. It's me I'm angry at for being so stupid, not you."

"And I bet if anyone had doubts about the guy when none of us did, it's you." He didn't know anything of the kind but figured the challenge was worth a try if it checked her self-doubts even a little bit.

She fell silent again.

Maybe Susanne should try to talk with her, he thought.

She cocked her head at him again. "You know, there were some things I wondered about. The night we responded to Elizabeth Matthews's code, Thomas seemed particularly peeved that Yablonsky had called the resus team. It struck me as odd how he kept pressing the point, ridiculed her even, when a simple reminder to check a patient better the next time would have sufficed. But of course he probably hoped that by browbeating Yablonsky, she'd keep subsequent calls to a minimum. That way there'd be little likelihood of anyone noting anything suspicious, at least until he had everything ready to pin the deaths on Stewart." Her brow furrowed. "Unfortunately, that made her explode about you."

"She would have done that anyway, I figure." He wanted to keep her talking, as if it might prevent her from sliding back into the hole she'd been in. "In fact, I wouldn't be surprised if Yablonsky hadn't already noted the increased mortality rate, being head nurse in charge of the records. Figuring how easily nurses could get fingered once patients started dying in unexplained numbers, she planned to make certain she didn't get blamed, whatever the cause. I just happened to be handy."

Her expression became pensive. "You know, there's another thing that sounded a little too neat—the way he practically echoed all the feelings I had about losing my father at the age I did when he talked about his own father dying. At the time, I suppose, I figured the similarity meant we were soul mates. And when we talked about growing up in the country, we seemed to share common likes and dislikes there as well. But he was adopting all my likes and dislikes as his own, to fool me."

"It might have gone deeper than just a sham."

"How do you mean?"

"Given how he practically lived his part, maybe he used your feelings to shed his own. He made your memories and emotions his, like pulling on a new skin."

"Jesus, that's creepy."

"I think a lot of how he presented himself came from inventing his new history on top of true events, then making it part of his own memories, which is why he never had any major slip-ups."

She held her index finger up, as if about to point at something. "But he wasn't foolproof, even in his pretending to help you and Dr. Graceton. At first he didn't have any ideas and I had to push him, then all at once he was Mr. Helpful. That struck me as funny too, that he didn't come up with his own ideas sooner. He probably thought at first that everyone going after you would muddy the waters, then got worried you'd find out too much, hence his getting closer to you so he could steer you wrong."

A little spark had appeared in her eye that hadn't been there before. By being able to pick holes in the deception that had deceived her so profoundly, she would gradually cut the lie down to size and, he hoped, become less fearful of being taken in again. "You see, J.S.? Now why didn't you just tell me that at the time? Look at all the trouble we could have saved. You're so clueless."

She gaped at him a full ten seconds, puzzlement scrawled in the furrows of her forehead, the sagging of her jaw visible even behind her mask. Then she started to giggle. "Wait a minute, Dr. G., you're messing with me."

"Damn right. And I'll keep messing with you until you stop being so hard on yourself. And I bet if Jimmy were here he'd give you holy hell—"

The sudden pain that slashed through her eyes stopped him cold.

"What's the matter?" he asked.

"Sorry, Dr. G. I still get really tired, really fast. Do you mind if I rest now?"

"No, not at all."

On the way out, he stopped by the nurses' station. "Has Jimmy Fitzpatrick been in to see J.S. yet today?" he asked the clerk.

The large ebony-skinned woman beckoned him closer. "Several times," she whispered. "But J.S. left orders not to let him in."

## 3:50 p.m.
## Erie Basin, Buffalo, New York

A light chop slapped against the bow of Jimmy's canoe, but the combined power of his and Earl's stroke kept the sleek craft on an absolutely straight course. A breeze from the west cooled the skin, and the dazzle of sunlight off the dancing aquamarine surface made it impossible not to squint, even behind sunglasses.

But Earl, seated in the bow, remained tense. He knew when Jimmy had invited him out here it wouldn't be for the pleasure of a Saturday paddle. "So are we making a run for the Canadian border, Jimmy?" he said, deciding to break the ice. Since setting out twenty minutes ago, his host had been uncharacteristically quiet.

"Actually, I wanted to tell you I had a job offer."

Not what Earl expected. "Oh?"

"Denver, Colorado. They need a hospital chaplain, and as a bonus, I get a little parish to moonlight in outside the city—ranch country, where I can do my rounds on horseback. Lone rider stuff."

"Really? Are you going to take it?" The thought of St. Paul's without Jimmy sobered him.

"That depends."

"On?"

"Whether I'm going to be carrying some pretty nasty baggage or not. I won't let my name hurt these people."

Earl paddled in silence a few strokes, digging the water

extra hard, reveling in the pull on his back muscles. "What about here?"

"No matter what, I'm resigning. You know I have to. I won't put you or anyone else in a position of covering up for me. Besides, my work here is done, with Wyatt stepping down and the young lions taking over. The question is, will that be the end of it?"

"You mean, am I going to help people figure out the complete explanation of what happened here? What good would that do anyone? Patients got the morphine they should have had in the first place. Nobody will be looking past Thomas Biggs to explain the corresponding shift in death numbers."

More silence, except Earl felt the surge of Jimmy's paddle make the boat leap ahead, creating its own small wake in the greater sea.

"How did you know?" Jimmy asked after a few seconds.

Earl exhaled, as if he'd been holding his secret like a breath. "There were two increases in the mortality rate on that floor. The initial one involved mainly people who were DNR, which meant they were likely near death and liable to have the most pain, and it occurred in the first three months of this year."

"So?"

"Thomas Biggs was doing one of his rural rotations in the Finger Lakes district. He couldn't have done it, and I had to cast around for another candidate. Thinking back, I remembered how you tried to fob me off with that story about the dark man when I wanted to take a close look at Palliative Care."

"Hey! That story's true, every word of it."

"Yeah, right. I also found it odd how you'd leapt to Yablonsky's defense during death rounds, since she personified the kind of indifference you detest. It didn't make sense unless you knew for certain that she hadn't caused Elizabeth Matthews's death. What happened? You were making your usual rounds when you slipped the people who needed it a shot of extra morphine, found the poor woman in agony, and for once her husband not at her side. So you gave her an injection, not realizing I'd already ordered a proper dose. At least you, or whoever else worked with you—"

"I'm not saying that—"

"Fine. Simply make sure your band of merry men, whoever they are, is disbanded before you leave. You do that, and I'm not going to be asking questions."

Jimmy said nothing for a few seconds, then chuckled. "Well, well, looks like you've a touch of the outlaw spirit as well."

"Maybe. Let's just say I'm willing to bend the rules when it makes sense. But I also intend to make you lone rider types obsolete around here. If there's wrongs to be righted, it'll happen legally. Get my drift? And that includes helping widows."

"So I can go to Denver without dragging along a potential scandal waiting to happen."

"You'll have no problems from me." *I wish you wouldn't go,* he almost added. Yet he knew in his heart that Jimmy had to leave. With him completely out of the scene, there'd be less chance of a misstep that might remind someone of his close proximity to the patients in Palliative Care.

"And to be thinkin' someone once accused you of not being one of the good guys," Jimmy said, and picked up the pace, forcing Earl to do the same. The increased speed made the waves clap more loudly against the red canvas shell that covered the cedar frame.

At each new level of speed, as soon as Earl matched his strength, Jimmy notched it higher, their breathing and the splash of water drowning out the sounds of the city behind them.

"What about you and J.S.?" Earl shouted.

"She needs time to trust herself again."

"And then?"

"I'll ask her to marry me."

Earl started to laugh. "Maybe you should at least court her with a few canoe rides first."

# Sunday, July 20, 10:05 a.m.
# Palliative Care

"I'm going home for keeps," Sadie Locke told Earl, her eyes more alive than he'd ever seen them. When she'd left a request that he drop by, she'd said she had great news.

"Really?"

"Yes! Donny's arranged for someone to run the Lucky Locke Two so he can stay in Buffalo, and we're moving into our old home, along with the nurses he's hired, until . . ." She shrugged, seeming almost apologetic for broaching the subject of her pending death.

He smiled and took her hand. "That's wonderful, Sadie. Absolutely wonderful."

"And I hear you're a new dad. I'm so glad your wife and the boy are safe. What's his name?"

"Ryan."

"And I hear he has a brother?"

He smiled. Evidently she'd been finding out all about him. He didn't mind—in fact, he considered it a good sign that she still took an interest in the world around her. "Yes. Brendan. He's six."

"A good spread. Too close in age, and brothers fight."

The small talk continued until he decided he'd better get back downstairs to Janet. "Well, I have to be going, Sadie, and I'm delighted at your plans—"

"Dr. Garnet, can I ask you a personal question?"

"Sure."

"You've seen people die. I don't know what to expect. Is it always hard?"

He felt stunned by the question. And at a loss about how to answer. "Well, Sadie, it's very individual. But as long as pain is well treated, and I'm sure there'll be no problem with that now, most pass away very peacefully."

"I hear some fight and hang on. I don't want that."

He thought a moment. "You know, there's one thing that's always amazed me. Some people make a decision it's time to let go, and then the rest just happens. It's as if there's a fundamental life switch that's in us to throw, if we can access it. Don't ask me how, but over and over I've heard a dying patient say it's time, and then there's no stopping the process. Sometimes in just a matter of hours. When that happens, it's all calm and very natural."

"Do you think there's a heaven?"

"Whoa, Sadie. Maybe you'd better talk to Father Jimmy about that."

"Nonsense. He's a company man and is going to spout the party line. I want to hear a skeptic's point of view."

He chuckled. "A skeptic?"

"You know what I mean. No agenda to push."

He let out a long breath. "I don't know. I figure there's something a lot bigger than us out there." He remembered the time he'd felt like a drop of water returning to the ocean, but shut it out. That wouldn't comfort her. "You know, another thing I've noticed is that people with loved ones around find it easier."

"Really?"

"Yeah. Not only the dying, but facing the unknown that lies beyond. It's as if the friends and family are proof they're not a nobody, that they've led a good life, and if there is a reckoning, it'll work out."

"Like me having Donny."

"Like you having Donny. I mean, already it's made a difference. You're almost glowing."

"I *am* happy he's here, and relieved he's staying."

"So you see—"

"But what about the stories of seeing people on the other side? Is that heaven?"

He chuckled. "I guess it depends what they think of you, for better or worse."

"So you're a hell-is-other-people kind of guy."

"Except heaven can be other people too, if they think well of you." He started to think his answers sounded pretty good.

*"No Exit,"* she said, almost dismissively.

"Pardon."

"*No Exit*. It's a play by Jean-Paul Sartre, an existential philosopher. Father Jimmy loaned me a copy. You're practically saying the same thing as that guy."

Earl said good night and retreated from the room, feeling he'd been whipped in Philosophy 101 by an octogenarian.

•

He lay in a gray zone.

I could see him below me.

Smelled the cloying, sick sweetness of his burns, felt the tube feeding oxygen to his seared lungs, and saw the glistening muscle that bulged through the deep fissures of his cracked skin.

But I floated above it all, no longer part of him.

Even the pain seemed distant.

But not the fear.

Out there in the darkness they waited.

Shrouded black shapes ready to take me, their silence as vast and overwhelming as the void behind them.

I didn't want to go there.

But I could feel myself being pulled inside out by their stares.

And one in particular who stood a little apart from the rest.

I didn't know him, but the ice in his gaze froze me with terror. I could feel the cold off him every time he drew near, and though I tried to scream, no noise came from my throat.

Yet he must have heard something, because he would recede a little, all the while looking at me with a hatred that putrefied any remaining shreds of life, further weakening my tie to the blackened husk below.

He moved on me again, sapping my resistance a little more.

I couldn't hold out much longer.

The shapes swayed expectantly.

And began to close in.

# Epilogue

## Monday, July 21, 7:00 a.m.
## Emergency Department,
## St. Paul's Hospital

"Nothing happened, you know," Michael said. He'd lowered his voice to a whisper.

"Nothing happened where?" Earl asked.

They were suiting up with the new Stryker outfits that had been delivered to ER over the weekend, accompanied by the long-expected directive that all critical care areas would have a resuscitation team dressed in them at all times. It was like stepping into a one-piece snowsuit made of yellow vinyl, and they were worn over the normal protective wear.

Earl felt hot even before he zipped it up.

"You know!" Michael said, his voice lower, but more insistent. "That business with the Baxter widow. I just met her for drinks, and we talked."

Earl really didn't want to hear this now. He'd just received word that six patients in a nursing home near Niagara Falls had come down with pneumonia over the weekend and, showing signs of acute respiratory distress, were en route to St. Paul's by ambulance. Provisional diagnosis: suspected SARS.

"Look, Michael, I was way out of line—"

"No, you weren't." He leaned his head closer as he pulled a second set of gloves over the first, snapping their cuffs over the sleeves of his new outfit. "I'd been quarreling with Donna, and here was a woman who didn't cringe when I touched her, even if it was just holding hands. But after you gave me shit . . ." He shrugged, his temples flushed pink above the mask.

Earl stopped struggling with his own gear and laid a hand on his arm. "Hey, I'm your friend and a buttinsky kind of guy. You had me worried."

"And Jimmy told me you'd talked—"

Earl silenced him with a glare. "That we never speak about, Michael, not now, not ever. You live with what you did there. I live with letting it slide. The rest died with Biggs. Understood?"

The man stared at him, his eyes melting into dark, melancholic pools, then nodded.

"How are you and Donna now?" Earl asked, partly to know, partly to snatch him away from such dangerous terrain.

"Better."

"Really?"

"Yeah. Janet's near miss really shook her up. I think Donna admitted to herself there were bigger dangers in the world than SARS, and decided that the idea we could run from them was crazy." He pulled the hood over his head. "Besides, she figures now that we're wearing these, I'll be safer. Nobody's caught SARS in one." His voice, heavily muffled by the Plexiglas mask, barely carried the foot of space between them.

Not so far they haven't, Earl thought, donning his own hood and immediately feeling stifled in the closed environment. He snapped on the portable air supply, and a cool flow into the interior of the helmet allowed him to breathe more easily. But the heaviness of the material cramped his movements and left him feeling claustrophobic.

They walked into the resus room, where Susanne and two of her nurses waited in similar garb. They would receive all the patients here, and be the only ones to care for them.

"We look like the cast from *Star Trek*," Earl said, raising his voice loud enough for the others to hear. They all looked so grim, he figured somebody had better lighten the mood.

"You've got more hair than William Shatner," Susanne cracked, and everyone's eyes creased at the corners, pupils sparkling in the gloom behind the transparent faceplates.

A distant rise and fall of approaching sirens tweaked Earl's usual surge of adrenaline at the sound, and the pit of his stomach tightened a notch. But today the familiar electricity failed to clear his head and charge up his clinical reflexes. Instead, he felt gripped with a growing sense of helplessness.

How long would they have to work like this?

Days? Weeks? Forever?

Neither would SARS be the last microorganism to emerge without warning, ready to take on the human species, outsmart science, and spread beyond their control.

The shrill wail of the vehicles swelled louder, descending on St. Paul's like an incoming swarm.

Surrendering to his worst fears, he thought of Janet with Ryan upstairs, of Brendan waiting for him at home. Having always believed that those dearest to him enjoyed an advantage against disease with his medical knowledge so close at hand, he felt the assumptions of what he or any doctor could protect them from shift once and for all. Even as he stood in the middle of ER, the stage where he'd spent a lifetime performing his special skills that could triumph over death, the foundations of his profession crumbled a little.

But he'd be damned if he'd cut and run.

Couldn't do it if he tried.

Didn't have a back-down gear in his psyche.

And if he stood fast, so would those around him, not just here in emergency, but throughout the entire hospital. His sense of domain extended to all of St. Paul's now, and he intended to exert his influence over every inch of it. Hurst could go to hell.

Through the frosted windows of the resus room he saw a blur of large yellow shapes as the ambulances arrived.

The accompanying noises permeated his hood—engines died, vehicle doors snapped open, people exchanged curt orders as multiple stretcher carriages were clicked into extension—but the sounds came across much duller than usual.

"Okay, everyone, it's showtime," Earl shouted, frustrated by how confined his own voice sounded. "Whatever we do for their breathing, let's also talk it up and soothe their souls. These outfits might smother speech, and those men and women may not be able to see our faces or feel the warmth of our hands. But don't for a second let a single one forget it's human beings taking care of them, not some damned robots."

Two attendants ran through the door with the first of the stretchers. On it lay a pale, elderly woman who wore an oxygen mask, chest heaving as she fought for breath. Her thin gray face elongated in shock at the sight of Earl and his team.

This wouldn't be easy, he thought.

## Author's Note

While *The Inquisitor* is a work of fiction, the men and women who comfort the sick and dying as hospital chaplains are very real. As Jimmy might say, it's not about religion, just one human's sympathy for another's fear and pain. To the good ones, and you know who you are, I say thank you.